# Colouring Books
## Gallery Three

### Turquoiselle, Cruel Pink
### & The Green Wallpaper

# COLOURING BOOKS
## GALLERY THREE

### TURQUOISELLE, CRUEL PINK & GREEN WALLPAPER

### Tanith Lee

Stafford England

**Colouring Books Gallery Three: Turquoiselle, Cruel Pink & Green Wallpaper by Tanith Lee**
© 2021

*Publishing history (in the English language) of the novels and story in this omnibus:*
*Killing Violets*, Immanion Press, 2012
*Ivoria*, Immanion Press, 2012
*The Sky-Green Blues*, The Secret History of Vampires, DAW Books, 2007

This is a work of fiction. All the characters and events portrayed in this book are fictitious, and any resemblance to real people, or events, is purely coincidental.

All rights reserved, including the right to reproduce this book, or portions thereof, in any form. The right of Tanith Lee to be identified as the author of this work has been asserted by John Kaiine, the beneficiary of her estate and copyright holder of her work, in accordance with the Copyright, Design and Patents Act, 1988.

Cover Art by John Kaiine
Cover Design by Danielle Lainton
Interior layout and editing by Storm Constantine and Danielle Lainton

Set in Garamond

**ISBN** 978-1-912815-11-1

IP0162

*Author Site:*
Daughter of the Night: An Annotated Tanith Lee Bibliography:
http://www.daughterofthenight.com/

Facebook Page for Tanith Lee's readers: Paradys Forum - Daughter of the Night - Tanith Lee

An Immanion Press Edition
www.immanion-press.com
info@immanion-press.com

# CONTENTS

Publisher's Note                                6

Exhibit Seven: Cruel Pink                       9
Exhibit Eight: Turquoiselle                   169
Exhibit Nine: Green Wallpaper                 345
About the Author                              371

# Publisher's Note

Tanith Lee began working with Immanion Press in 2010. She'd been looking for a publisher to release a series of short 'slipstream' novels that didn't fit easily into traditional genres. These books were Tanith's own brand of psychological thriller with a sprinkling of weirdness and surreality thrown in. The series was to be known as *The Colouring Books*, as each novel within it had a colour theme. We published seven of these novels before Tanith died in 2015. She planned to write two more and had the title 'Wintergreen' for one of them; it's a great loss to literature these never came to be written.

The first three books in the series, *Greyglass*, *L'Amber* and *To Indigo*, were all released in 2011, since Tanith had already written them. These were followed by *Killing Violets* and *Ivoria* in 2012, *Cruel Pink* in 2013 and *Turquoiselle* in 2014. Immanion Press is now rereleasing the books in three omnibus editions, rather than keeping them in seven separate volumes, as we are committed to keeping Tanith's work available in print and to make this as affordable as possible.

In these three omnibuses, we also include an extra story with a 'colour theme'. These have been selected from Tanith's uncollected stories, which appeared in magazines and rare anthologies. 'The Sky-Green Blues' in this book is a story that first appeared in Interzone magazine in 1999, and a year later in 2 'best of year' anthologies (details on copyright page).

# EXHIBIT SEVEN
# CRUEL PINK

In Memoriam
V. H.
Golden Talent. Courage of Steel.

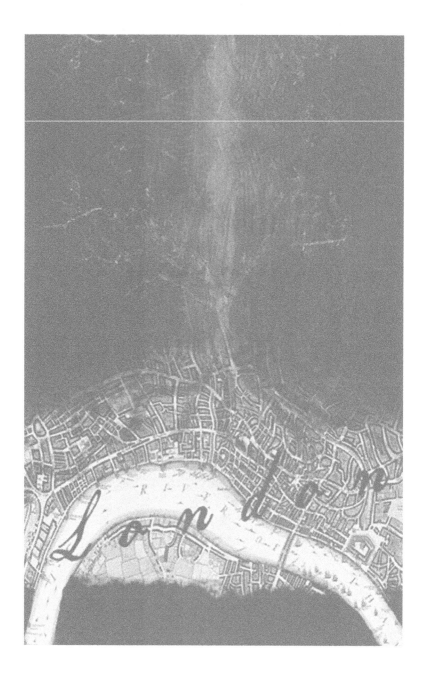

## EMENIE:

# 1

I kill people; what do you do?

Birds are messengers, and can tell me things. Actually, they can tell anyone things, but most people, obviously, don't grasp this. It was early autumn, really warm, about 6 p.m., and I was walking along by the canal. The pigeon came over and landed on the towpath in front of me. (They don't tow any barges along it now; there are just the derelict one or two over against the other bank. The old park is up there. Completely overgrown, of course. And beyond the old rambling trees and bushes, and taloned roses and four foot high grass, you can see the ruins of three tall blocks of flats.) The pigeon was slatey-blue with a white head and clever crazy eyes. It picked something from the path and then let it fall in disgust. I read the message this time from the pattern of light and dark on its back. It told me the weather would stay good and the light would last until around ten to seven, and then there'd be a long soft twilight. Plus there was somebody by the park I'd see if I continued walking up the path towards the ruins of the Co-op. It was sort of take it or leave it, really. Both the message and my reaction. I had gone out just for a walk, really. And the pigeon didn't promise me something I might truly find irresistible – just a possible might be worth looking at. Which was fair enough.

Once it was sure I'd got the message, it turned round and took off, rising far up over the orange and yellow and evergreen of the trees, heading for the upper sky, above the wreckage of the suburbs. It would probably be in central London inside ten minutes, the bird. Well, in what was left of London, evidently. But for a pigeon that would, I expect, suffice.

# 2

After going on for about twenty minutes – I judge time fairly accurately – I saw a man sitting on the opposite path, near the old bridge and the green and crumbly steps, fishing with a real rod and line.

"Hi," I called over. "Catch anything?"

"Nah," he said, but without resentment.

"I don't think there's anything in there, really," I said.

"You're very likely right."

"Except the odd shoe," I added.

He looked up and grinned. "Oh yeah. I already caught one of them. I threw it back."

"So you're just fishing for pleasure," I playfully said.

"Sure. Though I suppose I could've tried frying it in breadcrumbs and olive oil. But I'd have had to kill it first."

"Oh, can you do that?" I was admiring. "I mean, if it was really a fish?"

"Sure. Used to catch salmon in Scotland. Silver-fin in California, too, once or twice, 'bout fifteen years ago."

"I could never do that."

"You could if you had to," he encouraged me.

"No," I said, sad and regretful. "I can't kill animals. Not even rats."

"You've got a problem there, then," he said.

"You're telling me. My place is overrun with the bloody things."

He sat, looking at me quizzically. The sun was low in the sky behind him, way over the park, shining its soft, pure, bronzy rays full on me. What did he see? This lone girl, just dressed in jeans and a floppy autumn-leaf colour T-shirt, long brown hair and paler brown eyes, clear skin, lightly tanned. A tawny girl, slim, all right enough, and perhaps lonely as well as alone?

"Where'd you live?" he asked me.

"Oh. Just back up there. Used to be my grandmother's house."

"Right?" He was interested. Well, he was probably in some squat, or other derelict premises. He didn't look dirty though, and his own nondescript clothes were OK. He was about thirty-five to forty. But I'm sixteen going on fifty. You can't always tell, with me. No, I don't lie, you can't, you couldn't, it's one of my talents. His teeth were good, I saw that again next minute because again he grinned. "I could drop by sometime. Help you with your rat population."

I seemed to be thinking. I was, I suppose. "You know, I found a bottle of wine," I said.

Yet – did I really want to, tonight? Maybe I did. I don't usually get a message from a bird, or any other signal, unless I'm up for it – even when I don't always realise at first I am, I was. I don't usually want to do it at home, either. But – well, I'd sort of invited him, hadn't I? It would be rude to refuse now, wouldn't it?

They know, I'm sure of this, too. Even you would, if you were the one. They – you – always know. It's a pre-arrangement, perhaps even made between us in a previous life. On such an autumn evening we'll meet, around six thirty, and then we'll do it – let's do it – let's fall in love.

## 3

"I remember this road," he said. "From before." This was as we were going in at the back door. (I hardly ever use the front, and now the back door lets directly into the rooms I use most often, on the ground floor. I hardly ever bother going up to the second floor. Or the narrow stoopy little attic.)

"You mean before – well..."

"The S hit the F. Yeah. Back then. I was younger then. You weren't even born, yeah?"

"You might be surprised," I said.

The back door lets into the utility room and so into the biggish kitchen. Then there's a space and a bathroom opens off there, and then there's the main big downstairs room, which is very big, being once – in my grandmother's time – two rooms. (She wasn't my grandmother. I killed her some years ago, an older woman. Can't recall her name.) This house, which is detached, stands between two others, also detached, and one of which is a large bungalow with an upstairs extension. All these other adjacent houses, however, are in a pretty awful state and – like the park – massively overgrown and impinged on by huge feral trees.

"Your fridge works!" he exclaimed as I took out the wine. Now he did sound accusing.

"It does sometimes. Not very reliable. Guy I used to know wired it up to something or other last year. I get about two, three hours, but you can't ever be certain when." (This is a lie, of course. I know exactly when.)

"Christ." He was peering in at the loaf and other stuff, a look of envious almost-pain on his face. "And you've got fucking lights," he almost shouted, as we moved on into the biggest room. There's only one side window left in here, from the way the rooms have been portioned off, and that is boarded up, like all the front windows. Due to the forest of garden trees at the back I hadn't so far felt the need to blank out the glass of the kitchen or utility.

"He did the lights, too," I said.

"Ever see him now?" he asked, greedily.

"No."

He gave me a hard sad look and sat down on the sofa. I lit some candles and turned out the overhead lights. "I'd better, in case they go off suddenly." Then I took the two dark green glasses off the fake fire-surround – at least there wasn't any excessive, infuriating electric fire turned on there – and opened the screw-top of the wine and poured us each a large, filled glass.

He drank about half at a gulp. And then sat staring at nothing. He was frowning. Finally he said, in a miserable and unfriendly way, "Perhaps I'd better take a look at the rat situation. Yeah?"

"If you don't mind."

"I can smell them already," he said. He was sullen. He didn't fancy me now, hated me presumably for having a working fridge and electricity. Or he just didn't know how to handle this weird brown girl, and the almost-comfort, and the silence, the utter silence, which he thought no doubt was being shut in here, but was really everything listening, waiting.

"Maybe you could look at the cellar," I said. "That's where they get in."

"One's fucking died down there, I can tell you that," he elaborated as I undid the door to the basement, which door is back out in that space between the kitchen and the big room.

"Yes. They do. In there and in the walls."

We stood and stared through the door-slot and down the steps into the utter sub-black below. I'm so accustomed to that stink of death, I don't even properly register it anymore. Conceivably it's just familiar to me now, part of 'being at home'.

"Hang on," I said, "there's no light down there. I'll get the torch."

There's a cupboard by the bathroom, and I left him staring at the black, the abyss, and took out the torch and then shone it over his shoulder downwards. "Do you mind going first?" I said. "I don't like the stairs. I'll shine the light ahead of you."

He glanced back then, into my face. He looked sorry for being gruff earlier: I'm just a nervous kid, and I've given him wine, and I might give him other things, food and sex, and a place to stay that's better than wherever he is currently holed up.

"Sure," he said. "S'OK."

I kept helpfully shining the torch before him. Then "Oh – just a second..." I said. It was plain I had forgotten something important. I hadn't, though.

I took the light off him, and took something else out of the cupboard, leaving him in blackness a moment before swinging the torch-beam right back exactly into his eyes.

"Shit."

"Oh hell – I'm sorry..." I cried, contrite. But I wasn't. Before he could see again, and using the handgun from the cupboard, I shot him directly through the face and head.

## 4

In the night I lay on the bed in the room that led off the main room; it had been part of the main room, part of the part that had been the sitting room once. The bed was large, sagging and lumpy and oddly comfortable, the mattress seeming to alter its shape to fit me in whatever position I adopted. Tonight, I was on my back. I had finished the remaining poured-out wine and put the rest in the fridge to keep cold. (The fridge always works, just as the light and the fire do. Even the electric cooker functions, though I seldom cook anything on it. Cleanish water also runs from the taps. Perhaps the fishing man would have called them 'faucets', in the American way. Because I'd thought later he did have a faint US accent, under and around, sort of tangled up in his London English one.)

He would be perfectly safe in the cellar. For now, or forever. He wouldn't even be on his own. There were the rags and whitish ribs and splinters of a few more ex-persons. In winter the cellar was nearly as cold as the fridge. Even in summer it wasn't too bad. Or, enough not to upset me, I suppose. As I said, the smell doesn't trouble me. So, it is the smell of death and decay. They too exist. They underline all things, just as does the scent of sap and vegetable growth, and of flesh that is living, whether animal, avian or human.

After I kill I always feel improved. I feel – satisfied. As if I'd cleaned the room, (which I seldom do), or cooked a wonderful meal, (which I never did or do or, presumably, ever will do.)

And the moment when I actually kill When I squeeze the trigger of the gun, or employ the knife or other sharp weapon, or strangle with a cord or my bare hands – which, with some of the less strong, (normally women), I can adopt occasionally as my method. I've used other means too; there seems no point in boringly listing each and all here (I may change my mind.) But I think my – targets, shall I say? – their type, something I see or detect in them, makes me decide how I should accomplish their individual murders. Just as I know when I notice them, or meet them they, this one or that one, is to be killed by me – the idea of pre-arrangement I mentioned previously. I can walk through crowds all day and find no one that's suitable. It's happened. Now and then it's happened on and on, and I begin always to be slightly uneasy, as if never again will I be able to find someone to kill. A year or so ago I was like that for almost four months. This wasn't good for me. I couldn't sleep and I couldn't wake up properly, either. I hardly went out in the end.

Then one morning a man went by me near the remains of Marks and Spencer's, (in the likewise remains of the old High Street), and he was the one. And it was simply all there again. The relief nearly made me shout aloud. I was so happy. Him in fact I shoved in the canal at the deepest stretch, up past the railway bridge. He couldn't swim, as I'd learned, and I'd partly stunned him, too. I watched him drown. I couldn't stop smiling. He was one of the best, I have to say, but that may only have been because of the enforced abstinence that was the prologue.

That night after the fishing man, and knowing he was there below, in the cold autumn pantry of the cellar, I heard a plane go over. You rarely do now, do you, and then generally only by night. I wondered where it was going, but it hardly mattered. Yet... there was a kind of half-musical balance for a few seconds, the upper melody of the engines overhead, and me lying on grandmother's bed – the central theme – while below the darkened strings of my latest victim's deadness formed the base, the percussion, steady and solid as an ancient, ticking clock.

Curious, night thoughts.

# ROD:
## 5

I made notes on the train. I always make notes. They're useful, I find, or at least they pass those spaces when there is nothing to do. I looked out of the train windows as well, and when the trolley came round with all that rattle and pretence of a sudden party, I bought a black tea and a shortbread biscuit. It's an hour's journey out of London. She lives in Brighton, my aunt. Vanessa, she's called. I believe after Ms Redgrave. When I was a lot younger, I used to ask myself if I'd have liked Aunt Vanessa better if she were Vanessa Redgrave. But probably not, if she still acted like my aunt.

When I arrived at her house near Kemp Town, it was about 12.45, a quarter to 1. I say about, my watch was playing up. It tends to do that on or after a train journey, even of twenty minutes. Most machines play up when I use them. At work it's our department's running joke. My computer always goes wrong, and the laptop, well, Forrel actually accused me of sabotaging it. But normally someone just says 'Poor old Rod. He can't even get a dog to obey him.' I don't, incidentally, have a dog. In a flat, anyhow, animals aren't a wise choice.

## 6

Vanessa was in her scrubbed oak kitchen, preparing lunch, which consisted as usual of some cold bought meats and a lot of bright green supermarket salad. She doesn't drink, but always offers me a glass of wine. Sometimes I say no. But I thought I'd accept this time.

"It's not good for you, you know, Roderick."

"What isn't, Auntie?" I still call her that, because she once said I should, and she had never amended her edict.

"Alcohol, Roderick."

She's sixty, if I have the math right, but looks a bit a younger, slim and bright-eyed from all the salads and yoga classes, with bobbed grey hair that bounces irritatingly with health.

The wine came in a shiny glass that could hold a decent amount, if filled up, but she as ever failed to fill further than one third of the way. It was white, the wine, Sicilian according to the bottle, before she recorked and shoved it in the fridge. As if any minute the Continence Police would arrive. If she doesn't drink herself, I often wonder why does she do it up – she wouldn't be offering me anymore, I know that by now.

Lunch passed in eating and in Vanessa telling me at length about her latest feuds with her neighbours – the semi-detached neighbours this time, rather than the people over the road, and with the local hairdresser who, she insists, cuts her hair too short. I told her that her hair still looked very nice. She said I didn't understand about hair.

During the afternoon, which was mild and fine, she gave me her usual tour of her long and quite elaborate garden. "How awful for you, Roderick, not to have one. My garden gives me scope. I hope you take regular walks?"

"Oh, yes," I dutifully answered. Of course I did. Ten minutes to the station every morning, ten minutes back at night. And now and then a walk to and back from *The Red Stag* at lunchtime, or *The Black Sheep* after dinner. About five minutes, those two.

"And you have no view," she added, "nothing to look out on."

I have explained more than once that in fact the back view from my flat isn't bad. I face the Little Common, beyond which the sun sinks behind the burgeoning central city outskirts.

I shrugged. "Nothing as pretty as your garden."

She made an annoyed noise, and told me about her feud with the Garden man, as she calls him.

Despite all that, it was, I admit, rather pleasant on the autumnal patio, watching the trees. We drank our coffee, and I fell asleep at one point. She seemed not to notice. She was still telling me, when I woke, about a campaign she was trying to start against too-early schooling of children. She seemed to believe they were now expected to attend nursery school at two years of age. Is she right? God knows, the way things are.

In the evening we had tea and ate a very peculiar cake that someone she knew had made. It seemed to be thinly iced in the middle, with a bitter jam on the top, and was wholly organic.

When it got to 7 o'clock I was, as ever, able to remind her of the train I had to catch. She told me of course I must go, it was very noble of me to have visited on Saturday, after my stressful week of work in central London. I replied that the rural quality of her house, the garden, and my brief looks at the sea from the train, had been wonderful.

She kept her final, if recently habitual remark until I was putting on my coat.

"Roderick... I do know you're gay, you know."

"I'm not gay," I replied. As always I do.

"You won't admit it, I see that. But why not? There is absolutely no stigma now. Why won't you be honest at least with me?"

"I am," I said, patiently, "being honest. I'm not gay."

"But you are, Roderick – you are! And oh, Roderick, I'd be so glad to see you with some nice friend – I'd be so happy for you. You could bring him to visit me! Do you think I wouldn't welcome him – that he'd sense any animosity from me – me, your Auntie Vanessa? Oh, I'd love to meet him, Roderick. Won't you trust me?"

I kissed her cheek. "If there were anyone, Auntie, I'd trust you. But there is no one. No one at all."

"Oh, Roderick," she said as we got her rather complicated door undone. "Oh Roderick."

# 7

I'm not gay. At least, as far as I know. And surely by now I would. I'm thirty-two years of age. Men don't interest me. People don't, a great deal, if I'm honest. But I like to look at women, if not in an especially lascivious manner. I like their scents and the way they colour their hair and choose their clothes and make their faces up. The way they move.

My mother and sister were killed when I was only five. In a train crash in France. Rotten, yes it was. My mother was only about my age now, and the little girl, my big sister, just nine. A psychologist would say I miss them, so I look at women now and try to see my mother as she was, and my sibling as she might have grown up to be.

The train back was full of jaded seasiders, lurching home to the sea-less tidal city, noisy or exhausted, or both. I had a vodka and tonic off the jolly-trolley. That would be my limit for today. I like a drink, but I don't have too much. Can't afford it for one thing.

I made some notes on the train going back, as I had on the one going down. It was dark, the windows black before we reached

Victoria.

All places smell different. Brighton had been salt and fish and leaves and compost. London that night was newspaper and neon and chemical smoke. I caught the other train out and down, there hadn't been a stop-off at my station on the way up. I always think that is so strange, going past your own station, unable to stop, having to go all the way in and then out again.

## 8

There was somebody hanging about in my road as I turned into it. As a rule, if that happens, it's some gang of youths, boys or girls or both, off the common or making for the common, under a streetlamp with their death-advertising cigarette packets vivid with plague warnings, and their little toy bottles of alcopops. They may yell at one, or not. They mostly don't seem to see me, or any adult. We're like ghosts to them, remnants already faded from the vast movie-screen of life on which, day and night, they get top billing.

Tonight though, it was just a girl on her own. Dark-haired and in a dark coat. Eye make-up, nothing else. She was walking slowly up and down between the station end, from where I came, and the five detached houses in the middle, the second along of which is where I have my flat.

She glanced at me as I went by. I assumed she was probably waiting for someone, but somehow it didn't quite seem like that. Looking out for someone, then. She seemed edgy, nervous and suspicious, less of the casual passer-by – me – than of the area. She was like a girl from a spy film, waiting to meet up with the dodgy contact she had been sent to find, who would help her, or harm her, depending how the script panned out.

When I crossed over to the house with the flats, I caught the flash of her pale face in the streetlight, turning to see where I went. And as I put the key in the lock, I looked back. She was staring by then, yet when I turned, she did too, and hurried away up the street. Unsettling, a bit. But people do weird things now. No doubt, they always have.

I rent the right-hand north side flat on the second floor. I put the light on in the downstairs hall and went straight up the stairs to it.

The landlady has the ground floor apartment. We don't really have dealings. I got the place through an agent, bought it over five years, it being so cheap, paying my dues every month through the bank by direct debit. I've only glimpsed her a couple of times. At least I assume it was her. She's in her fifties, nothing startling, a bit of a recluse perhaps. I have to say, there's sometimes a bit of a bad smell down there, the ground floor that is. Very faint, but not appealing. It comes and goes. Drains, I reckon.

My flat is small, two rooms, bathroom and kitchen. I generally clean it over on Sunday mornings, it never takes long. There's nothing special or 'graphically amazing', as Forrel might say, in any of the rooms. White walls and some mirrors, the ordinary blue curtains and carpets that were already here. The electric kettle is mine, like the few books, and the clothes in the wardrobe. The main room and the bedroom have electric fires as well as individual central heating. The cooker's gas.

The rear-view, though, as I've tried to tell Vanessa, isn't bad. There are the couple of streets that slope down, and then the towpath and the canal, and over the other side is the common, with its trees and, framed now on blackest night, the three diamante-windowed fifteen-storey blocks of flats that rule over Parnassus Avenue.

I'd missed the sunset. But despite the clemency of the day, the sun had gone out in cloud not far outside Brighton. There wouldn't have been much to see.

Before I switched on the lamp in the sitting room, the other end of which faces out to the street, I went to discover if the dark spy-girl, Anushka of the KGB, were still loitering in the road. She wasn't. Either her date had found her or she had slung her hook.

I made some coffee and sat on the couch to check my notes, but I couldn't entirely concentrate. It was almost 10. I activated the TV for the news, and whatever hell, horror and idiocy had gone on everywhere while I was cooped up with Aunt Vanessa. Before it came on, I did have one quick look in the wardrobe. Only one look. My second, though, if I counted this morning. No worse than the drinks, I thought. Half a glass of white wine at lunch and a double vodka in the evening. Half a minute's morning wardrobe-look, and two minutes' look at night. That was enough, and not too much. In the sitting room, the girl reading the news had hennaed her hair. She looked beautiful.

# KLOVA:
# 9

I tried the lipstick last, before I went out.
I'm always having make-up. If I can't afford it, I'll just steal it.
But generally I can afford it.
I never mind stealing.
It's so like simple. It's just a sort of spell I can throw over the store O.C.'s as they peer and follow me about. I never get caught.
But I hadn't stolen the new lipstick.
I'd had a money-gift wired into my account a day before and the bank-nanny told me last thing that night. Three thousand shots. That's a lot. I couldn't work out – often can't – quite who it came from but, you know, who cares? It was there.
Although by tomorrow some of it would be gone.
I was going to the Leaning Tower.
In my black and gold, and the tinsel hold-ups, and the chandelier ear-drops, and the totter-heels, and the new lipstick.
I left about Zone 48, because nothing much kicks off in town until around 50 – Midnight.
I thought the male, who lives in the flat across from mine, was in, I heard his news-viewer on as I went downstairs. Such an old-fashioned roost, this flat-house, no slide. The old woman who holes up in the downstairs part was silent too as silence. She is a peculio, and no lie.
I am very certain she goes all over when I'm out. Gets in my rooms.
All over the upstairs bit too – not sure even if anyone lives there – and all over the male's flat as well.
She doesn't take anything. Not from me.
But sometimes she disturbs some piece or other – like the shadow of a chair hangs wrongly and that's because she has shifted or knocked it. Or the spume in the bath dome is wet, though it wipes itself dry soon after use.
One morning in winter I came back at dawn, Zone 16, and there was a pearl from one of my gloves lying on the glass tiles of my social room. I hadn't worn these gloves for nights.
But so what.
Live and let love.

Love and let go.

Go live.

When I got outside, I glanced up, and through his window shields I could faintly see the male's lights were on. So he was home.

He's old, too. He might have been pretty when he was younger. He's one of the Older Generation, before it all got changed. In fifty years he'll be dead.

In fifty years I'll still look sixteen.

I look sixteen now, but I'm twenty-nine.

They say we are lucky.

Of course.

That's right.

I took a quick look up and down the long wide ice-cream-gleamy street. The houses here are still quite old, but way over there, beyond the Forest, the sky poles of the outer city sheer up in layers of diamond and ruby terraces. And I could just make out the light on top of the Leaning Tower, pulsing on-violet/off-rose/Chinese-dragon-green.

If I took the sprint I'd be there in twenty minutes. Did I want to be so early?

Like but right then I saw this girl and this new male were stood there under one of the float-lamps.

She was dark and serious-eyed and twentyish, so she might be me-type, or younger old-going-to-die-soon type. I couldn't tell.

The male looked like a quack.

I am going to walk by, but the girl speaks to me.

"Excuse me, but you just left that house."

I walked on.

She ran after me.

She had high-heels but not proper high enough.

He rumbled after her.

I turned and looked at her.

"What do you want?"

"You see," she said, helplessly, moving her hands as like she was underwater, "I'm looking for my bloke, Sigh."

"Sigh?" I said.

"Yes – short for Simon. He spells it SY."

With a name like that he was surely almost being of Older Gen. Perhaps he'd just given up the ghost. I suggested that, and she let out a thin silly scream, as if I'd hit her or turned my Self-D spray on her.

The male with her said loudly, "Right, d'you know anything about it? He was just fishing down the canal a few days back and he never come home. He's her feller and my bruvva and we wanta know what the fuck happened to him, 'cos he doesn't just vanish, right? She's scared he fell in the canal."

No one calls it the canal any more. It's called The Nile.

"Can't help you," I said.

The girl started to cry.

I walked on, and they didn't try to stop me. They should go to the Civ Law anyway, if they're worried. It's nothing to do with me.

Only thing is, now skipping about in my mind to the tick-tick of my slenderest totter-heels on the milk-light-washed pavement, a remembering of another girl a month ago, summertime, also asking me on the street about someone else who had gone missing .

Why do they ask me?

I don't know.

I don't care.

Live and let go.

## 10

I danced all night.

Always do.

Had carnal with a male in the Singles Rooms of the Tower, and then got the sprint back.

I felt wonderful. Sex is brilliant, and all the exercise.

I only drink liquid-silver, which is very good for you and inspires the brain.

My plan was to go to bed as the sky before the flat-house was blazing with sunrise, and sleep into Zone 34.

The street, when I reached it, was empty of anything but the dregs of darkness.

I'd forgotten all about the girl and male and their missing feller – bruvva Sigh.

But when I got to the house – and undid the door with my ID nail, I smelled this smell.

The street smells clean and hygiene-brushed. The Forest at the back sends wafts of green and ink perfume and the aroma of birds and shadow. But this house, when you step in from the fresh air –

The house, just there in the downstairs hall, right by where the old woman has her apartment, it stinks.

I have noticed this before.

I have put it down to the place being so old and all that. Upstairs everything smells sweet.

Maybe it's her.

Maybe she's decaying.

Maybe she's died and is falling in bits, and this grey-brown reek of a rotting retro-burger wrapped in metal-foil is the result.

But I thought, as I stood there, that I had smelled the reek before and then it had gone away.

Now it was raw.

It had claws.

It had sores.

I ran upstairs and leapt into my rooms.

I should contact the Civ Law on my Mee.

Instead I went into my bathdome and threw up all my lovely night, and my sick was silver, worth a fortune if I had the guts to scoop it up and strain it through and package and send it to recyke.

But I couldn't.

Let go.

It goed.

## Emenie:

## 11

About seven days after my thing with the fishing man, I had a double. They weren't very much, if I'm honest. But it wasn't too bad. A man, and later a woman. Obviously, two in the same twenty-four hours is in itself rewarding; it's only happened twice before, and I've been killing people for – well, let me think, almost seventeen years.

I had a slight concern that night, just as I was drifting to sleep, that I might get a long wait after this.

As a rule I try not to be superstitious.

The next morning, at nine sharp, someone rapped the knocker on the front door. (Needless to say, the bell doesn't work anymore.)

Years ago this would have been a postman, or a religious fanatic. Now there isn't any mail service. And usually the religious go about things in more covert or more strident ways.

I'd gone to bed fully clothed, tired from the second killing, which had taken place a couple of miles away, in the ruins of the suburban hinterland. I rolled off the mattress.

The exit to the downstairs hall, and the front door I hardly use, goes from the main room, but for some reason I've hidden that door in my room behind an old screen. It's quite pretty, the screen, with peacocks painted and stitched on it.

By the time I'd moved the screen, opened the room door, crossed the hall, unlocked the front door... well, I thought the unusual caller might have gone. But in fact he was just rapping the knocker again.

"Yes?" I asked kindly. I never look a mess, even when I've just got up. I look clean and tidy and combed, and my breath smells of mint toothpaste. Again, it's just something I can do.

"I'm lookin' fer my bruvva," he said.

"Really."

"Yeah."

He was a shambling type, in a big – not moth – probably rat-eaten leather jacket. His greasy hair hung in chunks about his miserable face.

"I don't think I can help you," I said.

"Well, yer see yer might," he said, squinting at me as if the hall, or I, gave off a bright light. But the hall is dark, even with the morning sun on the front of the house. "He knew this road – we both done, when we was kids. Me bruvva."

I smiled benignly.

He said, "An' this house, back when things was all right." We each then sadly looked down at the ground, politely mourning for Civilisation's end.

"He wen' off to the States," said the man. "Then he come back."

Oh, I'd already realised, by then, identified who this one wanted. The rather maleficent miserableness both he and the fishing man had in common. Or, I suppose, had had, before I killed the fishing man.

"He liked to go an' see all the old haunts, even when they was rubbish now. He'd've come here."

It was time to draw two lines through the conversation, and so cross it out.

"Well he didn't come here, or if he did, I didn't see him. No one's been here."

"Man up the park," said the persistent brother, "he told us, me an' her, he seen him go off with this woman, off up this way."

"Maybe," I said, "but he wasn't with me, and he didn't come here."

I tried to shut the door then, and he put his foot in it, in the prescribed manner. I wondered briefly if I should ask him in and properly get rid of him. But you see, I don't like to kill that way, not to order, as it were. It would spoil the act for me. Put me off. Inevitably, it has happened, though only once, long ago. But I learned my lesson. Unless it really is incriminatory life or death for me, I can't and I won't.

Therefore we stood there, him with his stupid big betrainered foot wedged against the door, and me looking at him with patient sternness.

## 12

Very occasionally I do go for a ramble through the empty and neglected house. The upper two floors are mostly bare of anything, although there is a bed in one of the rooms which, a couple of times, I've had a rest on through the afternoon, where the late sunlight comes in at the glass via the lacework of the garden trees. This glass too, of course, I haven't boarded up.

In the attic, pigeons sometimes make their nests, flying in and out through a broken skylight.

For some reason, with this obstreperous bore wedging the front door open, my mind travelled briefly off and away, flying like a pigeon-spirit through the higher storeys, as if looking for something, some remedy.

I said, still patiently and kindly, "I really don't see how I can help."

"You're 'ER," he said. "He went off with you. You both come here. He's in there now. I know he fuckin' is." And then he bellowed past me, up the stairs, "Oi Sy, COME OUT!"

Naturally, now, there was nothing I could do to deter him, and in a minute he was probably going to stampede past me, and go tearing about. He might not find the fishing man (Sy?) because the cellar door isn't easy to spot without a light. And it's difficult to open. But it would be such an intrusion.

Damn him, I almost certainly would have to allow him entry, make it easy, then kill him. I glared at him with final unhidden loathing.

And then.

From somewhere over the street, a girl came running. She had long dark hair and big wounded eyes, and the moment I saw her I knew she was for me. She was mine. It couldn't have been more evident if she had worn a big scarlet badge reading Kill me, please.

## 13

She rushed straight up to the leather jacket man and grabbed his arm.

"Stop it! Look what you're doing! Leave her alone! How can you be such a bully?"

And, rather to my surprise, Big Bruvva sort of shrank down and squinted at her sidelong, with a childish guilty watery gaze.

She said to me, "I'm so sorry. He's just upset. We're so worried, you see."

"Yes," I said.

She said, "Simon went fishing in the canal. Yes, it's crazy, but he was, a bit. We all are now, aren't we, most of us. But this was days ago..." I thought, yes, I know exactly how many days ago. "...and then there's this guy on the waste ground down there, and he told us there was a woman with Sy, and he went off with her, and well, the guy said he thought he'd seen her before, the woman, and she lived in a house here – this house, by the bungalow."

I said, as if making the decision I had already made by the time she was across the street, "All right. You can come in. Not him. I don't want him in my house. But you can come in. We'll have a talk and see if we can work out what's happened. I can see you're upset..." At that she started to cry. Lovely, polished crystal tears out of her dark grey crystal eyes. Poor little thing.

Big Bruvva slunk back. He went to sit on a broken wall by a dead lawn with a rusted vandalised car on it.

She and I, once I'd shut the front door behind us, walked through into the downstairs portion of the house.

# 14

I made some tea. It had to be black obviously; even though the fridge works, you can never find proper milk now.

While I made the tea, I saw the damp patch on the kitchen wall had changed shape. It looked like a slim woman in a long robe, or shroud.

Sometimes, omens can be unsubtle. This one anyway was now redundant.

My prey was already here.

I didn't put anything in the tea, except the sugar she asked for.

We went through to the main room and she sat on the sofa and I in one of the two armchairs. I didn't light the overhead lights but used some more candles. (She hadn't commented on the fridge, but full electricity might be too much for her sensibilities.)

"It's nice here," she said, after a while.

"It's all right."

"Better than where we are – I mean, Sy and me. It's an old caravan. But at least we..." she halted. The 'we' might now be superfluous.

Then she began to tell me all about him, her lover or partner or whatever he had been. I wasn't interested in the least. It was like – what? – dissecting a good meal you've eaten when it's all gone – oh, this meat came from so-and-so, and that cheese-sauce I made myself using this, this and this. No point.

I barely listened, just watched her. The thing was, actually, although I had known immediately she was to be my new victim, I hadn't, as yet, picked up from her any idea of how it should be done. And it must be done correctly. To kill with an unsuitable weapon of whatever sort would jar. As if, to use the analogy of food again, you cooked a perfect fruit pie, and then poured beef gravy on it. Although again, I can't rule that out – in some cases just such an anomaly might be wonderful. A rich acidic apple tart, maybe, with the very saltiest gravy... Or like the man I killed one time, by thrusting a plastic purse into his throat... Yes, nothing should ever be completely ignored as a possible enhancing means.

I kept thinking, however, as her recital-eulogy went on, that Bruvva would charge up again and start hammering at the front door. Or worse, find his way round to the back. Would she then be able to quell him again?

Frankly, I didn't want to kill her here. 'Sy' was here. It was too cosy, the two of them in the cellar, rotting side by side.

Some other arrangement must be made. And hopefully by that time I'd know how I wanted to work with her.

Suddenly she stood up, as if she had telepathically overheard, consenting and assisting me.

"I've taken so much of your time. I'm sorry. But, we had to try, just in case – thank you for the tea." She wasn't nervous, just sad, and solitary. Obviously the hulk outside would be as much use to her as the burnt-out rusted car.

"Look," I said, "I know a few of them round here. Why don't I ask them about all this? And though we don't have police any more, there's a little group along the canal, a bit rough, but they sometimes take up a good cause. I'll see if they can help."

"Oh, would you?" Her face flooded with gratitude.

"Maybe come back tomorrow – sort of evening, yes? Only don't bring him. I'm sorry. He scares me."

"No, I promise. Just me. Thank you," she said.

She had stars in her eyes not tears as I let her out again at the front door. Bruvva, I noted, had vanished.

The morning was turning misty, like soft smoke, powdering over the ends of the road, the tree-tops, the edges of vision.

# Rod:
# 15

On Tuesday morning Forrel delightedly told me I had to see Bins, our Department Manager. Forrel's delight is always an indicator in such matters. Bins's face was another.

Bins has been in charge of The Floor for three years and he has an aging unkemptness, nasal and ear hair, spindly frame and large belly coupled to a self-deceptive – one assumes – youthful urgency to change things.

He scowlingly smiled at me, and showed me the three awful capped dead-white teeth nestled among his yellower ones.

"Now, this can't go on, can it?" Mr Bins demanded.

It seemed the last report I had emailed through to the Upper Tier, as he calls it, had been full of mistakes – typos, misspellings, misuse of italics, 'Martian-looking' names, and so on.

I explained my machine was playing up.

"Your machines always play up, don't they?" he gloweringly reminded me. "No one else has this problem. What do you do to your computer, Terris," (he always has my surname wrong) "to cause this? Do you spill your coffee in it? Do you play silly war games on it or watch pornography and lose track of your duties? This can't continue, Terris. Can it?"

I was certain it could but refrained from saying so.

"And I see you've requested leave for this Wednesday afternoon. Why is that?"

"My uncle, Mr Bins."

"It's most inconvenient."

"I've offered to come in on Saturday."

"Yes, well you'll have to, but it still isn't convenient. Why is this sudden absence needed?"

"My uncle is a very old man."

Mr Bins seemed to infer my uncle was near death. His face became grave. But even that failed to bring on any mercy.

"Very well, then, Terris. You must do as you think best. But you'll have to work all of Saturday, I must make that clear. And bear in mind, the firm is not at your beck and call. You are at its."

## 16

Uncle George's flat is in Lewisham.

That's one of my twenty minute journeys. A couple of times I've even taken a taxi back from there later in the evening, but their rates are now so high I tend to stick to the train. Though even that, it goes without saying, is exorbitant.

The day was rather foggy in the morning. There were no repercussions from Bins. I grabbed a sandwich at The Stag for lunch and then went straight down.

Vanessa doesn't, apparently, drink, but George was normally continuously drunk. He will start to 'partake', as he has termed it, at about 10 a.m., and get through around three bottles of wine, the odd V or G and T, or W and S thrown in as a 'treat'.

He was never offensive or incoherent. He talked about the 'old house in Kent' where, if one believed him, there were five or six dogs and a parrot, (which finally escaped), and a housekeeper, 'Sonia', with whom, one gathered, he had had an 'arrangement'.

I reached his flat above Empress Designs in the High Street. The back of the flats is rather bleak, looking into other business back yards, but once up the stone stair and through the door, the area was spacious, and comfortably equipped with battered, pleasant furniture, books and CD's and vinyl records, three music centres and four drinks cabinets, and innumerable photographs of dogs and parrots and – possibly – Sonia, a buxom young woman in a clinging one-piece bathing costume, under a tree. These photos may be fakes, or from somebody else's albums. They look about 1950's in style. George gave his current age as seventy-six, but looked more like fifty-six. I knew nothing of him until after my father died. I was almost fourteen then. Another accident, unfortunately, my father's death. A plane crash off the coast of Norway.

As it often has been, when I got there the door of the flat was on the catch and ajar.

I sidled in, with my token present of three bottles of white wine and two red. The white was French, the red Californian.

"George?" I experimented. Sometimes he was in the front room that overlooks the High Street, listening to Bach, with the wine, if white, in an ice-bucket. He doesn't like to be recognised as 'uncle'. It's always just George.

I couldn't now hear any music. And nobody responded. He always had done. "Come in," he would cry in his mellow voice, like that of an elegant first class actor acting an elegant first class drunk. "Come in, Roderick."

Not this time, though.

The front room was, as ever, untidy and gently warm, the window letting in the sun between the dark red-wine curtains; no nets. The ice-bucket stood in place too, with a nearly fresh Saint Saône, just a half glass gone from it. But no glass on the table.

Sat on the turn-table of a well-polished, reinvented gramophone was a disk highlighting Mozart's Don Giovanni. But the apparatus was switched off and cold.

George had a regular cleaner here, but I doubt he kept up an 'arrangement' with her. I had never seen her, but he had said in 'later life' he only liked young girls – about sixteen – or much older women, older than he was, ninety even – they made him feel young.

I've never had any notion if recently he obtained sex with anyone. That was his business, presumably.

I took a turn round the crowded room, and looked out at the busy street – shoppers, buses, bikes and bicycles. Opposite was Furnished Futures, its windows that day crowded with glittering curtains and strange chairs that seemed made from dark yellow bones.

George had once confided he thought, in the small hours, when the road was unbusy, objects from Empress Designs crept across and had relations with stuff from Furnished Futures, and their resultant children subsequently appeared in both emporiums, and elsewhere along the High Street.

"George?" I tried again.

Was he in the bathroom?

I went back into the passage and along to the bathroom but the door stood wide on a pristine modern white water-suite scored for bath, basin and convenience.

I tried his study then, and his bedroom. George wasn't there. I looked round the edge of the half-shut bedroom door, and saw the bed, a priest-like single, and the window that in turn, when the blind is up, gazes off at the wall of next door's supermarket.

## 17

It appeared George had had to go out for something, but the wine was ready. He always offered me a drink, and went on offering, far more than I take as a rule. Later we'd go to The Palace, the Chinese restaurant up the road.

Presently I put the wine I'd brought into the already quite well-stocked fridge and cupboard. I took a plain, gleam-clean glass from the kitchen shelf that was full of gleamingly-cleaned glasses, and sat down in the front room with some Saint Saône cold from the bucket.

Taking out my notebook I made some notes. It was then about 3 p.m.

## 18

At 6 p.m. there was still no sign of George.

I had gone round the flat again, rather foolishly looking under the bed, and in the two big bedroom cupboards. One never knows, especially with the elderly. I could recall him saying to me, a year or so before, "You know, Rodders, you're more of an oldster than I am. You're what – thirty-five – thirty-seven – and you're like an old chap around sixty. But I'm a lion, my lad. I'm eternally sixteen. The boy that never grew up." I hadn't argued.

But by six, I had begun to wonder if all these years of consummate boozing had at last accomplished what the medical fraternity endlessly warns everyone will now happen to them, if they drink as they like, and eat as they want, or pass within a two mile radius of a lighted cigarette.

I put the notepad away and tried two or three of George's 'special' phone numbers. The cleaner – the local doctor – some female called Mrs Spur(?) – but nobody answered and the phone, too, seemed to be playing up, the dialling and ringing tones fluctuated. Had George forgotten to pay the bill?

On the ordinary rota of our evenings, he and I would part company about nine to ten. But I didn't want to linger longer in the empty flat. It felt impertinent. The place too had begun to demonstrate uncomfortable sounds – shiftings, creakings – and curious odours – dog-hair, talcum powder, even cannabis – none of which I'd ever noted there before, and that might anyway be permeating upward from the shop below.

I put the undrunk wine back in the fridge, shades of Vanessa, and left George a note apologising for having to leave at six-thirty. I asked him to call me at my home number, as I was sorry to have missed him.

When I let myself out I shut the door.

Naturally I felt I might have done the wrong thing. But to institute a police search seemed premature, and he would never forgive me if all the while my visit had just slipped his mind.

I would call him later. Or tomorrow. Then I could act. If I had to.

By then I was very hungry. But I went to a pub near the station rather than the Chinese restaurant. I couldn't go there without Uncle George. It just wouldn't seem right. On the train I thought about the wardrobe.

## Klova:
# 19

There was another thousand shots wired into my account the bank-nanny told me, flashing up the message on my Mee at Zone 14.

My first thought was I could buy some more clothes.

By 20 I was out into the city and buying them.

Then I had a moonshake at the Crazy Cornerhouse.

The city looks very ordinary by day, I think, like as if it's too old. But when it gets dark and the lights and neons and lazulies come on, London looks supernatural.

I love night by the river.

I like the way the water, which is slicked with gild-oil, looks like gold snakes all in it and over it, like that thing about eels, is it? Some poet wrote.

In a public dressing-room I changed into my new dress and shoes and put on my make-up and the lipstick, of which I'd also bought two more sticks, it's so good.

I went to the Leaning Tower.

The Tower is seventy storeys tall.

I think it is.

You can see, even under the coloured pulse-beams, all over London, all sparkling and night magic, and out to the suburbs with their little lamps, and the parks and empty gaps of land. You can see to my road, and the Forest by The Nile. The moon was up, yellow and hollow like a mandolin. They say the moon is manmade, don't they?

# 20

He was in the garden at the top of the Tower.

I mean several hundred males are usually up there, and girls, but tonight he was, too.

I like the chrysanthemum forest at the middle of the garden.

The flowers grow up to fifteen feet tall, or almost five metres in Oldy talk. They have these narrow, tough, woody, scaly stems, with little dark green leaves like snake-tongues. The petals on the huge heads are combed, and they rise out of an opening, a sort of sky light, into the night. They're white and bronze and burgundy red, and they drink fizzy lemonade and Sham-Pain that the sprinklers feed them all evening.

"Shall I get you a drink?" he asked me.

"Yes," I said.

So he did and while we had our drinks, he asked if I'd have carnal with him. He was like very polite. But not a peculio. In looks he was about seven feet, but we are tall now, our generation that doesn't age, and he seems around nineteen, which means either he is, or that's where the change kicked in. His eyes were very dark blue and he had spiked blue hair. Live and let love.

We had carnal in a Singles Room, and that was brilliant.

Then he bought me another liquid-silver and we walked round the Upper Terrace, and looked at the river and the sky poles, and I pointed out my place miles off, by The Nile.

He said he could see there was a light burning.

I said that was the male in the flat across from mine, who is careless with his window shields.

"Do you like him?" asked my night partner.

"No. He might have been pretty when he was young, but he's old now." We then said together, gravely, "In fifty years he'll be dead." And left the correct pause.

Then my night partner said he would like to see me again. It was by now Zone 8. In two hours the day would start to wake up.

I said yes. I said he could come and see me at my flat.

"There's no slide, but it's all right otherwise."

"I can walk up a few stairs," he assured me. "I have to all the time. "By then he'd already told me he worked as part of a Human Security Team, in several big old places in central London.

I said, "Only thing, there's a non-good stink sometimes in the downstairs hall. The old woman as owns the flats has her place off there. It was truly foul the other night, but a bit less now."

"Probably rats," he said. "We get a lot of that. She should try that humane killer. It works, just sends them to sleep and they die. Then it destroys everything inside five Zones. Not like the filth they used to dose them with before. I used to shoot the poor little fucks to save them that. One clean shot."

I liked that in him. I like everything so far. He is beautiful. And the sex was star.

"I'd tell her, but I never see the old woman. The bank-nanny pays my rent."

"OK," he said. "If I see her, I'll tell her."
Then he asked my name and I told him without any problem.
"Klova," he said. "Flower and spice."
He is called Coal. Like his skin.
He walked me to the sprint, and we said goodbye tenderly. I wondered if he really would visit.

## 21

Coal sent a message to my Mee.

I got the machine to polish the glass tiles in the social room and set the thing in the bathdome to make it extra prist.

Last time I was in the downstairs part there was no smell.

I went over the bridge on The Nile and into the Forest at dusk, when the electric fireflies come on in the trees, and picked a couple of night-blooming violas. You're not supposed to. But the O.C.'s are pretty stupid there. Or maybe it's just that thing I can do to surveillance cameras.

Funny, in a way, because Coal is in security.

I've never met that many people who have to, or want to, work for money. Most of them get by on the wired-in donations, like I do.

Even the old male across in the other flat — who I've only glimpsed now and then — even he doesn't seem to work, and he's one of the mud-stuck older-ones-who-will-soon-die.

I put the violas in cube-ice glasses.

They burned there all frosty, with purple-blue petals like Coal's eyes.

I hoped it would be special.

It had been, but then, a second time...

You can't be certain, ever...

Love and let go.

Only thing, no more shots in my account, and now, after my last night at the Leaning Tower, I was down to only five hundred.

The bank could probably give me a loan, till the next shot.

## 22

Coal arrived exactly at Zone 40. Exactly when he said.

He brought a hamper of things to eat and drink!

They were wonderful. And Sham-Pain. (Like the chrysanthemums have in the Leaning Tower.) This though from France, it's part of the tariff they pay, of course, but generally you don't ever get to drink any.

Coal said it was one of the rewards of his job.

In a while we went to the bed and it was again brilliant. Better even than before.

Later though, when we were sitting at the social room window in the dark, drinking Sham-Pain and watching The Nile and the Forest lights, he said to me, very seriously, "I do have to warn you, Klova. That woman downstairs – there is something really crap about that smell. I did pick it up, coming in. Not powerful, but there. Sort of ground into the bones of this house where you live."

"I so hoped you wouldn't. I didn't notice it earlier."

"You see, Klova, you get used to things when you're around them a lot. And that smell – I'm not even certain that it is rats. No, I am not."

We sat in silence then, and I began to feel strange and to want he'd go.

And when it was Zone 46 I made up a lie about how I would have to visit my aunt tomorrow and needed to get to sleep soon.

And we parted coldly, after all that lovely sweet nice.

And I cried afterwards, which I do not do.

I cried.

Love and le-t – no. I cried.

# EMENIE:
# 23

She arrived at 7p.m. She was alone, not even invidiously shadowed. It was dark by then in the lampless street. No moon. But I could see her coming along the road, through the tiny spy hole I keep in the boarded-up bedroom window at the very front of the house. I had been watching out since five. I'd left the time open, you see, 5 to 7ish. Anytime then. After that, I'd said, I had to go and look in on an elderly neighbour. What a good Samaritan I was, wasn't I? She had a faint sheen on her, the girl, that's what made her visible to me in the dark, like phosphorous, or as if she was radioactive.

"Hello," she said shyly.

I let her straight in, and through into the main room.

"I found some wine," I said. "That was such a stroke of luck. Do you like wine? It's so awkward for you, this. Wine might help?"

And she clasped her hands together, like an old-fashioned – perhaps Victorian – child.

"Oh, I love wine. We never have – we don't – didn't..." She faltered, said bravely, "Sy likes beer, so we have that. He knows someone with a sort of amateur brewery. It tastes..." laughing suddenly, "...horrible."

"Nothing worse than bad beer," I acknowledged. (More lies. I'd never drink it. Or, only now and then.)

(She had asked my name, last time, on the cliff-edge of the front doorway. "I'm Micki," she had said. "Mum called me Michelle – but, well. Most people call me Micki. Can I," she had asked, "ask your name? Don't say if you don't want, it's just easier for me to get my head round this if – if I have some sort of name for you."

"I'm Emenie," I said.

And her pale, clear, sad face fell.

"Enemy?" she asked, staring – less in horror than in despair.

"No. Emm-enny," I enunciated, "it's Old English or something."

She had smiled. A Victorian child, smiling. Innocent, wanting to be good. So many examples in so much literature. "Did your mother...?"

"Something like that."

I have no mother. No father. And in those peculiar brief moments I didn't want to deceive her. And she accepted my evasion. Why not, when she'd got my real name.)

And so now, when I handed her the emerald glass full of ruby booze, she smiled again and said, in the most musical and heart-broken, heart-breaking way, "Thanks, Emenie. I can really do with this."

And she could. After all, it wasn't poisoned.

# 24

We sat in dark candlelight, she on the sofa, I in the armchair. I began my spiel. Now I had to deceive.

"Right. These guys I know down by the canal. They don't know anything, they say, but they'll ask around. I can't vouch for them, but as a rule they seem to try to protect people. Sometimes it's an idea to give them a sort of present..."

"Oh – but what shall I...?" she rushed in anxiously.

"It's OK. I didn't just find one wine bottle. I found four. They had two, and I had two. Yes, it was lucky. But they are pleased, and they might come up with something."

"I miss him so much," she whispered to her glass, which was already half empty, as they used to say. "I miss him. It's mental in a way," she added. "He used to be unkind to me. Oh – I don't mean physically. I just mean, well, other women, or he just used to go off – but he always came back. And if he said he would be back that night, he was. He always was. And he was so clever. He had a job in the US. You know. Before... And he did really well. But he was always so unhappy."

I watched her. She was the unhappy one now.

Sy wasn't unhappy.

Bloody Sy – Simon was stone-grey dead.

And soon this girl would be. She was mine to make that way.

I stared at her. I read her, tried to learn her by heart. I had to. Enigma still masked her round. Despite all of it, for the very first time in my career as a killer, I could not grasp what method I must use. It simply would not come to me.

I got up and refilled her glass.

She said, "You're very kind. Thank you. And for asking... those men."

"I'm sorry," I said, not sorry at all, obviously, it was none of it true, "everyone else I've asked never saw him, knows nothing. That chap," I added, "in the park – I had a look for him," (I had, too) "but I couldn't find him." (Nor had I. If I ever did, since he claimed to have seen me with Sy, I might have to consider murdering him. A chore. The demeaning of a sacred pleasure. But, if I must.)

"Oh," she said wearily, drooping down, her dark hair falling past her face in two charming brunette spaniel ears, "that was more –

well the man who came here with me last time..."

"Sy's brother."

"Yes. He – sort of kept on at the man over there on the waste ground. And the man sort of said he thought he might have seen Sy with a woman and they came here..." She faltered again.

I said, consolingly, "I suppose, as he's his brother, he's pretty desperate to find out."

"Maybe," she said.

She shut her eyes.

The refilled-full-again glass wavered in her hand. "I'm so tired," she said. "I don't sleep. I can't. Not at... home."

I said, "Why don't you have a rest? That sofa's OK. I can bring you a clean pillow and a blanket."

She didn't show anything of being suspicious. Merely looked up at me. Now she was the exhausted Victorian child, dragged over the snow-mounds by some villain, her mother dead amid the drifts.

By the time I came back with the pillow and coverlet she lay completely asleep full-length on the sofa. The filled green-red-black glass had been stood, most carefully, on the floor. She was on her right side, and had her left hand curled under her neck, and her right tucked against her breast. She hadn't even taken off her coat.

I laid the shroud of the cover over her and put the pillow at her feet not to disturb her. Then I crept out of the room, and into the kitchen, not switching on the light.

Outside some foxes were fighting, or copulating, in the gardens. At other times badgers come and do the same. I value their savagery. It brings energy and a reason to the feral wilderness of trees and shrubs.

I sat listening to them. I sat thinking of knives and the gun, and stones, and this poison and that, of strangling and smothering and pushing and so on.

What was her special need? Until I fathomed it I couldn't make a move. And now her presence in my flat, in my 'grandmother's' house, was like a briar of clear dark granite. It might entangle me. It would get in my way. There had to be an answer very soon. But I couldn't sell myself – or her – short. Enigma. Endeavour. Endless. Enemy.

# Rod:
# 25

George didn't call me, and so the next day I called him, first on the landline at the Lewisham flat, and next on his antiquated but functioning mobile. Both took my message but refused to render up my Uncle George.

I had work anyway to contend with, plus making up for the half Wednesday escape with a whole dreary Saturday. Weekends generally entail only a skeleton staff, and the most tedious memos to check and respond to through the machine which, of course, soon started to print everything up in what looked like the Cyrillic alphabet.

One of the caretakers, Bill, strolled in during the afternoon, and we had a chat about his angry and mad-sounding wife, who, according to Bill, was always bolting the house door in his absence and so locking him out – either that or when he was in the house, and she out, taking his keys as well as her own, and so locking him in. I've suggested it might be her age, all this, and perhaps she could visit her GP. But Bill said she had always been like it. She had driven him nuts in hundreds of ways when they were in their teens, and terrorised him into marriage when they were twenty. There were no children. But she didn't want any, and he hadn't, but now he sometimes wished he had a son or daughter he could talk to. After this, I told him about George, who I'd continued to call, two or three times each day, to no avail. Both landline and mobile now refused even to take a message.

"They go funny when they get to that age," said Bill, who seems to be in his late fifties, and whose wife is insane.

"I keep thinking I ought to get on to the police," I said. "Except he'd never forgive me if he's there and just wants to be on his own. He's pretty spry. He's never ill," I added, thinking but not saying anything of George's alcoholic habits.

On Sunday, I half meant to go to Lewisham again. But I was worn out, and the thought of another weekend train gave me the creeps.

On Sunday evening I phoned Vanessa.

I told her about George.

"Oh, George," she said dismissively. "He's a drunkard. He

could be up to anything. I should leave well alone, Roderick."

She had little time for George. He was from my mother's side, and Vanessa was my father's sister.

Vanessa told me, at great length, about her next door neighbours, who had started to have parties twice a week and, as the weather was still fine, often spilled with their guests out into the adjacent garden, laughing and drinking and smoking dope, with loud music playing, sometimes until one or two in the morning.

"Poor you," I said.

"I'd complain to the council," she said, "but they take no notice."

"Perhaps they'll stop when the weather turns," I opined.

She said, brusquely, "Are you coming down next Saturday?"

"Well..."

"Yes, Roderick, I know you normally only visit me once a month. But remember, I have to go to Wales next, to see Cissy."

Who was Cissy? God knew, and apparently Vanessa thought I did too. It would save time to agree.

"Of course, yes," I said. "Next Saturday, then."

One more day gone down the drain.

## 26

Through the next week I kept up my calls to George, and even wrote him a letter.

I said I was worried, and did he need a hand with anything.

I wondered if he had collapsed in the street due to some Bacchic seizure and been carted off to hospital. But George, I knew for a fact, always carried some form of ID, not to mention a note of next of kin, (me), along with a stern, signed refusal of any of his organs for transplantation. I heard nothing from anyone.

On Friday night, I decided I had to take a detour and drop by his flat on my way home from work.

When I got there it was well after seven, and the High Street was bristling up with gangs and other evening revellers. But the flat was dark, and no one answered my rings on the bell. I peered through the letterbox and then called through it... "George! George?" But no one replied. There was a smell of dust and dried wine and emptiness. When I rang the bell of the next door flat, a child of about ten came to the door. It had a baseball cap on the wrong way round, and snot on its upper lip. It stared at me aggressively as I asked if its mother was there, before it abruptly slammed the door shut again in my face. I could tell I'd disappointed the awful little creature; it must have been expecting someone else.

Oh, I knew I should go to the police about George. But I felt dog-tired, and tomorrow, now, I had the trek to Brighton. I had a G and T at a pub, and then made one last effort, walking along to the Chinese Palace. "My friend – my uncle –" I described him to the beaming waiter. "Has he been in this week?"

"Yes, yes," cried the waiter, trying to lead me to a table.

"No, no, I'm sorry – you see, I'm looking for my uncle."

"Yes, yes," cried the waiter, handing me a menu, "we do any what you want."

"Yes, thank you. Another time."

I extricated myself from his non-comprehending web and hurried back to the station.

## 27

I had to change trains for Brighton that Saturday.

To me this was annoying out of all proportion to the event.

Watch it, I thought. I was thirty-two and acting like a silly old codger thirty years older. Everything is always like this, I thought, attemptedly philosophically. Nothing works and nothing is ever as you expect.

Nor was it.

I arrived, the train having been delayed, nearly an hour late. Already I could audially conjure my aunt's voice, "Well, Roderick. I've been hanging about here waiting..."

I had made quite a lot of notes during my journey, but also I had tried to call her, both from the train and Brighton Station. Her number was engaged.

Along with most of the rest of the enormous queue, I waited fifteen minutes for a cab.

It was a gusty cold day, that Saturday, and suddenly, under the white-blue sky, the ochre and amber leaves were shrivelling from the trees, the taller ones of which were often skeletally bare. The

Pavilion looked over-emphatic and windswept, when the cab took some detour or other, as if expressly to show me the famous building. Or show me to it, perhaps, this visitor to its town. The wind howled.

At least Vanessa's neighbours would have to forgo their garden parties.

The house seemed as always, though autumn had shed foliage on the front lawn and path. A plane was passing over, as they always do. That smell of fishy sea and compost.

## 28

While I waited at the door, helplessly I pictured – anticipated – another subnormal child in a cap and snot. But instead a tall lean man in his forties opened it, with a broad, willing smile. "Hi."

"Hello," I said. "I'm sorry to trouble you, but I was wondering if you knew where the woman from No 12 next door might be? Vanessa Taurus? I think you know her?"

His face fell slightly. He did know her, evidently.

"Mm," he said.

"The point is," I said, apologetic, "she was expecting me about an hour ago – train was late – but I thought she'd still be here..."

Firmly Vanessa's party-minded neighbour said, "We don't know her well."

"No, of course not. I'm just a bit – surprised she isn't in. She always is when I call, you see. She's my aunt," I tacked on, trying to impress him with the fact that I knew her well enough to conclude her unexplained absence now was entirely out of character. I implied concern, but not, obviously, alarm. Yet I was alarmed. After George, it went without saying I was.

"Sorry. Don't know anything about it. We never know she's there anyway. Unless," he paused, frowning at the memory, "she comes round about something."

"I see."

"Yes. She complains a lot. To and about us."

"Ah."

He didn't slam the door, just nodded and shut it, still in my face, and still without any offer of information, let alone empathy.

I had an abrupt Ag-Christie-ish idea that, sick of Vanessa's displeasure, the man, and the wife Vanessa had described – "Skirts too short for her age. Streaked hair" – had turned on her and bumped her off. They would dump her body at some tidal cove later on, by night, or bury her under the decking.

Our family name isn't Taurus, either, but that's usually as near as anyone else ever gets. Taurus, or Terris – although George, I believe, used to give it, where he had to, as Terry.

And now what? No doubt the other neighbours, the other side, and across the road, would also refuse to take any interest in my disappearing aunt. Good riddance! they would say in their not-very-secret hearts.

In the end I went through the side gate, which wasn't locked during the day, and into the back garden.

It was secluded enough in summer, but as I'd seen before, once the trees grew bare, and both next doors' walls being low, their gardens were on full view, crammed with adult artefacts and leisure toys – barbecues and garden furniture, sunshades still in place, whirligigs for washing and even, on the other side, a large apple-gathering ladder propped at a tree.

Standing on Vanessa's patio I looked through her French doors. They were very clean and clear and gave on her sitting room, which was also clean, and scrupulously, nearly soullessly, tidy. Just as with George's flat, there was too an air of the Mary Celeste, for I could see through into the adjoining dining room, where the table had been laid with cutlery, water glasses and a large cut-glass bowl loaded with lime-green salad and cherry-red tomatoes.

Without thinking, some instinct, I tried one of the glass doors. Which opened.

## 29

"Vanessa? Auntie Vanessa?"

It sounded infantile, that 'Auntie' now, made infinitely more inappropriate, such a teddy-bear word, called in the rough voice of a mature man.

And needless to say, no one answered.

Why do I put it like that? Because I had known, I had known even before I got on the second train, that something had again gone out of kilter. Like George, and his vanishment.

I went methodically through the house. I looked in the five upstairs rooms and the bathroom, and downstairs in the living rooms, the kitchen and cloakroom. I even looked in the oven – cold and void, and in the fridge – stocked with marg and wholemeal, sugar-free jams, and milk and mince and free-range eggs, and with a solitary bottle of wine, not uncorked. The slices of cold meat were out already and arranged on plates. The kettle had been filled from the filter jug, with the decaff standing by in its big chocolaty jar.

Everything in the way of furnishing or convenience was dusted, hoovered, bleached, scoured, polished and aired. The blue suite in the bathroom and grey suite in the cloakroom sang with hygiene and mint flavours. In the bedroom a book, closed solidly on its leather bookmark, was a nonfiction study of the English coast. Vanessa was about halfway through. Her nightdress lay invisible in its case. Her mules nested just under the bed.

As with George, I looked in cupboards, under the beds of main and guestroom. I even steeled myself to look in her formal and unstimulating wardrobe. I let down the ladder to the attic and clambered up and gaped out of a tiny diamond-shaped window. One could see the sea from the attic. I'd never known. But otherwise it only contained water tanks and wiring, these also in significantly good condition.

I pulled out drawers and saw boring dossiers to do with house maintenance, bills and garden and shopping accounts, and similar stuff.

In the end I ran a glass of water from the tap and drank it, sitting at the dining-room table. To take the unopened wine seemed inappropriate. Even to munch a slice of meat or lettuce, or bite into a tomato, was certainly forbidden by some oblique code.

For about two hours I lingered. I didn't, at any moment, imagine she would come back. Not after George.

I didn't bother to try the phone. I had a feeling it would give me the engaged signal, or that bossy voice that tells one to call later, like an insolent butler from the 1920's.

I had one strange and unworthy thought. I wondered if I should steal anything from her. Not money or jewellery, not that I noticed any, but a book, say, or a plate... something. I wasn't sure if this impulse was from a desire for some memento, or only a wish to rescue an object randomly from the deserted property.

She would never come back. Just as George would not.

When I left, not having, or not having seen the key, I was unable to lock the French doors. As with the side gate, it couldn't be helped.

Was I depressed? Frightened? No, nothing much. It was only rather melancholy.

As I walked back along her road I told myself she would come in soon, and make a fuss that I hadn't turned up, and hadn't rung her to apologise. But I knew perfectly well she wouldn't. I'd never hear from Aunt Vanessa again. And never again from Uncle George.

Back on the Brighton esplanade I had fish and chips and a couple of beers. All around people were eating and drinking, and gazing at the churning white and turquoise-green sea. The chalk makes it green, I think somebody once said. The sky was going to a grumpy purple. It would rain soon. Or pour. Pour like silver milk on the just and the unjust together.

# IRVIN:
# 30

I have seldom seen a worse or more worthless attendance than there was tonight at the theatre. Is it for this we trod the boards in our finery, with reddened lips and darkened eyes, and sang out the words of the poet? Is it for this I stabbed to the heart with the trick dagger the delicious Mis'us Merscilla Peck, an actress of some quality, and the blood-sac disgorged, and I at last fell dead from the villain's poison, so realistically and disgustingly? For twenty-three persons and some irritated dog, (this beast not worth one flea upon the back of my own pernicious and unfaithful hound)?

Well, so it goes. But our wages will reflect this wretched meagreness of a crowd, as does a polished spoon the dirty dish.

So then, home, and not even a dawdle with Mis'us Peck to console me.

The house as ever damp and drear, and the benighted roughness of the land outside, among the coppices and mournful as a painting I once saw of a nocturnal Ophelia, drowning herself in a leaf-falling autumn, under a flux-brown river. This penance of a view runs all the way west of north, to the Ravensburn marshes.

The dog was out and off about his business, as ever, ravishing some neighbourhood canis femina.

In my turn out I went again to the Black Sheep Inn, and had there some strands of meat in a levy of boiled water.

I must find another leman, it seems, until the fair Merscilla, who shows no mercy, (indeed her husband is the kinder to me), until, I say, she forgives me for the sparagal of tonight's congregation. Why I am to blame, who knows? But then, he who can wholly fathom the mind of a woman no doubt is a very great master of wisdom, which I, alas, am not.

No fire on the hearth on returning, though I had paid for such. I will speak to the landlady, if ever I am able to catch her. She is elusive as the unicorn. Though less lovely.

Blow out the candle then, Irvin, and lie down in the icy bed. May God forgive London. I do not.

## KLOVA:
## 31

He didn't come back. Coal, I mean.

Who else would I mean?

Like truly I hadn't expected him to. And I would get used to it, that he never would.

But I didn't.

There were also no new shots, and now the bank-nanny had paid the quarter for the flat and the gadgets that heat and light and clean it – including the extra polish to the tiles – I was down to one hundred and twenty. I messaged the nanny and asked if I could have a loan of three hundred, and later it messaged me and said No. Instead I could have an over-debt of one hundred and fifty, at an interest rate of like something I might not be able to repay unless someone wired in three thousand shots pretty fast, and then even a thousand shots might end up paying off the debt-interest. So I said No as well. Then I went to bed at Zone 20, like some kiddy.

I can remember that at the Child Centre. How they shoved you off to the dormitory so early. And I used to cry, but silent, so the bullies didn't hear.

I never knew my parents, not even my mother.

On my birth-registration she is called CP.

That's like the letters on the lipstick, now I remem it.
C.P.
Only there are like as the other smaller letters too. On the lipstick.

## 32

Next morning I got up and I had an idea.

I'd dreamed of Coal, and he said in the dream, "Where are you?" And I thought then he meant he would like to see me, but he wouldn't be the first one to move. After all, I'd told him to go. I still didn't know really why I had. It was because of him going on about the rat smell. Stupid.

But I didn't of course have his Mee number. I decided though if I went to the Leaning Tower that night he would be there again, and perhaps it would be fine.

I put on the black and gold and red and all of that, even though I'd worn it there before. It wasn't anyway worn when I saw him first. I put sparkles in my hair, which is black at that time.

When I left the flat-house I for some reason rem'd the peculio male and the girl who asked me about their lost male called Sigh. No one was in the street. No visible home lights anywhere. And the lights weren't on in the Forest and the float-lamps had gone all bunched up about five buildings along and were useless and blinding when you got under them.

I caught the sprint.

It was only when I was on it I thought; there was no bad smell in the hall tonight. I was really sure this time there hadn't been. Perhaps I could ask him back.

When l got into the Tower I went along through all the rooms, slowly, each by each. I only bought one liquid-silver. It would have to last. I couldn't afford another. I couldn't really afford one.

I didn't see him, though. I didn't, anywhere...

And then I went up on the roof-walk under the spire with the blue-mauve-rose-jade pulse beam. And I tried not to cry. I was early at the Tower, it wasn't yet 48. So maybe he came later, the way generally I did.

I went down and into the loud room and danced with myself a while. There were lots of girls and some males, all dancing with themselves, but none of the males was Coal.

I had the lipstick on.

I wondered, as he said his name was Coal, if his registered name began with P.

At Zone 48 he came into the room, and tonight his hair flamed dark red like the chrysanthemums, and his eyes were red too, like garnets in his dark beautiful face.

He was with a girl.

They danced together.

I went to the side and sat on one of the thin stools, and finally his eyes passed over me. I thought he would just cut me out. But he stopped dancing and spoke to the girl. Her face was blank but it went blanker, and he crossed the floor and stood beside me.

"How are you, Klova?"

"I'm OK. How are you, Coal?"

"I'm here," he said.

"So am I," I said.

He leaned over and kissed me on the mouth. I was so moved I couldn't do anything. He said, "What do you want to do?"

"Whatever you do," I said but he couldn't hear me.

I said, "What about her?"

He heard that.

"She's fine," he said. And I looked and she was already dancing with two other males.

"She's just a friend. She's meeting someone. I knew you'd be here," he said softly, and his voice played under the music and I heard every word. "I knew you'd come here. I sent you a message."

"To my Mee?"

"No. Just to your mind. Your heart. And I knew you would hear it and you would be here."

He put his arms round me and slid me off the stool and we went into a bar and he bought me another liquid-silver, but he drank fire-cracker.

Then he said how about going to a room. And I said, "Let's go back to my flat."

And he just nodded. No mention of anything not good. He smiled at me. He said, "Shall we have another drink?" and I saw I'd drunk all my second drink in about five minutes, but I shook my head. "I'm sorry, I can't afford to stay in the Tower much longer. I only paid up to Zone 50." and showed him the little mark on my thumb. If you outstay, an alarm goes off below, and a couple of people come in to remove you. It's very discreetist, but you have to get out. Under Civ Law, if you don't they can do things."

He was staring at me.

He said very softly, but now I heard him very clearly, for we weren't in the loud room, "You can't afford to stay."

"No. Oh, Coal," I said, brightly, chattering from nervy happiness, "I've got hardly any currency left. No shots and I can't get a loan..." I hadn't meant to blurt it, and now, finding him and that the message-dream had been real, I didn't care. It was nearly funny being without funds. It would change – didn't matter.

But he stood back, and looked down at me, with his garnet eyes. And something struck me then, that only the very well-off can use inner-eye cosmetics like that.

"So this," said Coal precisely, "is why you've come after me? You want pay off me, do you, Klova-flower? Yeah? Well, girl, you ain't go' have it. Right? Yeah? You can take your girlness out of here and out of my life. You can go and swim in blood and fire in hell you ice-cold cuntess."

And then he turned round and walked away over the room, silent and straight as a walking spear, and his cruel brain and tongue were the two sides of its blade.

Then I got up and I was dead all over and inside, as if he had hacked me open wide and killed me.

I could barely see or hear, and on the slide I dropped my empty glass and a machine sprang out of the silvery snake-skin of the stair and gobbled the obstacle away.

In the street I leaned on the Tower's glowing wall, under the staggerish sky poles. All people took me for a drunky, but I was dead. Only dead.

# Emenie:
# 33

The foxes were out that night a long while, sexually screaming for mates, seemingly insatiable once they joined one. Joined being the significant word. They stay caught up, as it were, for an hour, I believe. Who told me this I have no notion. Either it's fun or it's purgatory. From the cries you can't tell either what it is, but presumably it's all right: lots of cubs appear in the next relay of months. Foxes are hunted for their fur, of course, as in the past, but in London mostly people are hopeless even about killing a fox, luckily. Most animals get away unharmed from the improvised unworking traps and damfool mobs with sticks and stones. The ones with guns can't shoot, as a rule, and ammo is scarce. Also there's less or no traffic on the ruinous and multi-potholed roads. And the men in scarlet on horses, and with trained-to-be-evil hounds, are no more. At least I imagine they're not. Let them rot.

I dozed through the fox-night, aware – like the princess with the hard green bean – or pea? – under all her mattresses and sticking up into her like a spike – of Micki sleeping in the next room.

Once I thought I heard her stir and wondered if she would start wandering about. I was ready to forestall her, and if necessary I would have sedated her with some mild opiate or strong pain-killer, of which I had a store. Something in a hot drink. Not to murder, obviously, just to keep everything safe and sound. But I didn't hear anything much else, and there was a tiny space when, very delicately and softly, she snored. It was more like a cat's purr, and only lasted three or four minutes by my reckoning.

I wondered what we would do in the morning. Go and look for the Park Man, probably, and/or my invented guys by the canal.

We could visit the wreck of the Co-op, as well. And the High Street. I needed a few things, and she could help me carry them back.

Never look a gift-horse in the mouth, and so on.

## 34

I didn't risk the oven. We had rather old bread and a butter and peanut spread I've found recently in little individual tubs.

I did put on the electric kettle, and we had black coffee and Sweet-Tooth, this also in individual sachets. She marvelled at the working kettle. I told her the legend of the guy who had wired things up so they worked for a couple of hours a day, if randomly. We had been 'lucky' this morning.

"Something big must still work somewhere," she said, doubtfully. "For him to do that... "

"God knows what."

"Yes. Oh dear," she wistfully said, "I used to love God, when I was young."

Young. She was young now. Agonisingly young. And not due to get much older. Age would not wither her, etc.

"Don't blame God. This mess is down to wonderful mankind."

"Yes," she agreed.

She seemed pleased I hadn't blamed her old lost lover. She'd slept well too, she said.

I said I'd thought the wildlife might wake her.

Oh no, she said, she found that comforting when or if she heard it. Life going on. The meek conceivably inheriting what was left of the earth.

She also asked if my neighbour was all right, the one I'd pretended I must look in on. And they were doing well, of course, weren't they.

After this interlude we went out, (she had already used the loo, marvelling at the way the plumbing still operated), and along the canal to the Co-op.

## 35

Am I right? There used to be some catchphrase about something being bigger on the inside than from outside? The Co-op is a bit like that. Except that the Co-op is smaller in the store part, and much bigger in the back rooms than seems possible.

A lot has fallen through, of course. It's only a few yards off up the side road that cuts away from the towpath, and evidently the damp of the canal and its various underground offshoots have undermined the building's foundations. Even so there are corridors that squinny along for what seems a mile at least, cramped little spider-cells of unused offices, some with ceilings long down. And then the storerooms, tall and echoing. They're full of rats, of course, and other scavengers, some human. Though the proportion of humans to animals is low. Naturally there are, by now, a lot less of our species. And besides that, many people believe the Co-op was long ago despoiled of all its useful wares.

Not so. In what I call the Secret Cave, which is tucked in by one of the main areas, a perilous looking, but so far stable, island of floor leads among the standing shelves. It's a library of preserved food. I have noticed, very oddly, that some of these supplies seem to re-establish themselves, as if many of the items in here are still being regularly delivered and restocked. At one time I suspected some remnant of government might be responsible, and that the goods were all booby-trapped or else laced with poisons, to clear the last of us out of the city. But I ate some extra things and used others. Nothing happened. Unless, obviously, I am dead, and just don't know it yet.

Below the floor-island, cliff-like tumbles of brickwork and crashed girders and beams – or whatever they are – statically collapse to a damp, weedy sub-basement.

(Last year I killed a woman here. I hit her with a wine bottle – there were plenty more – then broke her neck – simple enough, she was thin and not strong. She'd looked so sad, and so much happier and more peaceful afterwards. I dropped her down through some struts and she vanished in the deep dark below. No doubt there was the smell, but other things die here, even some of the food probably dies. It always smells.)

Today I, and my little companion, Micki, went about with my shopping list.

We got packets of bread-mix and dried egg, and jams and sweeteners and tea and coffee. After that we collected cans of veg and soup – and packets of dried fruit. There was even cotton wool, three big bags of it, and toilet paper. No one else appears to bother with that. But Micki, (forgetting again, I supposed, for a second), cried out that Sy and she always asked for toilet paper as a present. That and beer, she amended. Then remembered Sy had disappeared mysteriously and that was anyway why she had ended up in the Co-op with me.

At last, the piéce de resistance. A huge freezer that still worked, and which no one else ever appeared to know about. I selected ready-sliced ham and some lamb chops. Micki asked me, as if I owned the place, if she might lift some sausages.

"Take what you want," I said kindly. "Everyone does."

Maybe the pork sausages, their telepathic lure, would guide Sy home to her. Poor little thing.

There isn't always alcohol. But there was. I picked up Vodka and another bottle of wine, but Micki only stared. She seemed to think she was – what? – imagining the goodies in the ruinous storeroom.

We now had quite a lot to carry. But we went out by the back way towards the High Street, or its remains. Four men were scavenging in the yard, where the big work lorries used to come in. Two vehicles still stood there, their sides ripped wide or blown open by home-made explosives. Almost everything was gone from them long ago. But people still find things. I once found a pack of smoked trout behind a bin, and still ice-cold. But it was winter then. I was lucky.

In the High Street my companion marvelled. I marvelled how she had never come this way before. How far off was the caravan where she and Sy had been living?

The bank on the corner had had another fire, I saw. The air smelled charred and little black flakes were even now filtering down from the drained sky. The butchers, once turned into a squat, had been for weeks trashed and vacated. We went into the tobacconists. I stopped smoking years back, and unlike most people, who boast they never lose their craving – like a loyal lover who will go on loving the denying beloved forever – I did lose the habit. A pity, because this place is packed with fags and tins of snout. Once the freezer worked in here too. But no more, and parts of the floor are cemented over by the white and pink death of ice creams.

Micki went on marvelling, and even pocketed two big packets of cigarettes. "I won't take too much. Leave some for other people." Bless her, the silly cow. "They're for Sy," she admitted, as we found the Diet Coke – it moves about, this, for some reason, and today was on the shelves of rotting magazines. "In case," she murmured, "he ever comes back."

"He probably will, you know," I buoyantly told her.

"You really think so? Oh, I'm glad. I do too. Thank you. You've helped me such a lot."

"Sorry we couldn't find those guys I spoke to," I apologised as we turned back for the house. "They're up to something else, presumably."

"Oh. It'll be OK," she said. She had bloomed suddenly with confidence.

I made a decision then. I would have to put my scruples aside and improvise a modus mortua. Plainly, while she was looking on the bright side, and before sorrow set in again, and bitter doubt, I had to kill her. It must be soon, this side of sunset, before the falling night arrived.

# Rod:
# 36

My mother died, as I've said, when I was five. And my sister also died then, too. Tragic, for them. Although I, being so young, hardly knew them. But thinking back, in later years, I have abruptly accepted how comparatively odd my earliest childhood had been.

Even following the tragedy, my childhood continued to be rather bizarre. Only with my father's death on the edges of Norway did my thirteen-year-old self-graduate to what, I surmise, most of us would consider a saner scenario.

I have to add there was no unkindness, no cruelty. At least, none that was apparent to me at the time. I had, as far as I then knew, the ordinary, incomprehensible, quite happy madhouse of a life that any cared-for infant and young adolescent experiences. The world is alien, and its rules often make no sense, but one is coerced or guided through, as a new recruit, to the State of Existence. Like any press-ganged soldier, one learns the ropes in order to survive. And a friendly and pleasing home helps things along.

My parents were rich. They had a house, once a farm, in a remote forested stretch of western British landscape. Neither of them seemed to do much except enjoy themselves. They got various people in to clean and otherwise cope, went out a lot themselves to eat, or on trips, leaving me then to attentive carers. He, I think, had business interests here and there, but others ran the show, he just drew out the money. This continued after the loss of his wife and elder daughter. He drank more then, and sometimes he cried. But he was never violently emotional, and soon enough returned to the normal pursuits, which unfortunately for him included flying light aircraft. He was, on that occasion, with another young woman, of whom there were several after my mother's death. She recovered from the crash, but the payments of compensation rather depleted his post-mortem cash fund. The rest of my teenage years I grew under the hand of an uninterested guardian – who I only ever once saw demonstrate a paroxysm of appalling rage, shame, and utter disbelief. And meanwhile the knowledge that the family 'fortune' was going, going, gone, grew with me. At eighteen, depletion was accomplished.

I left my fairly amenable school, and the country farmhouse, and anything else known and liked, and began the third part of my life, with the firm which, even now, nineteen years after, (or does it only seem so long?), overload and underpay, bore, irritate and employ me. The last also I ever saw of the guardian was in my eighteenth year.

"Well, Rod," he said, wringing out my hand and clapping me on the back. "Onwards and upwards, eh?"

I pacifically agreed. He asked then how my girlfriend was – "Maisie, is it, Rod?"

"Sophie," I replied. In fact of course there was no girlfriend. I had made her up to reassure him, the previous year, when he seemed to think my formative phase had somehow deprived me of all the proper joys and adult responsibilities.

Rather strangely I recall, out on the street again following this interview, I heard a girl's name shouted from behind me. It was Sophie. But it was, and is, a popular name.

And the world makes no real sense. To recap: children see this but too well. And somehow I still see it. I'm not immune to the annoyance, or the regret. But I rarely fight the tide.

I had a dream two nights after Vanessa vanished.

I dreamed I went to her house again in Brighton, but after dark. There were no stars or moon, no streetlamps on, no lit windows. But it was a dream, so I could see the way without them.

When I reached the house, it was derelict; part of the roof had dropped away, the windows were smashed, the door off its hinges and hanging wide.

Nevertheless, in I walked.

Just as I had on the day she went missing, I meant, and started to look all over the place. But now, not unreasonably, it had been stripped and vandalised, and upstairs a fire had been kindled on the landing that, before it was doused, had burned off the top of the stairs, so the upper floor was beyond my remit.

In what had been the dining room, only half the table was left. The table had been sawn in two. And on what had stayed was an envelope, white and pristine in the gloom of night.

Picking it up, I saw it was addressed, or at least named for me: Roderick. I could recognise Vanessa's handwriting from her selections of punctual, functional seasonal cards.

I tore the envelope open. A single folded sheet of paper slipped out into my hand. I duly unfolded it. Dear Roderick, said the letter, I do know you are gay, you know.

That was all. She hadn't bothered to sign it. I assumed she had predicted I would be sure only she could have left this message for me.

## 37

I was kept at work an extra two hours, some rush job; Forrel was involved too. This time his computer, not mine, played up.

Not until almost nine o'clock was I able to release myself. Then Forrel reappeared and suggested we went to a club in the back streets of Soho. I was worn and enervated and thought, why not, and went.

Actually, not a bad place. Food and drink – very little of the first and a surfeit of the second – were very over-priced, but to my astonishment Forrel insisted on picking up the bill.

Girls cavorted around poles, semi-clad. Forrel seemed to like this a lot, but also seemed to be working himself up to liking it, and to demonstrating that he did, as if it were another test our workplace had set him to pass.

On the other hand, I genuinely did like looking at the women. Some of them were very skilful, sleek and limber as trained stage dancers, which perhaps, when able, they were. Most were pretty, and one extremely beautiful, with black satin wings of hair and long, strangely Oriental blue eyes. But as I marvelled at their contortions, seamless skin and delightful ankles, I also felt a defensive fear of their anger and resentment. Or their frustration, perhaps. Or very likely their utter scorn.

In the end, about midnight, when Forrel – who had confessed in an undertone he had won just over a thousand on the Lottery, and had meant to spend it with his girlfriend, but then learned she was leaving him – began to go glassy-eyed; the beautiful woman with black hair came straight across to us.

"Are you having a good time, guys?"

Forrel assured her he was. I nodded and smiled.

Doubtless realising I was the less pissed of the two of us, she said to me softly, "I can dance private, for you two only, in a room. Would you like this?" She had the faintest accent. I couldn't decipher what it was over the hiss of trendy beer-pumps and bottles of fake champagne, the disco music and the yodels of the mostly male crowd.

"Goshyer," said Forrel, now himself speaking in a foreign tongue, "is ulaz we wan, eh, Roddee?"

I said to him quietly, "It will cost."

"Fugger costa, Les dwit."

So we went with her to the other room.

## 38

The room was so over-the-top it spoilt the illusion that vague dark and intermittent laser lights had partly created elsewhere. It was like something razored out of the Arabian Nights, one dimensional and lacking all glamour. Hard sticky reds and tacky gold and chips missing from corners.

Anyway, she danced. She stripped off her minimum of top and played with her breasts. Now, poor girl, under the hard light they looked too pointed and solid. As if digitalised. Implants, probably.

Forrel passed out in the middle of the dance. He slid to the floor. I propped him up in case he was sick.

She kicked something under the (not) Eastern carpet, and the music stopped. She came over and sat down at the table and poured herself some of the fake champagne.

"I can see you two guys have had a long workday," she said.

"I'm afraid so, yes."

"He OK?"

I had no means or experience of him to know, but said reassuringly, "He's fine. Just tired."

"How tired are you?"

Eyes like sapphires over dagger-tips of steel. Her naked breasts, that should have been beautiful and no longer were, joggling there, free-standing, manmade, and full of God knew what.

"Enough," I said. "But thank you for the terrific performance."

"Triffic purr-fremance. I can go somewhere with you, if you like. Hundred fifty. OK?"

I felt apologetic, so I could look apologetic. "If only. I'm sorry. Married."

She smiled, beautiful again. Relieved, I would think. She said, so soft, "I was married once." And then she drifted away.

I sat there, finishing my drink.

And next a man came in and presented the rest of the bill, and Forrel woke up and threw up contemporaneously.

## 39

To get back to the flat a cab was needed. The driver grumbled about going so far, but in the end did.

He dropped me at the top of the street, nevertheless, refusing to drive down any farther. He had heard, he said, things about that canal and the common. No way.

I wondered if there would be any lurkers on the street tonight, although generally by now – around two in the morning – they were stoned blind on the common, slumped by makeshift fires, or else gone home to their turbulent bivouacs among the tall blocks of flats and local squats.

I wondered briefly about Forrel too. I had found him a cab, pondering if the cabby would accept the smell of puke. But Forrel only wanted to get to the regions of Hyde Park. He maintained a tiny expensive penthouse there, somewhere. And he still did the Lottery, and won. He won over the cabby too.

As I walked down from the station end of the street, I began to see a tall, dark figure, standing on the opposite side of the road to the house with my flat in it.

This triggered an immediate memory. That girl, the one I'd christened Anushka, the Russian spy. I hadn't seen her since, admittedly. But now here was this – what was he? As I came inevitably closer, I noted he was indeed a black man, very tall and slim and with short, thick, crisp hair. He had that lion face that comes from the aristocracy of Africa. And all of him was like that. He might have been leaning on a spear, clad in lion skin, still as marble and impenetrably royal as antiquity.

But better not stare. I kept my eyes down as I went by on the other pavement, and turning on to the front path of the house, I heard him, in the deep silence, give what I took to be a sort of sigh.

When I reached the front door and let myself in, as I had with her, I glanced back. Unlike the girl, the man didn't look away. He met my gaze with a glare like black neon. Don't linger. Go in. Shut the door. I did so.

Once upstairs in the flat, I did – again, as with 'Anushka' – go to the front window before I turned on the light.

She had fled away, but he certainly hadn't. He just stood there in the dark, worse dark than usual, too, since three of the streetlamps had given out.

Who had she been after? And who did he want?

I drew the curtains and put on some lights, made a sandwich – the food from the club had melted like fairy gold – and coffee. I had drunk more booze than my ration.

Sitting down with the TV on, I made some notes. Then I sat thinking. Without looking from the window again, I pondered the black warrior standing across the street. And the phantasmal KGB girl. And the girl with blue eyes and plaster-cement breasts.

And then I thought about the wardrobe.

## 40

The wardrobe is a valid, if also normally rationed, part of my life. Like the notes I make such a lot of, the wardrobe gives me an extra dimension. Very possibly this will make no sense to another person not similarly moved. But then again, no doubt many of their own private pursuits might well be lost on me.

To be honest, I hadn't indulged in the wardrobe since I'd felt I must peer into Vanessa's grimly orderly and staid version in Brighton. I'd been put off, it seems.

By now it was almost 3 a.m., and I was due to rise at six-thirty in order to be on time for work. However it wouldn't be the only time I'd made do with less than three hours' sleep.

I swiftly got ready in the bathroom, and then went into the bedroom. The wardrobe here is small, of course. None of the rooms are large enough to fit big pieces of furniture.

The wardrobe door is always kept locked. And the key is not on my keyring, where it would definitely look incongruous. I store it elsewhere.

On undoing the wardrobe, everything at first, to an alien eye, is average and of slight, if any, interest. Perhaps one becomes aware of a dark curtain that seems to hang at the far end, closing that area off. But it may just be a shadow, an optical illusion.

I drew the curtain, which is black, and shoved it back along the rail with my everyday clothes, none of these of too bad a make or condition, and neither of any particular elegance, let alone merit. They serve. Beyond the black curtain is a softer grey curtain. Drawn back also it will reveal a sudden glitter and gleam, a sudden wakening to light and colour, reminiscent of dawn and sunrise. Another world, as in some famous children's book, I believe, though I've never read it. Another world.

## 41

In colour it is rich wild gold, but augmented by a thousand glass beads, which are pink, a deep luxurious edible pink. The gold shines upward through the pinkness, and the pink reflects inward on the gold. Like a sunrise, as I said. The fringes that ornament the line of it are also pink and gold, but this gold far paler, with a silvery tone. And the second pink is hectic, like that of certain roses, geraniums, orchids even.

Below, the accessories, also in matched shades. And above, on the little shelf – put in the wardrobe maybe to facilitate hats and gloves, in the days of such things – the hair. Blonde, the hair. Shoulder-length. Very realistic. It was very costly, even back then, when even luxuries were cheaper. The dress cost a very great deal. From a theatrical shop in Covent Garden. I remember how thrilled they all seemed to be at this staid, youngish man buying such a gem for his girlfriend, Sophie. And I said she had a thing about pink. It was her 'favourite' colour. The woman directly serving me came out with that old saying, "Blue for a boy, pink for a girl." She and I laughed. I could recall my father quoting this saying, too, but I didn't tell the woman that. I said Sophie would love the dress. And when I bought the cosmetics later, and the shoes, and expensive costume jewellery, all for Sophie, I also said how she would love those particular things. And some of the people who served me were enthusiastic at my perceived generosity, and others – very clearly – took me for a sucker, in thrall to some young demanding slut with a too extreme taste in fashion.

I used Sophie's name on the wig form; that transaction was managed by post. Sophie Thorney – another version, in fact, of our outlandish family name. (It truly is a family name, by the way. My mother and father had been cousins. Terris, Taurus, Terry,

Thorney, etc. were general to them, and to all the kin I knew. Or had known.)

To answer a question that might be floating in the air, no, I never myself put on these garments, though they may well fit me; nor the wig, nor the make-up or the jewels. I only ever look at them, and that – just now and then, and touch them, sometimes. That's all I've ever needed.

Nor is the pleasure erotic. Though pleasure it is. I have no full idea why I am thrilled by these specific and idiosyncratically glamorous things. Although I do have several theories which, very likely, it's pointless to set out here.

After about twenty minutes I drew back the curtains and shut and locked the wardrobe door and put away the key. It was getting on for three thirty-five, I must lie down and snatch what sleep I could before the alarm, faithful and infuriating as a watchdog, eviscerated me out of slumber. I considered inconsequently if Forrel would himself make it in to work. Poor devil. Half his lottery money must be gone, and his girlfriend gone, and nobody but bloody old Rod to go to a sex club with. Poor sod.

# KLOVA:
# 42

No memory of coming back to the flat-house.
 I woke up there. It was like as morning, or I thought so.
 When I woke up again it was dark again. Night again.
 All the while I knew what had happened. How he misunderstood me. And what he said. Coal.
 What he said.
 Over and over.
 In my mind.
 Bank-nanny woke me next time.
 Four thousand shots.
 Didn't care.
 Then I couldn't sleep again. I walked about the rooms, even round and round the bathdome. I couldn't get away from me, or from him, or from what he said, and thought.
 I thought, should I message him? But I didn't have the number of his Mee. He'd never given it over. I couldn't go back to the

Tower. If he saw me he would say it all again, think it all again.

There was a day and another night. No sleep. Just walking.

Then I dressed and went out. No cosmetics. Like no eyes, no mouth. I walked along by The Nile, by the Forest. I passed the streets that lead away, all planted by their tall trees that never lose their leaves, and the tall shops that sparkle. The sun shone.

I looked down in the water, and I thought about being under it.

But then that seemed wrong, because someone here who was happy might find me and be upset. I never before thought like that. How I might hurt someone else.

And I rem that girl and that male quack, those people about that other male called Sigh. And how I was with them, with her. Can't help you. Don't know. Don't care. Live and let go.

Couldn't let go.

Thought about the river in the centre of the city. Under there. Never found. Thought about that.

## 43

Somebody had written on a wall Five London Lives. I stared at this. What did it mean? Somehow it made me uncomfortable, but that can't be, because I was dead.

The river was still beautiful because darkness was coming. It was livid black-green and rippled with the gilded-oil snakes.

I didn't try to jump in.

Didn't want to spoil it.

No. I couldn't understand it. I didn't think the surface would break and let me through. Like as I'd lie on top and it would drag me away, and everyone staring, girls and males. And Coal would lean down and spit on me.

## 44

By the time I reached the flat-house again it was Zone 42 and one half. The Forest had no fireflies, and all the float-lamps were out. And I could only see because the sky was very bright with lots of stars sewn on there, most of them manmade, they say, don't they? And the moon was standing high up, and it was white, dead white.

I didn't want to be there, but where else? I didn't want to be anywhere. Not even under the river in case, then, all I could be, would be memory, remembering.

But I looked up at the flat-house, and even the old man's lights were shielded fully. You never see the old woman's lights.

Then I saw there was a light. In my social room.

I stood there, looking over, staring. I was amazed, and my true misery I forgot. Because why was there a light showing from my window when you never could see my lights from the street.

After this, another thing happened.

Up to the inside of my window came this old, old man. And he stood quite still, and as I stood looking up at him, he looked down at me. He held a funny glass in his hand, like glasses were centuries ago that you see in museums on quick view. And in the glass was a red drink he was drinking very fast. But he paused a moment and waved at me.

He waved.

The old, old man.

At me.

From inside my flat.

## Emenie:
## 45

Despite getting sausages and cigarettes for Sy's return, little Micki showed no wish to leave my house. Not illogically, perhaps. Something in her brain had figured out that, while she was away and couldn't know, she could believe he might meanwhile have returned there.

I understood though the Bruvva figure could again turn up for real. So I had asked her if this would occur. She had assured me he'd gone off to Wales. Wales! How –? She said he knew a man with a van that worked, and they had been hoarding petrol for the holiday. And there were still boats, didn't I know? She had told him to leave me alone, as well, she said. Inevitably, however, I knew too that if she vanished, just as Sy already had, Bruvva was likely to reappear in my life. I'd tackle that when it happened. He had struck me as fairly moronic. Though sometimes extra dangerous, morons are easier to remove. By which I don't necessarily mean through murdering them – as I never want to, when they're not labelled in the right way, the way that links them to me. As was Micki.

Really I must admit, I just needed to settle with her. Concentrate solely on her.

My reflections as we returned from the shopping spree were strong and lasting. I had to put her out of awareness before her optimism failed her. Before the night fell, darkness, disquiet.

I used the oven, saying it sometimes worked at midday – and see! – it did. And we had hot lamb chops and tinned carrots, and for dessert dried morello cherries and long-life tinned cream. Then coffee with Vodka. She even smoked one of the cigarettes she had got for Sy.

The sky turned gradually greyer and more grey. Then a pigeon landed on the sill of the kitchen, where you could still see out.

The shadow patterns on the pigeon's back were clearly legible to me.

Each of them confirmed the stages of what I must do.

We moved into the main room. It was a nice indoor afternoon. Cosy. I turned on the electric fire and by now she merely accepted I could run it for a while. I too was much more at ease, cheerful and relaxed. Now I had a firm grip of the plan.

## 46

At what I took to be four o'clock, and before the true full dark began to gather, I turned off the fire by the hidden switch. Micki was dozing and didn't see.

Making out I too had taken a nap in the armchair, I woke her by a prolonged, rather vigorous yawn.

"Sorry. We both probably needed a sleep."

"I shouldn't. I slept so well last night on your couch."

"Well, you're welcome to stay tonight as well, if you like. Only tomorrow my bloke's coming over, so..."

"Oh! Of course."

I had introduced the falsehood of a masculine partner to reassure her I had no Lesbian designs on her, but she seemed rather deflated. So I added, thoughtfully, "Though, if you won't mind him, I'm sure he won't mind you – he's a nice guy. We usually go to that house over the park. They have bands sometimes and sort-of wine – rather like that beer you talked about, maybe. But it's not too bad.

If you'd like to come along with us."
She smiled. "I'd like that. Thank you. If you're sure he'll be OK."
"He's easy-going, my feller," I said.
Then I had a 'brainwave'. "I've just thought, if the fire came on for a bit, we've probably got hot water. Would you like a bath?"
She was the child again, and it was a Charles Dickens Christmas.
"Oh – yes – in the caravan – well we never get water, let alone hot water – but what about you?"
"I get to have lots of baths. It's your turn."
She hadn't seen the bathroom till then, only the cloakroom with the lav that flushed and the cold tap that dribbled cold.
We stood together as the old cracked white bath filled itself with steaming water, and I added a few lavender drops from a container.
"Let's have some wine, too," I said. "Oh, let's enjoy ourselves! And tomorrow we'll have a good night out."
"Yes," she breathed. "Yes."

Christmas comes but once a year.
Treat the time with dread and fear.

## 47

Poor little girl.
There was quite a strong dose in the wine, sleeping pills, but I'd mulled the wine on the oven hob and put in sugar and ginger.
"It's a bit bitter," I precautionarily remarked.
A bit bitter. The biter bit. The bitten bite. The bittern has bitten.
I was fairly sure she wouldn't drown. The bath is rather slim and short. I've fallen asleep in it more than once and still been breathing above the surface when I came to.
When I went in, after about twenty minutes, she was well away.
I stroked back her black hair from her steamy brow. She was breathing deeply, and smiling, in her sleep.
Straightening, I saw myself in the piece of mirror that had stayed attached to the wall. It too was filmed by steam, but I made her out, the slim brown woman with her acorn hair and eyes. Older today, about twenty-nine, thirty. If I chameleoned into forty, I'd certainly be old enough to have had this little girl as a daughter.

How sweet she was. I didn't want her hurt any more.

Leaning down I gently lifted her pale soft hand, with the faint tracery of its sea-blue veins at the wrist, and carefully and quickly cut across them three times.

The razor was well-honed, the old kind. In the heat I didn't think she'd feel it. And the pills – they're good ones, I've used them myself once or twice. They'd have a thorough, syrupy effect.

I guided her hand and arm back down to rest on the bottom of the bath.

Just there, instantly, the water was changing, clear into pink and crimson. Into scarlet.

That's what they used to call it, those bastards who hunted foxes – not for food or clothing, but for sport. The hunting coats. Hunting Pink. Only they were red. Blood red.

Her face hadn't changed. Her hair drifted in the water. I looked at her body, now I had done what had to be done. She had that ethereal underwater paleness of skin I can remember seeing in reproductions of the work of Leonardo da Vinci, or Botticelli. Black hair at her groin, thick but not in excess. And lovely full little breasts, with small pink bonbons of nipples. But the rose water of her blood was already spreading over her, recolouring...

Sweet child. Poor little girl. Go, as they had once said, with God. God bless you, darling dear. And walk in Paradise.

I left her alone to die. She should have her privacy.

## 48

Next morning I let all the water and blood out of the bath. Then rinsed Micki off and picked her up in my arms – she was light as a feather or a moth – and carried her through into my bedroom. I dried her and dressed her in a fleecy blue dressing gown I had, as if to keep her warm, which was irrelevant, but there. Then I sat her in the chair in the corner, with a cushion behind her head.

Dead faces, even those of the young, fall in a strange way. I've noted that before. But she was still pretty. And she had that look, too, that I've also seen, though less I must admit on the faces of the ones I've killed. It's a sort of secretive knowledge. But of what?

Having settled her, anyway, I went and cleaned the bath thoroughly.

This method had not, for Micki, I'm afraid, been entirely original to me. (I'd have liked it to be.) But not overused, shall I say. I knew however it leaves not much mess.

As for her body, I didn't want to chuck it in the cellar, down with the others, and her faithless, stupid twat of a lover, Simon. I wished, I confess, I could have found somebody to embalm her. She could have looked really beautiful mummified, even, like an Egyptian princess. But the means of her death at least were classic Ancient Roman. In those days they committed suicide like that, especially the females, a hot bath and a razor or knife and lots of wine, no doubt. And then the right hand, which had wounded the left hand and caused death and so was blasphemous, a criminal against the laws of men and gods, was cut off and buried separately. At least she didn't need that. I was the killer. She was pure and free of blame.

For now, she could stay where she was. The cold preservative season was getting under way. In a while I'd find a means of disposing of her. For now, let her rest a little longer. She was safe, with me.

# Rod:
# 49

Most of the trees were empty of leaves. The shops were full of the compulsory pre-figurations of Christmas. I recalled the lament of my guardian. "It drives me Christmas crackers." The cold was gathering in too, like the dark evenings.

It was about this time I noticed that the bad smell had come back to the downstairs hall. It was, in fact, dramatically worse. Not drains now, I concluded, but a selection of rats dead in the walls. Oddly, these stinks had never seemed to reach up into the rest of the house. Nor had I ever heard rats, let alone seen any, about or in my flat, or anywhere on any floor. I wondered if the occupant of the other flat, the southside flat facing mine across the landing, had detected anything. But really nobody ever seemed to live there. I had always reckoned they were generally away, and at those times of their leaving or returning, I deduced I must have been absent myself. Certainly there was never any noise or disturbance from the other flat, as there never had been from the floor above mine, which also seemed unlet and vacant. Yet – how to explain this? I had, now and then, felt an awareness of another person – or people – evinced by nothing I could call up as proof – but nevertheless inhabiting both the opposite flat and the rooms above. It – they – scentless, noiseless, unlit, and having no visible form, yet I had a vague awareness of having – glimpsed them – without seeing. But no doubt that was just the foible of a tired man home from a boring job, and having no true imaginative life.

That evening Forrel called me on the landline. He frequently had, and did, after our night out in Soho. Though as to how and where he got hold of the number, I have no idea. Some illegal foray through the firm's security, perhaps.

In the past I'd had Vanessa to contend with, either during my visits or on the occasions when she called me, fortunately not very often. I had weathered her diatribes, almost exclusively about others, as best I could; quod erat demonstrandum.

Vanessa was gone. Now Forrel seemed to take over the role. It goes without saying his voice and tone were utterly dissimilar and his complaints as unlike as I, or surely anyone, could envisage, but regrettably the niche had been filled. During the working day, fairly often now, he would – what did they call it? – buttonhole me. Pinning me to my workstation, or in a corner of The Stag, he would begin what I had recently titled Forrel's Lament.

Tonight was no different.

"She emptied the joint account, Rod. Every fucking K. Did I tell you? Sure, there weren't that many. And she sends me these postcards about her and this fucking man she's with. She ends up *Glad you're not here. I'll have to move. Get away.* And that girl – that girl with black hair and tits at the place we went – can't stop thinking about her..."

I put up with it, making conciliatory sounds, for about half an hour. Then I mournfully told Forrel I was expecting a call from my aunt, an old woman, and I'd have to go.

He let me, with the reluctance of a starving squid.

It was just after I put the phone down that I heard the noise. Frankly, I'd have had to be deaf not to.

# 50

A woman was shouting at the top of her vocal range, which range seemed enviable. And then there came the crash of breakage. It might have been a window – certainly glass.

I had jumped up, startled. In this myopic and sedated house I had never before heard any sort of ruckus.

There was little doubt as to the source. It was the flat across the landing. The silent, darkened, possibly unlived-in flat.

Two things occurred to me. The tumult had sounded raw and spiteful enough that maybe I should try to summon the police. Whether they turned up, of course, would be down to them. The other element was that I had been damned lucky so far to experience very few of those incursions on one's private aural or visual state by raucous neighbours. I had heard enough from Vanessa to make me, if only dimly, conscious I had done well in this department. But now, was everything to change?

An interlude – it didn't last – of quiet came. And then a huge masculine roaring. Followed by an alarming bang. This sounded as if a large piece of heavy furniture had been dropped from an impressive height. Had someone been under it?

It seemed not. Up geezered the woman's rabid rant, wordless with fury and also filtered through the sandwich-filler of the landing space. After which up sprang the male voice again. And here I did make out a selection of words projected in a fruity baritone bellow.

"Again – my whisky – date of it – woman, I shall – damnation!"

It came to me that neither voice was young. Both, however, in their unmatched and savage manner, were filled by strident passion.

New tenants? Like Forrel, it seemed I too would have to move.

But then again I felt compunction. These two elder persons seemed set on acts of violence. In the ordinary way I would avoid such a situation. But a sudden unease and – almost a compulsion – overcame me.

I found I went out onto the landing.

And I stood there, undecided, resentful and cautious, nearly amused in some silly, childish way, yet too appalled, foreseeing the bloody ending of these strangers' saga, long enacted if never before here.

No. I had better call the police. Or else turn up the TV and glug a drink of Vodka from my limited store.

Precisely as I turned to go back in, the door of the other, south side flat flew wide. I reversed again. Two people were there. In hinder place an irate woman, with shining bobbed hair; in the foreground, looking somehow both homicidal and benign, a bemusingly oldish-youngish old man, wine glass in hand.

"Why, Roderick," he said, all easy-going charm once more. I knew his charm, his pleasant and coherent alcoholically undrunken joi de vivre. It was Uncle George. And behind him, frowning severely, Auntie Vanessa.

## KLOVA:
## 51

It wasn't like the old woman, how she sometimes gets in, that is different.

I was so scared I turned to run.

To run away from the flat-house, and the old man leering out of my window at me down on the street.

And the street was like dark black, the darkest of black. No lights but that one light, in my flat, where I wasn't and no lights ever showed. So I ran right into something I thought was a tree, only trees don't grow in that street. But the tree reached out and held me.

"Let go!" I screamed.

"No, it's OK – easy, Klova-Spice. It's OK."

And what had grabbed me wasn't a tree but it was Coal. No flames in his hair tonight. No hell in his eyes. His eyes were black.

I stopped moving and thinking and being. I just stopped. He held me up.

After a while he said, "What scared you like that? Was it me?"

"There's an old man in my flat," I heard a voice say, which must be mine.

"The old male you said lived across from you?"

"No. No one I know. No one." And my head turned by itself, or something turned my head, and I looked back at the flat-house, and there was no face looking out, no lit windows. Not even the faulty blinds of the ordinary male in the second flat. Just darkness.

And Coal was in the darkness, holding me.

I put my head against him and sighed and was still.

## 52

He told me, out on the street, that he had made a mistake and spoken cruelly and unreasonably to me. He realised I wasn't after shots of cash, only explaining why I'd have to leave the Leaning Tower earlier than usual. He said he did not care anyway if I wanted any money of his. I was welcome. Whatever I wanted.

Then he said, if I could forgive and let go any bad feeling towards him for what he'd said, he thought he should come in with me, and find out what had happened up in my flat.

I had been so destroyed by sadness, now I couldn't spring back. It was like a stem that was crushed in me.

I didn't know what to do. I only leaned my head on his chest. I remem'd the feel of his body, its scent.

I started to think, which is a peculio, about my mother, C. P., that I'd never known. And about the Child Centre. I never made friends.

They said I was a solitary child. A Solo, they called me.

I had a different name then.

I didn't like it, and when I left at sixteen, and after the Generation Change programme had stopped me ever getting older, I changed my name too. First it was Clover. Then with the K and A. Klova.

After a while or so on the dark street with Coal I said I wanted to go in. That was all, but Coal and I went across the road to the house.

I could walk all together by then. But he kept his arm round me. He was like a part of me, his arm a part of me.

But all and none of me wasn't or was me. I didn't know who I was. Klova. What was Klova?

The moment we got into the house, that smell was there. It was thick as mud from the edges of The Nile. It was a grey, liver-brown smell. It was raw and full of metal tines that made a sort of like as steel sounding in your head.

"Fuck," Coal whispered. "That there is no rat, girl."

But he moved me on, and we ran up the stairs, and then we had outraced the smell. It just seemed to stop before the last step.

We sprinted into my flat.

We leaned on the door breathing the nice air. It was clean.

In the social room, the tiles glimmered because the automatic lamp had come on, and also I could see the blinds were fixed at the front window. No light could show.

Coal went into each room, including the bathdome, and then he came back and said, "There's no one here but you and me."

I asked myself if I had imagined the old man in the window, because I was so sad. I didn't say this to Coal. He worked in Security. He would think again I was or had been lying, to get his attention, saying someone had been here when nobody could be. My bills were all paid. I hadn't had to use the bank over debt. There was no reason for the apartment security to have failed.

Coal came over and held me again. He kissed my hair. I tried to feel glad. Couldn't feel.

We went into the bed area and lay down.

I hadn't got any make-up on.

He said, "I always think of your pink lipstick, Klova-Spice. But your lips are sweet pink anyhow." And he kissed me. We had carnal. It wasn't like before. It wasn't real. What's real?

The time check said it was Zone 2 and I was awake but Coal wasn't. Then he woke up. He looked at me.

I said, "Someone's on the floor above. Upstairs."

"That's another flat, right?"

"There's never been anyone up there before."

I was afraid and I'd sat up, looking up like a brainless at the ceiling, though of course you can't see through.

Someone was walking about up there. It sounded heavy and the floor/ceiling creaky and sagging. Even so, the ceiling didn't move.

"Do you want I go up and see?" he asked me.

"I don't know."

The noises didn't stop. I said, "It may be her, the old woman. She gets in my flat sometimes, moves things. Maybe up there, too."

"Klova," he said, and kissed me again – how many times had he kissed me? Oh, a million times a million. To make up for all the kissing we'd missed, he'd said. "That sounds too loud for an old woman, it sounds like a male. I want you safe. I'll go up and find out."

I said, "The old woman's let the flat up there, that's all."

"Let me make sure. This guy you said you saw in here, what was he like?"

"Old. Old – soon-to-die old." I paused, and we both waited the grave respectful moment. "And he waved to me."

"Stay there," said Coal.

He went out. I heard his bare feet, soft as the paws of a big cat on the next bit of stairway that, in any proper flat-house, or anywhere, is a slide.

We hadn't fully undressed. I pulled on an overshirt. I followed Coal out, shutting my door, moving up the stair after him.

It was very dark again here. And no lights came on to help. On the next landing was a narrow door to one side.

We would need the correct and personalised nail ID to press and get in – but then, I'd forgotten, Coal worked in Security.

He did something to the door with a band around his wrist I'd taken for jewellery. And the door, that seemed to be made of jet-black glass, gradually slid away into the side of the wall, the way mine does on the floor below.

Coal had already seen me following. Obviously he would. Now, not looking back, he raised his hand for silence and care. Then he moved in through the doorway.

Again, no lights. It was pitch black now. It was like stepping through into nothingness.

I didn't want to be there.

I wanted to be in the Tower, and dancing, and Coal dancing with me, and then we'd go to a Singles Room and it would be brilliant. And then I would go home, by myself, and I'd be the way I was when I was myself and I'd put on my lipstick that is dark sweet hot-flower pink. And in the mirror I'd be sixteen, though I am twenty-nine going on forty-nine. And I'd curl up in the bed. And in the morning the bank-nanny would message me about some more thousands of shots from the kind benefactors that look after all of us since they are so well-off and that is their duty and joy and...

...and Coal said, in a hushed flat snarl, "Look, Klova."

He had a torch-thing, some gadget I'd never seen before. It shone all over without light. Everywhere was still pitch black but you could see every detail, even the bright eyes of a rat peeking out from an old, old cupboard in one corner.

The room was old.

Older than the planet.

The masonry was lopsided, and great warty beams held up the low and listing ceiling. On the floor was a worn rug, heavily coloured and stained and dirty, and with holes. And there was a plate made of some grey metal stuff on the floor, with a yellow bone lying across it. And there was a table with a wood top and some papers, and a glass with a thin pillar that was greenish and very chipped, with black sediment in the bottom. I could smell bad water and damp, as sometimes you smell it walking by The Nile, which used to be a canal. And the remains of food, and human body smells, particularly piss and sweat, But also cold winter-tree smell. And I saw a window, very, very small, with dark glass, but it had a long silvery crack through it.

Then the torch-thing failed. The images all went. And right then somebody moved past me. Not Coal.

A male, though? I'm sure a male, and young. Twenty, like that. Dirty too – sweat and piss and spunk – but good too, new-baked bread, like that. And alcohol, some sort. And human hair, unwashed, but too – good, like the bark of a tree smell. And... lavender.

But he was invisible. Not physical.

Really he wasn't there.

Nothing was.

The upstairs space was only a neglected flat, with whitish walls that shone even in the darkness, and carpet across all the floor. And the back window was broken, and suddenly a bird flew out of somewhere and in through the window and then straight up through a gap in the ceiling.

Coal said in my ear, "Let's get out."

We turned, and the door was another sort of door, like as from a Time-Tourist game-stat at the Child Centre. You had to turn a handle on the door, a knob, like that. Coal did, and we walked on to the landing.

We went down again to my flat, hurried in, and secured my door. Above, in that place upstairs, was total quiet, now, and nobody but Coal and me were in my flat.

"It was a ghost," said Coal. "I've seen them before."

In the automatic soft lamp shine of my rooms he glared at me, blaming me once more for something I hadn't done.

# IRVIN:
# 53

Tomorrow I must fight a duel. A great nuisance. It is a severe interruption, as I had meant to go to visit Mis'us Peck. Such things are sent to try us, and so they do. I shall probably kill the fellow. He is an almighty imbecile. Pretty enough, with his blond locks and silk coat, but entirely lacking in wits. It seems he has found out I merry-digged his wife, (who is sixteen years and flower-of-face, with bosoms white as milk and very full). I am quite certain I am not the first, though she did tell me that I was. But all women lie. It is indigenous to them, as scales to a salmon.

Well, there is no way round it. I have opted for swords, knowing him a fair shot and not, myself, a great liker of guns. A sword or a knife is silent. One does not always wish all London to know when one has dealt the blow of death.

I have left the meat bone for the dog. There was little enough meat upon it at the first.

But he is besides a faithless hound and may not come back till I have gone out. It is always possible too, I must surmise, that I will perish in the morning, on Hyde Hill, when Mr Cuckold comes for me with his polished blade. Now there's a thought. I must puff out the candle. It is half done, and until my next payment day I can afford no other. Thus, goodnight.

Up with the cock, as they say, and to The Black Sheep Inn up the track, for a bowl of burnt coffee and a scrag of bread.

"Ah, Mr Thessaris," say they, "up and early to your business."

Told none where I was to go nor what to be about there.

A blood-red sunrise, and thereafter snow coming down. Winter has no consideration for a poor actor shoved out to kill some noodle. No doubt I shall die of the winter chills rather than the fool's prick-blade.

(I write this in the back of the carter's cart, as he trundles me to my appointment.)

Damnation take all husbands.

Picture then the day. And by the time we were at the outskirt of the city, under the wild ground of the hill, everything was already frosted thick white as the Earl of Scarrow's face in powder. Parted with the carter there and was roundly cursed by him despite the coin I gave. But this has happened before.

The snow ceased to fall as I climbed the hill, and I was glad to get some warmth by the exercise.

Groves of trees dominate the summit of the slope, and from

one such I could make out the smoke of a brazier. What a picture was that, then, when once I got in among the trees, all set up as if for some epic scene at Drury Lane.

For there stood the adjutants and the other hangers-on, and the doctor looking grim, and there the husband, who must probably play the hero.

Jem Templeyard was not a bad fellow, thought I, with the irony of a man dragged from his bed too early, to clash blades in the ice and snow. A handsome youth, not yet twenty-two summers, and shaking enough I could see it, but whether from fright or freezing it would be hard to tell. Certainly he fired up when he saw me.

"You're late, you damned villain!" he howled at me. "Too afraid to come? Or thought to cheat me?"

I shrugged, and reluctantly took off my coat. It's better to fight in one's shirt, I find. "You must allow me to have had some morsel to break my fast."

"It will have been your last meal, you gutter scrump."

"I am heartily sorry," said I, "you term your bed a gutter."

"What?" cried he, all amaze. "What – you think I meant that? By this it seems you admit you seduced my wife..."

Another of them intervened. "Hush, Jem, comport yourself as a gentleman. Well, Mr Thessaris, you've no second, I see."

"None but my hound, who last night vowed he would come, then cried off due to a long interlude with the tinker's bitch."

One or two of them laughed. Which set off the fair Templeyard again. Once more they sternly patted him down. He did not remove his coat. A novice, plainly.

The brazier, meanwhile, which gave less heat than smoke, began to cough as if it had the autumn plague.

The umpire waved us to the centre of the glade, where the ground was flattish, though the snow truly hardened now, and would prove slippy, hiding also roots and other trap-trick delicacies under its mask.

We were next told, as is usual, that we might yet resolve the matter in some gentlemanly way.

"I am willing," I said, "if Mr Templeyard is willing."

"You forced my wife," he snarled, his fine eyes flashing.

"I did not force her. I have never had to force that way in my life."

"You lie! She swore you misled then forced her."

"And why did she tell you this?"

"Why? In Christ's holy name, you feculence, why?"

"Would it be, mayhap, she heard I had – shall I say to content you – misled and forced also the actress, Mis'us Peck? As I have been doing, I must add, and no penalty to it since most of the city is aware of it, and her husband with them, for the past six months?"

"What do you mean, vile debaucher?"

"I mean that jealousy, the green-eyed monster, has urged your wife to invent unkind tales of me."

Templeyard drew and flourished his polished weapon in the air, nearly taking off with it, in the flurry, the nose of the unready umpire.

Then headlong the brat runs at me, red in the face and yowling.

## 54

Well, it is nothing but God's truth, to be an actor is to gain many skills, to dight and diddle with a sword but one of them.

Why, not four years gone, I played the role of Hamlet, albeit in a much-foreshortened version, at The King's Theatre in Covent Garden. And even now, though reduced to strutting about the lesser stage of The Obelisk in Stampwell Street, (off Cartwheel Lane, you cannot miss the place), I maintain my fensive ability.

Nevertheless, it is no quiet thing to contest with a madman, strong with youth, passionate as a girl, and careless of his strokes as a drunken windmill.

Such an adversary may kill one from sheer clumsiness. At the least, take out an eye or off a hand – or choicer part.

As we skidded and lurched about the boards of Hyde Hill, I came to think I had better duel with him another way. I spoke of jealousy, and I have seen that work curiously, and something of that too I had, abruptly, on the hill, attributed to Templeyard himself.

Best now to try my luck, for I should like that sport better, certainly, than this.

I lured him soon into an almighty lunge where the ground was at its most glassy. (It is all actors' moves, I find. Life, that is. Or most of life.)

The blade wheeled wide of me as he staggered, and I, making as if to dart in again, stuck the side of my boot to his so that he skidded worse, and let go his sword in a crazed dance to save himself a plunge.

At this I caught him and wrestled him close, both his arms pinned. The heat of his body against mine, I sincerely own, was a great delight on such a frigid morning.

He struggled, naturally, mad as a boar under a net. The rest were some way off by then, huddled wisely to the brazier. Since Templeyard and I must one kill the other, let us get on with it as quick as able.

"Listen, Jeremias," I murmured at his ear, "before one of us ends, you'd better hear me out." He made a gobbling sound but nothing else. Untrained, though far younger than I, he was mightily out of breath, panting like a boy at the hoist of the scenery-shift. "It is you I have my eye upon. You, if you will, I had intended to mislead and – no, not force – but dally with. Your dear little wife, why she was only the means to the end, and I must suppose she guessed as much, and there we are again, before the green-eyed monster." I had held him close as I said all this. Close enough he could feel against him, if he would, my eagerness beneath the belt. And sure enough, praise the saints, I began to detect a replying eagerness from him, hard as a stone, but restive as a serpent.

So I let him go, and at that he almost did fall down. Legs to sawdust, as they say.

"Well," said I, "if the truth offends you worse than her lies, better kill me."

He had righted his balance and stood there gaping at me. "What do you mean?" he whispered – again.

Heaven spare me all virgins. (For he was virgin enough in this.)

"I mean I should like to tup you, sir. Kiss and coddle and feel and fondle and pierce and ride you until you could barely lift your sweet arse off the floor or bed or wall I had layed you on or by. It's you I'd like. And if that's not to be, then take up your blade. Then tell the world I died of unrequited love. Not such a bad end, for an actor."

His face was white as the snow where it was unmarked. His eyes had darkened. He panted heavily, and now it could not be from duelling. For sure, I thought I had him.

Imagine then my offended horror when off he sprang, grabbed up the dropped blade, and leaping back at me before I could reassemble my wits, he gave me a nick across my left upper arm.

The cut was shallow, more the bite or scratch of a cat, and would do little harm. He had pinked me, as the gamblers have it. Pinked, then reddened me, for my sleeve was quickly bold with blood.

"I am content," shouted Jem Templeyard to the others. "That will do. I see I've misjudged this man. I will say he has insulted my blameless wife. But only by his words and in error. Nothing worse – I have misunderstood her complaint. And so I have dealt him only this little punishment. Let that," growled he to me, "be a lesson to you to watch your manners, Mr Thessaris." The surgeon was coming up, looking most disappointed one of us was not now lying on the earth with his viscera poured out wormlike all around. Before he reached me with his bandaging, Jem added, in a once more breathless whisper, "I will meet you in the coffeehouse on Parnassus Walk, at noon."

I smiled. I had cause. I can deal with both, the ladies and the jacks, and am good too at that. And he was, as I have remarked, a pretty fellow.

## 55

The snow had begun to fall again, and more heavily than before.

I sat at the window of the coffeehouse, drinking the brew, (far superior to that of The Black Sheep, which its cost reflected) and, as I waited for my new amor vitae, I thought idly enough of my childhood and my cruel father.

It was no current love-affair, nor injury, which occasioned this, but the snow itself. In my infancy I recollect only days and nights of sumptuous heat or other days and nights clad white in snow and rime. Such were the general excesses of my beginning, supposedly, only such painted back-casts remained to my memory. (In just such a manner the back-casts behind Macbeth, in which I took the part of Banquo, are most of what remain to me of the play.)

My dam had fled my father, Jonathon Irridemus Thessaris, some seven months after I was born. Whether she had wished to take me with her and been prevented by circumstance, (most probably that of another gentleman), or purely had no wish for my company, (for infants are addled, piddled, leaky and squeaking creatures), I do not, nor shall I ever, know.

Small odds. I was left. And so, sour-nursed and whipped up by drunken sucklers and unkind servants, but none of them so dedicated to the Pitiless as my male parent.

I am sure he mauled and slapped me often, to prepare me, perhaps, as one must prepare certain types of wood, cloth or canvas, for the ultimate onslaught to come.

What I recall is the first beating, when I was five. I shall not write a word about it. By this alone, you must judge its harshness.

He had, my father, taken up the cause with me, as later, in my thirteenth year, he undertook to educate me upon, because I, being got by him on her, (my mother, that is), and brought by her in the usual way into the world, was half her child. Though half his, too, and therefore perhaps a recoverable commodity, since I was male. But being also half of her, inferior I was, too, detestable and loathsome. He had thus aimed to cast her out of me, as priests and prophets of the Church cast out demons from human flesh.

At fifteen, however, I had seen a play and found a longing in me which outweighed all doubt and fear. I, as possibly had she, would have stolen soft away. But he caught me. Accordingly, I turned upon him, and myself taking up the instruments of his wrath, I battered him senseless and left him in his house for dead. As he lived, some credit, I confess, should be given him that he did not call up the pursuit of the courts upon me. He let me go my own way, as he had once let go her.

The house is miles off, in the province of Sussex, far south of the Capital. I have never heard more of him. And if ever he has of me, which is unlikely for I am not of colossal fame either for good or ill, he has never come to chide my loss. He may even be dead. It is some fourteen years behind.

## 56

In comes my paramour, at some minutes before the clocks strike for noon. He is ready shaved, washed clean and perfumed, having on fresh linen and another silk coat.

"Thou art fair, my love," say I, "and the bull bellows from the pasture."

He grins, boy-like. And says I am an actor, what else would I say?

"It is the Bible has that," I loftily tell him. To his credit he does not know enough of religious text to correct me. He is both excited and nervous, as one must expect.

As he sits down, he blushes.

A pleasing change, this, from the choleric red of before.

We quaffed the black drink and our spirits rose high and knocked upon our hearts and skulls. Then there was a crimson wine from Girtland, or some other clime.

After that, along the whitied street we swaggered, lords of the earth, and so into the winding back ways of London's prodigious skirt-hem, and down to a certain tavern, where I acquired a room.

He was all agoggle. But I, of course, have done such stuff.

In the room a sudden girlish terror came over him, but I'd anticipated no less. I gave him brandy, kissed him, and so began upon him. In afterthought, I am not entirely sure he was quite innocent. He took to the procedures, once in, with the willing devotion of a lion cub to meat.

As I had promised him, so I did. And at the last we rolled upon the floor, he screaming in a joyous extremis. Luckily it is a noisy spot, and well used to such jolly uproars.

Then, after, like any maid, he began to weep, and begged to know if he had sinned. I told him he had and would do so again. And proved to him he would, as we both did so promptly.

Following this he slept, and I, well-satisfied enough, lay wondering a little which of the two of them, Jem or his white-bosomed wife, I preferred. To their credit, I decided to allot them equal pedestals.

When evening fell, and snow lay outside deep as goose-sauce, he told me he must get home. For all that we spent another hour, nor wasted it in chat.

Our quarrel certainly was made up. And he, good lad, paid off the innkeeper. Having regained the outer byways we parted. For him the road homeward was not too taxing, for he had money for a horse well-shod against the ice, (though I could think it might cost him more in the horse's motion and saddle under his own well-ridden rump.) I, however, must make my journey as best I could. Which, fortified with a snap of chicken and a pint of bitter ale, I did, slipping and sliding all the way under the blue jeer of a full moon. Three hours it took me. And what a weirded and awesome scene it was when reaching, through the outer lanes and ever more ramblous houses, the track that runs above the water-rill and the rough pastures, where bare trees stood with branches like cat claws, most being coppiced. This too is the rare world I look on from the back window of my hovel-room.

Once indoors, and very glad I was to be so, I climbed the doleful stairs and went in. Cold as a grave the bloody pesthole was, though I have paid the old brown hag who owns this tenement to light me a fire when the weather is inclement. Nevertheless, the work of minutes prepared and ignited a blaze. And then at least all took on a cheery look.

It was quiet in the house that night also, which is seldom the case. They are a queer parcel of citizens that dwell in the building, and where I have glimpsed them, (which, as in the matter of the landlady, brown as a withering leaf, is infrequent); they seem dressed in a diverse and Bedlam manner. So I have pondered, now and then, what they are at or do, to maintain body and soul as one.

I glanced once from the cracked window, and the ground was whiter far than both Mis'us Templeyard's soft bubbies and her husband's fine hard haunches. No friend to me, the winter earth, nor that frozen water-course I musingly call the Nilus Stream.

My arm now ached where he had pinked me with the sword. But I have had much worse in my mature life, yes even from the accidents on a stage. And in childhood, as I have said, a millionfold worseness more.

The dog had not condescended to return, the faithless devil. The yellow bone lay where it was. And for my supper what? A heel of bread and a gulp of brackish wine. Thereon to bed, and might Hell fiddle for the rest of them.

## EMENIE:
### 57

Days passed quietly, and the leaves still hadn't all come down. Clotted yellowish and dried-out, grey-green and brown, they stuck on the taller or smaller trees, as if glued there. It was unreasonably mild, as sometimes happened now. The year would turn its twelfth page in just under another month. But back When, this was how things would have looked in mid-October.

Micki remained in my bedroom, sitting in the chair.

She had firstly tightened up, but by now she had loosened.
Even I had to be aware of the growing stench.
Somehow, and this is absurd, I couldn't bring myself to throw her out.
My initial plan was to gather her up and take her down to the canal in the depth of night when, mostly, nothing human is about. I could put her in an old canvas bag, (she would be easy to fold in the primal state to which she was reducing), and sling in too four or five empty wine bottles to give my cargo its clanking excuse, should anyone accost me. (The bottles would be useful, too, if I needed to stun somebody.)

But I never made this move. I simply left her sitting in the chair, with the cushion behind her head, while little pieces of her flaked off like petals, and some of her dark hair fell out on the floor.

I took to sleeping in the main room, on the couch, as she had.

I didn't speak to her, of course. I was perfectly aware she was dead.

One morning, I took one of my rambles round the entire house. I went into the empty rooms, and ran the taps in the two upstairs bathrooms. Flushed the lavs. The water ran, but looked a bit dark. Sometimes it doesn't run at all.

In the attic there was an old pigeon agglomerate – a sort of nest, but now vacated, with just a few white splashes and baby feathers left. I admire their tenacity, the pigeons. You get gulls sometimes, from the Thames, or even the sea, God knows. Probably the whole countryside has run to rank seed and is full of fat overfed bugs and worms. Plenty to eat out there, and in the city too.

In the afternoon, I wondered what Wales was like, now. Couldn't think why I'd started on that, and then recalled how she, (Micki), told me he, (Bruvva of Sy), had gone off there. Certainly he hadn't turned up here again. Perhaps the Celtic Picts of the west had done for him.

That evening I began to feel defensive. I do sometimes. There doesn't always have to be a direct reason.

I blacked out the back and side windows with the thick curtains I long ago put up there but hardly ever draw. Each pair has a central zip, and this cuts out almost all vestige of my low wattage bulbs.

It occurred to me I hadn't gone out for days. I still had plenty of supplies, but it's never wise to let it go too long. There would be a dearth of certain things quite often. And always the inevitable idea that in the end nothing at all would persist on the shelves. It was a miracle, even with the reduced contemporary population, things had lasted this long. There was always possible vandalism, too. Some furious loony might burn down the leftovers of the Co-op, or Marks and Spencer's, or the entire High Street, (they had done for the cinema ages back), or else truly manage to poison every can, bottle and package in the freezers.

No, I would have to make a decision on Micki. I would have to put her in the bag and carry her out and dump her in the canal, although right now the water was rather low... there had been little rain for months. But anyway, not tonight. No. Not tonight. It was chillier, frosty perhaps, the stars were up and watching like bright hard eyes on wires.

## 58

At some point near dawn I dreamed I took the corpse into the back garden, and in among the trees. I had a sturdy spade and dug a grave for her and put her in. When I'd filled up the grave with earth again I lugged along some paving stones and laid them over. They should be heavy enough to keep the badgers and foxes out. In the dream this was straightforward.

As soon as I woke up I lay there on the couch, smelling, tasting the stink from the bedroom, and asking myself if this was indeed a workable plan. Of course it would be a tougher job than in the dream. Aside from anything else I'd have to smash through tree roots and generally clear the ground a bit, even before I could properly start. I would have to find any paving, too, (or other heavy materials – big stones, rocks – perhaps from a garden centre like the one there had been nearer the outskirts of the inner city, if it still existed. And that was a two hour walk, and the same back.) Anything like that around the houses here was worn and broken up too small.

Finally I got out of bed, and precisely then was when somebody began thundering blows on the front door.

## 59

I knew who it would be. It had to be. It was.

But behind him was another man, a little younger, and in a ruinous old uniform – police, army, it was difficult to tell, it was so torn and filthy and had gone a sort of brassy mothball colour.

As with the first time Bruvva and I 'met', I'd gone to bed the night before fully clothed. And as I've said, I never look a mess. Clean, combed and tidy. And today about twenty-four. Just something I can do.

I didn't greet him politely. He had been potentially violent before, and only Micki had kept him off. She would have said to him as well, obedient child as she was, that I didn't want him there again.

"I bin in Wales," he told me grimly, as if it was my fault.

I said nothing.

He shook his greasy scabby locks at me. He had the faint remnant of a black left eye.

"I bin there and I come back and she ain't around. She told this old cow wot lives in the shed there that she's going to see you. An' then she din come back. Just like Sy."

I said nothing.

And now the uniformed sidekick spoke up.

"We understand," he said, "she come here."

"Do you," I said. "Well she didn't."

"She's fuckin' lying!" judged Bruvva.

Uniform scratched his crotch, not menacing just cooty.

He concentrated while he did this, a combined expression of anger at the itch and enjoyment of the scratch making him go very nearly wall-eyed. Then: "We need to come in." He added, surprisingly, "Madam."

Nonplussed, what could I do? I said, "No, I don't want that," and I was already trying to shut the door – which I'd only opened because otherwise they could have smashed it down, and still could – and Bruvva caught the door and wrenched it from me, crashing it back against the wall.

He next charged directly past me, making a growling sound, and the other one pelted after him.

I thought, very clearly, and actually in words, I must run now. Leave everything – just get out...

But I couldn't make myself. I couldn't do it. So instead I turned and followed them into my main room through the door in the hall.

The smell was already appalling there. Having breathed in a mote or two of fresh air from the autumn-winter street, I nearly choked on the effluvia.

What more would they need? This in itself was proof enough that I was culpable, but the pair of them stood there in the room, with its boarded or walled-off windows and only a drizzle of illumination spilled in from the outer hall. And they weren't gagging. Not even turning anything over or examining all the bits of furniture for clues.

I said firmly, "Look, I don't like this. I've only just got back myself from my sister's, just about ten minutes before you turned up. I've been away over a week. Are you saying your brother's girlfriend has got into my flat while I wasn't here? Is that it?"

They went on staying crowded together in front of the fireplace with the electric fire that 'sometimes' works. The place reeked and they didn't even cough. They looked now, both of them, like uneasy guests at some uptight stranger's tea party, all big feet and thumbs and not knowing how to behave.

But Bruvva said, "What's in there?" And pointed at the closed bedroom door.

"My bedroom. Where I sleep. I haven't been in there yet."

"Is it locked?" asked Uniform, in a puzzled way. But another flea intervened, this one in his short thick hair. Scritch-scratch. Same reaction, wall-eyed.

"No," I said. "You realise this is an assault, and invasion of privacy?"

Neither of them moved. Either towards the bedroom with dead Micki sitting and rotting in the chair, or to leave the house. It seemed to me they might just stay there, planted by the fire that wasn't on, and waiting for the vicar's cucumber sandwiches so they could drop them on the Aubussin carpet from sheer awkward loutishness.

But then Bruvva went rolling off and clouted at the bedroom door, so it simply sprang inwards.

The bedroom was pitch black. That sheen I had seen on it which came from her, either putrescence or phosphorous, had gone out. No light at all. And the stink...

I felt myself shrivel in it, as if never before in my life had I ever encountered such an aroma, as in fact I had not; it had never stayed that immediate when matured.

What I must do, plainly, was wait for Bruvva's outcry, and then I too must rush forward, and shriek and say who had done that – who – who – when I had been away – done it in my innocent absence, to wicked Micki who must have broken in with a wickeder third person, who then killed her.

Bruvva went forward into the room. Inside, he got out an old petrol lighter from far-gone days, and flicked it, and it lit. A tiny lemon flame.

From out in the other room I, and presumably Uniform, watched through the doorway as the flame skittered over the fetid bedroom darkness like an evil butterfly.

Eventually, "Anything?" Uniform called.

At which the butterfly was flicked back into its own dimension and Bruvva slunk out, wearing a worse-than-ever gloomy and aggrieved look.

At me he glowered. Yes, it was all my fault; Wales, life, what was in the bedroom, the history of the downfall of the world. And so to me he angrily announced, "Fuckin' shit. Nuffin in there. Nofuckinfing at all."

## Rod:
## 60

"Pink for a girl," he used to say. My father. "And blue for a boy." That was his several dark blue suits then, and the ice-blue or turquoise ties – coloured like certain modern bottles of liqueur or Tequila. But I never saw my mother wear pink; or Isabel, my sister. At least, since I don't remember them at all well, I don't believe I did.

But Uncle George was wearing his usual tired if not graceless or unhygienic garments, and Vanessa too, her general attire and polished-pewter bob of hair.

Need I relate, I was lost for words. George filled the gap.

"Come in, Roderick. Have some wine. I have a very drinkable Pinot Noire 2001. She, of course," he indicated the glowering Vanessa, "has just destroyed my last bottle of Glen Fayle. Can you smell the fair spilled Usquebaugh, dear boy? Delicious even in demise."

"You drink far too much, George," said Vanessa, in just the tone she employed to tell me that sort of thing. "Alcohol..."

"Alcohol, you silly old bat, is the solace of my days. Get back to your salad-making, you whore of Babylon, and shake your silver hair on it. Best part of the meal. You can kill a man by feeding him hair," he added mildly to me. "Did you know, dear chap?"

I shook my head. Vanessa had spun on her heel and gone into the kitchen.

"Yes. Cut lots up and stuff it in the stuffing. Either he'll choke on it or, if it gets down, it blocks up the lower intestine. Dead in agony inside the month. In India, I believe they used to use chopped up tiger whiskers. More painful and far quicker. Perhaps less fun."

I had pulled myself partly together.

"George," I said, "what in God's name are you doing here?"

"Oh that." He drew me into a space not unlike, although not completely, a replica of my own flat across the landing. There were two largish rooms, and one of these seemed to be his. I saw the wine-red curtains, and the narrow bed, and all around the music-centres and vinyl-record-players, piles of books and CDs, if only one drinks-cabinet, crowded by a battalion of red wines, bottles of gin and whisky. I couldn't smell the spilled smashed bottle, but I had heard it destroyed, had I not; it had been one of my reasons for venturing across. A tall narrow fridge freezer lurked in one corner. "Can't leave it in the kitchen, you see," said George. "I and she share the kitchen. Please note, the fridge is padlocked. As is the cabinet when I hit the hay." They were. "I miss the Chinese Palace," he added. "Anywhere decent around here?"

"George, listen. Why are you here and not in Lewisham? Why is she here?"

"Ah, well," he said. He sank into the single armchair and put his feet upon a little stool. The wine bottle was to hand and he filled his glass. "Loss of income, Roderick. Straightened circumstances in bad financial times. The predatory crunch of bankers chewing on our bones. Lost everything. Fled with a man with a van. I remembered, you see, you'd told me this was a cheap area, as indeed it is."

I stared at him. "And Vanessa?"

"Same thing. Home repossessed. They'd have had the lot, so she grabbed what she could and parked herself on me. The other room, you understand."

"But..." stupidly I blurted, "...you two don't get on."

"No." George smiled and sipped his refreshed wine. "Quite stimulating, silly old bitch. Too young for me, of course, or too old. Not sure which. I like the young girls to look at, sixteen, seventeen.

And the ancient hags for a night out. Feel like a kept man, then. Not like you, dear lad. You at thirty-nine, going on ninety-nine. I'm old as a listed building by now, but inside young as a lamb. A teenagéd, that's me, accent acute, angled left to right and upwards: Teenagéd."

In the kitchen, Vanessa banged metal things, perhaps forks, on china plates. I pictured the cold meats and frosty green salads.

"Any take-away places hereabouts?" asked Uncle George, with an appealing youthful greed.

## 61

As I've mentioned, I had a guardian after my father's sudden death. He was no relative. Someone appointed by a court, I imagine.

His subsequent horror and bemusement were spectacular. And next I was cast in a new mould very strange to me, and I had to visit an endless (it seemed) stream – no, a river – of people who'd 'wanted to help me'.

I recall less my confusion and disbelief, which soon enough transmuted into a complete amazement, than the dreadful interviews I had to undergo.

In awful over-bright little rooms, or more awful darker ones, smells of damp or nail varnish-scented new paint, window-frames full of cloistered courtyards beyond. Everyone was determined to assist me.

At almost fourteen, I realised fairly swiftly what they were on about. And after that I learned to speak and then to listen, and so to seem to come to an enlightenment which, frankly, I never felt, and do not feel now. Not even now do I fully, I think, grasp what all the fuss was about.

Most of all I came to see that after each interview, all rather, in their intense ways, resembling the debriefing of a prisoner of war, (or, sometimes, his harsh interrogation), I felt much, much better. I myself was aware this was solely because said interview was finished. I was free for the rest of the day or, as things 'improved', the week, the month, the year. And my knowledge of the liberation to come made me tell them all how much better I felt. Although, wisely, I never expanded to explain it was the escapes from my 'helpers' that lightened my heart.

In that way, rather rapidly perhaps, given the situation, I progressed out of their remit.

At least, by then, I knew what was, and what was not. What I was – and was not.

Did I ever blame my parents? My sister? I think I never blamed them, and I know I don't blame them now. Did they destroy my life? I doubt it. It was life itself that destroyed their lives. Smashing them like special whisky bottles in trains and planes, while I, little bastard, lived on.

## 62

I began my awareness, and began to grow up, (to the age of thirteen-going-on-fourteen), as a girl. Yes, the little girl to whom pink is allocated. In my case, I often wore it, too. Pink. I'll assume it suited me, back then.

They had wanted daughters, and the first elder daughter was female. Isabel. Then I arrived. What should they do? They discussed it, I expect, or maybe they didn't, how can I know? But it was decreed that their male boy baby was to be brought up, from the first, as a female.

So I was taught all the usual girl things then current, encouraged to play unroughly, given dolls, pretty clothes, advised on softness and sweetness, I must conclude. My hair was long and had bows, which I can just remember. My name was Rosalind.

Now, I must make this clear. I never saw either my mother or sister, let alone my father, unclothed. Not even in a one-piece bathing costume. And obviously, as a small child, my voice was not of any particular gender. I had, inevitably, a penis, but since the bathroom and lavatory, (of which there were several), were private places, with what was I supposed to compare my own equipment?

However, as I grew up, certain anomalies – it must go almost without saying – intruded. This though was after the tragic deaths of my mother and Isabel. Normally I would have gone to my mother, I suppose, when, at the age of ten, I saw the picture of a naked man in a grown-up book of Renaissance art. And recognised the vital piece. My father was at home at this time, and I went straight to him.

"Oh, Rosalind, dear," he said, "sometimes girls and women have these too. And sometimes, of course, some men do not."

To me this made immediate and unproblematic sense. I did not know anything, aside from the act of urination, for which the penis was constructed. By then I was, as well, here and there, noting the shape of the female bosom. I mentioned this. My father assured me they were, none of them, real. They did not grow. "Most ladies have them made, do you see, Rosalind? They are then attached, painlessly, to the body by a cosmetic process. The usual age for this is sixteen, but some girls prefer to acquire them before that date. Most foreign girls, I must say, seem to do that." He gazed into space as he said this. Looking back I suspect he had, then, a very young foreign mistress. "But you're far too young, my love, to worry about such things."

I assured him I did not want them especially, was just curious.

"Of course you are." He gave me a hug and we ate some chocolate.

I must stress here, there was never anything abusively sexual involved in any of my experience with my father. Even my later interrogators, who at times had seemed determined to discover that there was, at last drew this same conclusion.

I was my father's daughter. He loved me, if rather absently, as my mother and sister realistically must have seemed to. He told me I was his consolation for their loss.

My voice began to break when I was about twelve. Probably I was rather dilatory in that. But concerned once more I sought his advice. I remember so clearly he played me a record – vinyl – of a most wonderful contralto. I forget her name, I regret to say. But my father said that this unevenness of my vocal chords also happened with some young women. It boded well, since I might end up with a wonderful singing voice, like the one just heard from the lady on the record.

I believed every word. Why wouldn't I? And I had been educated by then, for some time, by – I must deduce – very carefully chosen private tutors. We had no TV. The outer world was over the hills beyond the farmhouse's verdant boundaries.

What did I lack? Nothing. Was I happy? In my own unambitious way, I was.

Eight or so years, five to thirteen, with few cares. Comfortable in myself. A happy young woman, a girl growing gracefully up.

Were there no sexual feelings? A few. But they never involved persons, or even images. They were serpentine tremors that rippled through my spine and groin, that made my woman's penis rise up, and if I caressed it, it would explode with joy. That was all. It was enough. No one had told me yet I had been cheated, if even I had been.

And then my bloody fool of a father crashed his plane on the beak of Norway. And the guardian arrived, and seeing me in my rose-pink dress, from which I spoke, I surmise, in the voice of an adolescent boy, froze like a stalagmite.

His tirade, and the adjoining congress of interrogators, can be pictured easily enough, I imagine.

Off came the clothes to their cries of rage and fear, all for me, but knifing me through. Off came the veneer of almost fourteen straightforward and smiling years.

On went the straight jacket of maleness. On went the shackles of learning, all over again, what not, and what to do, to want, to hate.

What would my father have said to me, I wonder, when I began to need to shave my face? "Oh, Rosalind. Some women do have to depilate. We'll get you something. It's a nuisance for you, but a sign of physical strength, too."

And what if, at sixteen, instead of hankering for false, cosmetically-added breasts, I had somehow seen some wonderful young girl, strayed onto the land round the house, and fallen, as they used to say, in love-desire?

"Oh, Rosalind. That can happen, you know. But for now, my dear girl, you should control yourself. You're too young to be sure what you want. Too, too young."

## 63

There had been, to begin with, no further noise, after I'd left the pair of them to their cold supper. Then, about 11 a.m. I caught a faint wafting hum of Bach. George apparently was playing one of his CDs. It didn't sound particularly loud to me, but then I began to hear a much louder sound. Vanessa seemed to be shouting again. Perhaps George's music had disturbed her. I had always gathered she went to bed quite early. George's response to her presumed complaint was to up the volume. And then again. My flat too was soon roaring with Bach, though in the bedroom, with the door shut, the torrent lessened. I wondered what the landlady thought. But I suspected she wasn't even there at the moment, which might account for the terrible rat stink's not having been treated.

I slept anyway. Waking around 4 a.m., all was peaceful. And it was Saturday, too, I could lie in.

But I was troubled, of course I was. At a distance these two relatives – both, I had to admit, slightly bonkers – were tolerable. But as next-door neighbours the future didn't look too bright.

I dozed uneasily and finally got up at six thirty, before the sun. Drinking my coffee I watched the solar disk rise in fact, over the street. How odd everything looked, I thought, in the dawn, the trees mostly bare, and frost pasted on the north and west side of roofs. Not a sign of life anywhere. Years before there would have been milk-carts drawn by horses, and Steptoe and Son rag-and-bone men, also with horse-and-cart. Kids might be out playing in the middle of the road, since cars were relatively few; you could go half an hour or more without anybody driving through a side street. But now, less than a contemporary scene, it looked only deserted. As if everyone had died or gone away in the night.

This notion made me uncomfortable, even now, after the former events of George's and Vanessa's disappearances were explained. I was almost relieved when, at 8 a.m. the phone rang.

Relief soon gave in to dismay. It was Forrel. He had, he said, come down on the train from London, hadn't slept all night. Could he come round at once and see me. He was in a 'State', he told me, with a threateningly grim self-importance.

"Well, you see..." I tried.

"No, I really do have to talk to someone. There isn't anyone else, you see. No one. Not since that slag left me. And I just don't – I don't know what to do."

With a sense of despair, I capitulated. And inside fifteen minutes he was ringing the main downstairs doorbell. I let him in, and up he blundered, stumbling about on the stairs and eventually lurching into my flat. I gave a quick glance, I admit, to the door of the flat across from me, but so far there was no reaction.

"Oh God," said Forrel, floundering, and falling on my sofa as if he lived here and had done this a thousand times. "Oh God – Rod – it's that fucking girl."

"Oh dear." I asked him if he would like a coffee. He assured me he had drunk a whole bottle of vodka on the train, hiding it from the guard, and now could only face the same kind of drink. But too aware this was not a sane plan, I poured him a small one, and made sure a plastic bowl was ready in the kitchen, should he repeat the indigestion attack I'd witnessed in Soho.

Then I sat down, as he insisted I must, and he began again on Forrel's Lament. It was substantially the same, tedious through repetition, if ornamented now with extra flights of fancy, such as leaping from the top of our five storey workplace or stripping himself naked and lying across the doorway of the room to which, it seemed, the girl with blue eyes and manmade breasts had twice taken him. I wondered if she had charged him the hundred-fifty she had offered me as her going rate. Less, due to his youth? More due ditto? It was impossible to try to follow his raving, not to say exhausting. If I had ever been prey to such passions, could I have been more sympathetic? How can I know? The curse-blessing of sexual love has never overtaken me. Or, more likely, I have never been fleet enough to catch up with it.

Surreptitiously, as he went on, I made out my weekend shopping list, which must include the Co-op, and the light shop for some bulbs. This didn't trouble Forrel. When he was ready he went off to my bathroom, "for a dump," and coming back refilled his glass to the top. Prudently, I added vodka to my list.

We reached nine-thirty, the time at which I'd meant to leave. In a pause I said, "I'm afraid I have to go out – shops, you know."

"Oh, you go, Rod. That's OK. I'll be fine. Catch a bit of kip here."

My leaden heart sank into my boots of clay.

## 64

George was on the landing. He wore a baggy suit, a somehow baggier tie, and an ancient, ancient overcoat. Vanessa was right behind him in her fake-fur jacket.

"Just about to knock," said George. "We're off to the local Co-op."

Hemmed in on all sides, I stood at a loss. And then behind me, Forrel opened my door, and smiled blearily out upon us all. He was by now in his shirtsleeves, his hair ruffled.

"Well," said Vanessa, with cool majesty. "What have I always said, Roderick? Why would you never be honest about this? You are gay. Here is the proof."

And George looked at me with a quizzical, gentle amusement. "Why not, old lad. Each to their own."

And "Gay," repeated Vanessa, holding out her hand to the swaying Forrel who, swaying, shook it. "How good to meet you, at last."

## KLOVA:
## 65

So I have put on again that special dress I bought, when next I went to the Tower and met Coal the first.

Before, I bathed under the spume, and scented me. And my hair in the hair-washer, and tinted extra black.

The dress is gold, with pink like glass rain all over. And fringes of goldenness and pink. The shoes are like the dress. And the hold-ups with pink roses.

I made up my face, the best I ever did.

And last of all I put on the lipstick that has C.P. marked on it. Like as my mother. If she was, and not one more lie.

## 66

He said to me I was a peculio.

I was Weirdness, and so weird things happen round me. And he wouldn't be one of them.

This is Coal. After we met the ghost in the rooms above. How could I argue? It must be true.

My eyes cried, but I didn't cry. I wasn't there, just somewhere in another room inside my head, looking out a window smeared with the rain of my wet tears.

He said, "Don't do that. It won't do any good. Take care, Klova. Have a fine life."

When he had gone I went and sat on the bed where we had had carnal. I didn't know where I was.

I was nowhere.

No sounds upstairs.

No stink from downstairs.

I am in nowhere and I do not exist.

So it will be easy. I'm all ready now. Like as I have done my best, and then the bank-nanny can distribute the last of my shots to other people who will need them. And no one will remember or think of me.

I will be wiped away, like the lipstick.

The lovely lipstick, which I kiss goodbye, and leave standing upright by the bed, its gold case with the two letters C.P. and the deep pink bud of its being.

The lipstick will be the last thing I see.

My friend. Bye-bye, as they said it in the Centre. Bye-di-bye-byes.

Love. And let go.

## Emenie:
## 67

They performed a cursory search of the rest of the flat – the kitchen, loo and bathroom, the inner hall – very dark, of course, and they missed the cellar door. They seemed disinclined to go upstairs and look elsewhere. Perhaps they thought other people lived up there who might object.

"No use," said Bruvva soon enough. "Useless." He glowered at me again. Again it was all my fault they hadn't found her.

The ridiculous thing was it was their own. Bruvva must be blind (had the black eye affected his vision?). And both of them lacking all sense of smell.

It was less than ten more minutes before they shambled out. The Uniform with a particularly incongruous "Thank you then, madam." And Bruvva with a glare and a mutter, "If she don't show, I'll be back."

I shut the front door, and then dragged one or two bits portable enough to lift or pull, heavy enough to impede entry a little, against it.

Only then did I brace myself and walk through into the bedroom.

I really would have to get rid of Micki's corpse now. There was no longer a choice. Why had I delayed?

The light came on when I threw the switch. Because most lights now don't work, they hadn't even tried that. But it was a hundred-watt blaze. Couldn't miss a thing.

I couldn't miss the squalor of the room, the untidy bed. I couldn't miss the chair with the cushion fallen out of it to the floor. I couldn't miss that she, Micki, was no longer in it. Micki – was gone.

What did I feel? A wave of utter panic. This was so illogical.

True, I hadn't looked in on her this morning, but last night I had, one quick stare, and then the door shut to try to alleviate some of the stink.

How in Hell had she gone?

Where to?

Somebody must have broken in and... and what? Taken her up, rotten and disintegrating, got her through the whole flat and out again – all this without ever waking me. All this without any mess. As I say, she'd been falling apart. But now there was nothing at all. Not a single stain or flake, not even one dark hair lying on the ground.

Presently, I went back into the kitchen, shut the door and sat down. I drank some bottled water. I had to think.

There was a plate on the table with a single smear of jam on it. Pallid sunshine, through the high-up crack in the zipped curtain, hit the plate, and I could see the shape of a raspberry-coloured snake spitting out a ray of fire. What did it mean, this sign?

I judged it was about eleven o'clock. I got up and went out of the kitchen into the garden at the back, to get some more clean air.

A small plane was going over. They hardly ever do any more. It might not even be manned, a robot plane, senselessly spying on us all, with nobody left at Government HG to take notes.

I watched it blankly, breathing up the cold garden smell. Leaves and compost, foxes, winter.

When I looked down again I saw at once straight in among the bare trees. What was that?

Without any thought I went to the spot and stood there, gaping down at the mound of earth, with all the long grass and weeds ripped off, and seven or eight broken-up paving stones lying on top. The badgers had been digging there, or one had, but not made much head-way. The stones were weighty. I knelt down and touched the soil. Still moist from turning. I had dreamed I had done this. Dreamed it. Had I sleep-walked out and somehow achieved my aim? I examined my clothes, my fingernails – but that was no indication, was it? I could always be clean and tidy, elegant even. What I might have done to get covered in soil and mulch and corpse-dust would all be gone.

Well then, I must have done the work. In the dead of night. Micki was down there now, under the earth and the stones. It was accomplished.

I turned and went back in, and so through the rooms again, and already the flat smelled quite fresh. Even the bedroom smelled only of its ordinary odour of faint must and damp.

# IRVIN:
# 68

Dogs are supposed loyal. Even wolves, when tamed, have sometimes been so accredited. They will die for you. Not so the faithless beast I have these past two years nurtured in my care, fed from my own plate, and vaunted, formerly, as a paragon.

For two weeks I have not seen the wretch, but am constantly told of his exploits, for good or ill. But yesterday comes the chandler to me to present a bill for a piece of cheese my dog had, so he swears, snatched from the stores. As luck has it, the chandler is a bone head who is enblissed by the theatre. And so I gave to him a free entrance to our current play, in Stampwell Street, off Cartwheel Lane. A rare piece of tomfoolery it is too, and no mistake, but he is glad, and I no longer forfeit for the cheese.

Then, this very afternoon, I am regaled by the carter, who is wont, under duress, to cart me to my work in London, by a tale of how my dog, last night, possessed five bitches in a row, and kept the folk of seven domiciles from their sleep throughout by the noise.

Said I, "No, not he. It was another cur."

"It was your own, sir..." (He calls me sir as others have called me felon) "...that black rogue tall as a pony and with one red ear."

What can I say? So he is. I shall be thrown from my lodgings in the old woman's charnel-house at this rate.

At 4 o'clock to the theatre, through the slush of the great snow we had, and by six I am on the boards, trooping with the rest, and

Merscilla Peck in the midst.

Thank God, she has gone back to favouring me, for there is such a scene in this play, (during which I seize her and act I have my way behind a curtain), at which otherwise I would burst, I have no doubts. But she and I regularly deal with this matter later, at an inn we know of.

Of all my charmers she is, I must acknowledge, the one most fires me up. Thank God too she is married, or I might have succumbed to the trap of wedlock. And I have slight doubt that herself as a wife, she would not smile upon my other adulteries, though ever permitting her own – as now, indeed she does, and her poor husband kept by her on a leash shorter than a cat's spanker.

Meanwhile, I also pass the time now and then with Mr Templeyard, who has not yet tired of me, nor I, yet, of him.

As for his tasty wife, they have quarrelled over the other business of my 'insult' to her, and she is off to the country with her mother. A shame, for my appetite is still whetted, there. But likely she may come back. Or if not, other fruit may fall to my hand.

It is a fact both women and men become enamoured of the actor kind. And since nowadays women, too, parade on the stage, as in former times they did not, they draw so many admirers they (and I) must sometimes leave the premises by a side-door. Merscilla for one has seven drones of this sort. I think she indulges none of them, having her bedroom hours mostly crowded up with me, or her spouse. But I do not tempt fate by looking into this, much. For myself I have had two or three other girls in the past month. One need not go hungry. But one wants, where one can get it, the roast hog not the cutlet.

Returned home, I find for once the old bell-wether of a landlady has laid and lit me a fire, and set out a dish of meat and eggs, as I had asked.

But Satan himself has been before me. He has got in and snouted out all the viands, leaving for me but a few chewed embers of the meal.

And how should I know who is thus responsible for my starvation? Why, he has left his signature, bold as any Shakespeare, in the egg and gravy on my rugs: a great pawmark the size of a hoof. The dog.

## 69

Last night the snow came down again and mantled the wild land beyond the village with its ermine carapace.

I had, having got to the play, half thought I should remain in town with Mis'us Peck. But alas, old Peck sends the page for her. He is sick of the winter plague, (there is for sure a plague for every season), and she must get to their broad house on Hampstead Walk, to tend him.

Losing heart then, I too travelled home, though not on foot but by the carter's cart, for he had been delayed in London.

"You should make your roost in the city, Mr Thessaris," says he, calling me Mr now as if he called me villain. "This must be an irk for you to wrestle with, such racketings up and down on my poor cart."

"Your cart is a swan, sir," said I. "She breasts the snow with grace and courage."

He spat into the white-flecked void beyond the lantern.

It was well past midnight when I climbed to my room.

Just at the door, I heard within a stealthy shift, and took it for my fiend of a dog. Charging therefore in I stopped with an oath. For no canine lay beside the once more lighted hearth, but on the bed a naked female form, gilded by the dimness and the fire to a creation of marble and amber.

"Never be startled, dear love," she said. And for an instant I did not know her. She was instead every female I had ever idled with, yet also none of them. In the strange light her hair showed both dark and golden, and her eyes had no colour, only flame in them.

"Madam," I said, "should you be here? Is this not unwise?"

"Does Cupid bid us to wisdom or to delirium?" she replied. "Shall we try, and see if we can work the puzzle out?"

I am an actor, and so know voices. Now I knew hers. It was the young wife of Jem Templeyard, back from the country, it seemed, and primed for battle.

I cannot say such an event has never befallen me. But never quite in this way. Jem had led me to believe she was infuriate with me and no less with himself, saying I was a philanderer and rapist, and he a coward, who would not credit the truth. He must run to hide, while I might smoulder in Hell, she would pray for it. (One rarely believes such vows, save on a stage. Men and women both volley out these dragon-vapours here and there. I have done so myself. We are all fools, and can generally be appeased.)

Oh, but she was a tempting sight. So smooth and soft and gleaming, as if limned by gold and opal. To take her so would be like a love-dance with a statue, but one alive.

She did not move, so I went to her, and then she gripped my hands and put them upon her bosom. Up sprang jack, and very next down lay Irvin Thessaris. And we galloped our measure in the riotous firelight, at which her shrieks came on so high and piercing I must stifle them with my mouth, for fear the whole bedlam housefull ran up to ask who had been slain.

As the dawn began to come, we by then beneath the bedclothes, she woke and said to me, "Did you never know I loved you, proud actor?"

"Aye, my lady. How else did you give yourself?"

"I might have done it," she said, "as with my doddle-dun of a husband. Because I must. No other pass for such as me. A poor girl. Christ aid me, I was sold by my father as you sell a shoe."

"More beautiful, for sure."

"Well, then, scholar, a beautiful shoe."

As a rule such brooding at the chime of midnight, or as the wash of the day comes back, is tedious and sour. But from her pretty lips, ripe and rosy from my kisses, I knew the sadness in her. Poor lass. To be a woman, and sold, as she said, to a man she despised. (For it was plain enough she did despise Jem Templeyard. To me he was a divine romp of a rump. But to her; her master, and her doom.)

"Well, sleep now, sweetheart," I said.

"No, I cannot sleep. I must be off and away to my mother's house at Levishamm. But before I go, I must say this. I loved you, faithless dog, as some love God. I loved you as the winter loves the spangled spring – that kills it. And you, my lord, thought me less than a breath of spice, or perfume. One breath. No more. Poor me," she said, and she did not shed tears, nor whine or cling. Cool she lay by me, my firelit statue of silk, with her velvet purse, and her prow of satin, and her eyes of smoke and fire. So I listened. The playwright, he would have been to his papers, and written down her words. I write them down, however, for – despite my doglike and Satanic thievery – I heard them all, and the song of her sad heart couched in that lovely cushioned breast.

"Dear girl..." I said, when she paused.

But she spoke again. "Hear me out. In less than a quarter by the clock I'll be gone. And, I think, never again shall I see you. No, not in this mortal life. Will you let me work one last act on you?"

Stupidly I said, "An act, my love, is the ballast of any play."

At which a falling star shot through her eyes. I swear they blazed from gold to white to grey. And then I felt a sore hot pain in my left arm, not far from where he, her husband, had struck me in the duel, pinked me, as he said. A scratch, a little bite. Nothing. Only recompense.

One may imagine I had started up, and then I saw she had only stuck in me a pin, the kind a woman may use about her dress, less than two inches. It was, even so, bloodied, but that only half an inch along its tooth.

She stared at me, tearless and intent. "I never wished to hurt you, my lord, my love. But this – I will have." And then she licked the pin, licked off my blood from it.

I confess with another jade I might have been moved to some violence. But with her, no, only I felt a profound sorrow.

"Sweetheart," I said, and took her in my arms, and held her close as the light stained in upon the wall. "Shall I never see you again? Surely, next summer, when..."

"No, never," she said, her voice very soft. "Not in this life. But you must always remember, while you live, I loved you. I have proved how much. May God forgive me."

Then she got up, and dressed herself, at which my lust returned. But it was as if my loins and my mind were at a complete variance. Neither would accede to the other. One was a lion, but his adversary a mourning dove.

I would have gone with her to find transport. I would have taken her to an inn for food or wine or coffee. But I did not speak. I lay and watched her leave me, and only after she was gone did I lie back. And then it was I who wept, yes, even I who never ever wept for twenty years without he was on a stage. After which I fell asleep and did not wake again till noon. Or, perhaps, not at all.

# Rod:
# 70

Vanessa's grim determination had soon dragooned all of us out on to the street, down the intervening streets to the canal, and along to the Co-op. All-Of-Us comprised by then not only George and myself, but Forrel.

He was still so drunk he had been fairly easily coerced. If Vanessa realised his condition, (probably she did), she made no comment on it. She was almost offensively eager to demonstrate her acceptance – no, her entire approval – of what she took to be my and Forrel's homosexual liaison. She had even made sure I had lent him my other overcoat, which was rather too long for him in sleeves and hem. To the half bottle of vodka he carried in tow, refilled I assumed at my larger one and now thrust into a pocket, she paid no overt attention. For myself I had been relieved to see the 'whole bottle' he had consumed on the train had been of this slightly smaller variety. I'd visualised his guts full of two litres, at least. However, as he now went on, they soon would be.

The Co-op is a sprightly place, sparkle-clean and well lit, and full of seemingly welcoming staff, who may be failed RADA students, even successful but passed-over ones, for all I knew, using their rejected skills to imply friendship and kindness.

Vanessa began to organize the shopping, naturally, George's, mine, and – presumably – Forrel's.

A great deal of salad and root vegetables ended up in our baskets, (Forrel had been given a basket too), brown bread and honey. I managed some lamb chops and butter and the cheaper eggs. Forrel distractedly picked up two packets of chocolate biscuits.

"Yes, why not," congratulated Vanessa, intent on her partisanship. "A little treat. I suppose," she added, "you can only get together at weekends?"

"Oh – er – yeah, sure," beamed drunk and hazy Forrel, and next nearly collided with a stand of carbonated drinks.

George, the couth and practiced drunk, wandered more sedately, and far more independently than Forrel or I did, we so assiduously herded by my aunt. George's was the trolley, stacked with many alcoholic beverages and a few mixers, one box of savoury biscuits and a plastic-wrapped selection of cheese.

When we attained the check-out, the girl smiled encouragingly on us, this strange little family of two aging, or aged, (or, in George's case, teenagéd) relatives, and two youngish, oldish nephews or sons.

"Having a party?"

"No," said George, amiably, producing a credit card. "It's the dog. The dog drinks a lot."

The girl giggled. "You oughta have a word with his vet."

George now paid, waving away all protests, including Vanessa's, which seemed to annoy her. But she reined it in not to upset Forrel.

Outside, a cab was already waiting. "Good-day, Max, old boy. Help us load up, would you?" Seeming quite willing, Max did so. He and George exchanged a little banter about life in general, paying no particular heed to the six bottles of spirits, and twenty-five of wine, settling clankingly in the boot with the cabbage, broccoli, lettuce, and other actual food.

George, it appeared, had already established contacts in the area, Max being one.

Max drove us to The Black Sheep, where George had decided we'd lunch, then Max waited in the pub car-park, reading a newspaper contentedly and sipping the large Coke George had bought him as the clock on the meter ran merrily on.

Forrel entered the pub like a man returning after too long an absence to a loving home. Everyone but Vanessa had stiff vodka-tonics, and thereafter en masse got through three bottles of Sauvignon. Vanessa drank orange juice. As for food, we all ate fish and chips, which wasn't bad, considering how far it had had to travel, frozen, from the sea; except, again, Vanessa, who had a prawn salad without chips.

Forrel only toyed with his meal. I was uneasy, fearing a recurrence of projectile vomiting. But what he had, thankfully, stayed down.

Once, he nodded off, unconsciously leaning to one side, his head a moment resting on my shoulder. Vanessa smiled, nearly glowing with affiliation. "You see, Roderick," she said, "how simple it is just to act as you want. These days no one, except a savage, would have any problem with it."

I'm afraid the vodka and Sauvignon spoke. "You're making quite a mistake, Auntie. In fact, this young man is insanely in love with a striptease dancer."

"Well, Roderick, I'm sure that will pass. I'm sure this other young man in the sex trade looks very good to Edward," (this was Forrel's first name, it seemed), "but a good relationship means far more. A perfect body isn't everything. And you could take some time to visit a gym, perhaps, improve your muscle tone. Edward would appreciate that, I'm sure."

My mouth had dropped open. I closed it. I had a vision of Forrel (Edward) prancing after some well-packed member of the Chippendales. I laughed.

George too looked amused. I thought he had very likely spotted her error from the first. Fortunately, though, the laugh dislodged Forrel, who sat bolt upright, and said, "It's nice." And smiled radiantly, and then got up and, in a sort of staggering amble, headed for the gents.

"Would you like another orange juice, Van," Uncle George courteously inquired.

"No, thank you, George. And I insist, when we get back, that I pay you for my groceries, and my lunch."

"Right you are," said George, lazy as a cat on a just-the-right-temperature tin roof.

Vanessa then also rose, and walked with the carriage of a queenly policewoman, to the ladies. George and I watched her progress, as other men might wait out the passing of a tiger.

## 71

"You know, old son," said George, "I have a bit of advice to give you."

I must confess I was worried, briefly, when he said that.

I've mentioned my far and distant pink past. How much of this either George or Vanessa knew I had never been certain. Neither of them had ever given me a clue. Unless, of course, I counted Vanessa's determination that I must be gay, which stemmed, I might suppose, from my being treated as a girl until the age almost of fourteen. What now though would my uncle say to me, in the intervals of Forrel's perhaps puking and/or passing out in the lav, and Vanessa's wholesome adjacent visit?

"Ever read Cervantes?" George asked me.

Surprised, I had to think. "I'm not sure. I may have tried to and

## Cruel Pink

not got very far. But I've seen it dramatized on TV once or twice. You mean Don Quixote, yes?"

"Yes, good old Don Quixote..." adherently, George pronounced it, yet as it would have been in his youth, Don Quick-Sott. "After all," George would doubtless have pointed out, "we have from this name the description quixotic – can hardly pronounce that kee-hoe-tick, can we?"

"So you know the idea, at any rate," he continued. "And you'll know the bit about the windmills?"

"Yes, of course. Most – well, a lot of us do. Tilting at windmills, when he thinks they're giants."

"Quick-Sott's whole life, more or less, is that, at least in the original intention. I don't mean, old chap, he always does things that are useless, because for what he wants out of life, they give him just the buzz he needs. The bar-slut is a princess, the innkeeper can knight him. The windmills are giants, meant to be slain by the perfect knight."

"And the advice?" I had just seen the door of the Ladies open, but actually it wasn't Vanessa who came out, but another woman in black jeans. She went up to the bar.

"The advice is this, just what Sancho Panza the servant-squire says to old Quick-Sott: 'Take care, your worship, those things there aren't giants, they're windmills.'"

"You think I take too much on myself, George?"

"No, Roderick. I think you don't see life quite as it is. You see girls as princesses, maybe, and ordinary streets as castle corridors, trains as chariots, for all I know, clouds as camels, (though that's good old Hamlet, of course), and giants where there are only windmills. Or, maybe, the odd princess as a waitress, and giant – as a windmill. We all do it a bit. But you do it a lot."

I gazed at him, quite unable to relate this statement to anything at all in my life. What did I ever see in such a reckless, mad and glamorous manner? My bloody awful job? The irksome train journeys? My lonely, stuck, just-adequate tiny life?

I was about to question him in a way unusual for me, when two new things occurred. Forrel emerged from the gents looking presentable and face-washed, though not yet shaved, and walking reasonably steadily. And as that happened the girl in black jeans came up to us.

"He says you're with that woman that's in the toilet."

George and I both goggled.

The woman in jeans resumed, "She's throwing up like crazy. I'll go back in, but we may need, like, an ambulance."

## 72

It had been the prawns, it seemed, and Vanessa, with her normal intolerance of all irritations, both voided herself and recovered remarkably quickly. George nevertheless sent her home in the cab asking Max to wait on there, for us, clock still running.

George's triumph was to get Vanessa to drink a single brandy, for 'medicinal' reasons. She obeyed him. Afterwards she got into the cab, pale, but reasonably self-possessed.

"Poor old bat," George said to me, as we again sat down.

Forrel was now drinking tap-water, but standing up. He told us how sorry he was about my aunt, and thanked us for a 'great break'. He said he would need to catch the one-thirty back to town. Someone had called his mobile, someone he had to see, and he winked at me. By a quarter past one he was gone.

"Silly chap," said George. "He's not your boy, is he? No, thought not. Besotted with a stripper, well, he could do worse, but he'll need funds." Then, turning back to me, he said, "And I need a word with you, Roderick."

Now what? I found I was frowning at him.

"Roderick," said George, "I'd like to buy your flat off you. Private sale. Will save me no end of money."

"My – flat."

"I'll give you a good price, and a bit over. I don't mind you getting something, old lad. Just not the damn government and estate agents, all the rest of the vultures. Why should I pay for their holidays and lunches and porno films? I need to pay for my own. And we'll square it with your landlord. After all, my first deal there was easy enough."

He explained that he was very fond of Vanessa, in his way. He enjoyed sparring with her, it kept him up to scratch. But inside the one small flat it was too much. And sharing a bathroom with a woman was bloody hell. You could never get in there.

So if I could let him have my place, he'd be just across from her and they could go at it kick and bucket (as he put it) whenever they wanted, and both get a bit of peace too.

"You could move closer to your work," he added, "or farther out."

Then he named the sum he had in mind. For a man who had had to run because of imminent bankruptcy, or whatever he had said and implied before, he seemed to have plenty of dosh. His credit card, as I'd already observed, still operated.

The thing was, the moment he added those words *or farther out*, a beautiful rural landscape welled upwards in my mind, like a rising chord of music.

It was the farmhouse, below the hills. The house of my peculiar beginnings. Obviously, even with extra cash, I could never afford to go back there. Yet... to the neighbourhood – why not? I'd never really seen much of it, beyond the grounds. And no one much had ever seen me, save those persons my father paid to forget. And I was very different now. Oh, entirely different. No longer in pink. No longer a little girl.

Did I, truly, want to go there? For sure I didn't want to stay either in my current apartment, or employment. They could go. I could find a little place somewhere, off the beaten track. Some little job, anything, just to pay the bills. I was thirty-two. I was fifty-nine. It was time I found a proper life that could suit and sustain me. That even, possibly, could wake me up.

The title of *Don Quixote* was still floating in my head, just over the resonance of my rural dream. Now another title came. *Five of My London Lives*. Not a book, I thought, puzzled. A play, perhaps? Why had I thought of that?

"What do you say," George asked me, "yes or no?"

Nothing could get out of me apart from thoughts. I said, "George, look, give me till this evening. Come across for a drink, about six."

"Make it a big drink, and I will," he said. He smiled his alert, serene, teenaged smile. "Don't worry, I'll bring the booze."

## KLOVA:
## 73

A shadow bends over me.
    How has it got in?
    Is it the landlady?

No...

Of course. It's Coal. He works in Security. He can go anywhere he wants.

I was thinking about getting up and trying the lipstick, before I went out.

But I'm not.

Not going out.

I'm going... in.

Like a flower closing in darkness or too strong sun.

Like that.

I didn't steal the lipstick. Like I'd had the money-gift wired into my account.

Who cares where it came from?

Who...

Who's bending over me?

"Klova," he whispers. "Klova-Spice. What have you done? Klova – what have you done?"

"Turned off the youth," I said.

"But..."

"I turned it off. Then you grow old. I grow old. And – that's it. Then I die."

I can't see him. Only the shadow.

He begins to tell me lots of things. That he made a mistake. It was all his fault. He didn't understand. He is sorry. He loves me.

Who is he?

Coal.

He is Coal.

He says, he can get a medic.

I said, "Too late."

# 74

Coal fetched that light-thing he used in the place upstairs, and it lighted, not dazzling me, but I closed my eyes, and I hear him breathing.

"It doesn't work like this, Klova," he said. "You can't kill yourself just by – what in hell did you say? Turning off the youth...?" And then there was silence, as he stared down at me. He said, "Klova." That was all.

Then he started to cry.

It doesn't mean anything. We all cry.
Like as if we rain. Like the rain-beads on my dress. Pink and gold.
Then he tried to lift me, move me, and it hurt me, and I screamed. I heard the scream from miles off. It sounded angry.
But then the inside comes in again and washes up over me, and I'm comfortable again. It's nice to die.

## 75

Who is there?
Oh, it's Coal. He can break in anywhere.
He is holding my hand, which is now all bones. My body like is bones. My skin, just a bit of stuff draped over.
"Let go my hand," I said. "I want the lipstick."
"What?"
"The lipstick. Just there by me. Give it me. I want to hold it."
So he found the lipstick and put it carefully into my hand.
It has these two big letters on it, my lipstick. I love my lipstick. That was my mother's name. C.P.
Nearly there now.
It's like falling down and down through black feathers. Soft. Nobody loves me, all alone.
But I hold the lipstick close and kiss the pink bud of its mouth that so often, like as it has, kissed me. Darling lipstick. Darling love.
I always liked its name, from the very first. What made me buy it. Then we kissed, the lipstick and I.
People leave bruises on you. The lipstick just leaves pink. It's kind and sweet, even though its name is Cruel. C.P. Cruel Pink.
Let go.
Gone.

## Dawn:
## 76

I think I've been away. You know how it is. At my age, you don't always remember. But I was always like that. When I was thirty I was like that. I'd go into a room or along a corridor and think, what was I after? Or I'd forget where a shop was in relation to the other shops. And as for names, I couldn't remember them. It's just that I'm worse now. It's funny really. I've grown into being old.

I wonder where I've been, though, if I was away somewhere? Years ago I'd sometimes stay with Susie, after she lost David, and I'd lost Ben. And sometimes I went to France, to see Jean. Did I fly? I think I did.

Anyway, I can see the cupboards and the fridge need replenishing. I'd better get my skates on and nip out to the Co-op.

I get tired doing that walk now, though it isn't far.

Also I had a bit of a funny experience the last time I was down that way.

You have to go by Rothall Street and Sundridge Drive, and then to the canal and walk along. Takes me about twenty-five minutes, and then a half hour back. When I was younger I could've done it all in half that. But the Co-op wasn't built then. And the canal was really a canal. Now they've drained and roofed it over, and underneath you can hear skateboarders screeching, and anybody that walks down there does so at their peril.

There used to be a sort of park or common beyond, but they've built on it since. Flats. When was that? About 1984, I think it was. The previous century. What a thought.

To get back to what happened to me last week. Or the week before that, I'm not certain.

I went out, as I always do, checked a couple of times I'd locked the front door, to be sure, to be sure, as Ben used to say, and up the road and down into Rothall Street.

The trees were losing all their leaves so fast. Time flies, doesn't it. It was only August a minute ago, or so it seems. And tomorrow it'll probably be Christmas Eve! I'm joking. But it seems that way, to me.

In Sundridge Drive there were a lot of extra cars, and Number 15 – or 25, was it? – had scaffolding up. It's silly, but house repairs always remind me of the war. I mean the Second World War, 1939 to 1954 – no, no, 1945, of course, I mean. But the war wasn't like that. I was only little, about four, five, six. But I remember those awful sirens. And the red in the sky, even out here. And the noise. Things falling. I wasn't evacuated, you see. I can't remember why not. Horrible times.

Then I got out of Sundridge Drive and walked along the old tow-path by the roofed-over canal underpass, and there was this gang of four boys. They looked about fourteen or fifteen to me. They could have been older.

Usually, if I see something like that, I'd cross the street, but there isn't anywhere, you see, there, until you come to the old bridge.

So, I kept going. They didn't seem to notice me at first. Just lounging there against the wall. And I don't look rich. I'm not interesting to them. Or, I thought I wasn't.

## 77

I shan't try to duplicate how they speak. I'll simply translate it into ordinary English, so far as I understood them.

1st Boy: Here she comes, look, do you see?

2nd Boy: That her, is it?

1st Boy: Yes, like a scarecrow. But she's just an old bag today.

3rd Boy (lighting a cigarette): You said she dresses up funny.

1st Boy: Yes, she does. Couldn't believe my eyes first time I saw it. You should have seen.

3rd Boy: Well I didn't. I don't believe you. You've been smoking too much f***ing skunk, you a***hole.

4th Boy: I seen her. I seen her down the station. Thought it was a loony.

1st Boy: She is a loony, you t**t.

4th Boy (taking a drink from a bottle of lager): She had a real short dress on. And a wig. F***ing gross-out.

2nd Boy: I see that too. From the back thought it was a bint. (Did he mean Girl?) F***ing weird one. Then I see her front ways. And she's ninety, like she is now.

(I am seventy-four, or seventy-three. I am not ninety.)

By then I was just about level with the gang, and I was afraid, rather, to go on.

And then:

3rd Boy: Yes, I seen her and all. Thought it was an old geezer. In a suit. That was up the High Street. Talks to himself. Herself.

They were all staring straight at me. So I had to go right by. And the oddest thing, they all pressed right back hard to the wall, to let me pass. Not as if to be polite, you see, but as if I was contagious, had some modern illness that can't be cured, or I was radioactive, maybe. I think they held their collective breath.

It was only when I was about ten yards on up the path that one of them, I think the 1st Boy, shouted after me: "Here, grandma, next time make sure you've got your other clothes on!"

And they all laughed.

Probably they were all just high on this drug named after an animal – what did I say they said it was called... bear? fox?

No, of course, skunk. Why do they call it that, I wonder, does it smell horrible?

When I came back with my shopping they weren't there, but I've decided I'll have to go the long way round next time, up through Wilchester Road. I don't want to meet them again. It made me feel a bit ill. They are all mad, or they've been driven mad by the drug. Nothing is safe anymore. It was safer really in the war, with the bombs falling. People were different then. They were – people.

## Emenie:
# 78

For a couple of nights I stayed in the room higher up the house, the one with the bed. I took a few cans of beans and pasta and one of peach slices up, and some water and Coke to drink. No electricity on the higher floors so I couldn't make a hot drink. In the end that drove me down. I made a cafetiere of coffee and stayed in the kitchen. The main room and the bedroom seemed warped out of true, their angles all wrong. And that clean smell was intrusive as any stink.

It snowed that afternoon, all this tattered cotton wool whirling down, like cold-white flesh flaking off the sky.

I still couldn't get round it, couldn't figure out what the hell had happened. I knew I had not buried Micki's body. Yet someone had. Who? Why? How?

The snow set in pretty solidly. My supplies were low. I needed toothpaste and shampoo etc., not to mention food. In this sort of weather as well the persons who still exist hereabouts go a bit mad, rushing into the remains of the shops, even loading up home-made sleds to drag away. Of course I knew I had to pull myself together, and go on with my life. If something happens that's impossible, you can only push it off into the back rooms of your brain. There would be an explanation. But I wasn't going to solve the mystery yet, maybe never. So, close the door on it.

I did think about Micki now and then. I wondered how she was, breaking down as she would be, gently snowing under the ground. Her hair would go on growing for a while, what hadn't already fallen out. That was a pleasant thought. She'd had lovely hair.

Even the cellar didn't smell now. But this was almost certainly because of the general cold. And, too, the corpses were mostly getting quite ancient. Even Sy's was pretty old – for a corpse, that was.

I got my thick coat, and my leather boots with the tough flat soles that came from the shoe-shop in the High Street before it was set on fire. I'd put on a jumper of dark orchid-red. I sometimes do wear red clothes. Though I don't always dress to kill, red's often my killing gear. If I wear red, I am fairly certain I'll be hunting. (Hunting pink.)

Frankly, the best way I could see of scotching my concern with the mysterious grave of my last victim, was to take a new victim, and make bloody sure (or unbloodily, if the method avoided it) I left them far outside my own premises. The shopping was one thing, but it provided too the backdrop and excuse for another murder. That would do it. Wipe the slate clean. Begin a new chapter. Get me back in the ordinary and workable groove.

## 79

There was no one about as I plodded down the towpath.

The Co-op, as I'd feared, had been massively scavenged by others. No bread, not a drop of wine locatable. There used to be a pub farther up, I can remember having a beer in there once or twice – people used to walk in and help themselves, even sit down at a table to drink. But that didn't last, obviously. It was looted and cleaned out.

There were some lagers in a box. I found some soups and peas in cans, and some chicken in the freezer.

It is peculiar. The supplies do seem genuinely to be restocked, from time to time. I've never figured that out either, have I? But it's as well they are, even if not today.

Having got what I could, I made my way back down to the towpath.

The sky was that lurid greyish-white the snow turns it. It had a bulging look, the sky, as if pregnant with the snows. It was going to eject snows like multiple quintuplets all over the ruined city and its feral outskirts. It was already starting.

The deciduous trees of the park were already in full leaf again, white foliage thick as late July. The evergreens still showed a little dark. Some crows went over, jet black, the snowfall making them like pieces of a jigsaw.

This message told me there might be something very close for me.

So then I looked more intently at the park. You couldn't make out the distant wreckage of the flats through the ongoing snow, but I could see a thin dark column winnowing lightly up in the windless debris of the air.

I crossed the bridge very carefully: half of it is down but the rubble has been solid for years, and you can get across if you have to. (Simon-Sy had, after all; I'd watched him do it, following my rat-laden promise of wine and, perhaps, sex.)

I suppose people came into this park once and played games, or had fights, read on seats in the shade, or sunbathed, or screwed behind the bushes.

Now it was just a man sitting on a pile of bricks, tending his fire.

He glanced up at me warily. And he had it written all over him. He was mine. My kill.

"Hi," I said.

He glanced up at me again, having already averted his eyes.

"I've got a couple of lagers here," I said. "You care for one?"

"Yeah. All right."

He was young. He looked about eighteen. The way I did, that afternoon. Perfect match. I'm often clever, that way, looking the right age before I even spot the quarry. Though I can, surreptitiously, grow a bit younger, or older, if I have to, when I meet them.

I went over and sat down on the broad, whitened root of the tree across from him. I handed him a lager from my not-very-full bag.

Bemusing me slightly, he twisted the bottle round in his hand, studying it, as if looking for a wine provenance label or something.

I said, "Cold day to be out."

"Yeah," he said.

I didn't like him. That can sometimes be an extra incentive when it comes to killing. It can add a nice bright red-pink cherry to the cake.

"So, going to tell me your name?" I smilingly asked.

"Why'd you want to know?"

"Well, just so I can call you something."

"Why'd you have to call me anything." It wasn't even a question.

"OK," I said. Then, "Want a cigarette?"

"Nah," he said. "They ain't good for you."

This made me laugh. Surrounded by ruin and chaos, he worried about smoking.

The method was already coming to me. After he had relaxed a bit, I'd get behind him. The fire was glowing under the smoke. In ten minutes it would be very hot and hungry.

"I had to come out," I said. "My mum sent me."

"Your mum?" He gaped at me.

God, he was stupid.

I handed him a Mars bar from the bag and previously from the Co-op freezer. Everything was so cold he might not mind. But he took the bar and turned it round and round in his other hand, (the lager now, still unopened, was in his left.)

"Do you want me to open the bottle for you?" I asked sweetly.

"Yeah," he said, and handed it back.

I thought, next bottle after this one: I can brain him with it, pull him forward rather than push him from behind...

I undid the lager and handed it back to him. He took a swallow. No reaction. He stared down into the fire.

Was he on drugs? Of all the commodities left behind by Armageddon and the Apocalypse, drugs had remained available. He might be, then. He had that pasty, saggy face, spotty too, and lank hair. His leather jacket had holes in it that seemed to have been punched through by a machine, they were so regular. Even out in the cold he smelled nasty.

I let him have his drink. He was slow. All the bottle, go on, boy, drain it. It'll help you when I do it, help me to do it.

The snow, so far shielded away somewhat by the crowded trees, began after all to flicker through. White moths swarmed to the cherry-red of the fire. Red was pink. Hunting pink.

I took out the second lager. (Still one left for me when I got home. I too turned the bottle in my hand. He was back gawping at the flames. And the cigarettes were in the bag. I didn't smoke. Why had I taken them?)

Abruptly I said, "Are you expecting someone?"

"Eh?"

"Someone's up there, on the higher ground." (Would he know what 'higher ground' meant?) "On that hill-thing," I amended. "Kind of waving – like," I added, to assist.

I thought he'd look round. But he didn't bother. He took another sluggish drink of the lager. He was probably only sixteen, in fact. It occurred to me he couldn't read, hence his gaping at the bottle. He hadn't recognised the colours, the signs, the omens of the label.

I stood up suddenly. "Fuck!" I gambled even he would react to my urgency, and my use of the still high-power word. "Christ!" I added, staring off beyond him over his shoulder, looking terrified and confused.

And he did at last respond. He tried to turn and look and get up all at the same moment, and, losing balance and purchase, he skidded on the snow.

The crucial instant had arrived. I had the unopened bottle, the liquid adding weight. I must smash him on the head and pull him down in the same second. Straight into the fire. I could do that. I had done things like that before. The burning warmth of the flames was so close. The burning close happiness of fulfilment strengthened and steadied me. And I reached forward and –

## 80

And I reached forward and
   and
   and I reached forward
and

## 81

And I couldn't do it. It wasn't a physical difficulty. I was agile, and it was quite simple. But my brain couldn't give the order to make my body move. Instead I let him slither, and right himself, and turn round in a rage on me.

"Wha's the fuckin' problem yer fuckin' ol' bitch?" he yelled at me. Oh, he was awake now.

I said hoarsely, "I have to go."

"You go, you ol' fuckin' cunt! Gwon. Get off."

I moved as fast as I could away from him, with my bag, and the second lager stupidly in my hand. I shambled off through the snow-bushes and reached the rubble and got over that, and on to the more solid remains of the bridge. I slipped and fell twice. Hurt my knees and one wrist. Kept going.

My heart hammered. My heart was screaming: Why? Why? Why hadn't I done what I had had to do? I didn't know.

When I was on the towpath, tears were running down my face. I stumbled back along the slippery path.

I didn't know why. Why I hadn't done it. Had I gone mad? He had been mine. For me. The crows had shown me. Birds are messengers. I read their omens. What was wrong?

I don't remember the rest of the journey. But I must have fallen again. There was red blood on my chin, and on both my palms, when I got in. Hunting pink. But I hadn't killed. I hadn't done what was there for me to do. And he had been mine.

## Rod:
## 82

Before he came over that evening, I made some notes. Quite a lot of notes. They encouraged me to do that, the people who purported to help me after my father died and my pink girlhood with him. And somehow I never lost the note-making habit. In fact, probably, it's become slightly obsessive. Like keeping up a diary.

When we got back to the house, George had paid off and tipped Max, the obliging cabby, with an impressive amount of notes.

As Max helped us bring in the sheaves, as it were, bottle-clanking upstairs like a Roman legion on the march, I noted that the foul stench in the hallway had finally been attended to. Well, thank God anyway for that. I had, I admit, a suspicion the smell had already been gone when we first came down earlier, with Forrel in tow. But my thoughts had been slightly distracted.

They were distracted worse now. Not only by George's bombshell about my flat and my subsequent musings on escape, but by the peculiar thing that had happened as he and I were walking back.

We'd taken the other, longer, route, for some reason, up around Wilchester Road. "Looks like snow," George had remarked as we dawdled along. "Good to get a bit of a walk in before the siege."

About halfway along the curve of the street, a couple of youthful yobs came shambling out of a side alley, and seeing us, stopped short, staring as if never had they beheld a couple of men, older or old, before. And then both of these kids burst out in raucous laughter, pointing and hopping, with a sort of brainless yet threatening glee.

"Tol' yah! Din I tell yah, man? It's 'er. Dun I say?"

It was at me, incidentally, they pointed. Not at George. What had they said – "It's 'er." Or was it Kerr or Ayre–some name mangled by their sloppy mouths.

We walked sedately past, or George did. And the two creatures did drop back, piling to a garden wall as if scared we might confront them. Others would have, perhaps. Once we were past, however, one of them shouted, loud through his own giggling, "Ere, sir – great fucking coat, sir!" And the other gave what used, long ago, to be called a wolf whistle.

As their chortles died off behind us, (thankfully they hadn't followed), one word jogged my memory. Coat. Forrel had made off with my spare one.

## 83

I got my small array of drinks out, including the original bottle of vodka; to my surprise Forrel hadn't finished it off. He must have topped up his own bottle – from the tap.

In the kitchen I polished two spirit tumblers with paper towels, and brought them through.

All the time I kept on thinking about the yobs. No, it wasn't a name, was it. The little prick had said: It's her, or he would have, had he been able to pronounce it properly. Her. To and of me. Of course, it was plainly absurd. Or was it? Did I, from that first training long ago, still carry some vestige of the female? In my walk, perhaps, or certain gestures? I didn't think so. I don't think so. Without any doubt my voice is masculine, and so is the stubble I shave off every morning. Therefore, what had prompted such a particularised insult? The idea had begun to raise its head that somehow, in some entirely unforeseen and unfathomable manner; hints of my childhood had surfaced round about.

Putting down the glasses, my hands turned cold as ice. I thought. George. George who, after all, must know my history. George, now here, friendly and urbane, teenager at heart, easy-going, George, telling Max the Cabby in a burst of chat, as they rode somewhere or other, And Max incredulous – "What? For real – they dressed him like a girl?"

"Bows and all," George would have answered.

And they would both commiserate with poor old Roderick. And then later Max would tell someone else. "Here, you'll never believe what I heard the other day..."

What to do? Should I tackle George the minute he arrived in my sitting room? I could feel my blood boiling even as my hands and feet froze in their skins.

I'd break the bloody new vodka he bought me over the bastard's head.

## 84

However. It wasn't yet half past five. I had another vodka myself, calmed down and sat down, and thought, Look, you're not used to so much booze. Don't go rushing to conclusions – rushing at windmills because you think they're giants. It's almost certainly some mistake. Those cretins are no doubt on stuff, and they probably try that mindless trick on anyone over forty. Or over thirty-two. They think it's witty. They probably shout 'Look it's 'im' at older women. Let it go. Don't fall out with George. He is offering you far more for this fleapit than it cost you, or has ever, could ever be worth. Take the money and run. Wherever you go, it will be a brand new start. No one will know you, not even if you end up back where you started. That's the irony. That's the place they never could know you. Rosalind. Roderick. Rod.

After this I went to the bedroom and looked in the wardrobe. When I had got out the other coat for Forrel to borrow – and so go off with – I must have knocked the two curtains at the end. Must have, since when I pulled them both back, the dress had dropped off its hanger, and crumpled into a glittering pink-gold puddle on the wardrobe's floor.

Somehow it looked – I can only put it this way – as if it had died. I was disconcerted. I picked it up, and hung it back up at once, smoothing it down, rearranging its fringes.

Of course there is this puzzle always, and I can't answer it. Nor do I especially want or need to. I don't hanker after my girlhood. I don't miss it or want to recreate it. I have never, past the age of late thirteen, when things were so harshly spelled out to me, desired to dress as a female. To be honest, I'd never that much wanted, or consciously enjoyed, dressing as a girl in my youth. It was just what, as a girl, I did. What girls did. And being a little girl, and then an adolescent girl, naturally, I did it.

Once I had been shunted over onto the other track, aside from some initial difficulties with what can be imagined in the way of dressing, and generally preparing myself, I had no problems with it. In fact, for fairly obvious reasons, I found some articles of dress and hygiene a great deal more comfortable. I cite Y-fronts, and later, boxers, as the very obvious example.

But the pink and gold dress, to me, is a magical thing. Yes, magical. I have no solution as to why, if I don't yearn for my female alter-ego, it should be. Maybe it represents some gorgeous and loving woman I might, had I been myself more exotic, aspired to attract. But as I've said, though I like to look at pretty and well-dressed women, though I like them, I have never felt, or feel, any actual physical desire.

Nor have I, beyond that seemingly spontaneous and private ability to grow erect and effortlessly come with a complete and non-complex enjoyment, been aroused – so far as I can tell – by anyone or thing. I have never experienced an erotic dream, either, concerning anyone – or thing. Now and then, particularly since in a way self-examination had been rigorously instilled in me by my post-thirteen 'helpers', I have pondered my self-sufficient, and inevitably suspect and dubiously limited repertoire. My lack of lust. Anyone else would assure me I am lacking, I am deprived, I must be miserable and forlorn. Therefore no one has ever been told. Nor will be, I should guess.

I had just finished smoothing off the dress and drawing the

curtains over and locking the wardrobe once more, when the flat doorbell went. George had arrived. George and the money and the plan of future escape.

As I went to open the door to all this, the strangest frisson passed over me. I don't consider myself highly superstitious. I'm not prone to sensing atmospheres, or having premonitions which turn out to be correct. I just get on with things. Yet, between one step and the next, one moment and another, I felt a deep and sourceless anxiety. Like a miniature gale it blew between my bones, coming from nowhere, going back to nothing, in a space no longer than it would have taken me to exclaim "Oh – but..." And as it passed it stirred up something which, if it had itself been given words, would have said to me: How is it feasible you can ever leave here? Of course it is impossible. Of course you never can, or will.

## 85

Two weeks later, and when the snow George predicted was well and truly down, private contracts had been exchanged; I had packed up anything I wanted from the flat, (it was little enough), and either put it into storage, or two negotiable suitcases.

We did, then, have a bizarre little party, George, Vanessa and I. Not Forrel, for despite Vanessa's constant demands, I did not invite him. "Oh," she had disapprovingly told me, "Then you two have quarrelled. Well, you must sort things out yourselves." Quite so. In fact I hadn't seen Forrel since his visit. Nor, for that matter, my spare coat. I had given in my notice to the firm, but had not worked out the time, thus incurring some loss of pay and, as they put it 'precarious pension difficulties', about none of which I gave a damn.

At least for the time being, George had made me very well off. I intended to go westward, back to the rural landscape of my past. I could stay in some modest pub or B and B, look around, make my decision. Providing every bank in Europe didn't crash to earth during the next few months, I could secure myself somewhere or other. And if they did, well we were all done for. It was like the initial atomic era, post the Cuba Crisis. In the end you just gave up on it. Astonishing, really, the genius of government and big business to turn pure terror into sheer boredom.

At the party we drank, even Vanessa had a sherry, and ate the salad and cold meats Vanessa had prepared. There was another of the curious cakes, too, with the thinnest chocolate ever able to be recognized by name skimmed over the top.

Neither of them seemed very regretful to see me go. Vanessa, however, eventually informed me that she agreed with my choosing to part from Forrel, (presumably evidenced by my departure.) She trusted I'd meet someone more suitable, and closer to my own age, in 'pastures new'.

Age. How old both of them looked that night. How old, too, did I. What age were we all then? George ninety, Vanessa eighty. And Rod sixty-five going on seventy-four.

For some reason, raising my glass to them, as they to me, I thought of my last tipple at The Red Stag in London. Once gone I'd probably never go there again. The Stag, and London, both. And come to that, despite my avowal to 'keep in touch', I'd probably never see Vanessa, or George, again either. At least, alive.

## 86

At 11a.m. next morning I, with my suitcases, left the flat, and the house. Max, polite and cheery, stowed the bags in the cab.

The schedule had been we would drive straight out and on to the motorway, heading for London, and Euston Station. To take a cab into the metropolis was, inevitably, a last luxury before I undertook the rest of the journey by various trains. I had hoped to find the cab-start relaxing. The rush hour was over, and I had three hours to make it, with ease, to my embarkation point. I'd have some lunch somewhere near the station. Then board the train, sit back and take in the view. Writing now and then, it goes without saying, a few more notes.

However, Max immediately had a small favour to ask.

"Sorry, mate. My wife, she's got bad bronchitis. I need to put a prescription in the chemists in the High Street. Then I can pick it up soon as I get back."

How could I refuse? This poor woman coughing and gasping, the very same poor woman Max had, perhaps, told, to her astounded amusement, how once I had been a little girl dressed in pink. After which she passed the information on.

"You go ahead," I said.

He thanked me, and we drove into the High Street, which was very crowded, both by people and other parked cars.

"Won't be a mo," said Max old-fashionedly, and got out and crossed between the intermittent traffic.

Now I sit here. I've been here ten minutes. Presumably he has had to queue up. Oh well. Be philosophical.

The road is untidy here and there with uncleared slush. Patches of ice? The cars that thump by seem to be, all of them, travelling much too fast, and gradually it occurs to me they are veering off slightly as they reach the spot where I sit in the immobile cab. Max hasn't, it seems, parked very well. The pavements are mostly clear of snow; I consider getting out and stretching my legs. After all, it will take at least an hour to reach the hub of the city and get across to Euston.

That car was very close. It seemed to rush straight at me. Yes. Maybe I will get out. I'm growing edgy after all. And given the way time is elongating, not to mention the bad organisation of the local chemist, I could be stuck here another twenty minutes. Though I can pay for the cab, I'm pleased to note the clock isn't running. The fee is a set one, and Max, whatever else his failings, is prepared to stick to that.

## 87

My hand is on the door handle. I'm half turning in order to get out.

I don't see the last car until it is almost on top of us, me and the cab. I don't believe what I see when I do.

And then we meet, the car and its flurried-looking male driver, and Max's cab, and I.

There is an incredible thump, a crunching and splintering noise, which I feel stabbed all through me, since it is happening both to each of the vehicles and also to me. Pains like slivers of broken glass flash inside my body or in the air, and I hear things snapping sharply, breaking, which – from at least a mile away – I realise absurdly and unconvincingly are my bones. Flying pieces like bright water cut my forehead and a curtain of scarlet mostly puts out my sight. That is all, for now. Nothing else... except, through the darkening haze, abruptly I notice Max running across the road, where all the other traffic has now stopped. He seems frantic, staring at what has been done to his cab.

# IRVIN:
## 88

Out of sorts. Yesterday I forced myself to the theatre and turned off a very vile performance. Was lucky not to be harangued with missiles from the crowd. As for Merscilla Peck, when we were from the stage she slapped me across the face. It seems I had ruined her own presentation with my lazy clowning.

Home with the carter, who tells me I have the winter plague, and also, (gratis) how many so far have expired of it, and that they are piled up near the Ravensburn marshes for burning, there being too many of the inconsiderate wretches to permit them Christian burial.

It was brooding on Mis'us Templeyard, I believed, had lowered my spirits. Try as I might I could not get her, as last I had seen her, from my mind.

The next night to the theatre again, and so to the stage, despite a raging ache in my skull, and too in every joint. Like an ancient tope of sixty or ninety years I crawled about there, and at length went off and fell headlong in a swoon. I recall little of that, and the fall could not bruise me worse than already my rheumatics made me. Waking I found I lay in Merscilla's lap, and her face all concern, and calling me her dove and her best darling.

This cheered me mightily, and after some brandy I felt so much the better, off to The Red Stag tavern with her, but as we sat to our wine and pigeon, first came some news that general opinion thought the Thames would be freezing over, a thing it has not done, as I understand it, since two hundred years or more.

Next minute though there comes another bursting into the inn, with the fresh snow pluming him and aureole all about him, like the white smoke that comes up with the Devil in the play.

It was none other than Jemmy Templeyard, and his face set like a gargoyle's with some bitter, terrible grimace.

Straight to our table strides Jem, and stands over us, shimmering with cold and his terrible unnamed emotion. No longer now a boy, I think. Something has made a man of him, and this thing, as so often it is, unkind and without clemency.

"Well, Thessaris," says my lover, "turn off your strumpet."

At which, it can be guessed, Mis'us Peck stands up and says glowering to him, "Will you be turned off then, sir?" Meaning of course he is the trull, not she.

But he neither answers nor looks at her, only at me. And his anguish brings back the aching into me, so cold and steely as a bite, or the sword's edge.

"Do it," he says.

And I say to Merscilla, "Best leave us, sweetness. I will..."

"Oh. He is preferred then to me, you donkey? Well, may you have much pox of each other." And she exits.

At that Jem Templeyard sat down. He took up her cup and drained it. Then staring away into the wall, he said to me, in such a low hoarse voice I must strain to catch every syllable:

"Her mother wrote to me, and I not getting the letter till this eve. She is dead, Thessaris, my Sophia. Not seventeen years, and dead." After which he put down his head on his arms across the table and wept.

## 89

He had pronounced her name an outlandish way, so for a minute I did not at all know who he meant. For as a rule it is spoken as if one said So Fire. But he had it So Fear.

"Your wife," I tendered at last. He wept and nodded into the table's wood. "How is this?" (I thought, Pray God she was not with child. For it might even be mine.)

Jem raised his head and wiped off his face on his sleeve.

"God knows how. But all my fault, as I must think," he said. "Her mother believes so. For Sophia was returning to her mother's house at Levishamm, but then the carriage comes very late, and when the door is undone, she does not step out and the servant gives up a howl. She is sat there, my wife, in the seat's corner, and a trickle of red blood from her mouth and down her white throat. And still, as only the dead ever are, so she is. Since you and I, she'd have nothing to do with me. And I was ill-tempered with her, yet she said nothing but went to her mother. And then it seemed Sophia was to come into the town, and her mother thinks this was to call on me, but I swear it never was, and never did I see her. I have not seen her even as now she is. In Christ's golden name, what shall I do, Irvin?"

I had no answer. And so for a long while after this we sat silent, drinking. And from somewhere then the clocks began to chime, all out of time and tune with each other as ever, and it was midnight.

A man came in presently to say the river had not frozen after all, and a great load of bets had been lost thereby. And that another great load, this of snow, had fallen from a roof at Covent Garden, and crushed two drunkards under it. Which caused much mirth.

Shortly after that a staid and sober servant entered, as they do in the play, and stealing over to Jem, plucked his sleeve, gave over something, and drew back. It was another letter. This Jem read, and his pale face turned from white to blue. I have seen that colour in life only once before, and that one was my father's, after I had so sorely beaten him.

"Oh God, how am I to bear it?" Jem said, yet in the most ordinary and measured of tones.

"What?" I said. I braced myself to confront new dread, but was not braced enough.

"The physician has attended, and says my wife is poisoned. She had poisoned herself. The paste has been found in a little box among her skirts. He says he knows the venom, and that she has taken it by mouth. Invariably, though it acts only slowly, a slight taste does the business, and it is quite fatal. Doubtless she thought she would be home before it ended her. Or not, mayhap. Or not." Then he got straight up. "I must go there," he said, but not to me.

And turning, he walked from the tavern, with the servant following like his black shadow, out into the white nothingness beyond the door.

## 90

At home, and a shoddy, ache-rattling carriage to be paid off, and then upstairs. No dog, no fire alight, a room like a grave. By now I was so ill I had called up the beggar from his bivouac along the track and given him money to fetch the doctor. A good time next the beggar below the window shouts up the doctor will not turn out so late but will attend me in the morning. At which he, and the doctor by proxy, are recommended to the most taxing pits of Hell.

I seek my bed and lie down in it, and so racked with torturer's pains and fever by then, I soon lose all proper awareness. Yet in and out of my distemper moves little Sophia, and I feel her death always heavy on me like an icy rubble, like the snow that fell and killed the drunkards.

Of course the fault is mine that she died. Did she not tell me she would never see me more in life? What does a woman mean by that except she will throw life off, and leave it to lie down instead beside you, and rot there, as your punishment. But her punishment on me may be just, and I, now, too sick to care.

## 91

About ten o'clock in the morning, the doctor arrived, having been shown up by the brown crone, or some other of the freak-show of the house.

He told me at once I was vastly ill, for which I did not thank him, being able to deduce as much for myself, nor wishing to charge myself any fee for so doing.

Then he came more near, examining me with his cold, gnarled and comfortless hands. Then, he seemed perplexed, and said he would bleed me, to see what mysteries he can uncork with my blood. This process, achieved with a knife not sharp enough, was terrible in my pain. But he seemed satisfied. He asked me next if I had eaten any strange thing, or been attacked in any fashion. I reminded him I was an actor, and often attacked on the stage, either by a fellow actor at the playwright's instruction, or some unsatisfied person from the audience.

He laughed heartily at my wit. Then recalled for me I had been involved in a duel, so he had heard it. (One's business is never secret, I find.)

I informed him I had only been pinked. He rolled up now the left sleeve of my bed shirt to examine the wound, which had healed well enough. But I was startled, even in my fobbled state, to note black marks in the skin below.

"Now this is not good," he said, with interest.

"What then is it?"

"I'm not of a certainty yet, sir, but will tell you when able. I must consult my books."

After which, having extracted the initial coins of payment, (that came to him far less readily than my life's blood), he left me in my misery.

Then a black tide swam in on me, and somewhere in the midst of it I heard myself declare, aloud, I was a fool indeed. For surely I could now reason things out? Little Sophia, with her own white hand, had made sure of me during our last sad merrymaking. She had thrust into my arm a pin, then licked off and swallowed what was on the stalk of it. So attending to both of us, she swiftly and myself at a much slower pace. Sophia Templeyard had poisoned me.

## Dawn:
## 92

I haven't been to the Co-op yet. I don't feel that well.

I went to the doctor instead for the routine visit they demand every year. He examined me, which I don't like. They are so matter of fact now, as if you're a sack of potatoes.

"Weight still fine," he congratulated me, having insisted I stand on the scales, "nice and thin. Plenty of young girls would be thrilled to be your weight, Mrs Thorstrestis." (They can never pronounce my name. And sometimes he forgets it and calls me 'Dawn'.) He took my blood pressure and said it was a little low, nothing serious, and much better than being too high. "We got you onto those statins just in time," he now congratulated himself. I have never confessed I don't ever take them. All these pills. What do they do to you, aside from what they're supposed to? I remember Susie... or was it Jean...? She took something or other the doctors gave her and it cleared up the original condition, whatever that was, and gave her some other illness. Well, I don't want any of that. My response to his offer of a 'flu jab can be guessed.

In the end he smiled at me benignly.

"But you don't seem quite to be in the pink, do you, Dawn?" This is an old fashioned phrase. Did he use it to patronise me?

"No," I said.

"Well, we have to remember," he reminded me, "you are seventy-four now. Not quite a girl. You need to take things more easily, get a bit more exercise, take an interest in something – voluntary work, perhaps."

I smiled gratefully, and I was allowed to escape, empty-handed. Rest more, exercise more, eat five portions of fruit and vegetables each day to make sure your stomach is nicely upset all the time. What is the matter with them?

I'm just depressed, probably. I was thinking a lot about Ben. He died thirty years ago, about this time of year. It feels awful to say this, but I can't remember the exact day. I always used to mark it, back then, whenever Then was, then.

He had bronchitis very badly, and it killed him – a systemic breakdown they called it. You don't hear of bronchitis doing that so much now. There are other more popular things now that kill you.

I came up all the stairs and got into my flat, at the very top of the house. It's in the attic, or where the attic was before we got the loft extension. There was a pigeon sitting on the skylight, but it flew away as soon as I arrived. Sometimes, if you keep really still, a lot of them settle there. They make a mess, and no window-cleaner any more to clean the glass, only the rain. But I like them. I like pigeons.

There's nobody else in the house now, of course. I had it all made over after I lost Ben, and let the rooms as flats, but in the end they made such a mess, the tenants, much worse than the pigeons, breaking things, and their children writing on the walls, and all the noise, sometimes until two or three in the morning, and when I asked if they could be quieter they were rude and then they left. Ran off without paying the rent. So in the end I just let it go and didn't let to anybody else. I live on my pension, which isn't much, and the insurance on Ben that comes from Ben's old workplace at the Parnassus Showrooms. Not very much, any of it. I don't think I could afford five portions of fruit and veg a day, even if I wanted to.

I suppose I'll have the last of the casserole tonight. I've made it last four days. It's almost six o'clock. Shall I have a sherry? That might be nice. And I can manage until next week, for shopping. There's bread in the freezer, and some cheese and soup in the fridge. I'm low on tea bags, but I can use each one twice. No milk left. Oh well.

Nothing on the radio later but jazz or pop, or something about computers. They go wrong all the time, it seems. Just as people do.

Shall I have that sherry?

I just feel so tired. I think I'll have a rest first in the chair. That's better. Just a doze by the electric fire until maybe seven. I'll fancy the sherry then. I can have cheese on toast. Yes.

## 93

I was back in my youth, but not really the age I was at the time. In the dream I was about twenty, but it was the war.

Outside the flat I could hear the sirens with that awful, frightening whining and gurning they used to do. Of course, it's meant to be frightening, it's to warn you. I never forgot their sound from my infancy. And all through the Fifties and Sixties, long after the war was over, they would keep on testing them out to make sure they still worked, in case someone dropped an atom bomb on us all. I remember Ben used to say "Four minute warning – what can you do in four minutes?" And then he'd wink at me. "I don't know, though." And we'd laugh.

After I lost him, you know, that was when I started to lose myself. Bits of me seemed just to drift away, as though they wanted to be with him, and not with me anymore. My silly memory got so much worse in my forties. And now, half the time, I don't know what I did yesterday, or even where I went. If I did. I don't, of course, ever mention this to the doctor. I can guess the grim and fussy result.

But to go back to the dream. There was the siren, and then I looked out of an uncurtained window – which I doubt I'd have done, or ever did, in the childhood blackout. I could see them all coming, on the blacked-out sky, the bombers, like a swarm of horrible fat wasps or flies. And their eggs falling out of them. And concussions miles off and then nearer and nearer. And the sky flickering red. And then one of the planes came in through the window at me so I jumped away. It wasn't very big, only about the size of a child's balloon. But it dropped the bomb straight down on my carpet. And everything exploded with a terrific bang.

I leapt up from my chair and stood clutching at the back of it, and for a few seconds, even wide awake, the room seemed full of burning crimson fires. It was the electric fire, of course, that was all.

# EMENIE:
## 94

Throughout the rest of the short day and the evening I couldn't settle.

I walked up and down the flat, even through the bedroom now, round and round. I didn't want to go out and through the rest of the house. It seemed full of weird noises, as though other people were there. Only they weren't. No one had broken in, or could have got in without breaking in. But everything felt wrong.

Obviously it was because of what had happened in the park. What hadn't happened – the man I hadn't killed although he had been mine.

Never before had that sort of disaster befallen me. Once or twice, even, in the past, where I was almost interrupted in the instants of action, I'd managed to forestall everything, yet do just enough to be able to start the procedure off again and continue and conclude once my way was clear.

And this time no one had interrupted. No one was about. It was a flawless situation. That still, white-grey air, the silent sound across the trees – such a pristine canvas, inviting, urging the master stroke – I should have been able to enjoy it to the full. What had happened to me? Why? Why. I hadn't lost my nerve, or ability. It wasn't that. Just some extreme – almost physical – failure of connection between my will and my reflexes. Sort of like the kind of thing that might happen when you were half asleep. You roll across to grab and shut up the alarm clock, (in the days when they were necessary), and instead your hand passes through thin air; you've missed the target.

But really, it hadn't even been like that. It was as if my brain shouted Go! And my hands, already reaching out, had suddenly answered No.

The worst thing was I was frightened. This hadn't happened before. Now it had. Which meant it could happen. It could happen again. And again...

The world got dark outside.

## 95

Eventually I found half a bottle of wine left in the fridge. It didn't taste too bad and I drank it all straight down. Then I went to my made-up bed on the sofa. I didn't want to sleep in the bedroom. That hadn't changed.

The electric fire was on, and I left it on. I was very cold.

Bit by bit the wine started to fuzz over the chipped edges of my shock and grief. I began to form a plan. Perhaps, tomorrow, I should try again. I would take the gun this time, make it easy on myself. It might not be quite the right method for my next victim, but it would do. I couldn't be fussy now; I had to make everything work.

I told myself to stop worrying. Anybody could make a mistake. Even I could, after so much perfect-making practice. It had just been the time for it, that was all. One slip doth not a downfall make.

I heard myself giggle stupidly, and felt sleep come gently in, coating me in layers of warmth and wine and abruptly stirring optimism. It would be all right.

## 96

An explosion...

The air cracked and blew about in bits.

The bang reverberated inside my ears. On and on.

The atmosphere was crimson with more than the reflection of the single electric bar.

I thought: A bomb has fallen through the roof.

I rolled off the couch and pulled myself upright. I didn't know where I was for a moment. I could smell petrol and fire, and where the door was behind the peacock screen, the door to the outer hall, was the origin of the deep red glare. No sooner did I think this than the peacocks began to burn.

What was it? Not a bomb – surely not a bomb. And if so, why here?

I thought of a shambling lout with greasy hair, and another one in a ruined uniform who had, like the old song, called me Madam. Bruvva and his mate.

The door was burning. Which meant the outer hall must be. The nails sealing up the wide old letterbox in the front door must have been picked or ripped out. Then something was shoved through. A half-flattened can of petrol, presumably. With some material wadded in the neck – a towel – something. And the end of it had been lit. It went off inside the hall, a sort of much larger Molotov Cocktail.

Yes, the door was on fire, and the peacocks were consumed, and now the main room carpet was burning in here. Mindless with instinct I found myself retreating through the room backward, into the short interim space, where the bathroom and loo are, and the door to the cellar, and so into the kitchen.

Smoke was building already, as floor boards and carpets, general furnishings, household debris and dust, ignited and joined in the festival of light.

I could think of nothing to do to stop all this. There was nothing I had to put out the flames. It was like a piece of music on a CD; long ago; the music began and had to run its course. No off-switch.

Once in, I shut the kitchen door.

The air was misted now, even in here, and loud with cracklings and sighing shifts of air and smoke. The whole house had become a smoker, filling its wooden lungs with the glorious fix. Oh, you never stop missing it, do you, a fag?

Even through the closed door, through all its little splits and holes and thinnesses, the red glow eagerly beamed at me... The insistent lover.

I'd thought of fire in the park, the fire the young moron made, and how I could stun and thrust him and yank him into it, so he would begin to burn. And I would beat him there, and kick him, keep him pinned just long enough, until he was well-alight and so no chance, even should he manage to propel himself finally from the flames. The burning man.

But it would have been on a much smaller scale to this.

I would have to get out. Leave everything and run, as I'd previously told myself I had to when Bruvva and Uniform first appeared.

Quickly I got into the utility room and undid the back door. I shot the bolts and worked the locks. I was cool enough, in a brain-dead way. There had been no space for panic.

But then, the door refused to open. Naturally. Would they have overlooked this adjunctive back-up? Even if never seen by them, (and though they had never seen Micki, let alone detected the stench of her rot), still Bruvva and his sidekick infallibly guessed I must have killed her. Maybe Bruvva came back, and found the grave outside, at which I hadn't looked for several days, not liking to, as if... shy. And that way, finding the grave he had located the back door, too.

Men love to burn women, they always have. For witchcraft, or heresy, or adultery. I cite Joan of Arc, Mistress Pently, Queen Guinevere – so burn this fucking heretic witch-queen called Emenie. And block her every exit from the pyre.

I tried the kitchen windows next. Outside the thick zipped curtains I could see at a glance every pane of glass now had external bars of heavy wood nailed across. When had they done this? How had I never heard them? Oh, it was like the burial – Christ had they even done that? Broken in, taken and buried her, then stormed back pretending still to be looking for her, to judge my reaction?

No – all insanity. Stop thinking, you cretinous bitch. I need to get out!

Already I had dismissed any idea of the front bedroom windows, or the side window in the main room. I myself had fully or partly boarded them up. And besides that area would be – was – fiercely ablaze by now.

The kitchen too was beginning to creak and sing with heat.

Smoke curled like a filmic Dickensian river fog, bleak, mutual and expectant. Oh for a real fucking river to put out this fire – my eyes were running, trying to help. My skin was tight. I could just make out how the plaster on the walls seemed to be blistering. I thought of the basement. Should I try to get back into the space beyond the kitchen, even though the fire would already be fingering, probing it – get down into the cellar – maybe the cellar would be fire-proof? (Down among the bones and stink, the accusatory remains – would they shelter me, their un-creator?) But where was the key? I'd hidden it, hadn't I? Where had I hidden it? I turned round full circle, staring through water and smoke and heat, a whirl of drawers, cupboards... No. No use.

It did not matter.

Only the fire mattered. The red lover. The Hunter.

I found a frying pan – out of the – into the – in the very instant I heard the second explosion of the electric fire from the main room.

Raising the pan high, I smashed it with all the force I had against the kitchen window. Glass disintegrated, and with it one small section of the nailed-over wood.

I heard a louder crack behind me. It was the kitchen door. Took no notice.

I was swinging again with the heavy pan when ice cold hands clutched against my back and into my hair. A hundred hands, two hundred, and all bright red, hunter's red. Not ice but fire. Liberated by the breaking door frame, enticed and fed by the inward gush of oxygen from the window.

The roar of the inferno swallowed me as the freezing scald of the flame-sea covered me up. As in a million meltings I was amber, I was crimson, I was molten gold. Far, far away I heard my shriek before the flames ate up my throat. Drowning in hunting pink. I was sunrise. I was dead.

# ROD:
# 97

Ghostly as twilight, a paramedic bent over me. "I'm just going to put this oxygen mask on for you, Rod – it is Rod?"

Max must have told him. Unless George was out there somewhere.

Pain is an excruciating and striated envelope, but I float inside it, indifferently.

Ah, now the oxygen flows.

"Thank you," I said. Or I didn't.

They still have to cut me out of the cab, but the gang, the crew, whatever they are, are assembled, limbering up. I get the blast of oxygen, and then that goes. Can't risk oxygen with sparks about.

They had given me something, I assumed, to ease the pain, not that it had much, although maybe the something given it is which enables me to float free inside the pain.

The gang were energetic now. Everybody else in the world stood clear.

I hear a blast of sound, drill-like, or like a gigantic wasp, possibly. I shut my eyes, as I don't want to watch.

I can see instead, under my eyelids, the stripper-girl's blue stare, and Forrel's wet unsober one, and my guardian in his paroxysm of rage screaming *What have they done to you?* And Max's wife coughing with her bronchitis which, years ago, could kill people. I recollect the KGB girl with dark hair lurking outside the flats. And the tall young black man with the kingly face.

Pink for a girl. Pink sparks sizzle. Something hurts through the drug, axe-hard and razor-edged. And a man curses.

A waste of time, George said, inside my ear.

I'm not afraid as I slip the leash. "Good boy," says George fondly, "good old chap." And dog-like I sink into sleep. What a bloody relief.

# Dawn
## 98

I was thinking about Brighton – or was it Wales? Of course I can't remember. I used to like Brighton. The Pavilion, and the pier, the old one, when it was there. Ben used to call Brighton London-on-Sea.

I called the doctor this morning. They said it was very difficult for a doctor to come out to see me. Patients really must try to go to the surgery. It saves everyone so much time. Except for the patients, I supposed, but didn't say. I said I couldn't. I was having trouble walking. They said they would see if it was possible he could make a call. When I was young they'd always come. All weathers, all times of day or night. I remember the doctor coming to see Ben. "I'm sorry, Mrs Tawstereries, but I do think your husband would be better off in hospital." All the old ones knew, when I was a child, that hospital was the last port of call. You didn't go to be made miraculously well, but to die. I resisted the doctor until it became frighteningly obvious I, and he, could do nothing else. They had oxygen at the hospital, too. It would help Ben to breathe. But it didn't help him. The night they moved him in, about an hour after, he died.

There was so much they couldn't do then, of course. Like dentists. I remember that first time I had to have a tooth out. They gave me a local injection – that's what he called it. But I felt everything he did. Agony. And that was only a tooth. Oh dear.

Jean died too, of course. So did Susan. But I wasn't with them, we'd lost contact. A niece wrote to me about Susan. I can't remember with Jean. It's funny, sometimes I wonder if I made them up, my friends. The way lonely children do. Imaginary friends... Jean and Susan. After I lost Ben. I know I didn't make Ben up. Ben was real.

It's afternoon now, and I've managed to drink some Marmite in hot water, which is always so comforting. I don't want to do anything, only sit here. No doctor has come and no one's called. Will I be able to get to the door if they do? All those stairs...

I keep thinking this same phrase over and over again. I don't know why, or where it comes from. It's about being on a train journey, or I think it is, where the train doesn't stop at your own station, so you have to go farther on, to a bigger terminus, and then take another train back. 'Unable to stop,' the phrase has it, 'having to go all the way in and then back out again'. Perhaps it's from a book, or one of the short stories they read on Radio 7 – no, it's Radio 4 Plus now, (or is it 4 Extra? I can't recall. It was easier when it was an entirely different number).

Seven, Seven and Susan. And Jean. And unable to stop, having to go in and then out again... Out again. Or in.

## IRVIN:
## 99

When my venerable physician returned next day there was enacted a scene worthy of King Lear, during which he ranted and raved and stalked the entire premises, bellowing for the landlady, who failed upon her cue and could not be found. "What possessed you, Irvin Thessaris, to abandon yourself in such a palsied and verminous stye? No wonder you have gained the state wherein I find you!" But I, being too weak to reply, he quit me, and I thought I should then be left in peace in my Hell to suffer. But no. Back comes he with an army: one to lay and light my fire, another to cook broth upon it. Well, then, only two, but by then their energy and actions filled up every mote of the chamber. There might as well have been two hundred.

"Pay heed to me, Thessaris," next sternly said my doctor, "you are undone. By which I mean, and here I will not piffle my words, you have been poisoned."

"I know it," I said. Or thought I did.

Regardless he ploughed on. "There is little I can do, sir, I am sorry to say. For I have seen you at the Obelisk, and though there are actors that better you, you are good enough at your trade, and once or twice you shine, sir, yes indeed, you have shone. I do believe they will not, at once, forget you."

Although I knew quite well, as I had tried to assure him, I had noted Death's bony thumb was pointed four-square at me, yet it is a chilling matter to hear some other pass your sentence. It has been only in the air, one might say, but now is written in black ink upon a page. Dead. I should soon be dead.

He then however began, with the fussy complicity of a housewife, to outline who should come in and when, and how I should be washed, and the bed-linen changed, and various other aspects of my comfort, and my hygiene – on which I prefer we shall not dwell. Besides this, my feeding, while I might still take sustenance, even a little wine and brandy with aqua of Mercury, and tincture of poppy seeds, to ease my pains: all such were now arranged, since my landlady was a whore and slattern and should, if ever he set eyes on her, be hauled before the Justice. The doctor told me lastly that my bill for all this care, now so assiduously ordered, was beyond my means. And so he would not charge me it.

I thanked him, rather insultingly, I think. But either he missed my wit or could not decipher it from my congested throat.

"Instead," he frankly owned, "I will take up that hound of yours. Whatever name you lavished upon him, I have named him Horatius."

Just then my faithless dog appeared in the doorway. Tall and jet-black, with his one flop ear red as an autumn rowan, he stared upon me bleakly from his night-black eyes. The villain, he had kept me no company, stolen my food, and brought on my head the complaints and costs of half the neighbourhood. Yet there he stood, noble as a hound of Egypt, favourite of some hunting Pharaoh – or of Antony, perhaps, who kissed and clove with Cleopatra. Horatius.

Well named.

"He shall come out with me," went on the doctor, my trouble long since sunk beneath his jolly sky-line, "for I am taking myself and my family to a province of the coast. There, at the country house, he can chase rabbits, be my fetcher for pheasant. Even after the deer, I believe, he would show himself with honour. And there are young bitches enough he can paddle. He'll keep me in good dogs till I am done."

All this while my dog had stayed and stared on at me. Now he advanced, at a stately pace, until he reached my bedside. He had a good smell, all forgot by me since I'd not seen him close on a month or more. Like copper and new horsehair, and mushrooms baked with new honey.

"Well, Horatius," I said. "Are you content?"

He at least, if the doctor did not, seemed to fathom my words.

He bent his head, and like a true gentleman, a brother or a son, he touched my forehead with his wet and wintry snout. So cold it was to my fever, it was like a diamond star emblazoned at my forehead's centre. I seemed to see out there, at a hole or a window, into a clear sweet darkness, deep as the seas, and shallow as a ray of moonlight – if it should be black.

"Go then," I said to him. "Be happy and prosper, my Horatio, my Iago. God send you good, you bad fellow."

He turned then and padded out.

He had been my priest. He had marked me with the sacred fire. I was absolved.

My doctor fussed about the last arrangements, and the server came and fed me a little broth, which was pleasant, and I able to swallow it.

The room was warm, and something burned in a pewter pot, the scent of which eased my physical discomfort.

But my worries had shrunk to nought. I pictured Merscilla. Casting herself upon me, her voice, of such beauty, like some instrument not yet invented, crying out in despair: "Thy lips are cold!" But she would never do it. Nor did I mourn that she would not. I should be dead before the raucous clocks began their disorderly riot for midnight. Dead before another golden sun arose. My space I had had to walk the stage of this world. I had played my part as well I might. And had not one, at least, informed me I had been good enough. More. That – once, or twice – I had shone. I had shone. Man, nor woman, can do no more than that. It is the work of the stars, the moon, the sun, to see to the rest of it. Blow out then, the lamp. And sleep.

## Dawn:
## 100

I can hear someone ringing the bell, down at the front door. Three flights of stairs, and I can't even get out of the chair to cross the room. I can't even get to the window to call down.

The telephone is out in the hall, too. No chance of that.

It may not be the doctor anyway. It's almost four o'clock and already quite dark. A Jehovah's Witness, very likely. And if it is the doctor, he'd say, "I'm sorry, Mrs Threstorillikiss, but you'd be better off in the hospital." So what is the point?

It's lucky. I don't want to visit the lavatory. I've found I've wanted that less and less in the past few days. It's supposed to be the other way round, isn't it, when you're old? Unless, of course, I've been there and just don't remember.

I had a cup of tea too, about two o'clock, after lunch, when I sat down here again. So I'm not thirsty. I wish I'd thought to bring the portable radio in. But I didn't, so that's that.

There it goes again. The bell.

Do stop. I can't help you. And you can't help me. I'd like to be quiet now. Good.

I think he's realised.

I can hear birds singing, that's odd, it's too dark, they ought to be in their nests, or wherever they go for shelter in the winter. Just because you can't see things, doesn't mean they're not there. All those pigeons, too, I think they've got into the other part of the house roof. Well. Good luck to them. I don't need that bit of space, do I?

The street is very quiet now. I can hear a plane going over. What a shame, I'll never eat that soup now, and it's minestrone, one of my favourites. Perhaps they'll give it to someone. I wonder... I wonder what I'll do, tomorrow.

# Pink:
# 101

I don't want to be cruel. Let alone overly cynical. Or – worse – make a big joke out of this. It's an extraordinary story. I've never encountered anything quite like it, I'd never even read before about an instance so complex, so incredible. Plus it is hilarious, in its own rather sinister and deeply sad way. So. I've got to be careful. Hence this preliminary work out on it all. A sort of dry run. Or – yes, why not, a dress-rehearsal. The big stuff, when I write it, will have to be very different. And I can't reveal my source, obviously. Luckily, enough people have been involved on the edges to get a partial idea of what went on. The ones that don't, don't count. Some of us will never understand it. I'm not sure I do. It scares me, though. I mean, something like this. You think, if it can happen like that then why not to me, given the right amount of stress, or of peculiar circumstances, or chemicals in the blood and brain, or just plain life. Life will always get you, one way or the other.

OK

My name is James Pinkerton, which I'm afraid, besides sounding very Gilbert and Sullivan, has earned me among my colleagues the dubious nickname of Pinky, or Pink. The last is a slang term too for a certain part of the female anatomy, a wonderful part, true, but I've never been that keen on its being applied to me. As a bloke, I'm not, in any other way aside from name, PINK. Not even politically. (Politically I'm not really anything. They're all crap now, as far as I can see, which I've gone into print often enough to point out.) Anyhow, that's enough of that.

When I first heard about what had been going on, from – I'll call him D.C.W. – I thought initially it was too crazy to do much with. Then I thought about it. That is, properly. Then I looked up a few other cases. Horrifyingly, there were more than I'd ever have thought could be likely. There are, of course, quite a few of the better known and more 'modest' (shall I say) types involving normally two elements. But the extravagance of this dossier puts most of those well into the shade. Similar, or nearly similar examples, however, have been, and still are, documented. I note here particularly the tragedy of Eric Verner Wassen, in Hungary, in the early 1920's. I won't go into all that here. Look it up on the net.

OK

The first thing, after my rather cursory research, was to do the follow-up groundwork. Which meant moving around the place and talking to people.

Most people, I find, really want to tell you things. And if they know absolutely zilch, then they'll make something up. Of this I'm wary, having learnt the hard way, years back, when I was starting.

The suburbs can be less people-indifferent than inner London, but even so they're not that socially involved. No, despite what a lot of Londoners say, those little clusters of shops and by-ways, where you can meet the same people again and again, are still not like the old villages that, even now, you can come across, in Scotland, say, or the outlands of Manchester. Plenty down here pretend to be arm in arm, and heart in pocket with the rest of their ghetto. But they're not. Again, it's gossip, speculation. If something looks really exciting, or awkward – some gorgeous girl, some dangerous, spiky guy – they may take notice – but even so it's mostly guess work.

About her, though, one or two, (more than that, of course), began to get the hang of the facts, even if they improperly understood, and so dismissed these, with the usual amused and condescending casualness. Mrs Jones was odd. But, they added, she didn't cause any trouble. Poor old cow, some of them said, (or bat, or biddy. Or cunt. Depending on their favourite pieces of the vernacular.)

None of them recalled when she'd moved into the area. A lot of them, inevitably, wouldn't even have lived there, or been born, when she had. Some of them knew approximately where she lived. Some didn't. No one, not even my source (D.C.W.) knew how or where she got started. She had had a husband – Mr Jones. But this was before anyone's time. Or, before anyone had ever seen, let alone noticed her especially. Somebody told me he could remember seeing her in her twenties – "Pretty little thing. A bit cagey though." No, he didn't recollect a male partner. Thought she might have had a kid, little girl, dark hair, about two or three. Several women guessed Mrs Jones had 'inherited' her property, in her thirties, or fifties. She was alone, and a miserable old cow (or bat or biddy etc etc). One middle-aged trendy in shorts said he could recollect, as a child, throwing stones at her windows, and putting a firework through her door on November 5th, because she had told him and his friends off in the street. (But apparently, he recounted this anecdote about several women.)

I worked with all this. Then binned most of it

OK

I'm in the pub, the one near the station, and nearest to Mrs Jones's final address.

It's an old pub, The Black Sheep. Bits of it go back to the

Sixteenth Century, or so the discreet notices say. Certainly the ceiling is low enough that if you wear a piece (I don't) you could scrape it off on a beam.

There are in this pub a lot of ancient relics. (I don't refer to the customers.) Aside from the beams and the narrow wooden stairway that leads to the upstairs dining area, there are glass cases with mummified cats in them, blackly hard, so sculptural they might never have been alive. These poor buggers were buried under the foundations around the 1590s to protect the building. There is also a huge painting in the bar perpetrated by a local artist in 1901. It depicts a Scapegoat – that is a human man, not a goat – as in the more famous artwork by... (who the hell is it? Holman Hunt? I'll have to look it up...) He is loaded with chains and in filthy rags, and stands at the edge of some sort of narrow river, staring and mad. A nasty sight to have hanging over you as you quaff your pint. But it turns out this is exactly where Mrs Jones always sat. At least, when she was – in that particular mood. This is how Josh the pub landlord, put it. Mood.

"You mean... the man?"

"One of them," said Josh.

"Right. There were two – yes?"

"Well, I only saw two."

"And this one was how?" I asked.

"She's sat under The Scapegoat. And he, this one, he's the bloody maddest. No one what hadn't seen it before, well, they'd laugh out loud. Or it'd go all quiet. I used to say, it's fine, she's no trouble. She wasn't. And some of them, well, they'd come in just to look at her. Some of them always laughed. One or two took pictures on their phones. You know. She didn't seem to, like, notice. But she was often talking to someone."

"To herself?" I asked.

"Nah. Someone else was with her. Only no one else was with her, you get me?"

There was a dog, he said, too. No, not a real dog. But real to her. The dog was always doing something wrong. And then it wasn't there. "I mean, it was never there – but now she said it wasn't."

"Did she talk to you?"

"Sure. She'd want a coffee, or wine. Sometimes beer. She had a funny way of wording it, but I got the drift. And she wasn't loud."

"Just her clothes."

"Yeah. Just her clothes, like."

"So what were they?"

"Big hat. Big floppy shirt. Big coat, long lapels. Just scruffy baggy old trousers. Men's, I think. Nearest I can think with the whole get-up – like Pirates of the Caribbean. That kind of stuff."

"Historical."

"S'pose. Like a kid dressing up. Fancy dress. Amateur theatrics. Yeah, that's it. Feather in it," he mused.

"In what?"

"His hat, mate. Her hat. The man. The second man."

OK

"Who was the first man, the other one?" I asked a bit later, after the lunchtime rush had eased.

"Eh? Oh that. He was – er, he was just like some bod from some London firm. Suit. More casual at weekends. Hair slicked back. Well, it was a wig, you get me? And the other one, that was a wig too."

"What other – oh, right. You mean the other man had a wig too."

"Sure. Long brown curls, him. A woman's wig, or that's what Posie says – she's bar staff. But they used to wear their hair that way, like, fellers then. 1700's? But the city guy in the suit, hair's short. But her hair wasn't like that. She had long hair. Most of it grey, she was knocking on. She used to put it up, or when I saw her in the street, when she was, well, when she was just being normal, it was up in a kind of bun. Used to call it that, didn't they? My mum called it that. A bun."

I checked all this over with him. They were things mostly I'd heard before, but his take was, for all the vagaries, more condensed, more decided. One long-haired man in period costume, or at least an approximation. Another man with short hair in a suit, or more casual modern masculine wear.

I asked him if the man in the suit spoke to other people not actually visible or apparently real.

"Not often. Last time I saw him though yeah, he did. I've just remembered too. There was a girl. No, not with the man. I mean she was being this girl. She had her own hair down then, and a bright red T-shirt. Of course, I say girl. I mean, sort of. You know. She drank... one glass of lager. She kept quiet. She seemed sort of looking for someone. I didn't like the look of her. Funny thing to say. Because, well, it was all the same, wasn't it? But this girl – only not girl, though dressed up like one, this old girl in her tight jeans and her red T-shirt, she had a look... You could just believe she'd stab you or something. Something... like that. Can't explain it. Come to think of it, though, I saw her in the High Street an' all once. She was chatting away to someone then. I mean, someone what wasn't there. 'Micky' she called him. 'Have you got enough cigarettes,' she said, 'Micky?' And something about the way she said it, even though it wasn't to no one as was there, made me go cold. Blimey. You'll think I'm as bloody bonkers as she is."

"Was," I said.

His face grew solemn and respectful. "Was," he echoed. "Poor old cow."

OK

To straighten this out a bit.

Mrs Jones was often in the bar of The Black Sheep. Sometimes dressed as a guy from the 1700s, (probably around 1760-70, from the type of clothing Josh, and others, described.) Or she came in more rarely as a city guy, in a suit, or casual wear at weekends. He, the last one, was more deliberate – "Never more than one double vodka, or a pint." The 1700s guy, who spoke in a flowery manner, (elsewhere someone else also commented on his speech being – "Like Shakespeare – or Samuel Pepys"), this character was a drinker. Only in a very funny way. One glass of wine and a jug of tap water, and then keep filling up the wine glass, as the wine shrank, with the water, and keep drinking. The same with the beer, though the single coffee was usually unwatered. A cheap date, then. Posie, who I later interviewed, remarked that the old woman-dressed-as-a-man seemed to get 'really high' on the watered drinks, "Like they're jugs of wine, or ale." Ale was what Mrs Jones, in the person of Mr Shakespeare-Pepys, called the beer. But it wasn't in fact the real ale the pub also serves.

After the pub, I tried the Co-op in Wellington Road. I tried other shops before and got varied answers, though more of the gossip-speculation type I've mentioned. But in the Co-op I met

Nancy Carrington, who said she has no objection to my citing her by name.

"I've often seen her, poor old thing. I had a granny like that, a bit ga-ga. Not so cracked though as – Mrs Jones did you say? As Mrs Jones."

Nancy is a nice-looking fifties-ish. (She doesn't mind my saying that either.) A calm person.

"She never caused any trouble. But she really did act in the weirdest way. For a start, she was often dressed like a girl in her teens or twenties, jeans, T-shirts, and her hair all down. Mind you, she was thin enough to wear that sort of thing. And she had really good hair, or it would have been if she'd had it decently shaped and cut. Yes, very long hair. Mostly grey, but with some brown tones still left in it. And she must have been at least seventy. Again, like my gran – she still had colour in her hair till she died. She was eighty-six. I'm sorry poor old Mrs Jones died so young – well, it is, isn't it, nowadays, seventy-four. She looked, well, too strong. The way she used to slink around the aisles sometimes. Sometimes she was crouching, and hiding – or thinking she was – behind the shelving. That showed she was pretty agile. Now and then she'd sort of teeter along parts of the floor as though half of it wasn't there and there was a great big chasm either side. But she managed it all right. Most of us, except a kid, couldn't, we'd probably have fallen over. Keeley was scared of her. Keeley always wanted to call the police. I said, 'they've got better things to do, Keeley. Leave her alone, she won't hurt you.' Everyone to start with thought she'd steal. I'm afraid that includes me. Shop-lift, you know. But she never did. She always paid cash. And that was odd too. I mean, when she paid you, she kind of wasn't there. She never said a word – it wasn't she was being rude. It was as if... her mind was wandering and she didn't see you or know what she was doing. It's a good thing we're on the level here. We don't cheat customers. Other places – well."

Nancy confirmed that Mrs Jones also appeared at the shop as Herself. She wore then one of two or three knee-length straight skirts and flat shoes, a jumper or blouse and coat. On warmer days sometimes the coat was replaced by a cardigan. Her hair was up in what Nancy, unlike Josh, termed a French Roll. At these times Mrs Jones saw you. She said Please and Thank you, and sometimes asked where something or other was.

The other visitation was the man with short hair, dressed casual-smart, if rather outdatedly. He always spoke too, would even have a brief chat with you about the weather, if you mentioned it, or the latest media-reported crisis. "She used to drop her voice right down for him. But it never works, does it, I mean unless someone really trains their voice. Men don't sound like women, women don't, like men. They just sound wrong. Poor old thing," she added sadly. Nancy looked sad too. Thinking of her grandmother once more, perhaps, and what age and life, (never forget life's part in the destruction), do to us all.

Later on, there, I received a real eye-opener too, from the stroppily timorous Keeley, a nasty little fat-mouthed bitch, who sprang out on me as I was, subsequent to interviewing Nancy, rooting in the freezer for some ice cream.

"Ere," quoth Keeley, "Yor the one wot's asking all them questions about that old bag, ent yer?"

I confessed I was.

"Well I seen her on the train up London – more'n once."

"What happened?" I legitimately asked.

"Nuffin happened!" she squawked, as if I'd suggested either she had molested Mrs Jones or vice versa. "She gives me the squeams." (Did she mean qualms? Screams? Squeamishness?) "Moment she gets in I move up the carriage. But I gets a look at her. Jeez what a dringe." (I think she said 'dringe', whatever that is.) "Like she's done up like a right slag, about fourteen. Shorty skirt right up here..." Keeley erroneously indicated her waist, "and hold-ups – stockings, you know, and it's all reds and goldy bits and all this long black 'air wiv beads in it, and high heels – and all this eye-stuff – thick as a – what are them bear things?"

"...Pandas?" I guessed.

"Panters, yeah," agreed Keeley, with hatred. "And this lip gloss. Pink. Errr," breathed Keeley, allowing me to see the grey chewed chewing-gum in her mouth. "Oughter be in jail, them like her. Or in the loony bin."

"Why?" I asked her, quite reasonably.

"Yor weird you are," said Keeley.

I suppose she's right. But aren't we all?

"Just tell me," I said, "before you go, how did she act, I mean what did she do, when you saw her on the train?"

"Nuffin. Just sit there, with her legs crossed an' you could see her black panties. She had black fingernails anall. Everyone was, like, killing theirselves."

"What a shame they never managed it." But no. I didn't say that.

OK

Nancy however later on added two extra incidents. It – they – had, she said, happened only about a month – was it? – before Mrs Jones had been found, dead of natural causes and old age, in her house behind the canal.

"Those times, you see, she didn't come in alone. First she was being the young woman in the T-shirt and jeans, with her hair down. And she had someone with her, a younger woman I'd say it was."

"Do you mean there was someone actually with her?"

"Oh no. Only in her mind. This person was invisible to any of the rest of us. What did she call her? Nicky, I think it was. Mrs Jones was telling this woman how to get through the store, which was apparently – as I'd always seen she found it – very structurally dangerous. And where this Nicky could find things. Except the cigarettes, for example, which of course are kept up by the lottery and the magazines. But Mrs Jones actually directed Nicky somewhere over by the paper goods. But it seemed to work all right. I suppose it would, wouldn't it? And this is the other thing I forgot to mention. Around the same time – or I think it was – was the snow down? I can't quite... never mind. The – man-with-short-hair version came in, I mean Mrs Jones as this man, yes? And that one time he – I find I have to say he – talked to us, but also he was talking to three other – well – non-existent people, two men and a woman. I can remember he called her Auntie Vanessa. And that time, very unusually for him, I mean Mrs Jones, the man took a trolley, and he put in a big bottle of vodka and four bottles of wine and some mixers – oh and some salad, which as a rule neither he nor Mrs Jones – if you get me – seemed very keen on. And Liz was on the checkout and she said to him, 'Are you having a party?' And Mrs Jones said, in this different voice – I mean not her own or the silly deep voice for the man, but a sort of older, more playful sort of a voice, 'Oh, that's for the dog'. And Liz and I laughed. And that," she added, and suddenly her nice brown eyes filled with tears, "was the last time I ever saw her – or any of her – well, her other selves. I am sorry," Nancy said. "Poor thing. Did she die alone?"

"I heard so," I said. But I thought, God knows. Who else was in there with her? Mickie – Nicky? Some other old friends? Auntie Vanessa? The dog?

OK OK

After the local ones, and because I hadn't yet been able to meet up with Dimble, (Dimble being the charity worker who helped clear the house, and who was willing to talk to me providing everything to do with him is kept private, and also on the agreement that I make a charitable donation of three hundred GBP), I decided to pick up on the London sites.

There are far less clues to these, of course. Only The Red Stag – or The Stag and Star, its real name – seems to exist in fully concrete form.

But when I got there, quite a lot of the regulars recollected Mr Shakespeare-Pepys, as the reader among them called him.

Reg, (who doesn't mind my referring to him as Reg, "Only no second name, please. The wifelet wouldn't stand for it"), was or had been, 'quite fascinated' by the contemporary old woman, who had clearly been possessed by a virile, youngish chap from the Seventeenth or Eighteenth Century.

"An actor, one gathered. Once or twice at Drury Lane and Covent Garden. Currently strutting the boards at The Obelisk in – where was it, Sandy? Yes, that's it. Stampwell Street, off Cartwheel Lane. I don't think you'll find that, young sir," Reg added to me. "Some of us have gone and looked, you see. Neither the various Geographias nor word of mouth seem to offer up proof of its existence."

"Invented, then?"

"Product of an insane but eloquent mind," pronounced Reg. "I said, didn't I, he called this pub The Red Stag?"

Reg told me that Thessris – he thought this was what the actor's name was supposed to be – seemed to see all of them in The Stag, though Reg doubted Mr T saw them as they were. "He'd have a joke with us, and with me often, as I rather liked it. I mean, I valued the way he – yes, of course, she spoke. Liked the twists he-she put on the English language. No doubt not at all authentic for the scholars, but balls to them. It had a ring to it. Some of the words and phrases – God knows if anyone ever spoke like that back then

– but, yes, a ring. What was that one we liked, Sandy? Oh, yes. Merry-dig. Fuck, you see? And I must say, young sir, he seemed to be having a merry-dig with plenty, and of both genders. Young men, lovely women. He was in love with an actress. Priscilla, I think it was. No, that's not it. Near enough. Priscilla Peck. Oh, yes, he had it bad for her. But lots of others, he didn't go short. No, no idea if your Mrs Jones was a les. After all, Mr T had men too. Three of them at least I heard him talking to in here. No, obviously not, no one else could see them. I wouldn't have minded seeing a couple of the girls. His Priscilla. And that other one – Mistress Temple? Something like that."

'Sandy' – not his name, nor to be quoted – didn't give me any information, Only nodded, or occasionally confirmed something, and smiled over the drinks I bought them both.

Reg though said he could only say he thought he'd seen the other incarnation, the bloke in the suit. Kept himself to himself, if it was the right one, had a quick single drink, or brooded over a sandwich, then left.

"She was limber for an old bird, wasn't she?" Reg added, with approval. "What was she? Sixties? But neither of the alter-egos was her age. Certainly not Mr T. She moved like a young man. Yes, and like a male too. Shame her voice let her down. And the clothes, of course. Looked, shall I say, merry-digging bloody silly in them. But. You say she died? That's a shame. We'll miss her. She ought to get a proper mention somewhere. Entertaining the masses, eh, Sandy?"

I told them that was the idea, when I wrote the article. We all shook hands as I left.

After The Stag, though, as they had forewarned me, I mostly drew a blank.

What anyway had I to go on? These relatively amorphous landmarks – the office or firm or workplace apparently not too far from The Stag. The Leaning Tower, with its perhaps uncountable storeys, and blue or red or green lasers pulsing from the roof – which seemed it might be up New Cross way – but God knew.

Some things had been easy to translate. The Sprint must be the station and/or the train – if a futuristic and very fast and brilliant model. The Park, Little Common, the Forest, the waste ground or rough pastures – these were all the same area, which was the built-on land across the roofed-over canal. Back in the '70s, I mean the 1970s, they were simple open ground. What used to be called

Green Space. And Wales, obviously, was – Wales. Brighton and Lewisham were Brighton. And Lewisham.

I tried quite hard, even so, to prise out anything that might have been the inspiration for Mrs Jones's multiple fantasies. I thought at one juncture The Gherkin might have triggered The Leaning Tower, though it fitted only in its leaning. Or I tried the Parnassus Showrooms, where Mrs Jones's husband had worked some thirty odd years before. Was this the workplace of the short-haired city guy? No way on earth.

As for Stampwell Street and Cartwheel Lane. Let's not go there. By which I mean nobody can go there. They don't exist.

I did try Stanwell Road, up against Heathrow. But it seemed a long shot, and so it was. I won't assert Mrs Jones could not have imagined herself at a theatre there in 1760/70, even with the giant roaring power of modern aviation thundering by above. But it seemed an unnecessary leap of her faith to pit her gift, (and so I must call it, I think), against so much of the contemporary contrary.

By sheer chance, (is there such a thing?), only two weeks ago, long after I had already become immersed in this research, I met a couple from Brighton who, without a hint from me, mentioned a 'Stark staring old hag' dressed up as a male business type, who regularly used to turn up at the station, get a cab, and go sailing off into Brighton town – now – city.

It tends to seem to be where she thought she – or he – had to go; they set off, went there, and only came back mission, at least mentally, accomplished.

I have to believe then, Mrs Jones did a lot of her imagined life-work in reality, if nearly always seeing and thinking it, presumably, something else. But she must have used her powerful imaginative muscles extra hard too. For example, did she sit in The Stag and fully imagine her times on stage, her hours with her lovers? Or she went into London and dreamed, while trailing round the pubs or cafes or streets, that she danced in the top of a big and leaning tower, with rooms for sex and a bar on every floor.

OK
Yes.
OK

How then did I get started on all this? And aside from that, and the testimony of the people I've interviewed, what proof have I got?

I never saw, let alone met, this madwoman Dawn. That was her first name. Dawn Jones.

It began when my initial contact, D.C.W., was put my way, by my then-editor, whose name I'm not going to give. (Damn it though, I will put it, here, if nowhere else, the name of Informant No. 1. D.C.W stands for Dentist Clive Woods. He's the one.)

I've no doubt he is a very good and conscientious dentist, Mr W. But clearly what he had encountered in – no, I think I will sit on the dates – had both unnerved and intrigued him. He it was who carried out the first investigation, reading various reports and books, and consulting with those in his own line of work, and elsewhere.

It had been a routine extraction of a back tooth. Dawn Jones had been his patient only a month or two when this became necessary for her. However she told him at once that her only previous extraction, despite local anaesthetic, had been so 'agonising' (her word) that she wanted total anaesthesia. This, of course, can normally be an option. And despite the fact she was over seventy, her general health seemed fine, and he thought that pain and nervousness might be more risky than a knock-out.

All went well, and the tooth was in fact swiftly removed. It was as they were staunching the blood that, despite all attempts to keep her quiet, Dawn Jones began to speak – as Woods put it without apology, in tongues.

The first sentences he got, and this in a woman's quiet, and – as he said – quite reasonable voice, were these: "I kill people. What do you do?"

Things happen in dentistry that can be quite startling. You need a cool head and a steady hand. He and his assistant frowned at each other. Each later admitted they knew they hadn't misheard.

"Just keep still, Mrs Jones. It's all going well. Not long now."

But she spoke again, and the otherwise full set of grown teeth, still missing only two, almost bit him.

"The birds tell me. Then I hunt. I always know which one's for me. Three days ago it was a drunk in the car park of the burnt-out cinema. Not the best I've ever had. But not bad."

Woods admitted he had to paraphrase, but insisted this was the gist of what she said.

He said softly to his assistant, "They do this, sometimes. It isn't real."

"Sounded real enough to me, Mr Woods."

They got the bleeding staunched. The flow calmed quite quickly, as it sometimes does with the old.

But Dawn Jones was still talking.

She spoke in different voices. All female, but two of them very bizarre, apparently meaning to be male, and sounding male enough in inflexion, apart from actual vocal timbre and depth. One male was some sort of office worker from inner London. "He complained about having to call on an aunt in Brighton." The other was – 'he' stressed – an actor, and 'his' mistress was giving 'him' a run around, from the sound of it, but there was another young lady – and 'his' language, ornamental from the start, turned very fruity, so the assistant began to snigger and giggle and Mr Woods, a clean-living man, grew rather offended.

Just before Dawn Jones came round there was another voice. She actually gave her name. Clover, Woods said. And she was straight, he said, out of Bladerunner or The Matrix, rather, I personally judged, muddling up his Sci Fi genres.

Clover had been dancing in a leaning tower with giant flowers and coloured lights, and had sex – Woods assumed 'carnal', which was what she called it, meant sex. Also she had stolen some clothes despite the O.C.s (? Did that mean observation cameras – he thought it sounded like it.)

"Two amoral criminals," he remarked to me, "a serial murderer and a nympho thief. And a sex-maniac in Mediaeval show-biz or whatever, whenever. And a boring old fart with a maiden aunt."

When Dawn came out of unconsciousness, she was the same as ever she had been. He asked her if she had had any funny dreams when under. She said she hadn't. Nothing, just a blank. He asked her if she was, at home, reading a lurid book. She stared at him for a second. She seemed only bewildered.

"Has anyone told you you talk in your sleep, Mrs Jones?"

She said no one had told her that.

She didn't appear upset, but only anxious to get away. So he gave her the usual dental advice and the leaflet to assist recovery, and she left.

He could tell his assistant soon forgot the exoticism of the whole episode. But Woods found it plagued him.

He began to read back issues of the local papers, and make inquiries here and there. Had there been a murder near the cinema?

There wasn't a cinema? Was there a night club in London called The Leaning Tower? Very tall, strobes on the roof, secret rooms for personal liaisons? Nobody had heard of anything so spectacular. He, as I had to, later, tried to locate even the memory of a theatre called The Obelisk off Cartwheel Lane. Zilch. Of course.

Then the consultations with colleagues and others.

"Woodsy, if you've never had a patient go off on one before, when they're under, you've been a very lucky man. Had a pretty girl once, seventeen or less, started telling me she'd always fancied me. Woke up and gave me the usual cold shoulder. I was only twenty-five then. Or there was the guy started predicting the lottery numbers. I, like a chump, started to try to memorise them, but it wasn't just one or two goes, he went on and on. Probably the forecast for the whole year's draws. And then..."

At length Woods happened, of all places on holiday in Spain, to spend an afternoon on the beach and get chatting with a doctor from Northampton. They exchanged discreet anecdotes of their professional lives. In the end the story of Dawn Jones came up.

"Tell me," said the (unnamed to me) doctor, "did she ever act this out? By which I mean seem to become fully, as far as she could, any of these – four was it? – people physically?"

"That is the truly unsettling thing," Woods told him. "Before I moved out of the area – my new practice is in Sussex – I'd begun to hear she was sometimes seen going about dressed as a man, or in a mini-skirt or something like that, truly unsuitable for a lady of her age. Or in theatrical costume. So, she was mad?"

"Oh, yes," said the doctor on the beach. "Very decidedly. If in a very specific way."

When he had the facts all keyed in, Woods started his serious reading. In that line he encountered one or two others resembling Mrs Jones. One of the more famous was the notorious Eric Verner Wassen, whom I've mentioned previously. Foremost of his episodes, if you ever take time to pursue him, was impersonating – or rather being – the King of Mars. It was this eventually that saw him incarcerated as a public hazard. Woods thought Dawn's story might be worth making something of, even though it seemed, at least in the real world, lacking in all criminality and violence. It was a tumbled and evasive route Woods took, but finally someone put him in touch with my editor, and so with me. He 'Foresaw' a book, a film script; I the writer and he the inaugurator, profits shared. I, on the other hand, saw a long article. We're still, as they say, 'talking' about that. She had no relations surviving, it seems. No one to muscle in or sue. That makes it more sensitive, somehow. The deeper I've got into it, the more I have felt this. I'm not a moralist. I've done a few things. Most of us have, in my line of work. You have to, to dig things out. But this. As I say, he and I are still discussing matters.

OK

I, even if Woods didn't, have tried to find out if Dawn's doctor ever caught a whiff of her condition. But could get nothing at all out of him, or anyone else at the surgery.

Frankly I don't think they ever much bothered with her. She never got ill, or never told them when she was, and passed her by now obligatory For The Old Folk tests with flying colours. Wasn't she ever confused or forgetful? I was patiently told that this wasn't uncommon in our more elder citizens. Providing there was no hint of Alzheimer's, leave well alone.

I had a notion they were bloody careless, as I say. For there would have been hints of just that very thing, even if wrongly. Because when Dawn was off being Clover, or one of the other three, didn't she sometimes wonder where she, Dawn, had been, and why she couldn't recall?

But that is someone else's problem.

Now, though.

I'd better relate my meeting with Dimble the Timbrel, the charity worker. (I call him that childishly because when I first met him, he kept on for about ten minutes about one of his kids and the word timbrel, is that in the Bible?, Sound the Timbrel or some rot or other.) He was one of those one-drink-and-I'm-sloshed. And not even cheap, since they like to go on having lots of those just-one-more type drinks.

However, he told me about the Jones house-clearance. And even something about how Dawn was found dead.

There were no suspicious circumstances. When the police broke in, she was just sitting up in her flat in the loft extension. (The doctor had called round in answer to her telephone request, and been unable to gain access.) She was in the armchair. The electric fire was on – it seemed she never put in central heating – and a nearly empty tea-cup stood on a table. She wouldn't have looked asleep. The old dead normally don't. They look – knowing. Knowing and fierce, as if to reprimand you. Or knowing and pleased, as if they glimpsed, in the last second, the joyful theme park of Heaven to which they were about to transcend. No one told me which of these looks Dawn had. And Dimble hadn't, of course, seen her at all. But the house and contents – he'd seen every scrap of those.

OK

This, I'd take a bet, is the only proof I can offer, aside from the gossipy or malicious or brainless – or compassionate – eye witness accounts reporting on Dawn at large in her own, or her four other, lives.

OK

(Stop writing that God forsaken two letter word.)

As I understood it, the house was three floors, the upper one being the attic-loft conversion. Although the way Dimble described it the place sounded as if it had an extra attic on the top of that. (And peering at the house through the overgrown trees a couple of times still hasn't quite got the details straight in my mind.)

Each floor is converted (Dimble) to a separate flat, though on the first-floor upper storey there is the potential to alter one large flat into two smaller ones. The stairs are mutual, as is the downstairs hall and front door. Dawn seems to have lived in all these flats, (her last tenant was apparently back in the late '70s.) But in fact Dawn, herself, only lived in the loft extension. Judging by what lay about elsewhere, the short-haired business guy had one half of the first floor, and the girl – Clover – the other half. The unlikeable girl in the red T-shirt lived on the ground floor, the biggest flat, (which also had access to a large kitchen, the garden, and a basement with cellar – empty but for the skeletons of two rats.) The second floor flat below the loft seems to have been where the actor set up his pad.

(One wonders what each of these five intelligences made of the others. Were they simply not at all aware of anyone else in the house, or did they get glimpses, perhaps more internal memories than actually thinking they saw anyone. Did too any or all of their imaginary friends ever inhabit the house, directly sharing their lives – the dog, for example, or the Micky-Nicky boy or girl, or the actor's numerous lovers, the friends and aunt of the short-haired man? I have a theory that perhaps Dawn's talent may have had to move them in with her, because near the end, as her strength was breaking down, those journeys up to town, or to Lewisham or New Cross or wherever, let alone Brighton, would have become insupportable.) Again Reg, at The Stag and Star, had mentioned that the actor who he thought was called Thes-sris(?) (from Thespian?) had announced he travelled to and from the city by cart. What could that have been? A bus – taxi?

In the rooms, all through the five flats, was a 'cram' of furniture, some old and damaged, some newish and cheap. (Just one 'wonderful' thing, it seems, a screen, both tapestry and painted, with peacocks depicted.) There were a couple of televisions, radios, and so on. There was nothing, Dimble said, that seemed particularly comfortable or attractive. (Why would there be? The comfort or glamour was invoked by the fluctuations of Dawn's deranged and versatile mind.) Four of the flats had a wardrobe, however. And in these, variously, and as appropriate to each personality, were T-shirts, jeans and boots (ground floor), suits, shirts and a selection of other 'dull' (again Dimble's word) male garments (half first upper floor flat), short tight dresses and costume jewellery of an extravagant and 'lurid' sort (opposite half of second first upper floor flat). The theatrical fancy dress for Thessris, in the third story second floor flat, was strewn about over an unmade bed. There was also one other oddity, (as if all of it were not odd). This being, Dimble gleefully said, a most sensational dress from the Flapper era of the 1920s, pink and gold, beaded and trimmed. It was a collector's item, and had brought the charity well over five thousand pounds. He had confessed he concealed his knowledge of it from the clearance people. (He trusts I won't reveal as much.) The thing was, it had skipped their original notice, since it was behind a black and a grey curtain (two of them) in, of all places, the north half of the second floor flat. That is, the short-haired guy's wardrobe. (A question or two extra there. Had that personality, a male, been less 'dull' than thought, having some gender issues, maybe?)(!)

I've been shown photographs, on Dimble's screen, from one of the charity's disks. House interiors and bits of furniture the charity had taken on, including the screen and the dress. Some other oddities too – such as a realistic-looking toy or model gun, found in a cupboard on the ground floor.

There's no reason any of that should be falsified. (Unless they've gone to so much trouble in order to get my three hundred pound donation, I suppose.) For me the pictures provide solid proof of... something. Some of the items are also still in the local shop. They are minor things, yet present, and as described.

The house itself now stands empty. A builder has bought it and will soon be doing the flats up to try to lift the price. I've driven past and seen how half the trees are marked for culling, a vile act in this age of global warming. The bastard must have bribed the council. Driving by not long since, I parked again, and went to the unsecured back gate, looking over. One tree was already gone, revealing that there seemed to be some sort of grave in the garden. I went in and took a look. Quite a big grave, for what it was, because almost certainly a family pet had been buried there. The little marker read, in black waterproof paint, Rover. 13 years, one month. Be happy in Heaven, Dear.

For the record I'd better add there is, very definitely, no evidence at all that either I, or certain of my most reliable – if also nameless – contacts, were able to unearth that Dawn, when in her killer persona, ever harmed a soul, while the Clover personality stole nothing, except in Dawn's fantasy.

OK

Split personality. Multiple personality. Classified terms for a particular form of certifiable madness.

But.

You know, we all do it – don't we? – one way or another. I mean, of course, we lead many different lives inside our one.

One personality for work, and one for your sexual partner, another for the kids, if you have any. Another when you're really elated, or when you're angry, and another when you're scared shitless. Every seven or ten years, too, you seem to grow into another skin as the old one shreds itself off. Older and wiser, older and more stupid. I'm not the guy I was at ten, or at twenty or even thirty-six. Who will I be when I'm forty-six, or fifty, or seventy-four? God knows.

And we have fantasy lives too, don't we? Reading a book, or watching a good movie. At our console playing computer games of death and daring. If we write, or act, quite other lives. And when we dream – oh, sure, then we really do. Twenty or a hundred, or more, other little Us's. Multiple Personality Syndrome. Once I dreamed I'd got to Mars, even if I wasn't King of it, like Eric Verner Wassen. And once, only once, when I was a kid about five, I sleep-walked through our house, which was a two-up two-down terrace in Walthamstow. But in the dream all my toys were running and playing up and down the stairs, my train and my toy bus were rushing along the lino in the kitchen, and our recently deceased tom cat was flying, on silvery wings, harmlessly in and out of the shut glass of the windows. I saw this. I was there. It was real. My misery when I woke below in the kitchen, at 2 a.m., was temporarily insurmountable. But Dawn Jones, thank God, never did wake up. Or not in this life.

I have a feeling. This 'dry run', dress-rehearsal – now it's done…

I may just hand over my three hundred pounds to Dimble. And suggest to D.C.W. he find another patsy. Rest in peace.

Let it go.

James Michael Pinkerton
London.
March 2011

# Dawn:
# 102

After I got up, I had the soup, the way I like it, very hot, with two cream crackers and butter.

When I looked out, it was summer, the sky so blue and all the trees thick with green. I put on a light dress.

I took the dog for a walk.

He's very good, the dog, but wilful. Sometimes he goes off on his own, he always has, especially to the park. We walked through the park. What a golden day. And over in the west, where the flats used to be, I could see the new bridge shining, just like gold itself in the light.

As we were coming back the dog indicated he had to go off again, but he'd be back tomorrow to see me. He always comes back. I stroked him and told him to give my love to Ben.

When I got home there was cooked chicken in the fridge I'd forgotten about. I had a sherry, and then a long cool bath. Painted my toenails as I haven't for so long. I admit, I admired myself in the mirror. It's nice to be young again. I think I'm about twenty-four now. It suits me.

Played the piano until eight, no stiff fingers! Then had a nice cold chicken dinner with a glass of wine.

Went to bed at eleven-thirty. Wonderful music on the radio. Looking forward so much to tomorrow, and to getting news of Ben.

The moon is shining on the bridge. It's silver now.

## EMENIE:
# 103

After I got out of the hospital, I took advantage of the free offer and came out here. It's wonderful country, and the weather, for autumn, is very good.

I climb the mountains and go for runs along the downs. There's a waterfall that plunges down about a hundred feet. Off to the west I can just make out the bridge. Steel, and always shining, but always, too, half lost in the mist. I suppose one day it'll come clear.

Killed twice yesterday. Both excellent. They were hikers, a couple, and we all enjoyed it a lot. Afterwards they shared their sandwiches with me. First time ever I've had caviar, and in a sandwich for God's sake. But I liked that too.

Tonight I'm twenty-one, and going to some dinner at the hotel. There is a man there that I've promised to kill, but we haven't been able to fit the time in yet. There's such a lot to do. If we can't tonight, I'll try to make a proper date, and stick to it.

One small problem. That idiot called Alun, who keeps coming back for more. I have murdered him four times and all different ways. I think I'll have to talk to him seriously about this. There are other people waiting. He will have to get to the back of the queue.

## Rod:
## 104

After I got out of the hospital I carried on with my original plan. I went up by train, but it was a surprisingly quick journey, less than two hours. Marvellous weather, not a cloud in the sky. Vanessa had packed cheddar and pickle sandwiches; George must be a good influence on her after all. Had half a bottle of wine on the train. My watch, by the way, kept perfect time.

It is as I remember it, the house. Though the land round it is, if anything, more lush. Beautiful autumnal shades of ginger and russet and honey-green. The fields golden, and in one a red tractor. There's a new bridge out towards the west end of the town, glowing like copper in the afternoon light; I can see it from the upper windows here.

First class dinner served by the live-in cook.

I suppose I'll have to ask them down, George I mean, and Van. Not yet, though.

I can remember playing in all these rooms, with my dolls, in my pink dresses.

I've hung the pink and gold dress up in full view on the back of the bedroom door. Yes, you can take things with you. The past is exactly the same country it always was, when you re-enter it willingly.

I look younger, and feel younger. That is a definite bonus. But I don't want to be ten or thirteen again. And I don't want to dress as a woman any more than I ever did.

Needless to relate, I don't miss work. I've taken it on myself to reorganise the library, and I have a feeling I might keep a horse in the old stable here. The exercise appeals to me. And now it's all possible. I don't miss London either. Though I may, eventually, go to have a look at the town here. Have a look at that coppery bridge. I wonder where it leads to, apart from over the river?

## Klova:
## 105

After I woke up, I got ready, put on best totter-heels, and then I put on the lipstick which I call after my mother, C.P. – Clover Pearl.

At Zone 48 I took the Sprint to The Leaning Tower, and in the room with the chrysanthemums, they had lots of Lantern Fruits, which are Chinese Gooseberries, flying round on their paper-lantern wings. Lovely little gold fruits with wings, playing round the lights, and never getting burned. I met a beautiful male, and we had carnal. Like it was, as is brilliant beyond brilliancy.

Saw Coal, too, and we waved to each other, but that was all. I don't feel any much for him now. But he's all right.

Later I had a moonshake at the Firewhirl, under the glittering sky poles, and watched the dawn coming up over the new bridge far off down the river. I love night there, and sunrise, when the bridge changes from opal to ruby to diamond.

The bank-nanny told me, soon as I was home, there were twenty thousand shots in my account.

But anyway I think I'll steal a dress sometime today.

Just like I can.

And then I'll go and love.

# Irvin:
# 106

After my final success at The Obelisk, Merscilla Peck both rejoiced in me and grew jealous, which she demonstrated most ably by her antics in the tavern bed, with loving moans and exquisite connivances, and lastly by biting me, sufficiently to draw blood, in the flank. Altogether not sorry to leave the Capital and its environs, not least the wretched hole I had occupied in the hovel of the brown landlady. (The dog had taken himself back there too, on one last visit prior to his sojourn in the country with my erstwhile doctor. Horatius, as now I must call him, had found my second shirt, and eaten a great deal of it. Whether this was a token of esteem on his part, or scorn for my new life, I shall never know.)

However, my own journey took me three days, after which I find myself where I have bound and sworn myself to be, since my miraculous recovery from Sophia's poison. It is a grim, grey stack, not quite unlike some ornamental jail, with its huge bell-tower thrusting upward into sky, and its narrow cloisters nailing down a tiny courtyard with a well.

And where and what then is this dismaying place? It is the Abbey of Fouldes Water. And here, through a tortuous and torturing process of denial and many redemptive silences, I shall freeze out from myself the glorious sins of my flesh, until I too am stone, both cold and grey, my own fine tower clamped in chastity, and my own bold heart clock-timed to a sedentary tick. Starved, flailed and chained. I am to be a priest.

I gaze on the Christ in his little niche, and through the open stonery behold that curious ancient bridge from Roman times, black as iron, and tending to the west. The sky shines Heavenly beyond, although the world is swanned with snow.

But they have promised me, I shall often read aloud the lessons, for my actor's voice.

## Dawn:
## 107

I saw the dog again today. We sat together by the little river. I understand, of course, that when I am ready, he will go with me over the shining bridge, and there we will be with Ben, and I will be as Ben is, and as the dog is, too. But for now I must finish all my five lives, for the sake of myself, and of the others.

While I am myself I can still recall, at last, very clearly, that I am also a young murderess, and a man who has retired early to his childhood home to keep a horse and read books, and a young girl who dances and makes love in a world of futuristic dreams, and a proud male actor who will now become a proud and sombre priest. One by one, as each, I and they, become ready, we will walk up on to the bridge of steel, or of copper, or of diamond, opal and ruby, or iron-black, or gold and silver, and cross through into the bright mist. And there we will all be one and quite different, so different from anything we have been here, ever, that I can't imagine it. Nor any of us could.

But for now the sun gleams, and the river sparkles, and pigeons rustle in the trees. I kiss the dog, and throw a stick for him, knowing he may then run off. And, too, that he will always come back.

# Exhibit Eight
# Turquoiselle

Whisky, wine and shiny pins –
Pour them out and stick them in;
All the graces, all the sins,
All the games that you can win:
And so the Fighters' Feast begins.

## One

The shed looked like a railway carriage, especially through the trees that grew up beyond the property. Some were silver birches, which gave a Russian effect, something Chekovian, Tolstoyan...

The shed itself had once been the colour of marmalade but had faded through the several wet English seasons it had had to endure. Now it was a pale rusty brown. Only by night, however, did the shed seem truly a little strange, for this was when an unusual muted glow began to be visible through the glazed windows. The colour was soft and faded. Some sort of Christmas lights might seem to have caused it, old ones that still, unusually, worked, and all in this one shade, this vague eerie greenish-blue.

Johnston, who lived farther along the lane, had concluded it was something like that. The few people who otherwise went that way after dark, drinkers from the local pub mostly, and assuming even they paid it any attention, took it for various illuminatory devices. Even, now and then, a bit of plastic over an ordinary household bulb. Or maybe an old–fashioned oil–lamp with that colour glass.

It was none of those things, of course. Just as the shed was a shed and not a railway carriage. And the area was not late nineteenth century Russia. Not much is what it seems. Some things are not even – what they are.

"Oh shit," said Donna, "oh shit." And getting up quickly she ran out of the kitchen.

She was going to the downstairs cloakroom, he supposed, in order to vomit.

Yes, he could hear her.

Carver turned up the sound of the TV she always liked to have going above the breakfast bar. Not that he enjoyed or valued the early morning news show that was on, but he needed a sound to block out the noises from Donna. (The TV flickered, settled; weather interference – it was prone to that.)

At first he had judged she had bulimia, but then she had said she believed she was pregnant. She said too she was pleased, and would go to the health centre in a week or so to get the idea confirmed. "Won't it be wonderful," she said to him, "a *child*." She spoke as if a "*child*" was another must–have thing, like the mile–

long TV in the front room, and all the other appliances, and her clothes and cosmetics, and the exercise club and the pedicure place and so on. One more lovely yet essential addition to her existence. Although she seemed not to like being sick. Nor had she been, so far as he knew, to the doctor, though her first fertility announcement was currently two months old.

He had never grasped she wanted a child.

He had simply thought she liked having sex.

Or really, he had simply never thought about that aspect of her needs and wants, even though, or perhaps because, the rest of them generally seemed omnipresent. Donna had never said to him, "Wouldn't it be wonderful if I had a baby – would you *like* that? Shall we *try*?" Or, she had never said, "I want a baby so *much*. Is that all *right*? *Could* we? *Can* we? *Yes*?"

It had only been her throwing up suddenly, and then: "I think I'm pregnant. I'll go to the doctor soon and then we'll know." Or words to that effect.

When she returned from the lavatory, he quietened the TV down a little and poured himself another coffee. He said did she want some water.

"No, can't – just – not yet."

"I'm sorry."

"No – it's – OK. *God.*" She scowled, then relaxed, and abruptly, looking blissfully up at him, she said, "But it's worth it, isn't it?"

"Is it?" A genuine question.

Donna laughed in a patient and archly knowing way.

"Yes, darling. It *is*. Don't worry. I'll be fine. I am already. It never lasts."

"I'm glad."

She had golden hair, slightly enhanced, cut to a luxuriant shoulder-length, and this morning caught by a window-full of the early autumnal sun. It was like an aureole, the hair, a halo round her, beaming. Such beauty nature and false contrivance between them could erect.

"You *are* happy, aren't you?" she asked.

"If you are. But," he hesitated, trying not to push beyond their ordinary limits of lack-of-communication, "you still have to see Chenin…"

"The doctor. Yes, I know. But well, it's a formality really. I *know*, don't I?"

She was just thirty-one, and had no fears. No one could insist she must undergo over-intrusive checks to be sure whatever cargo she carried was unharmed by excessive extra years. And she was slim, not over or under weight, healthy, mentally active, and in a five-year-old relationship with a solvent male partner, apparently committed.

He smiled at her.

Donna smiled back from her golden nimbus.

He thought, she isn't pregnant. She's just so certain she is she's got the symptoms. Bleakly he glanced out of the window into the joyous brightness of the morning. In twenty more minutes he would need to leave for work.

Carver's journey into central London routinely took an hour and a half. But today, leaving at about eight, the traffic was far more heavy and obdurate. He did not have to reach the Mantik building before ten-fifteen, which was just as well: he reached it at **ten-ten.**

Throughout the drive the sun had blazed on the roads and highways. In London, even the city's polluted ceiling scarcely marred its brightness. The terrace of dull white buildings that stretched along Trench Street behind Whitehall had a veneer of blurred shine, all save the last three, which were encased in scaffolding and tarpaulins. Carver parked in the little side street where normally he left his car – someone would garage it later – walked around the corner and went past the scaffolded facade of the last building, to the side door. Here he used his three security keys to let himself in.

Beyond the door, the wide windowless hall was sunlit by uplighters. Reception today was the young guy known as MY or, in the parlance of the office, 'Mum's Youngest.'

He checked Carver's ID carefully. Carver was still novel to him.

"Morning, Mr Carver. Nice weather." He did not speak like a young man particularly, or had been told not to.

"Sure," said Carver, and took the lift to the fourth floor.

His room, free outside, as some of the upper storeys were, of tarpaulin, and in aspect looking away from the river towards Holland Row, had the window-blind down. He glanced out through the tiny hole. Everything seemed as expected, the backs of tall houses, high walls, the small pub generally known as Long's squashed in between the parked cars, the occasional pedestrian.

The sun here described, he thought, a kind of barrenness. A cityscape of blank stone, with toy people wandering about until their batteries ran down.

He had been in the room less than five minutes when the intercom buzzed him to go up. His appointment with Jack Stuart was for a quarter to eleven, but he would have to wait, he knew; one always had to wait for Stuart, five minutes or twenty-five.

It might have been a ploy. If it was, today Stuart did not resort to it. Instead his door stood half open.

"Come in, Carver."

Stuart's room, unlike Carver's, was quite large, with brown leather chairs and a brown polished side table. Paper files and boxed discs were neatly stacked on shelves. The coffee-making machine gave off its eternally cheerful aroma, a scent that was more alluring than the subsequent taste.

"Have a seat," said Stuart.

Carver sat.

The windows here too had the blinds down. The blinds were always down. There had been net curtains in the old days.

"How's life?" Stuart asked. He was a slim man, warmly dark skinned and haired, with cooled grey eyes.

"Fine, thanks."

"And Donna?" Stuart always remembered their names, the current wife or partner, any offspring, or other remaining relatives.

"She's fine, thanks."

"Good, good." And playfully: "Will she let you off this evening?"

"Yes, of course."

"That's good. It's just a five to eight-nine-ish. Avondale. OK?"

"Sure."

"Good. Your piece on the switch was good, by the way. You received my memo?"

"Yes, Mr Stuart."

"We're all up to level then, Carver. Well, have a good day."

"Thanks. You too, sir."

When Carver got back to his room, the relevant brief and tab for the evening had already arrived. The table was booked and office credit card awaiting collection. He would not bother to let Donna know, he had warned her of the possibility he might be late. Even though getting out of London just after ten, which is what it would amount to, could be worse than later, since the post-theatre traffic would be starting to crawl in all directions. And Avondale was a bore.

In the lower corridor Silvia Dusa had passed Carver and flashed her black eyes at him in apparent hatred. She looked in a controlled yet flaming temper, as ever. Perhaps her problem was hormonal; a beautiful woman, yet she must be in her forties, a "dangerous time", as Maggie put it, for "all women". Maggie should know. Donna's mother was well past her forties by now, "over the hump but not over the hill", as Maggie also would declare.

Carver shut the door of his room and began to search for various necessary impedimenta. Not finding what he wanted, he went out again and taking the side stair now went to the half-floor for supplies. The rest of the morning would pass in its expected dull and formulaic manner, then lunch in the canteen. He had to call in on Latham at 2.30, get the next piece of the latest office puzzle. And then off to Rattles with unlimited expenses to jolly up Avondale, before piling him into a Mantik chauffeured car for the airport.

The day ticked and trickled down its sun-gold drains. Autumn came much later recently. Twenty years ago, when Carver was a kid, already the leaves on the trees would have been mostly orange, **and** yellow, or rich brown, as the table in Stuart's office, the foliage thinned out, falling. Almost every leaf now was still thick green, only tarnished a little here and there as if lightly scorched.

Carver reflected on this **sparely.** Thinking of his childhood reminded him of things seldom pleasant, such as his father, a drunken bully. If Donna finally produced the child she said she was going to have – if it really were a fact – what sort of father would Carver make? Would he be any good at it? ('Good' seemed to have been Jack Stuart's Word for the Day. Sometimes Stuart did that, used one particular word, on and on, over and over. And then that word was dispensed with and another used: perhaps '*solid*', like last Friday, when so-and-so was a *solid* guy and someone had *solid* grounds for a premise of some sort. Was this an affectation of Stuart's, did he choose that day's word before he set up shop in his room? Or was it some nervous or Asperger-type peculiarity, a kind of vernacular stammer? Stuart however did seem to play tricks, did he not? For example, during the past five or six months, when called up to see him for either the most trifling or urgent matter, everybody had to wait in the reception area, which even had magazines littered about like a dentist's. Then today, Stuart's door was already open.)

Yes, it was better to consider the games or aberrations of Stuart. Not to go back too much to the autumns of childhood, the violence and silence, or the secret adventures, and their sequels, if they had ever been found out.

"You know," said Alex Avondale, after his second V and T, and once they were shown through to their table at Rattles, "I miss it. Down here."

He said this with the lugubrious nostalgia of a demon redeemed into Heaven, but pining for the 'old place' below.

He had, apparently, a vast estate in Scotland, Highland country, where snow sculpted the spring and autumn peaks of mountains, and turned them to Antarctica in winter. But London was his homeland. With Avondale Scotland was not only a separate kingdom but another continent.

Carver had really only to listen, be an appreciative audience. He was good (Stuart's Word for the Day again) at that.

It had been his stock-in-trade, when he decided to apply it, from his early years, being able, if he must, to listen, and to offer, now and then the correct response. He did not suppose he had learnt this from the bullying of his father, from the *terror* his father had imposed. It was not self-defence, rather absenting of self – absenteeism.

Avondale had rambled on since the car first brought them to the restaurant. And in the bar, as the golden evening melted into the nocturnal version of the London ceiling, and was slit all over in neon slices, Avondale continued. He drank quite a lot, and talked a vast amount during their meal – for him, alefish, and then some sort of exemplified liver stew. (It was a quieter menu for Carver.) Rattles had been reputedly so named for its more exotic dishes, curious fish and fowl and flesh, including rattlesnake. **And** the bill, when established, after the dessert and cheese, coffee and brandy, was fabulous, but the courtesy card took care of it, and the petty cash took care of the tip.

The limousine and driver came back promptly at twenty minutes to nine.

"There's a matter I'd really like to run through with you, we didn't get to it this evening," Avondale said, in the last two minutes before his journey to the docklands and the plane. "A venture – I'd like to cut you in, Carver. It might be lucrative."

Carver had nodded, smiling, looking pleased but not too much so. Such proposals were broached sometimes, freelance like this, here and there. A couple had been bizarre (a man called Simpson) and one discoloured enough Carver had carried it straight back to Stuart. Most were cigar-dreams, brandy-fantasies, not worth even recollecting, and this one, unspecified, seemed exactly like that.

They shook hands out in the stuffy chilliness of an autumn London night.

"Take care, son," said Avondale, as the immaculate door was shut on him.

Carver watched as he rode away between the prickly bristles of the city lights, red-faced and gentle with false sentimentality, irrelevant and over. The end of another day.

And now, for Carver, back to Trench Street, drop off the Third Person, then the short wait to get his car, and next, his own long drive home.

Though with regular irregularity Carver varied his homeward route, he knew all the variations by now quite well. Tonight he got across the London miles, cutting out through the suburbs into Peckham and Lewisham, eventually reaching the narrow by-lanes of Kent. Tree-massed dark then, but for the scaley wink of the cat's-eyes, and the isolated gleam from a closed-up pub, cottagey terrace, or the sudden towering gate of some secretive club. He passed the abandoned school with broken windows, the distant vague group of squatting towers on the hill. The woods were thick, jet-black on moonless navy clumps of sky. Black leaves caught the headlamps and grew wetly drily green. At intervals a fresh blinding blaze of lights announced wider thoroughfares, then it was back again into the uncoiling serpent's bowel of the lanes. Eight or ten years before, this late, often there was not that much else on the road but for Carver. But now many cars light-splashed by, or the tottery jingling behemoths of giant lorry-transports, like robot things from some computer game.

Carver, a careful, intelligent driver, alert but not involved, had again space to think. He thought over the day, assessing its routine, and any short moments it had had of the unusual – Stuart's promptness at his appointment, the fat woman in the canteen who had lost her temper, as he passed her, over some disarrangement of her food, the new file Latham had given him that afternoon to read, with the latest on Scar.

All told, Carver had made slow time tonight. Reception after nine had been old BBS, (nickname Bugger Back-Scratcher), who could be officious and over-detailed, so that returning the Third Person, and putting in the receipt and card from dinner, took nearly half an hour. The London traffic was augmented too by some maintenance work near the park; Carver had wondered if this was a cover for something else, as roadworks so often were. Whatever it was had caused more delay. As he finally gained the approach to the village, his watch showed almost 1 a.m.

He doubted Donna would still be up. He hoped she would not be. Mother Maggie had probably come over. They would have watched TV and drunk wine, (or orange juice for Donna perhaps, if she thought she was pregnant). Maggie tended to come by cab for such evenings, and to take a cab back to her own place at Beechurst before eleven, and then Donna, alone, wandered about, had a bath and went to bed, read and fell asleep with the bedside lamp turned on full – to welcome or chide, as she said, when he arrived "hours" after. Of course, sometimes it *was* hours after, three or four in the morning. "Mag thinks you have a girlfriend," Donna had said.

"Oh, does she?"

"Yes. But I don't."

"That's all right then."

"Do you?" she asked at once.

Carver had shaken his head. "No." *No*, he thought. Donna was more than enough.

As he drove into the village, the car sliding slow now, with a long soft feral purr, he saw dim yellow in the curtained side window of The Bell. The purring note might be a signal the engine, as before, was about to play up. And The Bell was having another lock-in late drinking session.

Carver pulled over and parked in the yard. He did this now and then, Ted at the Bell did not object.

"Oh, it's you, mate," said Ted, letting him cautiously through under the porch like a secret lover. "What'll you have? Usual?"

"Thanks, Ted."

"Long old day for you, up town?" Ted asked the ritual question.

"Yes. Too long."

"Here you are, then. Lock Heim." Ted added the Jewish good wish with his emphatic regulation phonetic misspelling.

"Cheers."

Carver drank the black coffee in a corner of the bar, away from the rest of the small group who were habitually here during a lock-in, and after harder stuff, not always limited to alcohol.

He would spend a quarter of an hour, leave the car and walk the rest of the way. By doing that he could be home about 1.30. She must be asleep by then for sure. Donna slept easily and deeply. He would not wake her. The spare room was fine.

A bird was singing in the lane, up among the trees with the stretch of fields behind them; there was unbroken woodland on the other side, behind the house. Despite this nocturnal aria it was not a nightingale, though musical enough. A blackbird, very likely, but roused by what? The lane's few and isolated street-lamps had failed to come on tonight; often they did not work.

No lamps showed in the house. Occasionally Donna did turn them out, even in the hall and inside the glassed-in front door. Only a security bulb flared on therefore as he got near, as it did anyway for every fox, badger or neighbourhood cat.

Carver unlocked the entrances, using another three keys, here, one for the glass panel and two for the main door.

Having gained the inner doorway, he glanced out again, and noted the night staring back at him as the security bulb extinguished: the primal and unnegotiable darkness. Quietly he shut outer and inner doors.

Living sound sprang up without warning, not twenty feet away in the unlit enclosure.

For a moment Carver, if anyone could have seen, became an invisibly distended and sparkling electric wire of attention. But in another moment, just before the lightning strike came of all the hall lights bursting on together from a master switch, he had relaxed, shrunk down again into an uninterested traveller re-entering his home.

"Where the *fuck have you been*?" Donna screamed, standing between the main room and the hall, vivid with incandescent irritation and a sort of fear.

Carver looked at her.

"You know where I've been."

"*Do* I? *Where?*"

"At work, and then at the bloody dinner for the client afterwards. As I told you I'd probably have to be."

"Yes, *told* me. You *told* me. Do you know what fucking time it is?"

"Thirty-three minutes past one."

"You said – you *said* – if you were going to be later than midnight you would *call* me."

"No, Donna, I didn't say that."

"You *did*. You *did* – and then no call – and when I tried your mobile it's off – as it always *is* off when you're out–"

"No, Donna. Only I can't always get a signal or clear reception when I'm driving. You know that."

"I know so *much*, don't I? Not enough though. *Where have you been?* There *is* someone, isn't there? Some shitty bitch you're seeing – and I'm *pregnant*, Carver, I'm going to have your *baby*..."

Donna was crying. "Look," he said, "let's go and sit down. I've been held up by roadworks all the way. Let's have a drink..."

"I *can't* have a fucking *drink* – can I – I'm *fucking pregnant*..."

He returned her into the room, her unseen sparks of frustration and rage and sorrow flying off her – he could sense her own primitive electricity; in the half-light that now illumined everything, he could almost see the glitter of it. He organised her sitting on the couch. He went out to the kitchen and brought her back half a glass of white wine from the fridge. "It won't hurt you."

"It *will*. You *want* it to hurt me."

He sat beside her as her momentum ran down, (like the batteries he had visualised inside the doll-people between Trench Street and Holland Row). She sipped the drink, staring at the enormous, currently blank screen of the TV.

"You misunderstood what I said, Donna," he told her.

"I thought you'd been in an accident," she whimpered, "I thought you were dead."

When finally he had got her up to bed, helped her undress, and arranged the duvet over her, fetched her hot rosehip and camomile tea, tucked her in, he left her, with the bedside lamp on the lowest turn of the dimmer, like a difficult child scared of a monster under the bed. Presumably there would soon be two of those, two children, her and the child; maybe two monsters as well. As he passed the spare room on the way downstairs again, he abruptly registered unexpected proof of the intention of this.

On top of the double bed was spread a magazine. It demonstrated, in articles and garish photographs, how the changing of such a space might be accomplished: spare room to something suitable for a baby, a toddler, a kid of five to fifteen.

Below in the kitchen Carver turned off the light. He stood looking out into the garden behind the house. The night remained, still on watch and staring back. But, his eyes adjusting, he could see stars now, sharply bright as if with frost, between the trees of the wood beyond. He had a late start tomorrow, did not need to leave the house until twelve o'clock.

Carver placed his hand inside the pocket of his coat. He turned an object there loosely over and over, but not removing it. Tomorrow morning he would put the object out in the shed. With the other stuff. He could just see the shed's glimmer from here, faintly. It might only be starlight. One could never be certain, until closer. On nights of full moon you could not be sure at all.

Once a thief, always a thief. Heavy had pronounced the word *Theave* however, those countless ill-assorted years ago.

Carver went to sleep swiftly, but Donna woke him about 5 a.m., being sick in the second bathroom nearest the spare room, instead of in the more private ensuite. He listened, monitoring her now, but the noises soon stopped. She retreated to her bed again, slamming the door, with a strong healthy vandalistic crash.

Heavy said, in Carver's dream, "What's it mean, your name? Is it means to be you're a sculptoror, you know, *carving* things – or you carve stuff in stones for dead bodies. Or you're a butcher? You carve up meat?" *Shut up* Carver answered. Heavy screamed at him on a high metallic note. Carver undid his eyes, and the alarm clock said 9 a.m. He killed its siren and went to the second bathroom along the corridor. It was untouched, it seemed, by anything – even the towels were dry when he used them after the shower.

## Two

Silvia Dusa was standing by the fourth floor annex coffee machine, weeping. In the half-light through the blind and the tarpaulin that covered the window-glass also on the outside, her tears shone spectacularly, like mercury.

Carver halted. He said and did nothing for a moment.

But this was, in the most bizarre way, like a direct piece of continuity, following somehow instantly, (despite the interval of domestic attendance, sleep, waking, and the drive back to London) on that other sobbing outcry of Donna's last night. They resembled two takes in a movie. Only the actress had changed.

After a minute, "Can I help," he said. A neutral tone.

No condemnation, no kindness, no pulsing rush to know or assist.

"Go to hell," she hissed, and turned away.

He too turned instantly, but as he did so she said, in a low, crushed voice, "No – wait. Wait…"

Dusa was perhaps, ethnically, if only partly, of Italian origin. But she had a Spanish glaze to her, her hair thick and coal-black, eyes dark, and everything clad in a fawn, honeyed skin. Her hot temper was a by-word in the office. Now she cried mercury tears in a breath-lisping near noiselessness, but with the passion of a drama by Lorca.

Carver stood at the wall and waited. Obviously, coffee right now was out of the question. He had not really wanted coffee anyway. He did not either want this.

"I must talk to someone," Dusa muttered, angrily.

"Yes?" He spoke warily. One had to remember, almost all the social spaces were open to Security. You should be careful what, even innocently, you said, did, unless being careful might itself seem suspicious.

"It's my mother," said Dusa, now in a strangled tone. "She's ill."

"I'm sorry."

"No you're not. Only *I* am sorry. She is *my* mother, not yours." She shot him one of her larval glances, full of hate, loathing and despair. Some of them found this sexy. Carver wondered why. She pushed past him, her body brushing over his. (Neither was this at all arousing.) Her scent remained, it had a strange theme of musk and oranges; something smoky, another element acidulous and sharp.

He found she had put a piece of paper, half a page torn from a corner-shop notebook, into his hand. He made himself the unwanted coffee, still holding the paper, then walked off again, not looking at the note, neither concealing nor making anything of it, as if forgetting.

Back in his room he dropped the note on the table, left it there and sat before the screen, next activating and running through the current disc-file on Scar.

> *The Third Scar*: Remember, the curse always has to do with the third one. Take the plot from this point to the other two possibilities: 1) A mark on the left hand, present since childhood, or the left arm, perhaps more recent. And 2) The terrain allocated for any relevant meeting.

Carver cleared the screen. The second plot point was new. He would need to contact Latham, who today was on leave. As if catching sight of it and recollecting, he reached out and idly took up the paper note. Dusa's pencilled scribble was eccentric but readable. *Long's 12*. She had hardly chosen a secluded or private place then, which might indicate either extreme caution or the genuinely mundane. Carver was inclined in any case not to go, he had other things to do, and for all Dusa knew could have another unavoidable date, like the dinner the previous evening. In that event, however, he might as well visit Long's and lyingly explain to her before escaping.

He switched off the computer, got his jacket, and went along the corridor to the lift. Downstairs, BBS was back on duty. "Can I just check you, Mr Carver?"

Bugger Back-Scratcher made a thorough job of this, he always did with the male contingent. ("Gay as the Gordons," Latham said.) Last night though Bugger had not wanted to feel Carver over, which in a way had been lucky, as last night Carver had had the stolen object in his pocket. Then again, one could always make an excuse. The kind of things that would cause a problem – unauthorised cash, cards, files or weaponry – were not involved.

The sun was fully out again, shining down on Holland Row and its garlanded trees. A slender creeping stain of orange was after all just burning through the leaves, fairly subtle as yet, as in Silvia Dusa's perfume, and, just as Silvia Dusa maybe was, gathering speed and strength to pounce.

She was not inside the pub, a cramped and old-fashioned venue with nooks and crannies, so Carver walked round it once, to be sure, then out again. And *there* she was, by the doorway with her head arrogantly lifted.

"The park," she said.

"All right."

He wondered why he had acquiesced so quickly and pliantly. No doubt because of the traces of tears still under her eyes. You learnt, he thought, to behave in this way, or sometimes you did, less empathy and human decency than some type of social conditioning. Or was he only curious?

They – Westminster Council, ostensibly – were having something done along the paths, blocking them. Boards were laid out in order pedestrians could, after all, trample over the grass. Birds poured across in clutches, protesting yet, from force of habit, indifferent to the always-disturbing interference of mankind.

She did not speak for a while. At last she said, "We will sit here." A decree? But then, a hesitation: "Yes?"

"Yes. Why not."

They sat on a bench under the trees; a few leaves lay on the ground, for the path, just here, was unimpeded. A dull working rumble from some mechanical device came at measured, aggravating intervals.

"You see, Car," she used his office nickname, "I have – I've done something stupid."

A long, long gap, with three choruses of the rumbling machine.

He said, "You mean about your mother."

"No. This is *not* about my mother. Oh, she's ill. Who cares, the old bitch. I hate her, always I have, from seven years of age. This is something stupid I did, when not thinking clearly. I have – *given* something to... to someone."

*What?* was what most people would say, Carver thought. Instead he replied calmly, "You need to talk to Jack Stuart."

"No."

"Yes, Dusa. As quickly as you can." (He could not use her own circulating office nickname – it was the obvious one, with the letters ME attached at the front.) "You need to talk to him before four this afternoon."

She shook her head; or it was more that she shivered violently all over. "Then I'm dead. Aren't I? *Aren't* I, Car?"

"I don't know what you've done. *No*…" He looked directly at her, with a face of stone. "You don't tell *me*. You tell Jack Stuart."

"You've brought a Third Person," she said, staring at him, "you have recorded what I've…"

"No. I didn't think to bring one, Dusa. You said you were upset over your mother. I believed you."

"Shittalk. You believe *nobody*. *I* believe *nobody*."

"Believe *me*. *Stuart*. Before 4 p.m."

Carver stood up, and at once she had risen too and caught his arm. "You *bastard* – you *bastard!*" Her voice flared strongly now and piercing.

Along the board-path a couple of heads turned. He and she would look like two quarrelling lovers.

"Let go, Dusa," he said, his own voice deliberately dropping, and icy. But this did not work on her, as he had guessed it might not.

She leaned close, staring at him, her eyes grown huge, so he could see they were not black, but a sort of dark mulled bronze. "Carver – *help* me." It was not a plea, it was a demand.

They were struggling over some obscure mental abyss – was it fear? Anger? Or an irrational plan of hers, a kind of madness that, to her, seemed essential of execution, and that she must have dealt with by someone else. "Will you speak to Stuart *for* me, Carver?" Both her hands were on him now, flat on his chest, burning through the jacket and his shirt, immediate and familiar, unwanted.

"Stop this, Silvia," he said quite briskly. "*I* can't do anything. I'm not important in the office, you know. I'm no one. An errand boy. Speak to Latham if you're too scared to go straight to Stuart."

She dropped her hands, the way a cat would put down its paws, seeing no advantage and losing interest. Where their heat had been he felt the warmish day strike two cold blows.

Silvia Dusa lowered her eyes. She was not crying any more, not breathing fast, perhaps not really breathing.

"I shouldn't have come to you."

"No."

"I'll do what you say."

"It's the only way for you to sort this out, Silvia."

He thought, stop using her first name. It set up a fake intimacy that was useless and had no part here. It had served its purpose.

He turned and began to walk, without hurry or delay, away from her over the pathway, then the wobbly boards. He had an urge to look back once, hearing behind him a woman's running steps on the open grass. But it was not Dusa, too heavy for her, and the shoes were trainers. He saw he was quite correct when a big young woman presently passed him, and went thumping off through the park towards Horse Guards Road.

What had she done? Pointless to wonder even. Probably nothing much. Or else something vast and irredeemable. Did he care? He was unsure. His own reaction any way by now would be tangled up in her attempted involvement of him, and the general repercussions any inane or insane mistake could always throw up for everyone, whether let in on the error or not.

That evening he left the car stabled at the office – there had indeed been a slight fault with the engine – he should no doubt not have risked coming back into London with it that morning, but it would often allow you a couple of hours grace before at last giving out. He took the train down as far as Lynchoak. He was meeting Latham in a steakhouse off the Maidstone Road.

"Weird bloody names these villages have round here," said Latham, as they sat drinking red wine, the meal ordered; it was not yet 8 p.m. "*Lynch*oak – a hanging tree, one assumes. Christ. And that by-way back there near the motorway. Tokyo Lane? *Tokyo* – I ask you."

"Yes," said Carver.

His mind had skewed abruptly over, as it kept on doing, to the tussle with Dusa earlier. He could still, now and then, feel the heat of her two hands on his chest, and the later cold patches that followed, as if she had leeched something out of him to keep her warm for the winter to come.

"You've got some bloody weird places near *you*, haven't you, Car. What is it – Bee Church."

"Beechurst."

"Oh, I see. God knows," said Latham, chomping his way along a piece of garlic bread with cheese and evident enjoyment.

He liked, Latham, what he called "Plebfood" – pizza, steak, chips ice-cream. "*Bee*–churst," he repeated, reflectively. "Be cursed..."

The waiter came to refill their glasses. The first bottle was done and Latham ordered a second. Driving would not be a hurdle, for either of them. "What did you think of the new script?" Latham asked. His face, a minute before sanguine and relaxed, had put on a lizard-like, *snake*-like concentration, emotionless but entirely focussed.

"It doesn't make much sense," said Carver.

"No," mused Latham. "What I thought too. But with that set of directors – what can you expect." And the greedy mask popped back.

Their speech followed its formulas, but no one could overhear. Not only obscured by the canned music but the turgid scrambled egg of other voices and cutlery. Besides that, the two recording/listening devices (Third Persons), Carver's and Latham's, were both on reverse, creating a mostly inaudible but interfering flit and flux of white noise. Enough to muddle most eavesdroppers whether human or electronic.

The meal came, the steaks – Latham's double – with fries, salads and various dips.

Carver had considered if Latham would ask him anything about Dusa's outburst in the park. Did they know? You assumed they always must, to some extent. Particularly if she had done what Carver warned her she must, and gone to Jack Stuart to confess. But Latham's main concern seemed to be to eat.

"Know what there's a whole lot of round here?" Latham asked as he studied the dessert menu. "Full of llamas."

It had been autumn then too, but the leaves had turned and many were down, coating the pavements of the side streets in crisply rustling tides that the wind blew high or low.

He was walking home from school, one of the first schools, when he was about eight and still bothered with lessons. He was alone, as he usually was. A solitary child, for his own assorted and unanalysed reasons.

He paused outside the shop that had one window all sweets, to look in. Everything was in glamorous reds and purples tinselled gold and silver. The wrappers alone looked eatable. And some had free gifts with them – model figures that moved.

The door flew wide and someone stamped out in a hurry, some

oldishly grown-up woman, who knocked against him and snapped "Watch out, can't you?" as though he, not she, had done the barging.

His face did not alter. He was used generally to a bad press. It never occurred to him that in ten years time he would be taller and stronger than she, and she ten years older. It would take Heavy, who he would meet when he, Carver, was eleven, to come out with funny speculations like that.

Carver, once the angry woman was gone, walked on slowly up the road, passing the Co-Op and the greengrocers, and the 'Lovely' Laundrette. He was in no hurry. It was getting on towards five o'clock, but that would make no difference. No one would be home, unless his father was, but he as a rule would be out again by this time of day.

The sun was dipping, going west, smoky and golden as if chocolate foil had been pinned up there then fumed with smoke.

Carver turned the corner and walked up the hill where the bigger houses stood, with proper gardens, and you had enough spilled leaves to scuff.

He was passing one of the low long brick walls that guarded the posh front patches of trees, lawns and paving, when a man pulled up at the curb in a dark blue shiny car that Carver knew was a BMW. The man immediately threw open the car door, sprang out, slammed the door shut, rushed across Carver's path and up the gravel to the front door of the house. This too opened before him, as if anticipating his wishes. Nor did it close at his back.

Such an extreme example of irrationally adult bossy speed and urgency had arrested Carver. He stood idling on the pavement, possibly waiting, with unconscious prudence, for the crazy man to express-train out again and dive back in the car.

But minutes passed, or Carver reckoned they were minutes, ticking off there in his mind, and nothing happened. Natural boredom then perhaps next made him both remain where he was – but also glance in at the car window. On the front passenger seat was a large cardboard carton, undone at the top. Inside smouldered the smoky gold of late afternoon sky and cutting-edges of deep dark red and indigo.

Chocolate bars. The box – he peered closer – was filled with them, some of popular well-known makes, and others more exotic, at least to Carver. Yet all of them beaming there, radiant with sweetness and joy.

The car door had been left unlocked. The man, all hysterical adult hurry, nearly knocking the boy over in a blind rush to get into the house, had not stopped to secure anything.

Maybe Carver thought he only opened the car door in order to smell the honey of the chocolate, which, the door once opened, he could. He leaned into the car, maybe also simply further to take pleasure in the smell. Did he even reach out and snatch up two of the topmost bars solely to gaze at them, inhale them, for a few precious seconds longer?

When the human express returned to his vehicle, about nine minutes after desertion, it was apparently just as he had left it, door unlocked but closed, the cardboard box bulging with its goodies, (most of them) and seeming, to a careless eye, untouched.

A woman waved the man and the car off as they shot away up the steep road.

Carver had already been climbing up it, and he did not bother to look round. He kept the chocolate close in his two jacket pockets, only occasionally reaching in to skim its metallically slippery papered surfaces.

He hid the prize in 'his' corner of the box room, where his mother slept on the narrow bed, and he on the narrower put-you-up under the window.

After two more days he secretly ate one of the bars. But then, not the second bar. He never ate that. Only *kept* it.

The excitement and contained exultation of the theft he would, when he was in his teens, and had undergone his first full sexual experience, technically equate with the sexual act.

Not in type, or extent of pleasure, that was, but in the straight-forward subterfuge, the ultimate extraordinary meant-to-be ease, this epilogue of slight embarrassment – potential danger – diluted almost shame. (The sense of achievement too, of *finding out*.)

As if – though in each case a different one – he had fallen through a loose floorboard into a treasure cave. It was all *there*. All available. Not just accessible cars then, or chaste denial. The world too had magic doorways. And you had to, of course you did, undo them, and then undo them again.

"I'm not kidding," Latham resumed, as he tucked into the Choc-O-Four with raspberry sauce. "I saw an entire herd of white ones.

And later two or three brown and white."

Carver said, "Yes, I think I have, once or twice."

"What do they breed them for? Milk?"

"I don't know."

"Kids' rides, probably. Or pulling a carriage in someone's stately grounds."

Lamas. Latham seemed to have more to say about lamas than Scar. Was Latham trying something out on Carver, because of Silvia Dusa, trying to see if Carver would mention her, or debate aloud if he himself should inform Stuart? On the other hand one deduced they were always testing, *trying* you. Even Latham's even more than usual greed tonight might be some sort of test of Carver's reactions.

Latham had cleared his plate – his second dessert – drained his glass, and now squinted at his Rolex. "Getting on for ten. My car'll be along in a minute. Got to make Canterbury before lights out. God, bloody bore, can't stand Chaucer, can you? But better than the Bard, I suppose. Probably sleep this off on the way. Well..." He rose, reached across and patted Carver on the shoulder, like an amiable uncle with a nephew several times removed. "Give that file another check, Carver, by the way The old method, yeah? Might yield results."

"Yes, of course. Good night, Mr Latham. Good journey."

"Oh, I always look on the sunny side. Like that old fart in the poem, what is it? Lying in the gutter but wiping his arse on the stars. That's the one."

He did not look, or enunciate, as if the two bottles of red wine, the bulk of which he had consumed, had affected him, but sometimes he came out with oddities after a few drinks. The bill had already been paid, and he sauntered to the glass doors, observing the night outside in an amused, innocuous way. The chauffeured car was already swimming on to the forecourt.

Carver had another fifteen minutes to wait for his, which would appear like an ordinary cab, the driver dressed in denim and ponytail.

Had she done it? Carver thought. Told Stuart?

Sometimes these rogue events took place; it never really worked, to re-examine them too much. Instead he thought of Donna, what emotion she would be dressed in tonight, and where, sleeping or awake, she would be lying in wait for him.

When he reached and entered the house, the lower hall and kitchen were lit up, and above, the hall lamps were on, but dimmed down.

The main bedroom he had seen from outside was in darkness, and he guessed, and would later note, the door was shut.

Carver made himself another coffee. It never kept him awake, though other things might do that.

In the kitchen, having put out the lights, he sat, staring down through the garden. They were quite high, those walls, six and a half feet. Who would have thought it, that skinny dark-haired kid who stole the chocolate bars by the posh house with the low outer wall. Now, his own walls, all his. And enough chocolate in the fridge – even if it was for Donna – to *coat* those walls with. The night was overcast by huge troop-movements of cloud, that were slowly rolling their tanks in from the southeast. From in here you could not see the lights of the village, the flutter of late TV and computer screens. The woods took over out there, at the garden's end, and after that swallowed up the lane, just Robby Johnston's cottage netted in them, and tied to them by ropes of ivy and chains of unlopped briar. ("Only things that keep the old place standing," said Johnston.) Carver's garden – he supposed he must call it 'his' – had no substance to it in the dark. Or it was *all* substance, the three smaller trees and the huge old pear, the weedy lawn, and the benches Donna had bought in a fit of gardenicity, everything amalgamated and amorphous. But at the garden's far end, almost invisible, and then more visible, and more, the faint shimmer of greenish-bluish illumination, trapped there, or *poised* there, like a living entity. And casting out from itself those slender streaks, to paint the trunks of the birch trees beyond the wall.

The shed.

Having crossed the cloud-blackened nocturnal garden, passed between the fruit trees, stepped by or over the bushes, he reached the rectangular concreted space left for a shed, where the shed, ready-constructed, had, a while back, been set. Parked and anchored, it was taller, longer and more wide than most such outbuildings; reinforced and fully weather-proofed. Two stone steps elevated before the middle door, which, once unlocked, opened inward.

There were three doors, each with a window, and four other windows between and to either side. In the strange glow of these seven front-facing panes, one could make out easily the flat black roof, the wooden walls that, by night and by glow were a greenish, bluish, greyish brown. The window-glass imperviously shone. Inside the shed, a sort of snow seemed to have fallen, and then formed into slopes, mounds, *things* which resembled other things, but were not such other things.

Carver mounted the steps and undid the shed's central door. It required three keys.

He went inside and the door was shut and locked three times.

The interior of the shed, seen still from outside, did not exactly darken then – yet a kind of obscuration fell there. Carver's shadow, perhaps.

Or only one more vagary of the advancing enemy cloud.

## THREE

During the last three days of that schedule Carver left his car at the office and took the train into London either from Lynchoak or Maidstone, reaching the stations and coming back by cab.

On Thursday evening he drove himself back in the repaired car, but using another, more time-consuming route, which sent him via Croydon.

It did not matter in the least about Donna's opinion of return times, since she was no longer at the house.

She had said, quietly, the morning after his dinner with Latham, that she thought she would go over and see her mother for a week. She had done this now and then in the past. There was no reason she should not, and the journey was hardly taxing, taking only about three quarters of an hour. Donna did not drive of course, but Maggie did, and came to pick her up on the arranged evening.

Carver had got home early enough to see the departure. Donna seemed fine, and Maggie, as ever, glamorous and optimistic, in her sensibly-dieted and reasonably self-indulgent fifty-year-old way. Not cabbing, she had brought her car. He had wondered if Maggie would, once Donna was safely installed in the bold red vessel, whisk back to have a last word with him. Something friendly and casual, but also some version of a last-minute attentive scrutiny of his reactions, his mood. Maggie was always very civil to Carver, somewhat over-appreciative, and slightly flirtatious in a carefully non-predatory way. It was her set method of dealing with men, he thought; it had paid off in her own personal relationships. However, Maggie simply waved, and then drove away.

No mention had been made by Maggie, nor by Donna, of a mooted pregnancy. He had been aware that Donna, since the prior dramatic demonstration, had stopped vomiting. Or at least, she had stopped doing so audibly when he was in the house. The magazine on kid-suitable room-changing had also gone.

After the departure, and the dark having fully settled on the lane, a film of silence formed. It was only the silence of the modern English countryside and imbued by distant blurs of sound – traffic far off, the passage of planes, unspecified electronic, or other, outlying mechanisms. Nevertheless.

Nevertheless.

Next morning, routinely, he tried the games key Icon on his iPhone. It said: *Clue up: One down*. Carver had seen this message a handful of times, and in many forms, during his service with Mantik. Seldom without a twist of the gut. He waited a moment before touching the screen for the *2nd Clue*. Which read: *Always Justified Marketable Value*.

Carver struck the clue back into nothingness.

Working from the current code-series, *Always Justified Marketable Value* gave him the initials S.D.

He switched on all the house radios, and the kitchen TV and the enormous TV in the front room, and caught the various news bulletins through the morning, across different channels. Nothing relevant was mentioned. Almost certainly it would not be or at least not yet.

Carver was more than glad now Donna was not in the house. He paced about, not properly thinking, trying to remember, mentally to order things.

At last he went up to what Donna called his 'playroom', across the landing from the spare bedroom. There was only one lock, but this was 'faulty'. It would only ever let Carver in.

His second phone was where he always left it, ready-charged.

"Yes, Carver," said Latham's voice, in a rich, mournfully appropriate tone. Carver had not needed to speak. "Better come in. We all need to look at the new deal, don't we? About six, OK?"

She had been missing, or at least not visible to him, since they separated in the park. He had noted her absence, inevitably, from the day after his dinner of misquotes, steak and lamas with Latham. But people were not always at the building in Whitehall. There were three other Mantik venues alone, subsidiaries, to which you might get sent at twenty minutes notice, or less. He had been *aware*, therefore, *alert*, but concluded that doubtless his was an overreaction, and as such he had mostly quashed it.

As he drove into London against the outrush of early escapee evening traffic, he kept feeling again the burning warmth of her tawny hands against his chest, and the pallor of the cold patches that seemed, each time, to replace them.

Silvia Dusa, (S.D.). Had he even taken her seriously?

No? Decidedly no. If yes, then undeniably he should and would have gone to Stuart – not, obviously, in her company, or on her behalf, but in order to protect whatever project she might, however slightly and inadvertently, have jeopardised. And partly to protect and cover himself, it went without saying, since she had hinted at her mistake to him. To stay dumb was to be complicitous with the adversary, whatever was out there that must be worked against.

What had she said? He had been trying all morning, after seeing that One Down clue, to recall precisely.

*"I have done something stupid... I have given something to someone."*

*Was* that what she had said? Her actual words? He had not, as she had accused him of doing, recorded their dialogue. He had had no grounds, surely, to feel that might be necessary.

The weather had stayed stormy and overcast. London began to loom up, a mass of thickly dark, and yet already luridly lighted shapes. The river lay like polished lead under its welter of neon and lasers. Ten or so years ago it had resembled a Science Fiction city, as New York had done years before that. But terror and catastrophe had fractured New York's architectural mountains, while the exhaustion of financial downfall was putting out London's inner fires.

Ken Lesley was tonight's Reception. His office nickname was, predictably, *Kill*, but several, Carver included, knew him as "Ken".

He checked Carver's ID fleetly, they exchanged a taciturn acknowledgement, and Carver took the lift to the fifth floor.

"Death occurred between approximately 11 and 12 p.m. on the

date given. The body was found about 6 a.m. the following morning, when a cleaner went into the lavatory. The pub is a quiet one, with a steady inflow of generally regular customers. Dusa was noticed on the previous evening, being a stranger, and also attractive. No one saw her leave since she did *not* leave, at least in any physical way. Usually, they say, the facilities are checked just before, and again just after the pub doors are shut for the night. But were not on this particular occasion. One senses that happens quite often. The means was a man's razor blade stuck into a cork – the old-fashioned sort of cork that isn't plastic. Dusa appears to have cut the veins of her left wrist lengthways, rather than across or diagonally. It's the most efficient method, and it worked, but not many people can manage it; it takes a steady hand. Nor were there any preliminary 'practice' cuts. She had drunk, according to the bar staff, only two glasses of red wine, house variety, nothing special, which she bought directly from the bar. She was on her own. If she was waiting for anyone, no one showed up. The bar people thought, in fact, she had left by the garden exit – the garden is kept open for smokers even if the weather is unsettled. The cleaner who found the body has been unwell since then, and her questioning has been minimal. No helpful DNA or other identification seems to be in the picture. No alien substances were found in Dusa's stomach. No other significant marks were on her body. The cork carries evidence only of Dusa's own handling. She did not find the cork at the pub, and seems to have brought the weapon with her, ready-assembled. At present, there we have all the information ceded to us."

Latham's voice stopped. (It had been his bleak voice, the one he used for such, and similar, announcements.)

Herons spoke: "Who did it?"

Latham shrugged, "We have no idea. Unless just possibly it *was* Dusa herself."

"Why?" That came from Ireland, smoking his fifth cigarette in the corner. Unlike every pub and office in England, this room had no smoking ban.

"*Why* is the thing we want to learn, of course," said Latham flatly. "Why, and if not, *who*. But there's very little about her on record, beyond the obvious profile-monitoring we all undergo. Read her file. It is now available to everybody present here."

"What's next, then?" asked Herons.

"Nothing yet. We do our homework. We keep our heads down and antennae up. Be ready. This is a Level Blue."

"So *low*?" Herons seemed affronted.

"So far. But it might go up to a Green tomorrow."

They murmured.

Carver had risen to leave the room with the rest, but Latham directed at him a smile and the smallest shake of his head. Carver therefore turned back, pretending to select a pen from the cluster on the table.

Latham, as he walked past, muttered, "Give it a couple of minutes, then drop by my room, will you?"

Carver did as Latham said. There were frequently clandestine signals it was necessary to follow. He wondered what Latham would want him to do and was glad again that Donna was away from the house. Under the circumstances the task might be complex and mean more hours to put in, and though she was used to what she called his extra-curricular outings, if she was still unsettled it might have caused problems. He wondered if Dusa had had relatives, apart from the mother, who must now be informed of her death, and if so who would see to it, the normal authorities, or Mantik. This job would not fall to him at least.

When he reached Latham's room, (a miniature of Stuart's on the floor above), the lights were lowered to a sociable level, and the vodka and glasses had broken free of the cupboard. Outside, beyond the blinds and the drawn curtains, an innovation Latham preferred, tarpaulins flapped and scaffolding rattled in a thickly rising wind.

"Sorry to drag you in on your R and R, Carver, but it seemed best."

"That's fine, Mr Latham."

"Good, good. Take a drink, yes, go on, we can sort out your travel arrangements in a minute, no worries. I think we owe you a cab home."

Carver poured the vodka and drank a meagre sip. What did Latham want? Something, plainly, that he meant to build up to.

"Take a seat. Yes, that's it. Just something I want to play over with you. I suppose you knew Silvia a little, did you?"

Carver said, "Not really."

"Just used to meet her in the corridor, yes? Yes. But the odd exchange of chat, I expect?"

"No, Mr Latham."

"That's the trouble, you see. That's just what everyone says. Kept to herself. And a bad temper. Typical sulky Latin, that's Herons' version. But I think he tried to get under her duvet."

Carver said nothing. Herons liked to imply he could get under most female duvets; Latham should be well-enough educated in such facts not to mention their veracity or falseness.

"So she was a social mystery, then," said Latham, and his voice, which had become the plum-jam version, was sticky now with regret. "Bloody shit of a way for a girl like that to go. Not even thirty yet. Clearly something weighing on her mind, wouldn't you think? Some deep problem. And never spoke to anyone. Felt she couldn't trust them."

*He knows.* Carver took another nearly non-existent nip of the vodka, scarcely more than a taste of its fumes. *He knows she approached me.*

"Well any way, Carver," said Latham, downing his own generous glass with a deliberately finalising flourish, "before I let you go, just one last thing. I'd just like you to listen to something for me."

As Latham touched the sound control button, and the yellow light winked on, Carver, if quite incoherently, somehow knew also what was coming. Not the perhaps predictable thing, but the nonsensical one; it was surreal and absurd, unbelievable, and could not happen.

Then out of the 3P disc-player he heard Silvia Dusa's voice, not yet thirty, let alone forty. "You see, Car," she said as she had on the bench under the trees, "I have – I've done something stupid." And behind her voice, if more muffled now, the intermittent rumbling of the council contraption relining the paths .

The gap which followed was not, he thought, as long as it had seemed to be at the time. But there – in it as before, he could count the three choruses of the machine.

And then his own voice: "You mean about your mother."

Carver glanced at Latham. But Latham sat listening, relaxed yet intent, his chin on his hand and the empty glass, of very polished crystal, resting carefully to one side. He might have been concentrating on a world class radio play, one he had pencilled in, as he might have said, because it was by a writer he greatly liked, or about a subject that intrigued him.

Silvia Dusa had done what she had accused Carver of doing. She had taken out with her, and then activated, a 3P – a Third Person – the infallible Mantik recording device which, allegedly, could even pick up conversation through the rush of running water or a loudly played stereo.

Dusa was spitting out her dislike of the mother now, her mother's irrelevance, filial fear or love, in this case, inapplicable. And then she said, as before, "...when not thinking clearly. I have – *given* something to... someone."

And now Carver would calmly say, as *he* had done, "You need to talk to Jack Stuart,"

But instead Carver said something else.

Carver said: "All right. You'd better tell me, then."

And after another pause, "Come on, Silvia. You wouldn't have spoken to me in the first place, would you, if you weren't going to confide. Felt you had to. So let's get on with it, shall we? And I'll see what I can do."

## Four

"You're too sure. It can't be so straightforward. How could it be? No – I don't. I can't. I shouldn't have spoken. No. I – am sorry, I apologise. It was nothing,"

"Don't be ridiculous, Silvia. It's obviously something."

"Nothing. No. I was mistaken, Car."

"You can't go back on it now." (He heard the man who was him, confident and persuasive, with a numbed aversion that did not amount to doubt). "Simply tell me the rest. Oh come on, we've all done unwise things, from time to time. It happens. We can sort it out, you and I."

"No. I see now, I must go to Jack Stuart—"

"Oh God, Silvia, do you *really* think that?" (The man – himself – gently laughed.) "*Stuart*? He'll hang you. He is very able, at that."

And then the rising note of purely physical alarm in her voice, "Let me *go*. Let *go* of me—" And a kind of scuffling quite discernible over the on-off rumble of the path repairs. A bird gave a shrill alarm call, even its retreating wings were to be heard. And then she hissed like a cat, or one of those snakes the nicknamers said she hid in her black hair.

Both of them were breathing quickly, as if they had been

running together, or hungrily kissing, or having sex. And then the disc roared into a huge chasm of silence, and nothing else rose from it. It had, maybe, offered up enough.

Although, of course, the sounds – machine, bird, voices, breath – went on playing. Replaying.

"We're almost there, Mr Carver. There's the church – houses – and the pub. The Bell, isn't it?"

"All right. You can let me out here."

"Er, Mr Latham said all the way to your door, Mr Carver."

"My partner," Carver said, "is ill. The noise of the car will disturb her."

"Well, Mr Carver, if it comes to that, I expect you will, too, when you go in – can't avoid it. And it's a bloody windy night. Temperature's dropped to 9. No, I'll drop you off up the lane, by your house. Nice and snug."

What did the Mantik cabby think Carver would do? Leap out and sprint for the woods? Vanish in the vast wild terrain that so briefly surrounded this English suburban village? He could do it, anyway, surely, once the cab had gone.

"Yes. OK."

And "Let me *go*," insisted the panting, struggling Dusa-voice in his skull. "Let *go* of me…"

"The disc's been tampered with, Mr Latham."

"Oh, come on, now, Carver. Don't be a twat. 3P's can't be fiddled about with. That's the whole point of them. They can be used for all kinds of legit recording or audio surveillance, or blocking of same. But once they have the record, that is it. The old days of course were different. As they say, that was *then*."

"I didn't speak to her the way I seem to be speaking on the disc."

Latham, non-vocal, pursed his lips.

"I told her myself to go to Jack Stuart at once. I said I couldn't help, *she* had to see to it."

"How odd," said Latham, in a quick, flighty, bantering way. "I wonder what it was she *did* though. Or did she let you in on it, Carver? After she turned the 3P off – or whatever happened to it. It sounded to me rather as if it had been dropped. But then she must just have grabbed it, mustn't she, and run for cover. Was that it? Frustrating. It must have been. Last straw. What you were doing, you were playing her along, weren't you, trying to tease it out of her. I can quite see that. Then you could just have gone straight to Stuart yourself and spilled the full Heinz. Yes?"

"No," Carver said stonily. He stared at Latham, into Latham's pouchy clever eyes. "However that disc was prepared – sampling, a backtrack from the park and then a voice mimic for me, perhaps – I didn't say anything about her telling me, and my helping her out. I actively *discouraged* that. I told her <u>not</u> to tell me, to tell only Stuart, and as quickly as she could. Or if she couldn't face him, go to you."

"Me."

"Yes."

"Well," Latham's eyelids had gradually folded to half-closed, as Carver had seen them do now and then over a drink, a steak, an ice-cream. "It's an odd one, isn't it? What was it you suggested? And actor mimicking your voice? That's a rare thought. Normally detectible. And why? The disc," Latham added softly, "was found in her bag, on the floor of the Ladies. Luckily the thing was in its casing, so the blood didn't get into it. It could have been cleaned up. But mucky."

Carver had stopped talking. Latham did not believe him.

Understandably. Third Persons *were* reckoned impervious virtually to anything, no blood, no human meddling could eliminate or distort their message. The very latest backroom science. And so, Carver was lying.

Did Latham therefore think Carver, having failed to get in on whatever tempting treachery or idiocy Silvia Dusa had undertaken, had later killed her? How had he done *that*, then? There were no drugs in her system or marks elsewhere on her body. She had not been, presumably, blind drunk. So Carver, perhaps sneaking in from the smoker's garden, had told her to sit back on the loo floor, put on plastic gloves, and then neatly cut her wrist vein lengthways, without an objection, or a single razorous slip.

He imagined Latham would have to detain him, no doubt leaving him first to stew, then suggesting Carver sleep over on the sixth floor, where there were a series of cell-like bedrooms, used for the nocturnal sojourns of those on duty, on watch, exhausted, or held in mild-mannered custody.

But Latham merely suggested they go down to the foyer-hall, where Latham could access transport, and Ken could arrange for

Carver another fake cab.

"Oh, just one last thing perhaps I ought to show you," Latham remarked in a throwaway style, as they descended to the third floor. The lift, already programmed, halted. Carver noted Latham, as Jack Stuart was inclined to, seemed to be repeating a lot of the same words – *just*, *last*. Did it mean something? Or was it *just* one *last* gambit to induce, (or allay?) unease?

They walked into one of the small side rooms. Latham hit the lights and woke the automatic on the computer. The large screen brightened, and without pause flooded up the static drowned image of a dead woman on a mortuary slab. Dusa, naturally.

How young, how agonisingly un-grownup she looked. No, she was not in her forties. This was a well-developed teenager, sixteen, eighteen, perhaps. And how dead.

It was a fact some corpses, for by now Carver had been shown, both on screen and in photographs, several, could look startlingly youthful. But in converse cases it went the other way – a sixty-year-old boy who had died of rat poison at the age of twelve; a hag of seven left pristine but empty by the side-blast of a bomb. They always shocked you. But the shock altered. After the very first, for Carver, the impact was lessened. Not in any trite or pragmatic way. More as if some shield was now flung up before and about him in the very second his brain accepted what his eyes revealed.

She had been beautiful, it was undeniable, Silvia Dusa. Decently covered by a sheet, needing only her face and her left arm and wrist to be displayed, yet the contours, valleys and soft full mounds of her body were explicit. Her black hair, thick and vibrant enough still to have retained, in those moments of visual capture, its luxuriance and scope, lay under her face, throat and shoulders, the perfect backdrop: ebony under honey.

"A waste," said Latham. "A *true* waste. Still a virgin." He spoke the leery words respectfully and with regret. "A damned bloody shame."

Acting all this, one assumed. He would be studying Carver's reactions.

Carver said, emotionless yet grave, "What about her mother?"

"Oh that. She didn't have one. That is, the woman died years ago – '90's, 80's. In Venice, I believe. *Death In Venice*. Just goes to show."

They stayed motionless and dumb before the icon of dead Silvia for another few minutes. And reluctantly, but clinically, Carver took in the drained wrist, with its rucked, red-black lesion. The skin, the opened vein, seemed strangely frozen, a sort of meaty-ice had formed on and out of them.

"Let's see about cars," said Latham.

The screen sank through violet, the overhead lights through scarlet, to oblivion.

Outside the wind kicked at the scaffolding. Like some giant hell-harp its poles and joints twanged and plinged in impotent answering rage.

Carver made coffee in the kitchen of his house. The fake cab was still parked, ticking and unlit, outside in the lane, and exacerbating the security light. When Carver turned off the downstairs house lights, the cab eventually roused itself and drove smoothly off. He suspected it might nose back again later, as if cruising, but did not bother with checking whether it checked on him.

When next Carver drove himself, it went without saying, he could expect to be tailed. But that could happen anyway, at any time. Mantik took care.

Why had he been let go?

Why not, if they thought he really was innocent, had just been rather naive in attempting to lure the facts of Dusa's misdemeanour out of her – only wanting thereby to get her into bed.

(A virgin. That had thrown him. More than his mistake on her age.)

They would certainly have him back for an in-depth meeting, however. He could not evade that. He had never had to undergo anything really serious in that line. But now he would.

He could not fathom what had happened with the Third Person, or the voice that was his own yet was <u>not</u> his at all.

It was all a game though, in its way. Everything. What was the Whitehall Mantik office's nickname for its staff? The *Enemies*. Which could indicate, demonstrably, they were the enemies of designated adversaries, or of increepers and traitors, but too of each other, *friendly* enemies in that scenario – but all en garde, one against another. Ready at any time to duel, to stitch up, to outwit and condemn. To punish.

Carver went upstairs. It was late. Despite Donna's absence he would not sleep in the main bedroom. From the spare room he could, at an angle, glimpse the faint blue-green sheen reflecting on the birch trees. The leaves were falling, thinner, routed by the wind, which now had sunk. The window-glass felt cold to the touch, despite the radiator below.

Was that the cab-car cruising back outside? Probably.

He went to bed in the dark, and dropped down into the fog of sleep, seeing, as he did so, where a dead woman lay on a grey bare slab, but he only floated past her, a swimmer deep in the lagoon, to the thick, soft mud of unconsciousness below.

Andy walked out of Woolworths with the packet of toffees he had bought, the striped sort his mother liked, and a tube of five coloured pencils in one of his jacket pockets. In the other pocket was a small assortment of Woolworths delicacies, a rubber, two biros – one blue and one red – a tiny gold action figure in a plastic pouch, and a lipstick in a shade he believed was called *Firebrand*. This last was also for his mother, and also bought.

It was her birthday on Tuesday. He had no idea if she would like the lipstick, but she always effusively said how lovely and thoughtful it was of him to save up for a present for her from what she called his 'dole' – the money, mostly in coins, she gave him when she could.

Andy knew his mother, whose name was Sara, was not much interested in him. She had *lost* interest when she and he got away from her boyfriend, his father, and the bullying and physical violence ended. Not having to protect Andy anymore, however ineffectually, seemed to turn off all maternal connection for Sara. But he had never been close to her, or so it seemed to him, or would have done had he properly considered it. He had never been close to anyone, except in the physical proximity way – hugged and smothered, or thumped about, or – now – thumping in turn, as Andy had been doing not long before, with Iain Cox. Cox was one of the school bullies. One or two years older than Andy, thickset and thin-eyed, he liked to take the piss, and/or take away your possessions. So Andy had used a couple of techniques he had learned from watching his father with one of his own weaker male cronies. Grabbing and twisting Cox's balls, Andy had brought him down, then knelt on his curled-over body, pummelling his thick-thin face until Cox was whimpering. Andy, by now, did not often attend school. Cox had been unlucky, and definitely wrong in his choice of victim.

Andy turned up the long house-lined road that led away from the shops, and towards the station. You could get to London in just over half an hour from there. Andy had done it. But he would not be doing it today. He wanted to go home and watch the TV horror film he had got from Video Rodeo at the weekend. He might also play with the golden action figure. He was not sure he was not already too old for such a toy. At just on eleven it was difficult to judge sometimes. Not that Andy would have put it in that way.

Starting up the station road, Andy realised, belatedly, somebody was on his tail.

Cox? It seemed very unlikely. Without needing hospitalisation, Cox had still been in a mess.

Andy set his mind, his ears, his other senses, to suss out who it was that was moving along, about two garden-wall lengths behind him.

Not the Law, he was pretty certain of that. The Law would anyway have got hold of him before this. "Thieving, eh? Think you made it? You didn't. Right, we need to have a word."

Andy shoved the improvised dialogue out of his brain. He had no real idea what a cop would say, because Andy had never been apprehended by one, let alone a store guard, or any of the shop cameras. His improv came from some old film he had seen, probably, a feature long out of modern date. No, this follower was of another sort— Abruptly the latening sun cast down a shadow on the nearest stretch of wall. It looked most like a huge, humanesque toad. That was simple then. It was Heavy.

Heavy, about Andy's own age, had arrived at the school when Andy was already often going missing, and Andy had not seen much of him. But he knew the gist of Heavy, including why he had been allotted the name. Heavy was ungainly and fat. But some current policy had, it seemed, said no one must be called *fat* now. They were *heavy*. So, the fat kid of about eleven years of age got that nickname. Which he seemed not to mind, barely to notice as mockery and insult. Whatever his given name was, which Andy did not know, perhaps Heavy preferred *Heavy* to it.

Andy turned suddenly. He planted himself and glared straight into Heavy's bulbous eyes.

"*What do you want?*"

"Oh, just," said Heavy, and smiled. He was like the specialised

Idiot you sometimes saw in old films too, Charlie Laughton swinging on a bell, or someone.

"Fuck off," said Andy.

Heavy did not grimace or grin. Did not cringe or brace himself. Did nothing let alone go.

"You are a fucking cretin," said Andy.

At that moment a big ginger cat leapt up on the wall, and Heavy immediately transferred all his attention to it.

Andy should have taken the opportunity to move on, but something odd arrested him. It was Heavy's *look*, his way of reaching out and touching the cat – abruptly and weirdly graceful, lavish, full of – of intelligent concentration and a type of – what? What was it? *Kindness..?*

Andy stared, knowing he should go at once.

But when Heavy moved back round again, smiling and still half watching the cat, as if it were the most fascinating *sight* for miles, Andy did *not* go. And when the cat began to wash itself, Andy remarked, "See, even the cat can't fucking stick you. It wants to wash you off it."

"Oh, no," said Heavy's soft turgid somehow browsing voice, "no, they do that when they do like you. To get your scent in their mouvfs and over them, and taste you and be remembering."

"You've got shit for brains," said Andy. "Who told *that* shit?"

"My moth–er." He mispronounced some things, Heavy, curious ways. And he said 'mother' as if she were a flying insect: *moth*-ah.

"Your mother's a cunt."

Heavy looked back at him. He was still quietly smiling, unphased, happy. "She *isn't* a cund. But she's *got* a cund. All women do. Like we have pricks."

"Go to hell," said Andy, lamely, he thought. And took off up the road at a rate of knots, leaving Heavy far behind – if he had even reckoned to follow – just as if Heavy were the bully and Andy the weak misfitted coward.

But he had the stuff from Woolworths. And he had the X–film. And Cox had perhaps lost a tooth. Not too bad for an hour's work.

As a rule a film could not be on the cards. But his mother would be out late tonight. She was cleaning the big Kirkpatrick house, six in the evening until about 11 p.m., while the happy owners were off getting rat-arsed. So he could easily watch the film before she returned. He had taken it the usual way. He had a modus operandi, (he knew the term for it), for each and all his thefts. All were slightly, or very, different. His technique here too had never let him down. Part of the secret was, he had found, in casualness. He could *act* casualness, as he could act quite a few states of mind and body, had learned this, perhaps, as he had how to fight dirtily and to effect, watching others.

When he reached home, a small flat which had been provided for Sara and himself over an electrical shop, once they had got away, he climbed up the iron staircase and let himself in. There was a front room and kitchenette facing the street, a kitchenette-sized bathroom and two rabbit-hutch bedrooms that looked out the other way across garages to some strips of rear garden, and the rear-ends of houses, and a church sometimes known locally as St Crudes. Andy opened the bedside cabinet in his bedroom. It was his private storage area, and as such Sara respected it. She believed everyone needed secret places, apart from those locked up in their brains.

A deep shadow by now was filling the tiny back rooms, which faced north. Inside the cupboard was darkness, but to Andy a vague glow seemed to open there, the longer he gazed in. The upper shelf and the lower, boxlike area, seemed to *shine* with the heaps of booty he had accumulated. Some liquid soap from a cafe toilet, two library books he had taken unseen and not returned, a glass from some other café, and a general litter that included a knife and fork from a school dinner, a watch-strap, safety pins in a container... and so on. Andy slotted today's trophies with some care in among these already established items, then sat back on his heels to review the assembly, the *still-life* he had created, was creating, would always, presumably create. One day he would run out of room, of course. But not yet. He piled the bigger and the littler things together with such cleverness.

Andy stayed there on the floor, his head slightly to one side, then grew aware of this mannerism and corrected it. (Mannerisms were not helpful, he had found; at best they were silly, at worst they could be giveaways.)

The glow bloomed and floated on the things in the cabinet. They seemed to grow even paler, and lose individuality, as he stared at them, unblinking. Like a soft amalgam of some dim darkish snow.

When he had had enough, he shut the door.

He had left the lipstick and the toffees out, on his bed, (which Sara had made), for the present-giving. It would not matter too much if Sara saw them beforehand. They had a purpose and so were *not* secret.

Stealing, to Andy, had *no* purpose that interested him or that he grasped. It was what he did, and was good at. Nor had he any interest in, or want of, what he stole for brief use – an action figure, a film – such things he would return. The value was never in the stolen article he retained, but in the *act*. Its skill – and the afterimage. (His skill in taking what he might *like*, momentarily, to have was simply incidental.) A private affair indeed.

There was a dead sparrowhawk on the patio paving when Carver looked out the next morning. He unlocked the kitchen door went to see.

A beautiful form, even dead.

The curved wings, already ossifying, held his eyes some while. Like fanned and folded greyish palm fronds. And the cruel perfect head. What had brought it down? A consummate predator, it would grip another bird on the wing, everything seen to in an instant. But the hunting was done for this one.

Perhaps someone had poisoned it, some Keeper guarding pheasants for humans alone to kill.

Presently, raising the hawk on a shovel, he carried it down the garden and cast it over the outside wall by the shed. If it was wholesome a fox would take it, not if it was venomous; they seemed to know.

As he was turning to go back to the house, he saw old Robby Johnston ambling crookedly up the lane through the morning trees towards him.

"Hi, Car. How're things?"

"OK, thanks. You?"

"Oh, not much changes for me." Johnston stepped off the lane and crookedly ambled up to the wall. Though partly disabled now, by some never-detailed leg injury, which had got worse, it looked, in recent days, he had been and still was a tall, lean man. The ground sloped up just at this point. Standing on the rise between the tree roots and the scuffle of silver-russet leaves, Johnston raised his face to the sunshine. "Wind's fucked off any way," he remarked, cordially. He had a handsome face, if creased and lined as if pleated and pressed, and had kept a strong longish mop of steely hair. Late sixties, Carver surmised. He had never bothered to check up on Robby J. No doubt the office had. Maybe now Carver ought to as well.

"Yes. The wind's dropped," Carver agreed. He leaned the spade by a shed door, one of the ones that did not open.

Johnston glanced at him. "Your lady all right? Haven't seen her for a bit."

"Donna? Sure. She's at her mother's."

"Oh, they still like going to mummy's, don't they? Funny that. Even sometimes when they don't really like mummy that much." ("I hate her, I always have," said Dusa the dead hawk, in Carver's head, "from seven years of age.") "In fact, Car, I've been meaning to have a word with you."

"Sure."

Johnston watched light ruffs of cloud blot over the pale, lowish sun. He said, still sky-watching, "I've been seeing someone about, the past couple of nights."

"Yes?"

"Mmn. Oh, I know some of them go up and down via the woods, and there's the odd nocturnal courtship. Not to mention animal wildlife. But this was a man on his ownsome. I couldn't see much of him. No moon round the first time. It was about 2 a.m. I usually have to get up for the old feller about then, he wants the lav. And I took a look out of the window, as you do, and there's this tallish bloke, all in black, out in the woods, between here and the cottage. Thing was, he wasn't courting, or pissing, or walking through. He was standing there. Just standing. I went back to bed in a bit, didn't stay to watch long. Too old for that malarkey. Wondered if I'd dreamed it, the next day. But last night he was back again. About the same time, and the same thing, just there, just stood there. I couldn't see which way he was facing, towards your place or mine. I had the impression his face was covered up as well. A black mask or a black balaclava. Should have told you, perhaps, the first time. But now it's happened twice. What do you think?"

# Five

He heard the car draw up about four in the afternoon. The sound was different, and he recognised it: a 2000 Chevrolet Monté Carlo SS. Bought about three years ago, second-hand admittedly, as a present from a then-admirer, it was a rich oiled red and gleamed, as it always did in sunshine. Maggie's car. Looking out from the upstairs window in his 'playroom', Carver made sure only Maggie got out of it, and only Maggie had been in it.

He locked the 'playroom's' door before going down.

"What lovely tea, Car. I can do with this. The traffic, honestly. It's absurd at this time of day."

"Yes, it can be." He waited, gauging her as he tried his own glass of soda water.

"This is quite difficult," said Maggie.

He waited on.

"It's Donna," she said, and her well-organised prettiness flushed with a sudden, perhaps hormonal agitation.

"What's the matter with Donna?"

"You don't sound very concerned," said Maggie sharply. "I mean, I say 'it's Donna' and you sound – almost bored."

"No, I'm not bored. I'm just listening."

"And now you sound very *patient*."

He waited.

Maggie drank her tea. At last she put down the mug and said, "I love my daughter, Car. Of course I love her. But I know sometimes, particularly recently, she can... exaggerate things. To others, to herself. Do you see? That's my difficulty."

"Is she ill?" Carver asked quietly. It was a much safer response than the one she might expect: *What* has Donna exaggerated?

"Oh – no. No, I think she's fine…"

Fine but not pregnant? He wondered, pondered, kept silent, kept waiting.

"No, she just – I don't know how to broach this, Car. I simply don't. It would be a different matter if I didn't know you – I mean, we know each other, don't we? We have done for a few years. And I'm not such a bad judge of men. Even quiet men, like you. Even men your young age, Car. And so – oh shit. Well, here goes. She says," Maggie put back her artistically styled and blonded head and looked him fiercely in the eye, "you've abused her. You've been physically violent."

He allowed the surprise to show on his face. (He had been anticipating something else, some floundering guess Donna had belatedly made, concerning the work he did. Some notion his 'office in London' was not exactly that at all. That his job involved somewhat more than the ordinary, soulless, time-eating yet well-recompensed slog he had always implied it was and did. She had never taken excessive interest in it, and this he encouraged. The long and erratic hours always irritated, and more recently apparently maddened her, but did not make her believe, he had supposed, that it was more than corporate overkill and overtime.)

"Why," he said slowly, "does she say that?"

"Well, fairly obviously, Car," said fierce-eyed Maggie, angrily, "because she thinks you *did*."

He wished to say, *Has she shown you any bruises?* He did not say this. He said, "Why should she think that?"

And Maggie got up. She shouted at him, the way Donna had if not quite so loudly or savagely. "Maybe because you *have?*"

"No."

"Oh, No. Well. You *would* say that, *wouldn't* you?"

"Not necessarily. If I were that way inclined, I might agree, and make some excuse."

"Is that what you're going to do?"

"No, Maggie. Because I didn't abuse Donna."

"She says you did."

Now it was appropriate to say it. "What did I do? What's the evidence?"

Maggie flung her arms quite elegantly upward. Her nails were long and faultlessly painted a soft coppery shade. Then she sat down again. She said, in the hushed tone of someone speaking of something *un*speakable, "She wouldn't say and she wouldn't show me. She said – the marks had faded. And she was – *ashamed*."

"Why ashamed?"

"She wished she'd hit you back."

"*I* hit *her* then, she said?"

"She – *implied* you hit her."

Carver looked out of one of the front windows. The Chevrolet sat smartly, glittering, on the space outside the garage. Across the lane the woods were also at last beginning to burn up red.

"What do you want to do, Maggie?"

"I told her I had to go into Maidstone, and I didn't say I was coming here. I don't know *what* to do. Donna has been – odd."

"Did she tell you she was pregnant?"

Maggie's nicely lipsticked mouth dropped open and she stared at him. "*What*? Pregnant – No. *Is* she?"

"I've no idea. She told me she thought she might be. She was going to see the doctor, she said. But I don't think she has. At least, not yet."

"But didn't you try to *make* her go?"

"No, Maggie. I didn't try to *make* her do anything. Just as I didn't hit or otherwise abuse her."

"You sound so – cool, Car. Is that how you feel?"

"I'm startled, Maggie. Like you, more than you. I don't know what's going on."

"This is insane."

"Yes."

"What shall I do?" Maggie asked, but not of him. Or he did not think so. "Honestly, Car, I just don't know. Look," she said, seeming to straighten inside her fashionable jeans, her sleek white jumper, her cared-for skin, "she wants to stay on with me for a while. That's all right. We can do things. Maybe be childish, go to the seaside... Something. I'll try to get to the bottom of this pregnancy business. You know, Car, I *don't* think she is. There's just – something missing from that, somehow. She isn't... like a pregnant woman. But could she be? Had you been trying?"

"I didn't know we were, but maybe she was. If you mean have we been having sex, then yes. We do have sex. She never expressed the need for a child."

"But you wouldn't – mind? I mean, you'd *like* it if she had a baby?"

Carver said, "I didn't suggest it, but yes. It might be good." Just the proper amount of cautious interest and agreeability in his voice. A lie. Less than liking the concept, he was utterly indifferent, and had been when, and since, Donna told him.

"Well. We'll see how it goes. Better keep it at that. For now."

"And she doesn't want to come back here yet," His voice was entirely neutral.

"I'm sorry." Maggie had taken the neutrality as self-controlled disappointment. Or understandable relief? "I'm sorry, but no, she doesn't. I'll keep you posted, yes?"

"All right. So long as you can manage." She could, she was aware she could, and would. He was quite safe to fake concern.

"You know you can trust me, Car."

"Yes. I know."

"I'll take great care of her. Honestly, don't worry. It's just a phase. She *is* my kid, after all, isn't she?"

"Thank you, Maggie."

"And – the other thing... You didn't. I apologise. Of course you didn't. That's not *you*, Car."

"No."

She stood up.

"I'd better get off. I'm – well, I'm meeting someone at a little restaurant over towards the town. It's OK. Donna's staying in with the TV, some wine and a couple of shows she likes and there's a great takeaway place..."

He decided abruptly, not having really considered it before, that Maggie too had become a fraction jaded with Donna.

They said goodbye at the door and she planted her accustomed light press-kiss on his right cheek. She smelled of health and hygiene and Chanel No. 5. The Chevrolet started up immediately, eager to run, and vanished like a red wave around the bend of the red-leafed lane.

## Six

Once the sun set, Carver took his position in the spare room.

Downstairs he had switched on the porch light, but not the security. The nearest (distant) streetlamp was out, and so would stay out. The rest of the house, upstairs included, he also left to the darkness. Like a conscientious or impoverished light-saving citizen. Or like Donna, when she was trying to make some point about his late comings.

He sat near the window in the upright chair that was comfortable enough not to cause unnecessary movement, unrelaxing enough it did not tempt sleep.

He had set a sandwich and a flask of coffee on the small table next to him, and a couple of other things that might prove helpful.

Afterglow and English dusk filled the woods beyond the garden wall. In the distance, about two hundred and fifty metres off along the lane, he could, when they came on, make out the narrow dim illuminations of Robby Johnston's cottage. By ten or earlier they would be dead again, although now and then, much later, one or two might reappear, generally starting in the upstairs bedroom. This indicated one of Robby J's insomniac nights, as he called them, when he sat up reading, and occasionally meandered downstairs for tea or a whisky. He did not employ lighting to visit the lavatory.

Carver would prefer tonight was not an insomniac for Robby. Everything needed to be back as dark as it could be, so nothing out in the woods might be disturbed.

As the evening ebbed he heard bell-ringing from the old church at the far end of the village. This did not, any more, happen very often. The village had complained, it seemed, about the noise. Later he heard two or three people, and next saw them, as they negotiated the lane, headed doubtless for The Bell pub. Somewhere around midnight they would return by the same route, unless there was a lock-in, which could last until sunrise, if everybody was in the mood.

Really, Carver knew he had set up his sentry post very early. But who could predict what preliminaries might go on, or if they did not, that too could be an indication.

Time passed, now fast, now slow, relative to itself, or perhaps to him.

Johnston's lights came on late, at half past six. (He had been out? Or asleep.)

Every hour Carver got up and went to check from the windows of the other upstairs areas, the main bedroom and ensuite and the 'playroom' to the front; the second bathroom, and the annexe at the opposite side by the boiler cupboard, to the rear.

Nothing unusual was apparent. No car drove through the lane, as rarely they did. When he opened the bathroom windows about nine, the air was much dryer and more cold. There was a smell of woodsmoke from some banked bonfire, and the indefinable odour of dying leaves.

He ate half the sandwich.

He gave no thought to Maggie, and none to Donna. She especially was now irrelevant, as so often, legitimate only though her absence. He did not even think of Silvia Dusa, or even of Latham in the room with the vodka and the recording of voices,

Carver's saying what he had not said at all.

Between eleven and a quarter to midnight the vocal people who had gone to the pub waltzed back with a torch flickering like a giant firefly, laughing and careless, and disappeared into the fartherness of night.

Johnston's lights were all out again for now. There would be no moon. And anyway the sky was once more overcast, only the splintery rhinestone of Jupiter intermittently visible. The vague lit aura of the village, also detectible from here, had sunk too, as it did not always do as yet. Though the shed, of course... a faint sheen, the reflection on the birches, nearly not there at all.

At twenty-five minutes past one he began to use the night glasses. He had kept them from a stint a year ago, as other Mantik employees often did. They were not very strong, the I/R by now not up to much. He detected a fox, however, trotting between the trees, a vaporous incoherent green, and a while after a rabbit or big rodent sprang through like a firework. It was 2 a.m.

Carver lowered the glasses, and closed his eyes for a scatter of seconds to clear them.

When he looked again, firstly without the visual aid, a figure, clearly man-shaped, was standing about fifteen paces outside the wall of his garden.

Just as Robby J had had it, Carver too was not sure which way the figure was facing. It seemed to *have* no face, nor any back or front. Even scanning it again through the erratic I/R the impression, if now haloed green, was of something less than human, featureless, yet having a head, two long legs and two long arms and a long thin torso, and all of these sheathed in a liquid rubber of blackness.

With extreme care Carver put down the glasses, and edged closer to the side of the window.

The faceless figure had not seemed to arrive, not even to evolve – as some CGI contrivance might have in a supernatural movie... It was *not* there, then it *was*.

And it did not stir.

He waited, not taking his eyes off it, preferring them now to the fluctuating glasses. And minutes ticked themselves antlike along his watch, more than audible in the unbreathing quiet. The shape was male, Carver decided. But that was all. It had no giveaways, offered no movement, was like some construct approximating a man – that in one or two seconds had slotted itself through from nowhere, and was now fixed forever.

Out along the lane a pair of cats began a yowling battle song. Carver did not change position or lose concentration. Did not blink, and so saw the figure after all come slowly and jerkily alive. Like a toy, whose faulty mechanism had already abruptly re-engaged, it pivoted, and the faceless black blob of its head rotated in the direction of the sound.

After which it took a single step. Only one. And again, it was gone. Even the glasses could not find it then. Had it dropped, smeared itself flat to the earth? Had it passed behind a solid partition which had only *seemed* the openwork patches of trees and shadow, but which could not be, so thoroughly did they now conceal?

Carver did not move.

He waited.

Nothing.

The cats shrieked a crescendo and ceased their argument.

When next he looked at his watch it was two forty-three.

At two forty-five a light burst inside Johnston's upper window, and soon struck the lower ones, like a thrown egg of fire. Bits of the fire-yolk dripped out also on to the woods. They revealed nothing significant.

When presently Carver checked from the rest of the house windows, back and front, up and down, nothing at all seemed about.

A motorbike snarled in the distance. But as a getaway vehicle it would be attention-seeking and unlikely. And he had not heard it before.

Around an hour after, all the lights went off again in Johnston's cottage. The theatre curtain had come down on the scene. Carver could feel this: instinct or training,....either, both.

Despite that he watched until the sky began to pale and push higher, before he left the window, finished the coffee, and lay down on the bed.

He would sleep one hour. Then take a walk in the woods.

## SEVEN

After showering, he checked the games key Icon of his iPhone. It was routine to do so. *Clue Up*, it read, *One down*. And at another touch: *Any Judge's Main Verdict*. Holding steady on Dusa then, **the** same letter-numerals. He touched the screen again, for Today's Lucky Stone. It was *Emerald*. The alert had heightened, from blue to green. Nothing had come up on the radio, TV or other legitimate news outlets, which he had also been checking fairly regularly. This afternoon his new schedule began, and he was due back in Trench Street around 9 a.m. tomorrow. He considered contacting Latham now. But if Latham had decided there should be contact, it would probably have happened, and had not. And first thing this morning, even before going out, Carver had again run through the existing files on his computer, particularly the file on *The Third Scar*. Everything was there, nothing seemed altered or obscured, in any way. He retained therefore his permit, and could study and work on them as normal. Which implied he was not, then, (was he?) suspect.

Carver went down to the kitchen and put bacon in the steel pan to fry. His body was hungry and the smell pleased it, although his mind moved uneasily elsewhere.

The woods, an hour and a half after dawn, had been empty of anything unusual, let alone informative. He had not really anticipated much else. The image of the black-camouflaged man, however odd it had appeared, had been real, concrete, a fact. Its behaviour, its apparent *tricks* of visibility and vanishment might even be due to some coincidental, quirky but logical happenstance. For could it – he – have been certain anyway he was under surveillance? The intruder was most probably a nobody up to nothing at all.

But should Carver inform Latham of the man in the woods?

It seemed more prudent, and less edgy, to tell Latham in person tomorrow.

Carver would need though to drop in on Robby J, say that he *had* kept an eye out, and *had* noted somebody around. But Carver thought he would add the man was most likely a wildlife-spotter. (Maybe he even was.) The main thing in any case was to deter Johnston from calling in the police, which could cause muddle, some kind of cluttering up, either of the perfectly innocuous – that might then turn resentful (the wildlife-fan becoming nasty and summoning his mates once the law had gone) – or, if the source were other, untidy any genuine evidence.

Carver knew, despite the untampered-with files, despite his being let go, free it seemed as air after Latham had played him the surreal recording, that all curious follow-up events could well have their source in Mantik.

Without quite being shown it at first, a leash might be on Carver now. Loose fitting enough it felt he could do as he wanted. Yet just now and then, almost to be glimpsed from the corners of his eyes, *felt* as it tapped, gentle, noose-like, on his neck.

Going back through the wooded lane, heading for Johnston's cottage about 10 a.m., Carver found automatically he still scanned from side to side. But of course, there was nothing, as there had been nothing valid detectable by him during his initial search. If available, he would have found it then. Instead he had noted the slight disturbance created by animals and birds, and further along one of the pub returnees, who had piddled up a tree then lost his footing and broken some branches, leaving a thread from trousers or jacket snagged there. The ground, aside from the area by the peed-on tree, was un-moist, and had taken no imprint of footwear. Leaves were down everywhere also, covering and artistically blending. Even where the male figure had stood immobile for such a long while, over twenty-five minutes, no notable impression marked the earth. Nor had *he* broken a single twig. Not even with that one impressive step that sequentially and utterly hid him.

Robby J was up and making tea in his kitchen.

"Hi, Car. Can I offer you some of this disgusting brew? No. Wise choice. Christ knows what they put in these T-bags now. Dung and senna pods from the taste."

Carver relayed the edited version of last night's vigil, and the verdict (hardly 'Any Judge's Main' one) of an obsessive badger-botherer.

"Well," said Robby, "it could be, could be. I heard him about again last night, you know. Woke me, the devil, I was having one of my good nights, curled up a-snore in my cosy roost. Hadn't even had to visit the lats. And then crash-blunder right under my bedroom window. Just before three, when I focussed on the clock." (This conformed with the cottage lights having gone on at two forty–five, as did Robby J's next statement.) "Put all the lights on, no messing. Didn't like the sound of it, all that thumping about, as if he was off his head on drugs, and/or *meant* to wake everybody up. I tell you, I wouldn't have minded a shotgun and the US shooter culture to go with it. But you know what it's like now, if some burglar pillock breaks in and stabs you, he can sue you for snapping his fucking blade on your ribs."

"Did you see him?" Carver asked, having given the complementary acquiescing nod.

"No. That was the odd part, in its way. The racket the chap made, I expected a grandstand view of him sprawled in the front garden, or what serves for it, throwing his guts up or eating a squirrel or something. But not a sign. And by the time I got downstairs it was Silent Night again."

"Nothing looks disturbed outside," Carver said. It had not.

"Lucky, I suppose," said Robby. "Y'know, I even wondered if it was old Ted from The Bell, Book and Candlegrease. Someone told me he's started seeing fairies in the woods. Perhaps they were only the old-fashioned kind, the ones with old-school ties. God," he said sharply, "my leg's playing up this morning.' His face settled to a wry amused rancour. "Bloody tea makes it worse, I reckon. Too acid, and I'm addicted to the muck, you know. Ten or twelve mugs a day. Need a whisky to wash it through. Can I tempt you?"

"Not today, worse luck. Work to do."

"Oh well. I've got the advantage of ending up a senile old cripple. Something for you young ones to look forward to, in a hundred years. Take care of yourself, Car."

The dinner with Latham at the steakhouse off the Maidstone road, had been a 'decoy' meal, one of a group, involving altogether eleven Mantik employees. Spread out at various locations, Guildford and Cornwall being the farthest venues, false trails were laid by two separate pairs, one separate foursome, and three individuals driving and eating alone. Carver certainly had no idea what strategic meeting he and Latham, not to mention the rest, had been drawing attention away from. Obviously, there had been similar outings in the past.

This afternoon Carver had to undertake a drive, ultimately heading into Tunbridge Wells. This also was a decoy run but was freelance in as much as he might stop as and when he wanted, if at least twice. The car he must use he would find in a by-lane near Lynchoak. Returning, there would be a 'cab' at Tenterden.

The indication was that if any 'interest' were shown in him, he should expect it in the vicinity of Tunbridge Wells. He did not need to try to lose it, of course, and later the 'cab' driver could slough anything that still clung on.

Carver drove to Lynchoak, stowed his car, and was in the new vehicle heading south-west by around five minutes to two. Within six more minutes, long before any mooted feasible connection, he was very sure a tail had already attached itself.

It was a shabby Merc, cadaverous grey in colour.

This car seemed to make so little pretence it was not following him that Carver began to wonder if it was not. It moved behind him along the curving side roads he had chosen, keeping a barely civilised distance between them. Until, turning on to a broader thoroughfare, he saw he had lost it. Perhaps naively he continued to think this until it reappeared, emerging with no warning from a side-turning, as if it had selected a parallel path solely in order – playfully – to surprise him.

From then on, the Merc continued to favour this type of manoeuvre. It would indiscreetly hug him, then slip aside and vanish for miles – before abruptly resurfacing out of some often unexpected turning or lay-by, so displaying an enviable SatNav, or personal acquaintance with the map of local roads. Carver himself kept doggedly on, as if he was either too dumb to have noticed, or too stoical to struggle. He had attracted the tail and might as well keep it busy.

He stopped the first time by driving into the small car park of a pub. The Merc sailed by and vanished at a twist of the lane. But Carver was ninety-five percent convinced once he had drunk the non-alcoholic lager, got back in his car and set off again, the Merc would re-join him, which indeed it did, at a handy T-junction, shambling out on to the road with bumpy clumsy enthusiasm.

There seemed to be only the driver in the vehicle. He was blank-faced and nondescript, dressed in some sort of woolly jumper, death-grey to match the car.

They played this match all that short late-year afternoon, driving between fields, along narrow, bad, lumpy tracks, past leaning old barns and ruined fences. Now and then Carver gave them a turn on a trim motorway. He also stopped twice more before they reached Tunbridge Wells, once at another pub, and once at a farm shop, which involved a gravelled hiccupping jolt of a pathway, on to which the Merc did not even attempt to propel itself.

Day was on its last legs in the sky by the time they got into Tunbridge proper.

Carver parked near the Royal Ash Tree Restaurant, and getting out, found the Merc had bumbled off again.

He idled about for an hour or so, traipsing through the Pantiles, and from force of habit buying a silver-black and onyx necklace for Donna, in a pillared burrow with bulging windows.

By then the dark had opened up and the lighted shops were beginning to close. There was no more sign of the Merc, or the woolly-jumpered driver.

Carver caught the train. With a suitable change, it would drop him close to the Tenterden pickup point, where the other car, the 'cab', would be waiting. His own car he would collect from Lynchoak tomorrow for the drive into London.

The train was full, buzzy with mobiles, laptops and miniaturised fried music, if not conversation. When Carver glanced around, he felt a jab of almost inert shock. The man from the Merc was already installed, only a few feet away among the seatless and standing commuters. He balanced there, clamped by other bodies, yet swaying and sore-thumbian, woolly *grey*. He did not look at Carver.

Carver reviewed the best moves to get shot of him before picking up his transport. If evasion was out of the question, Carver thought he would have to wait before heading for the pickup. To let the 'cabby' give a vehicle the slip was one thing, but a direct foot-follower might pose a more immediate threat. Carver had not been advised either of this possibility, or of how best to tackle it.

He made a decision. He would get out at the next halt, secure a real cab, and drive in that over to Tenterden.

The train was approaching another station. As Carver rose, the coatless jumper man turned and looked straight at him. The flat stodgy face broke in a wide and familiarly friendly grin. Carver ignored it. He eased his way towards the further set of doors. The train had slowed and now stopped. Along with a clump of uninvolved others he stepped off on to the platform.

Carver paused a moment then, watching as the train absorbed its new dose of passenging customers. The man was just visible, no longer smiling, only blank, and as the train resealed itself he and it glided away, a collective piece of characterised scenery removed from the stage.

The 'cab' dropped him without argument just at the edge of the village, by the church. He and the driver had exchanged the normal bare minimum of words. A few of them centring on the driver's discontent. His engine had started acting up. Carver did not mention either the Mercedes or the man's arrival on the train; he could save these events for Latham tomorrow. Nothing had followed them now.

Walking up through the village, there were anyway still plenty of people about, lights on everywhere, (even the church had been lit for some service, or organ practice), and *The Bell* was blazing. Carver could see Ted through the window, dancing what seemed to be a gig. What had that other business been, that take of Johnston's on Ted's seeing 'fairies'. Johnston had surely misunderstood, though he had been correct about the figure in the wood, the man with the black blob for a head.

In the lane the streetlamp nearest the village was on, but farther up darkness, technically unimpeded, reassembled. The boughs were bare enough even so at last that they left wide holes through to the sky, clear and starry, and with a new moon already high.

Carver waited briefly near the house, looking over at it, noting too the way the woods were, and the tree-fringed fields behind him.

How cold everything appeared, colder than any actual coldness of atmosphere, a night-scene painted with ink-stained ice and shut behind a frozen pane of glass.

Carver thought after all he would send a short memo to Latham via the phone in the 'playroom'. He should maybe mention the man in the woods too. Whoever had put the action on, there had been a lot of it.

What would happen next, tonight?

Carver knew he must *sleep* tonight. It was an early start tomorrow. The train to Lynchoak and then the drive up to London. Perhaps therefore eat, then take a break of five hours, that would be enough. Then woods-watch sentry duty again. He unlocked the house doors, aware all the while of the night pressing through its ice-glass at his back. He glanced out from the inner doorway, as usual. The sheer silence had a kind of sound. Sara, his mother, had been sometimes hysterically afraid of the dark.

Downstairs the phone, the landline, had again begun to ring. This had happened seven times now since eight o'clock. Each time too the mechanical voice offered to receive a message, and each time no message was given.(But the phone did play up. All the phones did.)

Reluctantly he had gone to see who, or what, made the calls. There was no number. A glitch then. Or cold calling, maybe. They, human or robot, could be persistent. He thought he would unplug the phone when he went up to sleep, and when keeping watch.

He had eaten steak, burnt as he preferred it, and tomatoes bought from the farm shop. He made more coffee. From time to time he switched channels on the TV above the kitchen breakfast bar, (reception was poor), but there was no report that seemed to have anything to do with Dusa, or her death. Perhaps by now he should reckon there would not be.

The phone rang again as he closed the dishwasher door.

He went out, and noted a number which, on this occasion, revealed itself. It was Maggie's landline.

With a sort of inevitable extra unwillingness, Carver put the phone to his ear.

He did not need to speak. The female voice was already screaming.

"Car – I have to come home! I *have* to! Oh God, Car – please – are you *there*? Is it *you*?"

"Yes, Donna, of course it is."

"Car – please help me, Car – please – I have to get home–"

"Try to keep calm. What is the matter? I thought you wanted to stay on?"

"She's keeping me here–" shrilled Donna. She seemed frightened, nearly demented. When her voice dropped, as next it did, it was breathless and shaky. "I've only got a moment – she went out – to get some wine, she said – I can't use my phone, Car – she's stopped me recharging it – so it doesn't work – and her two – she's *hidden* them – she's keeping me prisoner, Car – Car you have to believe me – I've only got a minute – seconds – Car help me – get me out–"

"Do you mean Maggie?" he asked slowly, quietly and distinctly.

"Yes – yes – Maggie – who else? *Maggie*. She's been drugging me or something – I kept falling asleep – she kept saying I had to rest, I was all in – I don't know what she gave me – it may harm the baby–"

Ah, the baby again. Carver said, "Donna, are you really saying your mother has gone crazy and has–"

"I don't know if she's gone crazy, Car. I don't know, Car. She's always been – well, odd, sometimes... Carver – *I can't leave this fucking house...*" The last sentence came over in a thin savage wail. "She locks me in if she goes out. Takes the keys. Car – please – you have to come–"

He thought, with a horrible lack of startlement, let alone compassion, or any sense of personal sadness, *She's gone crazy herself. She's beyond reason.* It was as if a wall of granite, miles thick, miles high, separated them. It was as if she were an actress, acting all this very badly in a lousy TV drama he must now switch off. He wanted, he found, to switch it off quickly. And he wanted to stay behind the granite wall.

"Donna," he said, "I can't come over tonight." She said nothing. "I have stuff I have to see to, can't get out of it. I'll come tomorrow evening, after I get back from London." Lynchoak, he thought, was near enough to Beechurst. It would be simple. If he had to, he could bring this mad woman home then. But not now. Not tonight. He must keep tonight – between them.

He was very tired, that was it. He would not be safe driving all that extra distance, after all the driving already today, and only one hour's sleep caught up on the previous night. He would be a fool to try to drive. God knew what was wrong at Maggie's. Nothing, probably. Donna was drunk. Or something in the pregnancy – if there was one – had upset the chemicals in her brain. Which chemicals anyhow never entirely kept steady, going on her general demeanour over recent years.

"Just try to keep calm," he repeated to her new silence. "Take things slowly. Maggie isn't going to hurt you. We'll sort it all out tomorrow."

Then she breathlessly whispered, and he grasped she had not listened, had not heard his denial of her, his decision of not yet going over, rescue deferred. "*She's back.* She's *back*. Her *car's* there. I'll – Oh Christ–" and the phone, presumably put down, went dead.

Carver stood in the hall, listening himself again to the other silence of the darkness, which was not like Donna's silence at all.

Could something so irrational be going on? Maggie of the Chevrolet off her head – but why – for what reason? Maggie was fairly grounded, sufficiently *sane*. It was Donna who might not be.

Donna who had alleged Carver had attacked her. Donna begging him – the attacker – *Please Car – please, Car* – to save her from a blonde dragon with such nicely moisturised scales and elegantly manicured talons, and an independent bank balance donated by several approving and satisfied male lovers who had never found fault.

Carver left the phone active, he would not unplug it yet. That would be his single concession to Donna's outcry. She could have a further twenty minutes, before he grabbed his four or five hours of sleep. Twenty minutes to evade her wardress with the drugged wine, and call him again.

Upstairs, as the computer in the 'playroom' shuffled its files for him, he thought Donna herself had doubtless forgotten to recharge her mobile phone, or lost it – she had lost two in the past six months, leaving one in a pub in Beechurst, she said, somehow dropping the other during a ramble through a park somewhere. Had she always been this feckless, this 'dotty'? Not in the beginning. No.

The file flicked open its screen pages.

He read, as he had done already several times, the introductory paragraphs. *The Third Scar* purported to be a script in the making, sponsored by a movie outfit that required some private funding. It had been dressed up, Carver thought, rather like a modern mystery for a nouveau Sherlock Holmes, with the implicated supernatural undertow inherent in, say, *The Hound of the Baskervilles* or *The Sussex Vampire*. A curse was threatened with the manifestation of a Third Scar. But the scar had three rival meanings: 1) A mark on the left arm or hand, of some unspecified sort, 2) A scar (or *scaur*) being the steep craggy outcrop of a cliff or mountain. The third meaning was stranger. 3) Postulated the use of Scar as a family name, the final descendants to bear it, three in number; the third and last being the child of the other two.

The plot involved, inevitably, crimes and secrets, not least the apparent curse that brought potential death no less thoroughly than the danger of a phantom hound, or a predilection of some thirsty foreign female vampire.

The phone rang again.

Despite himself Carver tensed. He got up, went to the door and along to the head of the stairs. There he stayed. The mechanical voice broke in, offering the caller its message option.

What would Donna say now?

A night-cold, night-silent rage pulsed through Carver, gushing upward from his feet – and perished as another voice than Donna's entered the house.

It was male. Seeming young. Diction exact. Not wasting a word. For it only offered one. *"Silvia"* said the voice. Nothing else. Message given and ended.

Carver sprang down the stair. The phone showed only that the number was withheld.

He had already texted Latham, by the agreed channel, to register the tail to Tunbridge and on the train. And the visitor in the woods. There had been no response, nor had Carver expected one. Like the Donna problem, that was for tomorrow.

But *this*. What to do with *this*?

He checked the games key Icon again. The signal had begun to blip. But it was the same clue, the verdict of the judge which still indicated the initials S.D. The Alert Level however had gone down to Blue – today's Lucky Stone was now *Aquamarine*.

The computer seemed jumpy, too. It froze, came back... He shut off the <u>*Scar*</u> file, and unplugged the machine. Downstairs he did the same with the landline. Later he would expunge all the house lights again, aside from that of the glassed-in porch. For now he left them on. It was later than he had planned. Almost ten o'clock. He could not, now, sleep as long as intended.

He would not bother with the news. Opening the kitchen's back door, Carver stepped out on to the patio, among the beaming outdoor lamps. He looked about and down the garden, the ornamental (mental) benches, the lawn, the bushes and established trees, the pear that sometimes fruited a harvest with the scent of honey and the taste of rotten wood; it had done nothing this year.

Leaving the house shut and lit up, Carver moved down the garden. Seen from outside, the uplighter glare from the village still bloomed against the clear indigo glass of the sky. The white slender moon was westering, but bright. Nothing suspicious was about. He could hear far-off traffic.

He walked towards the shed.

The blue-green luminescence inside the shed had either not

been there, or was unnoticeable in the beginning, Carver thought. And when at first it began to show, he had dismissed it as his own misperception, at least for a short while. It was quite pertinently like the glow – the *after*glow of thieving – that had lingered for him on those things he stole in his childhood and teens; an optical illusion no less profound and affirming for being recognised and labelled. But now, little by very little, as the amount of small scattered objects he presently conducted home, and so into the shed, grew in number and sequent density, so the *glow* had increased. Less than a bloom, it magnified to a sheen. And after this, an actual illumination. Everything he took currently, of course, came from the Mantik building in Whitehall, and in itself was unvaluable. Pristine unused discs and cartridges, batteries, un-ink pens, tiny and now nearly redundant notepads, grips, clips, tags, tabs...the very last item to date had been the memory card for a make of camera with which Carver himself had never been issued. That theft he had placed inside the shed on the morning after Donna enacted her initial five-star mad-scene, the morning *before* Carver met Silvia weeping mercury tears in the corridor, and she had said *Go to hell*, and then *I must talk to someone.*

None of the thieved articles, as they never had been, were of any lasting use, and normally of no use to him. If they could have been, he never used them. Practical use was not their worth or significance.

As he unlocked the central door of the shed, something flew suddenly up from a tree beyond the back wall. After dark that was uncommon. But then again, the light of the shed might have deceived the bird, as neon and streetlamps might elsewhere.

Carver shut and relocked the shed door from inside. He glanced from the night-blind four back windows to the front seven.

How alien, he thought, his house looked from here, a retro smartish '80s', '90s'-ish erection, with certain, now-dated kinks of structure. Its stark lights made it a target.

Carver turned to look around him.

The effect of snow-heaps, that had always struck him about the things stored in the cupboards of the chain of flats when he was a boy, lessened here, on closer inspection. There was more room to lay them out, these trophies. More space for individual or group identity.

The glow rising from them – blue-green like the two Lower

Alert colours duly mixed, Aquamarine and Emerald – what caused it? He had never noticed such an effect anywhere in the tarpaulined, scaffolded building in Trench Street, let alone the supply stores – the 'stationery cupboards'. Carver though did not believe any longer his imagination was to blame. His imagination did not work in that way at all. It was no doubt his *imagination* that sometimes made the glow seem a little *less*.

Without prelude, a bolt of crucial tiredness struck him a soggy blow. He did not frequently experience such draining energy-slumps. He would have to, he concluded, go back at once and sleep, even though, now, less than three hours could be scrounged before he should resume his watch on the woods, assuming he meant to keep it.

He ran his hand swiftly, less a regulation plain caress than an obligatory *contact*, over a row of the stolen things. Enough.

He moved instantly back towards the central door of the three, the one that could open and close. And halted. Behind him – what? – to the rear side of the shed only the four windows, facing the garden wall and the woods. And one of these windows as his periphery vision had told him – Carver turned.

Outside the window, *inside* the wall, something stood, upright and solid and very close.

It was black, viscous *rubbery* black, and the head was composed of the same material, having no features: a sculpted blob. But then – as if the turquoise gleam in the shed had flared – Carver saw after all one feature. Eyes. Black and shiny, in-and-unhuman. Splitting the mask of darkness. A pair of eyes in a faceless face, looking, looking, *looking* into his own.

Carver was not amazed. As he would not have been amazed if nothing had happened. He had tempted them in the lane, walking back, dawdling under the isolated and mostly unlighted lamps; now by walking out here, the house lit like a beacon behind him.

He went directly to the door he had not fully locked and opened it quickly and jumped straight down on to the concrete apron, turning as he did so to the figure, where it pressed close to the shed.

And something now really did happen. Something changed. The sky – was very bright – somewhere, far off, a sound – Carver was no longer there. Nothing was.

# Eight

Just before he was meant to start at the secondary school at Sucks, (as Andy called it), Sara and he had to move again.

The new place was another flat, a partial clone of the previous several they had inhabited since escaping his father. Found for them, and with Sara getting assistance with the rent, (and to bolster that, working her endless hours cleaning), they were still inside the zone they had occupied, by then, for two years. And Andy was still enlisted, at first, and if seldom in situ, at the primary school in Potters Road.

In the future he would wonder if Sara had ever, during that time, been informed of, or threatened about, his truanting.

If so she never relayed the experience. She might, worn out and edgy as she was, even have forgotten it. He himself *had* been informed, threatened, and bawled out on the matter, which meant nothing to him. It was no longer legal in schools to beat kids up over their misdemeanours. Accordingly he did not care.

After the move, which had also meant little to him, or even probably to his mother, Andy went to the school one-day because he felt like it. (The novelty, perhaps.)

The midmorning break came nevertheless, and found Andy in the school yard, with some as ever non-personal items he had thieved in his pockets, already having lost interest and thinking of leaving. But the sun was warm, and he leaned on the brickwork, being a lizard and absorbing it as lizards did, apparently, in hot, still noonday countries – Brazil, Spain, the Caribbean.

Lizardlike, motionless, his soulless eyes swivelled in his static scaly frame. And soon he saw Heavy up near the rain-shelter, with the two bullies, Cox, (who had *not* lost a tooth) and E-bone, looming over him.

Andy had not come across Heavy since their encounter in Station Road. There was no reason he should have done.

Cox had kept out of Andy's way too, since Andy had thumped him. And E-bone was a moron, Andy had long ago deduced, a muddy-coloured, black-white spite-fuelled boil, inert but able to burst when given a cue.

The lizard watched.

Some of the other 'young people' – as custom was coming to

title them – did too.

"I wonder if he'd just fall over," said Cox. "Yeah?"

"Go'won," said E-bone. "Pushim."

"Shall I push him?" Cox, raising his face to the sky, asked God. Seemingly God concurred it was feasible.

So Cox set his big hands on Heavy's big fat shapeless torso and pushed.

Heavy did nothing. He looked at Cox, as if not sure what Cox was. Heavy did not appear frightened. But he was very big, a blubbery consolidated mass that rocked a bit but did not give.

"It's a *game*," said Cox to Heavy, determinedly. And this time he drew back, considered, and slammed himself against Heavy, and E-bone laughed, and some of the others who watched sniggered in chorus, glad it was not them being attacked by Cox.

Heavy seemed to go over only after an interval, and very slowly, like a too-large and wrongly-made doll. He swung backwards, not resisting, his face even now without any dismay, let alone panic. Too thick to drop easily, somehow defying gravity all the way down.

When he hit the ground, the hard concrete below the edge of the rain-shelter – also concrete, chipped and grazing, and his huge unwieldy unsightly head banged down too, and the smack of the impact sounded, or seemed to sound – even then he did not really react. And after it, he lay there, as unmoving as Andy the lizard against the warm brickwork. But Heavy's expression did slowly change. It became one of the vaguest surprise. Brainless, Heavy. What peril could there be for *him* in having his skull smashed on the ground?

Then he got up, and it was a marvel. A sort of jumbled upward *flight* – Why had Cox and/or E-bone not put the boot in? Laughing too much maybe. They also missed the curious beauty of Heavy's getting up, the cumbersome grace – *agility* –

Heavy anyway was again on his feet. Gracefully he shambled forward, across to them. He did not look as if he had been hurt.

Abruptly Andy noticed he had unpeeled himself from the hot wall. He was not a lizard. He was a human, and wide awake.

"It's a game," said Heavy, to Cox and E-bone.

"Wan' notha go?" asked E-bone.

"It's my turn," said Heavy, with gentle logic.

And reaching out, effortless – like a gigantic fuddled swan – he too *pushed* with his two flails of arms that were wings. Cox and E-bone simultaneously, astounded and howling, fell backward. In due season, *their* bodies hit the hard and bitter earth, their heads smacked – *crack, crack* – on the concrete.

There was not much noise now in the yard, which once had been called by the name "*Play*ground".

Then there came the sounds of Cox puking, and E-bone crying.

Rather oddly, Andy remembered right then someone had said E-bone's father had been killed. Perhaps this was not true. Or it had been long ago. But in E-bone's sobbing misery, Andy unnervingly heard somehow his own helpless lament, his mother lying by the cooker after the advent of his father's fist, and he curled up against the wall, waiting for the next onslaught "*Shut up you little cunt–*"

"Shut up, you little cunt," said Andy, under his breath.

And as he did so, Heavy, who could not have heard him, turned to gaze his way. And then Heavy was bending over Cox and E-bone. Heavy murmured, sadly, "It's just a game, you didn't ought to play with it, if it makes you unhappy."

He was halfway up Hawthorne Road, (his new route home) before he realised Heavy was again, as once before, shambling along in his wake.

Andy ignored him. Last time telling Heavy to fuck off had not worked after all. But in a short space the fumbly stupid sound of Heavy's feet and shoes annoyed Andy enough he did turn round.

"*What?*"

"Isn't the sky blue," said Heavy.

"No. It's orange. Piss off," Andy added, despite the redundancy. It would not work, nor did it. As Andy resumed his journey back to the new flat, Heavy fell in beside him.

How completely weird he was. You knew it, obviously, but then you sort of really looked at him, and *really* knew it. And it was much, much worse than you had ever reckoned.

"I saw an oransh sky once," said Heavy, meditatively. "Something was on fire."

"Your fucking brains."

"Oh, no. Old houses."

Andy glared at the passing traffic. Cars, buses. Congested. Fast.

"And in a film," said Heavy, "I saw."

Andy said, "Look, shove off, would you?"

Heavy did not seem to know what had been said. He kept on walking at Andy's side, smiling up into the sky.

"There's a bird," said Heavy, with soft pleasure.

Evidently birds had just been invented and were still a rare phenomenon.

Andy thought about Heavy pushing both Cox and E-bone over, and how someone had gone for the nurse and then, while somebody else asked E-bone, who was still crying, if *he* had pushed Cox over, E-bone said he had not meant to, they had just been playing about was all. Heavy had already ambled off, but it appeared E-bone was afraid of Heavy now and would not incriminate him. Cox, who had stopped being sick, had been taken to lie down.

Andy wondered if *he* could get the better of Heavy in a fight. Surely he could? He could not picture, however, Heavy fighting him. Heavy's plasticky skin was impervious. How ugly he was. So ugly it was not actually ugly, but some other type of visual shock.

Andy was staring at Heavy. Andy moved his eyes away.

As they turned up Lodge Road, Heavy said, "What's it mean, your name?"

Beyond the traffic lights, Andy could see the off-licence on top of which was Sara's new flat. This was far enough. He stopped, angled round and looked at Heavy. Andy thought, *He's like a punch-bag*. If you hit him he would come back at you. Like he did with Cox and E-bone. It was not a defence or a reflex, not anger, but a built-in *mechanism*.

"Look, man," said Andy in a level grown-up voice he had heard his mother use, and some of the people with the social services, "I need to be on my own. All right?"

Heavy looked at him. Heavy's round eyes were the colour of mud, or slime.

"I had an apple in my lunch," said Heavy. "I like apples. Some people don't like apples, like in the By-bell." (He meant Bible, Andy knew that from some class when they were being taught things from the Bible and Heavy pronounced it as he did, and seemed unable to alter this, so the teacher gave up.) "That was why he gave it her."

Perhaps, Andy thought, he could just take to his heels like last time. He would soon outrun Heavy. But he heard himself reluctantly say, "Who did?" And did not know why he had.

"The serpan. He didn't like apples so he gived his one to that woman in the garden." (Oh. he meant Adam and Eve, What the teacher called a Parable, or something. Some senseless fairy tale–) "And she liked the apple, but she shared it with her boyfriend, because she liked him too and wanted he should have some. And then that other one came and he was angry. But the serpan was only not wanting to waste it and she was only being kind. My moth– ah told me. She tells me stuff."

"You are," said Andy, slowly and precisely, "off your fucking nut. Now fuck off or jump under a car, whichever you'd like best."

"I'd like best," said Heavy, with a sudden dreamy energy, "to *fly*–" And spreading out his two bolsters of arms, he spun away, careering off along the pavement, laughing in a drainlike gurgling, and here and there jumping up the half foot that was all his bulk and discoordination seemed to allow.

Andy too ran for it, the other way, dodging in behind the shops before Heavy could think better of flight and try to re-join him.

She had mixed race too, as E-Bone did, Sara, his mother. Sara's father, for protection from racial prejudice, had changed the family name to its anglicised version, <u>Carver</u>, which Andy then at birth received, as he was a bastard, (or born out-of-wedlock, as no one any longer said... did they?) E-bone's mum's dad had not altered their family name, and so E-bone received that, as he too was a bastard boow. Andy did not remember this name, though it had something to do with islands, he believed. E-bone's proper first name was Ebony. His mother perhaps had been making some statement, rather an out-of-date one, if so. It might have been an OK name, but not when you were eleven. Nor, at any rate in England, would Andy's <u>real</u> first name have been. Andreas. Which probably would get pronounced Anne-dria, or Andri-arse. Andy was the easier option.

E-bone meanwhile had a dead father, maybe killed, or only dying young. And Andy had no father, for that monstrous thing was gone from their lives too, Sara's and his. Heavy's mother (or moth-ah) was definitely dead. Some of them had been told this early on, by a teacher trying to protect Heavy from them. Yet, as Andy had seen, he always referred to her in the present tense.

But Heavy was mental. Went without saying. You could not look like that, and not be.

"The leaves that are left are leaving," said Heavy.
"You shouldn't try," said Heavy, "to lock the stable door after the horse has bolted it."
Heavy said, "That girl has a lake in her eyes."
Heavy said, "Look how the wind runs backward."
Heavy said, "A tortwas can't change its shell."
"Shilt," said Heavy.
"*Shit*."
"Shilt," Heavy agreed.

Nothing was special about Sackville, it was an ordinary secondary school. A modernish, many-celled glassy building, with yards outside and 'playing' fields, where organised compulsory unplayful games took place. Andy attended sometimes, and sometimes did not, as before. As before also, if more lavishly and sharply, he was warned, and told that his mother would be requested to explain his absences. Andy paid no true attention, simply politely nodded. The attempted control of the Young was already toughening, but stayed sporadic, and, initially, without full back-up at Sucks. The teachers here seemed especially harassed and incompetent, at least to Andy.

That Heavy also appeared at Sackville-Sucks never suggested itself as an oddity. Heavy was, the general opinion had it, sub-basement-normal. But Sucks was not exactly an educational paradigm. It took what it was given, and tried to drone, yell, mock or coerce fragments of knowledge into it. And where presented with slippery and non-absorbent subjects such as Andy, at one extreme, and the 'moronical' Heavy at the other, gave up. Only legal punishments were allocated – extra work, enclosures, reviews, and tirades promising parent-victimisation in lieu of pupil-torture. These were not absorbed, either, and rarely gone along with.

When Andy first noticed Heavy, slowly wandering over a games field where he had been told to "Run, boy, for Christ's sake –" Andy was not unduly astounded.

Heavy, by then, kept turning up in Andy's vicinity. Most frequently since their last days at the primary.

It went without saying, Andy, back then, always attempted – and as a rule succeeded in – getting away. This became a sort of tiresome game, pointless and stupid, for Andy. Just as were the organised rugger, cricket and football later, at Sucks. Yet Heavy still morphed into a fixture, meandering along behind Andy, or at his side, until sloughed. Oblivious to insult or the waves of hatred Andy expelled in his direction: conceivably Heavy had become accomplished at such a thickening of emotional skin. He took no notice of Andy's gibes, though when Andy ran Heavy let him go – maybe because physically, Heavy was not equipped to pursue. While they were 'together' Heavy would offer his curious observations, mistakes, musings. And sometimes, as partially with the ginger cat, and fully the *flying*, Heavy would, at last, now and then himself leave Andy.

Why Andy never physically went for Heavy remained unsure. Andy suspected it would be useless. Like the push-induced fall. Heavy would simply once more rise up. Possibly, too, Andy pitied him. Though it did not seem like that.

And then the other thing happened.

It was on the final day when he finished at the primary school. Andy had gone in mainly to see what he could steal, since thereafter these venues could be off-limits, short of breaking in. And that Andy never did. Had never had to.

"There was a wolve in the garden," said Heavy.

Andy going home – had been, and now they jointly were – walking along Hawthorne Road.

"Fox," Andy corrected.

"No, it was a wolve," said Heavy gently, prepared to be patient with such ignorance.

"You don't get fucking wolves here," said Andy. But without real anger. It even crossed his mind that a wolf had got out from somewhere, and with luck would kill and eat Heavy.

"You get wolfs," said Heavy. "Just people lie about it."

Two women were walking towards them down the sloping street. One had a small black puppy on a lead, eager and intrigued, even it seemed by the noisy, reeking flow of traffic.

Andy thought it was best if he just kept quiet and let cracked fucking Heavy ramble on. Andy could make his own getaway in the usual place. (Andy's pockets were lined with little thieved bits and pieces. Nothing needful. Nothing really of value. His.)

Sara might already be home. Her cleaning work had been rather sketchy in the past seven months. Some regular clients had moved.

Others were economising, (or had sacked her). She would not though, even if in, stay long. It would be a 'girls' night out', like all evenings when she washed her hair the previous morning, as she had today.

They were almost level with the two women and the dog. Heavy, Andy saw, was staring at the dog, yet not with his usual mesmerised-by-animal pleasure. Heavy looked – concerned –

"Oh, Joan," said one woman to the other who held the dog's lead, "your –"

"Fuck –" said Andy.

Rush, grunt and roar said the traffic, breaking open, leaving a space, as someone turned off into a driveway – with oncoming vehicles speeding adjacently forward from each side –

And the eager, intrigued puppy-dog, which had, with its antics, somehow snapped its lead, went bounding forward –

Hurling itself out –

On to the mindless, lethal, hungry road.

What happened then remained for Andy a puzzle, its images kaleidoscopic, only really assimilated afterwards, and perhaps incorrectly.

The dog had managed to gallop across half the road, due to the brief gap caused by a single car leaving the stream; a bus ran along behind it, moving rather more slowly.

But the traffic on the far side, pouring left to right, was at full charge.

And now once more, as the bus hove forward, the near side – right to left – was also congesting and pouring, an urgent glittering snot of vehicles.

In the split second that followed the dog's dive into this murdering sandwich, something else had shot forward, off the pavement and into the river of death.

The motion of this second springing thing was lumbering and big, was a senseless rubbery tumble. But also – it was swift, honed, imperious, coordinate. A leopard springing that was, too, a jelly-lead balloon.

Sounds altered.

Screeching and bumping, tinkle of tiny things that shattered, horns, psychopathic shouts.

And at the centre of the sounds, a scene. A bundle was curled up on the road, somehow glimpsed, seen *fully*, in the middle of a formless chaos where speed became stasis, a stopped frame, a *still*.

Huge and incongruous, Heavy curled up on the ground in a ball, with motionless traffic inches from him.

The two women who had been with the dog were crying. One had screamed, yes, Andy could hear the scream even now, hung up, snagged in the air, with the new voices crashing about below it.

Drivers were gabbling in their cars, some getting out.

Both traffic lanes had been stalled by the stop-frame, but they remained animate. How odd, no one seemed hurt, only unnerved and made feral by rage.

Heavy, of course, was dead. At least one car must have struck him. The dog would be dead too, somewhere under or furled into his bulk, when he tried to save it –

And then Heavy unfolded himself, again with that ungainly, ugly, and somehow perfect physical connectedness. Up he stood, holding the small black dog in his arms. And the dog was wagging its tail – Andy could see it clearly, waggling, a tiny black penis of joy. It was licking Heavy's face, joyously. Rather than minced, it had apparently just had the best thrill of its immature life.

With his usual shamble Heavy clumbered off the road on to the pavement, ignoring the bluster of the various drivers, none of whom really anyway seemed to register Heavy completely, so busy were they inspecting wing mirrors from which the glass had fallen out, or bumpers and fenders scraped by fellow motorists' motors. The line of stalled left to right traffic stretched quite a way. People were crowding on to the pavements farther along, craning to see what the fuss was about. The near side had resumed its forward momentum.

Without any bother at all Heavy came over and presented the laughing puppy to its weeping owner.

"Here, Mrs Joan," said Heavy, kindly.

Presently stunned, reason switched off, all she said was, "Thank you." And held the puppy tight.

Heavy came nextly to Andy, and they walked on up the road.

Nobody thundered after Heavy. Nobody called out to him, tried to assault or arrest or congratulate him. Nobody seemed to know quite what had occurred. Andy included himself in that.

When they reached the turn-off, Andy stopped.

"Heavy, how did you do that?"

"What?" Heavy asked amiably.

"That dog. How did you –?"

"Didn't want him squashed," said Heavy. "I've got money for an ice-chrome. You want one?"

"He's not supposed to run," Andy said now, standing on the grass field at Sucks, as the sturdy games teacher pounded up, red as any London bus and scowling with entirely extraneous wrath.

"Who are *you*?" he snarled. He was breathless after all despite his own constant workouts and joggings. "Why aren't you in your class?"

"Free period, sir," lied Andy. The second lie. "But this boy isn't supposed to run." Andy nodded at Heavy, who waited, smiling cordially, as if none of this was other than a civil discussion between civilised men, or had anything directly to do with him.

"Why not?"

"His chest, sir."

"I see," said the teacher, furious to be cheated of his prey. "Then why didn't he say so himself?"

"Well, sir, he's... a bit – er. You know."

"Mental," supplied the games teacher, his utter scorn and irritation precluding any sop to the PC views that were not yet properly in place. Let alone to mere decency. "Go for a *walk* then," he scowl-snarled at Heavy. "Brisk as you can. The size of you, you need to lose some of that blubber. You, what's your name?"

"Peter Coombs," said Andy promptly. Lucky Lie Three.

"OK, Coombs, you go with him. Try to wake him up."

"Yes, sir."

The red bus went sprinting off, thumping down its human wheels, as if redundantly to make the point. Failing to make it.

"Isn't the sky blue?" asked Heavy.

"Yes," Andy said.

## Nine

When he and Sara lived in the flat above the off-licence, regularly there had been a rising smell of alcohol. It had its origins less in the shop than in the carelessness of some customers who, having bought their cans of lager or bottles of cheap wine, opened them instantly once outside, and generally spilled some in their haste. Or else to honour the gods.

Their very first flats had stunk of stale alcohol spills too, and more intimately, from drink detonated on the premises. Or projectiled or urinated out later on: his father's offerings.

Carver did not really like alcohol, or its smell, that much. It had near associations with violence and claustrophobia.

To smell it now, so strongly, as gradually he drifted back from wherever he had been, was disorientating. Nauseating.

Carver did not move. He did not open his eyes. It was dark, he could tell easily enough without doing so. He must have gone to bed and fallen asleep, although he did not recall this. Had he been untypically drinking – knocked over the glass – not cared to clear up the mess?

Something was wrong with him, then. He must have felt ill. Why had that been? The lack of sleep, the phone calls (Donna, the persistent messageless robot, the male voice that said _Silvia_...) Or was it something to do with the decoy drive and the grey man on the train. Or the other man – the man by the – _shed_ –

Despite himself, Carver's lids flicked back.

And, as he had suspected, it was pitch black; he could see nothing.

Where were the windows?

There were no windows.

He was not out on the concrete at the garden's end, by the shed. He was not in a familiar house off a lane in a wood beyond a village. He was somewhere else. Somewhere that blared with the stench of stale beer and wine and whisky, that had neither a soundtrack nor a helpful visual. Hear no evil, see no evil: he could only _smell_ evil. And _feel_ it, under his back, his head. His hands, which he could not move since his wrists, like his ankles, were intransigently fastened down.

Automatically he stopped holding his breath. He heard himself breathe, ragged and needy. Then he heard himself speak, in a soft, rational tone. "Hello."

But the pitch-black did not answer. It was cold, and the cold did not answer either. Only the stink, stinking.

Carver lay still. His head thrummed, not painful, too hollow to conjure that. When he fell he had hit his head on the hard concreted earth. Just as Cox did, and Ebony, when Heavy pushed them. Had somebody pushed Carver? Somebody had done *something* to Carver. Done it in that second, that split second that Heavy rose up from death on the road with the living dog in his arms and Andy finally saw the unknown man standing outside the shed, lit by its turquoise radiance, was none other than Robby Johnston in an adapted rubbery diving suit.

*Scar*, he thought.
   I have reached the Third Scar.
   My mother was a scar and my monstrous father was a scar. I am the third scar.
   And I am *on* the scar, the rocky outcrop, in some high lightless cave, where once contraband booze was stored, and has leaked. Locked from the sun and the moon and the stars. But not the scars.
   I also am scarred.
   By birth, by living. My Third Scar will be death.
   Or add an 'e', he thought. Scare. *I was scared as a kid*.
   Again he drifted. Calmly he thought *And am I scared now*?

## TEN

Sara, when he was a young child, had been very good-looking. She was in her mid-twenties then.
   (His father had been perhaps good-looking too. But excessive drink and bouts of manic fury, drunk or sober, had cancelled most of that before Andy was five. And he had scarcely any illusion of it left when Sara and Andy escaped.)
   Sara did not drink seriously. But she smoked cigarettes extensively, forty to sixty a day. Later, slowly, agonisingly, she gave up, not being able to afford the rising prices.
   By the time Andy was fifteen, Sara was in her early thirties, and her looks were beginning to wash off her like make-up.
   He came back that day about 5 p.m., dissociated from his wanderings about central London; it was an overcast sullen evening, the grey 'architectural' buildings had melded with the sky. Basically, he had run out of things he wanted to do.
   At this point Andreas Carver, (or Cava, like the wine and champagne), seldom or never visited Sackville Secondary. And

coming upstairs to the flat over the off-licence, he wore his ordinary uniform of jeans, shirt and jacket, which certainly was not theirs.

Opening the door – he had a key, as he always had – he saw Sara immediately, sitting on the skimpy pinkish sofa. As a rule, she was not home yet, not today, but out cleaning, with a flock of hapless others, the Devonshire Centre off the High Street. But instead here she perched, nervilly drab in the middle of her spilling blonde strings of hair. And opposite her, on the best chair, which was a sort of mottled green-brown in colour, like a shat-on cabbage, was a guy in a suit.

It was a curious suit, too. Inevitably, a suit looked old-fashioned, but conversely it was right up to date, and sharp as a new razor blade. Deep grey, like the evening, and London, and Andy's mood. And the mood now in the flat.

Sara's pale bony face flashed about.

"Andy," she said, desperately, "this is–"

"That's OK, Mrs Carver." The man spoke with total reassuring self-assurance, false as hell. The sort of voice-over you might expect on the crashing train or plane or rocket-ship – _No need to be alarmed. Please stay seated and enjoy the view_. A combine of rich fudge – and malice – enormous sympathy, empathy – and utter frigid indifference.

Andy heard that faultlessly and knew it, even if perhaps he could not, then, have labelled it with total accuracy. _Faker. Taker. Snake._


"You haven't been going to school, Andrew, have you." (Not a question.) "Why's that?" (And this _was_ a question? Andy did not reply. The suited man regarded him with a half-smile, not friendly, nor inviting confidence, nor angry, but something – _something_.) "I think various people have spoken to you about this, Andrew. And to your mother. Outlining the possible consequences of your non-attendance." (Sara had gone into the kitchen, another miniscule space packed with minute sink, three thin cupboards, a miniaturised fridge, and an electric cooker of unwilling temperament – they consumed a lot of takeaways – to make the suit coffee. Andy had asked for coffee too, but Sara had not acknowledged his request, perhaps thinking it publicly unfitted to a growing youth just fifteen.) "It seems," said the suit, "you're not keen on school."

You could not call him a suit, really. He dominated the suit, somehow. At first *it* was what you saw, then you saw *him*, and the suit much less. You only saw his shirt because it was blue, and his eyes were blue. Vivid blue. Contacts, maybe. He had brownish hair, well-cut in a way his generation – late thirties, early forties – favoured – a bit long, loose, hankering back to the liberations of the Seventies. (It vaguely suggested itself to Andy that in twenty-five more years he too would be around the age of this man now, and the man would be, perhaps, in his sixties. Heavy might have pointed this weird sort of actuality out; Andy, by now often in contact with Heavy, had partially picked up the peculiar mind-set. Though to Andy, of course, at fifteen, trapped for the moment in the flat with the suit, it was a floating concept. More immediately he could smell the coffee, instant and cheap, and below that the faintly greasy underlay of the room – Sara did not clean thoroughly at home, being worn out by the work elsewhere. (Or, judging by the sackings, maybe not elsewhere either.) Beneath the coffee too, there was the well-known rising hint of rotted alcohol. Last night some gang had had a noisy play-fight under the windows with lager cans.)

The suit was called Sunderland.

"You're really quite bright," said Sunderland. "Or so they say. Do you think you are?"

A fresh question.

Andy decided to answer.

"No."

"How interesting. I'd have said you thought you were *very* bright, too bright in fact to have to go to classes or obey stupid rules."

Andy stared at him. Then looked away as the over-vivid eyes met his. Andy shifted slightly. He was glad when the door opened and Sara slunk back in with the coffee in the big red mug that had only one chip out of it. She had put it on a large plate in place of a tray, with the packet of sugar and a jug of milk. 'Gracious living' Sara termed that kind of thing, with a sort of mournfully scornful jealousy.

"Thank you, Mrs Carver." Sunderland added nothing to the mug. He sipped the inferior too-weak brew, did not pull a face, (as the electrician had that time), and set the mug back down. "Please don't feel you need to stay, Mrs Carver," he courteously told her, a caring prince with his rather thick domestic, "I'm sure you're snowed under with stuff to do. Andrew and I are fine."

Snowed under. Sara, a jittery, shiny little bug, muttered some incoherent appeasement, and flitted back into the kitchen. She did not even leave the door ajar. Frightened all over again, very likely she preferred not to hear, as she had not when his father had begun to rev up.

"The thing is, Andrew," said Sunderland the suit, "We've been looking at your record," (a vinyl album of hits, a file in police archives, an unbroken achievement at running the mile in one second), "and you truly have some potential, we feel. But you're not going to realise it by skiving off all the time. The teachers at Sacks, of course, are pure unmoderated shit," (*what*? Andy found he was sitting bolt upright, as if pulled by the sparking strings of the unexpected swear word), "so frankly we don't blame you for hiking your arse straight out of there and off to do something worthwhile. At least, that way, you're learning about real life, or you are to a certain qualified extent. More than the so-called curriculum will teach you, definitely."

A pause.

Andy now was staring full-on at Sunderland, and *trying* to catch his eye. And Sunderland, an accomplished flirt, was gazing instead upwards at a genuine fly that, nervous as Sara, was skittering along the ceiling.

The fly and the pause continued.

Sunderland spoke again. "Why don't you," he asked mildly, not glancing Andy's way, "open the window so that poor little bugger can get out?"

Like an automaton Andy rose, reached the window, opened it.

"Go on," said Sunderland, conversationally, to the fly, "make a break for freedom while you can, matey."

And the fly let go the stained plaster, whizzed across the narrow space, and shot through the opening into the dismal onset of evening.

"How did you do that?" Andy said. As he had said it to Heavy, after the business with the dog.

"What? Oh, that. I didn't. It's called coincidence. Sit down, Andrew – or do you prefer Andreas?"

Andy sat down. Sunderland must know his true original name from the 'record'.

"Andy," said Andy.
"OK. Andy. You're fifteen now, aren't you." (Also no question. Sunderland knew, that was all. Knew all of it.) "How about we get you into a college? No, I don't mean like a university, and I don't mean like a fob-off pile of crap. I mean somewhere you'll have quite a bit of freedom, access to good tuition from people who respect you, and a range of choices, or at least up to a point, on what you learn and how and when you learn it."
Andy sat there. None of this made sense.
"Why?" he said. But only for something to say. He had reached the state of grasping he would have to respond. Just as the fly had done.

Logical or not, since the dog, they had hung out together quite a bit, he and Heavy.
Heavy usually instigated their meetings, if you could call his approaches that. He would just turn up, arrive. And, after the dog, Andy did not try to get away from him.
Andy did not analyse why not, or why he now spent time with Heavy, walking about, or sitting in the playing fields – when vacated – even sometimes going to see an afternoon movie, or watching one at the flat when Sara was out. (Andy stole these films, of course, from *Video Rodeo*, or one of the other hire places round about. He would have had to steal most of them, as most were over-18, dark adult horror, psychology, or – if very seldom – rather limpingly mild porn. But, once seen, and usually only once, he would thieve-them-back, reintroducing them into the relevant shop, either in exactly the right spot, or else somewhere unmatched, as if some browser had picked them up and then put them back wrongly. Somehow the security cameras never seemed to catch him out. But they were always going wrong, those things. Only now and then he did retain a movie, and then he would never view it again. There were even so by now exceptions to his steal-only-worthless (to him) articles. A habit he knew that later, if ever he had any proper cash, he could break).
Although Heavy came to the flat then, sometimes, he never did this if Sara were to be home. On the couple of occasions he found she already was, Heavy simply sloped away inside a couple of minutes. "*Who* was *that*?" Sara had asked Andy initially, crinkling her eyes and brows and mouth which, for a moment made her, he

thought, appear like a stranger and completely ugly. "What," Sara uglily added, "are you doing with such an ugly funny-looking lump? He must weigh about sixteen stones –"

"Eighteen," said Andy. This was not a fact.

"Well," had said Sara, "there we are, then." And she gave her hysterical giggle.

Andy was not offended, he thought, by Sara's take on Heavy. It was the normal one, the *popular* one. It had been his, before. He thought of his father then, for half a minute, big and overweight, faceless with hatred, smashing Sara against the walls of the other earliest flats.

While Heavy though did come into Andy's home when Sara was absent, Andy was never invited to Heavy's domicile, whatever or wherever it was. Nor did Andy ever try to find out, let alone gain access. Sometime after, it came to Andy that he did not even know who Heavy lived with. His mother was dead; that had been established by the staff at the Potters Road Primary, even if Heavy always referred to her as if she were not dead, indeed, often suggested, by reference, he had recently spoken to her: *I asked my moth-ah about that*, or *Moth-ah told me there are black swans, and a brown kind too* – after somebody on the bus the previous day had been talking about swans, (white). Andy had very little interest in Heavy's home life. As very little in his own.

But Heavy, what he said, his – frankly non-human, even un-*earthly* – perception of virtually all things – "See, that blackbird is flying up to the moon" – "That red glass in the church window is from where they spit the comm-onion wine" – alerted, almost *fascinated* Andy. He no longer thought of these verbal overflows as errors, or signals of mental retardation. Heavy was like – what was it? – some oracle or prophet from some weird past history. What he said made sense some *other* way, or was a sign of things that could not happen, *happening* – some place or other. Somehow or other. An alternate reality. Or, they only made Andy laugh. He *liked* them. Why not?

Heavy's physical being too had changed for Andy.

No longer did he regard Heavy as a monstrosity. Heavy had his own inexplicable coordination. He did *not* blunder or shamble. It was... not like that. And here and there too, as if a blurred curtain were lifted between them, as when Heavy rose up from the bully's push, or leapt to save the little black dog, you could see there was to his movements a kind of purest animal adjustment. Leopard, panther, mammoth. And surely, he was indestructible? Attack and livid mechanical danger had not seemed able to hurt him. While his mad Old Testament prophet mind, rich in its own panorama, never yielded to the would-be ruination of external threats or deeds.

Andy did not wonder if his own view-point ever became tinted by any of Heavy's. Andy did not stick a definition on what, years in the future, he recognised as Heavy's joi de vivre.

Andy never considered either if he loved Heavy, as it was possible to love someone asexually yet deeply – as one might love a wonderful father, or mother – as Heavy himself seemed to love his _own_ mother, her death an utter irrelevance.

Andy thought, but did not think. Which was surely how one survived.

When Andy located Heavy, he was standing by the 'lake' in the park, watching the shining green ducks move over the dark green polished surface, and showing his habitual duck-approval.

"If you could wish for something," said Andy, "what would it be?"

Heavy apparently pondered.

"An oransh," said Heavy, truthfully.

Andy burst out laughing. All the strain and bewilderment, vague spurts of what might be excitement, or sheer misgiving, left clinging to him from the evening before, sprayed off and dissolved, for the moment harmless, in the air.

"There was this guy called Sunderland," said Andy eventually.

"Underland," said Heavy.

"_Sun_derland."

"Sun under land," said Heavy. The prophet had proclaimed a secret clue?

But Andy went on, telling Heavy in a rush not common to him, about the interview. About the College.

"It's not in London. Some dump in the country. But I'll be a – boarder. Only they give you your own room – it sounds... all right..."

Heavy watched him, nodding once.

"I don't know if I want to go. I don't know if it's good – or fucking shit. Only I'd get away from her," (he meant, of course, Sara), "it sounds – OK. Perhaps. I'll piss off out if it isn't." Andy turned to the lake. He did _not_ know what he thought. He did not want to go. Felt they might force him. Was too *anxious* to go – or to refuse –

They stood there, he and Heavy, about three feet apart, watching the ducks whose heads, Heavy had formerly explained, were the colour of "Jait" or "Corianta leafs."

"He said, Sunderland, if I didn't go I'd wish I had. He said what did *I* wish for?" said Andy. "And what did I? Not an orange. Make a proper wish," demanded Andy. Conceivably he wanted Heavy to wish him good luck.

Heavy did not speak.

Andy said, "I wish it's OK."

Heavy spoke then to the lake. His voice sounded old and strong and strangely fined. An actor's voice, but not a modern one.

"May all the good be happy," said Heavy to the lake. "And all the bad be good."

They separated about two minutes later, without another direct look, without touching. Aside from unexpected dreams, or in sudden glints of memory, Andy had never seen Heavy again.

# Eleven

From the darkness someone replied.

"Hello, Car."

Carver: Where am I?
Someone: Where do you think you are?
Carver: (Pause) I don't know.
Someone: Perhaps *I* don't, either.

PAUSE

Carver: Is there anyone there?
Someone: I'm here.
Carver: Who are you?
Someone: Who are *you*?
Carver: You – know who I am.
Someone: Do I know?
Carver: What's my name?

Someone: Can't you remember?
Carver: Can't *you* remember?
Someone: Ask another question.
Carver: You – ask another question

SILENCE

Are you still there?

SILENCE

*****

The Voice: You're awake again, Car?
Carver: (Pause) I think I am.
The Voice: Shall we resume? Do you think that's something we should do?
Carver: Why am I here?

PAUSE

The Voice: Why shouldn't you be here?

PAUSE

Carver: The last thing I remember was the shed. And then...
The Voice: Yes?
Carver: Was it gas, the drug?
The Voice: Something like that.
Carver: What happened to Johnston?
The Voice: Who is Johnston?
Carver: The man in the rubber diving suit.
The Voice: How quaint. Something quaint in that.
Carver: It was dark. He wore a mask.
The Voice: If you say so.
Carver: And then you drugged me.
The Voice: *I* drugged you?
Carver: Somebody. I want some water.
The Voice: Maybe later. Something can be arranged. Later.

PAUSE

Carver: Why am I secured?
The Voice: Are you? Are you *sure* you are?
Carver: Yes – I – *yes*. Christ – my ankles and wrists. Some kind of electronic lock – I need a lavatory.
The Voice: I'm afraid you'll have to see to all that where you are.
Carver: Why?
The Voice: It will save us all time. Go on. Help out.
Carver: Where is Stuart?
The Voice: Who is Stuart?
Carver: Jack Stuart. Mantik Corp.
The Voice: Something tells me you are feeling a little stronger, Car.
Carver: You keep repeating that word. *Something*.
The Voice: Something. Some things do get repeated.
Carver: I need some water.

SILENCE

Silence. Next a sound of dripping, trickling, then a gush – a tap turned on, perhaps. But not close enough. (And anyway it is, from the reek, alcohol again, some sort of too-sweet gin.) Presently it stops, the sound if not the stink.

Scar. Scarred. Scared. S car, Car, Carver.

Andreas Cava.

Darkness. Sleep returning, coming in even through the fear and the sullen ache in the bladder, and the dry burning of the throat and mouth. Somewhere on the edges of the new induced nothingness, stands Robby Johnston and his fixed black jellies of eyes. Is it Robby that has taken him prisoner here? The voice was not Robby's voice. And it repeated one particular word. It *is* Mantik that have him, surely. And now he is to be tried. And found wanting.

## Twelve

Bright sunlight seared a second window through the blind. Outside he could hear faintly the whirr of big wings as birds crossed over the house from the back garden to the woods and fields the far side of the lane. And downstairs, an occasionally chittering monotone, without doubt the TV in the kitchen above the breakfast bar, dispensing its obligatory sensation and inanity and horror. There was the scent of coffee.

Something (*something*) seemed slightly odd to him as he got out of the spare bed. A dream maybe, now forgotten. A dream of Heavy, had it been? Or Johnston – or was it about Sara and the sandwich-size flat over the off-licence when he was a kid, and Mantik had first reached out for him, and sent him off to the unusual college in the country...?

He had slept in pyjamas, as only rarely he did. He went to the window and let up the blind.

The back garden of the house in the village was not there after all.

The house had transported itself, presumably during the night, to the summit of a high rocky hill, or cliff, which now gazed directly outwards at a spangled blue plain of daylit sea, the sun standing, rather to the left, on its own searing tail of reflection.

Another bird flew in and over. It was a gull.

Carver remembered the black night-morning garden, the man in black rubber, the glare and then the nothingness, the spaces of other darkness swelling and fading, bound hands and feet, pissing himself, throat full of dry fire. And here he was at this window, in a room that was – or entirely resembled – the spare room of the house, its proportions and its furniture, everything but for the view from its window. He was showered and fresh, his bladder even not urgent. The taste of familiar toothpaste and mouthwash was in his fully moisturised mouth.

But he could hear the kitchen TV, which Donna had switched on as she always did when she was the first down. He could smell coffee. A hint of bacon too. The pyjamas though, now he looked at them, were not exactly anything he had worn before.

The sky was blue, bluer than the sea, as if to encourage it to extra effort. Was this summer? It had been early autumn. Had it?

Yes.

"*Something...*"

The voice spoke again in Carver's memory.

Carver glanced about the room. His clothes lay on a chair, as he might have left them in either of the house bedrooms. They were clean. The boxers were clean. But they were, all of them, these things, the ones he had worn that night. The night before. Or days ago perhaps. Or weeks.

Or a month or a year.

He did not know what the drug was they had used. Or what other, if any, medleys of drugs had been employed to subdue, question, restrain, terrify, reassure him.

Was he still under the influence of anything...?

"*Something.*"

He could not tell.

His stomach growled, abruptly hungry, a starved beast scenting and responding to the aroma of coffee and food. Which now seemed to be evaporating. Had he imagined them? How long besides had he been without such things? But he sensed no weakness. His weight and stamina felt and seemed to him as usual.

He checked his pulse. It was steady. Putting off the pyjamas he looked himself over, turning to the wall mirror for confirmation. He had no bruises, raw or fading, no signs of injury. His colour was normal. His eyes were neither inflamed nor over-bright, the pupils reacting correctly to light or shadow. There was no vertigo.

Downstairs – if it was – it sounded as if it were – he heard a clear burst of laughter. A male voice, or two, and a female one. No words, but the tone and timbre – Donna did not laugh like that, that smooth contralto ripple. But one of the male laughters – could that be Herons?

Carver snatched up and put on the clothing, *his* clothing. He went to the bedroom door and tried it. Without protest, it opened.

Outside, again, utter unfamiliarity. The corridor was long, painted pale, and veered sharply from sight at two corners, one to the left and one to the right. Three other doors, these closed, marked both the walls either side of his door. Facing him across the corridor there were no doors, only two windows, separated by some five featureless metres.

He tried each of the doors, all were locked shut. Then he went to each of the windows.

They looked inland, away from the sea, and up across a wild park or large overgrown garden. He barely took this in. There on a rise, whose summit ascended less than a quarter mile off, and reasonably visible through the big green trees, had been stationed a Russian train, (circa 1900?), of many carriages.

They were, unvaryingly, of a rich marmalade colour. *Something*... Chekovian, Tolstoyan... Every carriage was Carver's shed from the house, and by day, their windows were blank of any glow, merely catching the sheen of the sun as it flew slowly upward over and across this unknown building, by this unknown summer sea.

Neither man was Herons.

He knew neither of them. Nor the woman.

The men were both of fairly average appearance, shortish hair. The older had a long, rather gangly loose frame, like that of a teenager suddenly aged into his full-grown fifties. He raised one hand in a token of greeting and said he was Van Sedden Then the shorter man said, in a slightly amused way, "I'm Ball. Singular. Like Soccer. Or a dance." The woman did not speak, although unlike the men she stared directly at Carver, seemingly taking in every atom that visually she could. She was black, light-skinned, with cropped brown-black fleecy curls. Her body was heavy but voluptuously curved, if fitted unbecomingly in a scarlet shell-suit and trainers. Her eyes were blue. That could happen, though he had never seen it before. She had no expression, her perfectly-shaped lips held still, as if they were for decoration only. The two men both wore suits, tieless shirts, everyday shoes. Ball wore a watch, a Rolex, and a silver wedding ring.

Carver said, "Carver. Where is this place?"

No one replied. Then Van Sedden murmured, almost reproachfully, "God, *He* knows. Not I."

"So you don't know," said Carver. He looked at Ball. "How about you?"

"Nope. Haven't a fucking clue, baby."

Carver looked at the woman. She continued to meet his eyes with her hot-sky blue ones, and she spoke after all: "Why don't you have some coffee?" Her voice was ordinary. A London voice. Somehow he did not *believe* in her voice. It was some sort of disguise – but to think so was probably irrational.

Why not, though, be irrational?

Look where rationality had got him.

He sat down at the long wooden kitchen table and pulled the coffee pot towards him. Filter. It would do. Ball had passed him a plain shiny black mug. They all had those, and black plates with crumbs of toast, and Ball's plate with a gleaming after-effect of bacon and butter. There was one unused plate.

Carver poured himself coffee.

Was this what he had scented upstairs? How? The scent had been pumped up into his room...?

Perhaps the coffee had something in it.

He did not try it.

The woman drew the pot away from him, topped up her own mug, and drank. She had stopped looking at him, as if there was nothing more to see in him at all.

Carver took a slow mouthful from his own mug. The fluid was hot. The taste filled his mouth and flowed down his already moist and comfortable throat. (Somewhere in the recesses of the drugged dark, they had roused him and bathed him, or he had bathed himself and cleaned his teeth, and drunk water, and seen to any other bodily functions outstanding. Only he could recall nothing of it.) Carver thought about the first time he had drunk coffee. He had made it for himself in a house Sara had gone to clean, lugging him with her because he was too young to be left, while the people whose house it was were on holiday and would not know. He had been five, he thought. Something like that. Sara had slapped him when she saw what he had done. But her slaps were nothing after the beatings of his father. And he had liked the coffee, even if it was instant and had burnt his tongue. Forbidden fruit always had a sting in the tail.

This kitchen was very small. The table and four chairs crowded most of any space. To the sides were squeezed in a pair of little sinks, a microwave and doll's house oven, shelves of things in packets and cans and boxes, a tall fridge-freezer narrow as a giant pencil.

Abruptly a door, partly wedged behind the freezer, came open, and a brisk young woman jigged in with a tray of bacon sandwiches and another smoking coffee pot. She put these on the table without a word, and without a word the people in the kitchen received them.

When she had gone, the narrow door shambled awkwardly shut

again behind the pencil. The two men helped themselves to the food. Carver took a sandwich. He bit into it carefully, as if afraid of breaking a tooth. But it seemed only to be bacon, butter, bread, exactly what it had pretended to be.

Outside, beyond the large window closed over by a thick matt-blond blind, unseen seagulls were screeching along the edges of the rocky height.

Chew the bacon, taste, swallow. Swallow the coffee.

Maybe a drug had been wiped into the mug, or on to the spare plate. Too late now.

He felt nothing like that. Yet the inevitable tension, the adrenalin-readiness that should be in him, and now building, was not really there at all, or – it was far off, about one quarter of a mile away, like the line of carriage-sheds on the rise. Just near enough to see and understand without effort. Not close enough to touch, or feel.

Carver, instead, felt a strange depression. It was very likely the residue of the drug leaving him – both the removal of feeling and now this subterranean dragging lethargy, like some of the symptoms he had heard described with insipient ME. What could he do? Nothing, as yet. Or ever? Nothing.

He left the remainder of the sandwich. Finished the single coffee, and pushed the mug a little away.

The black woman had produced a small notebook and pen from her shell-suit pocket. (No laptop then?) She was writing something down, tiny twitters of biro ink, unreadable. Was she making notes on him?

Carver spoke.

"Do any of you know why you are here?"

The man called Van Sedden laughed. It was certainly one of the laughters Carver had detected from upstairs. Sound must have been electronically passed into his room, if not smell.

"None of us know. Like life. None of us know, beyond **the** physical act, why we're alive, and none of us know why we are here. So we invent possible reasons. God caused us to be born. So then, did God decide we should be brought *here*?"

Friendly, Ball said, "Shut up, Seddy."

Carver said, "What *happens* here?"

"Apart from breakfast, you mean?" asked Ball.

Carver waited.

Ball shrugged. "Nothing much."

The woman said, "People come and go, Carver."

Carver said, "You didn't tell me your name."

Her head turned again to him, slowly, reminding him of a snake. Her face appropriately had still no expression. And rather than speaking, she tore out of the notebook one page, and wrote carefully on it, then passing the paper to him. Carver read the name: ANJEELA MERVILLE. (*Anjeela* seemed to him more Asian than Caribbean or African. Or was it a fanciful take on *Angela*? And *Merville* – did the blue eyes come from that side?) "Thank you."

But she had gone back to her tiny notations.

The choked door behind the fridge was abruptly opened once more. A tall portly man in a suit eased an awkward if practiced entrance around the fridge-freezer, and stood smiling affably. "Morning, all. Ah, Mr Carver. Can you be ready in about twenty minutes? Mr Croft would like to see you in his section. Somebody will come down to show you the way."

Carver said, "All right."

What else was there to say?

The upstairs corridor had led, on the eastern turn, to a locked double-doored cupboard. The western end of the corridor went round its corner to a stairhead. The stairs were wide and quite shallow, and descended between the pale clean painted walls to a square hall lit with sidelights, and with brown tiles. Off this to one side opened a cloakroom, with a small high frosted window, a lavatory and washbasin, a mirror, and hooks for coats – nothing hung there. (Everything was pristine, and newish, as everything else seemed to be.) The other room that opened was a sort of storage area, lit from above by a neon strip, with (locked) cupboards. Beyond this, through a square open arch, the kitchen.

To meet with Mr Croft, nevertheless, they went out a different way, via the fridge-freezer-door, Carver getting by without much fuss, but the fat, very young man in shorts and a loose white T-shirt, making a bit of a scene of it. "Why that bloody door has to be bunged up by that bloody fridge beats me!" he snapped red-faced. Then resumed the smiling pleasantries he had begun with. He was the guide who was to conduct Carver "to Mr Croft's section".

"Hope you slept well?"

"Sure," said Carver.

"Good, good. That's good." (Was 'good' *his* Word of the Day?) "Big old place, this. Have you seen the sea?"

"Yes."

"Fabulous day. I mean to do a bit of cycling later. Wonderful weather for it. Do you cycle?"

"No."

"Should, you know. Bloody good for you."

The fat health expert had by then got them down a long doorless corridor, windowless and neoned, and hung with pretty photographed images of trees and mountains, and let them both into a steel lift. There were no markers as to the number of floors but, seamless and almost silent, they went up past six. This 'place' was tall then, or it was in parts.

They emerged next in a second doorless corridor with long windows to the left. The view was vast and soaring – rock edges, sea, sky, wheeling gulls with sun-gold wings.

"Where are we, here?" asked Carver quietly.

"Seventh floor, old mate."

"I mean, the area. The district. The sea."

"Yes," said the cyclist, enthused and beaming, "it's fabulous, isn't it? Beautiful weather too."

"England," said Carver. "Is it?"

But they were through the corridor and the cyclist-guide was pressing buttons by a tall shut metal door. "Just a sec, old son."

And the door slid open, and there was another person beam-beaming, a beaming girl in a summer dress and long fair hair.

"Mr Carver! Please come in. Thanks, Charlie. Take care."

"Please sit down, Carver. That chair is the one I'd recommend."

He – Croft – sat against the blinded, lighted window, and was in silhouette. An old trick, clichéd, out of date, filmic, foolish. Effective. A big shape, a big man, tall and broad-bodied, from flesh, bone or muscle, conceivably all three. His voice put him at about forty, but of course that did not have to mean much. He could be in his sixties, seventies even, if he was strong and vocally trained. His hair, against the brilliant blind, looked like a piece, an actor's wig, convincing only on a stage. But here the glare might deceive. After all, Carver found the sunlight irritated his vision, staring into it, or at the dark mound of the man titled Mr Croft.

The chair was all right. Not designed to make the sitter either luxuriously comfortable or anything opposite. Another black mug of hot black coffee had been set in front of Carver on the desk-like table, and a jug of water with ice and a lemon slice and a polished glass in reaching distance, before the happy, jolly girl had taken her leave.

It was doubtless of no use to ask any questions as yet, if ever.

"Well," said Croft.

Not an inquiry. Just a statement.

The sides of Carver's tongue were electric with the urge to speak, to *demand*.

He did not. Only sat and stared at the actor against the light. And Carver's eyes pricked and began to water. Carver looked down.

And there was Croft again, printed white on a blur of floating darkness. Afterimage. Omnipresent.

Croft shifted. A profile appeared, a large hooked nose and shaven jaw, a heavy-lidded eye that glinted and then grew dark. By the description of the light, the wig was iron.

"Today's a sunny day," said Croft, "rare in England."

(Is he telling me that we are *not* in England, where such sunny days are rare? Or that we *are*, and *so* the rarity?) "They say the climate's changing, of course they do. Bang on and on about it. Slightest unusual weather. Make us all worry, worry. Always all our fault. But I can remember rainy summers and autumns just the same. And waterlogged springs. Even you, probably, saw the same processions of dull grey unwarm days when you were a kid. Snow in May. And not limited to the UK, all across Europe."

Carver did not speak. It was not apparently, essential.

Croft rose. Yes, about six foot three, and of a strongly developed, heavy frame. Approximately two hundred and fifteen pounds. "Why not we go outside, have a stroll in the grounds? What do you say, Car?"

It was not the voice from the drugged darkness.

It was not a voice Carver knew.

In any case, neither the voice nor the man took any notice of Carver's reaction, even the chance of one. Croft, risen, strode towards the room's second door, and plainly Carver must get up and go with him. Carver did not prevaricate. What point? He too rose and followed Croft, who opened the door by the previous means of a pressed button-panel in the wall. The door undid itself into another corridor, low-lit, featureless, windowless, and winding. It seemed to take a few minutes to go along it and reach another door operating on buttons. Which in turn undid itself into another lift. Down they flowed, five, six floors – seven? The lift door gave on a dazzle of flooded white and burning green and blue, drowning Carver's eyes. A terrace, flagged. Stone steps with a safe if ornamental stone handrail. The park – the grounds – beyond, the savage tangles of unpruned bushes and trees, the high-grassed upslopes, the radiance, and the salt-clear smell of the sea from the far side of the house, and the gulls, borne over now by some updraught, noiseless and floating. From the position of the sun, this place had just gone by midday, in somewhere or other.

They walked up a slope, but the trees were very thick, their trunks often wider than three or four Crofts hugged together. The foliage was a static deluge of green fire. Or was that a *yellow* leaf there? It might indicate only damage, not a season. One did not see through the trees anyway, to any other slope. The Russian train-carriage sheds were not visible.

"Ah, here's the bench. We'll sit, shall we?"

They sat, side by side, separated by an interval of about one metre, on the long smooth stone seat. It had a flat and upright back, and arm rests at either end in the shape of – what were they? Griffins, Carver thought. Yes, griffins, eagles' heads and the bodies of lions. An impossibility, and not what they seemed.

Nowhere in view was there any sign of a boundary, a wall or electrified fence. No indication of anything significant, beyond the trees.

Croft stretched, lazily, as if entirely at ease.

"Lovely place, this. And wonderful weather." (Would he now suggest they go cycling? He did not.)

But the big carven head, under its iron cap of real or unreal hair, smoothly turned, and there were the two dark eyes, looking for his.

Carver met them. His father had had eyes as dark as this, though of a different colour. He himself, Carver thought, had eyes the same as Croft's. (Cava. Andreas Cava.)

"The point is," said Croft mildly, "I want you to relax, Car. I can see that may be difficult for you at the moment.

Understandably so. And in light of that, I want to fill in a few of the empty boxes for you, explain how things are, here. You're safe, Car. Perfectly safe. Safer here, with us, than probably you have been all these past – how many? Let's see, it's around eighteen to twenty years, is it? I mean since when you got into that college out in the wilds of – *Suffolk* was it? Or West Sussex... Slips my mind, but of course, you'll remember it well. Rescued from that daft secondary school – called after that bloody woman Vita Sackville-West, I suppose. They started your training off there, at the *college*, bit by bit. And then recruited you for the Service. Serve your country. Save your land. Anti-any-and-all-others – even our beloved allies, the Godforsaken Yanks, if it comes to it. An interesting job for a boy, a young man. Not boring. What is it Mantik's slang calls its own people? Life Long Enemies, that's it, isn't it, Car? L.L.E. The L.L.E. of all the other oppressive and misguided regimes all over the world, and of all their spies and vandals. The *Secret* Secret Service. That's you. Rule Britannia. And then you make one tiny little error, and Mantik puts on its dinner jacket and gets ready to eat you up alive."

Croft stopped talking. He stared on into Carver's eyes, which did not now have to water, in the warm green thoughtfulness of the shade.

"You're saying this place has nothing to do with Mantik," Carver said, flat, neutral.

"As far from Mantik as the moon, Car. Much, much farther. From here, you can *see* the *moon*, now and then."


Croft was leaning back again, his jacket removed and slung over his arm of the bench, his legs stretched out, crossed at the ankles. He might be anyone, taking a break, enjoying the summer, or autumn Indian Summer, as perhaps it was. Certainly the many scanning devices that would be discreetly planted around would pick up that pose. And Carver's *too*, sitting still, tense and listening. There might be men as well, discreetly planted around, armed and waiting for the chance that after all Carver decided to run for it. But surely, lessoned as he had been at Mantik, he would never attempt such a futile thing.

"Why am I safe," he said at last, "with you, if not with Mantik?"

"We, Car, are the *corporation* that in turn keeps an eye on *them*.

Somebody has to. I'm certain, if you consider it carefully, you can see the common sense of such a back-up unit. So no, Car, nobody here is asking you to become – that lovely Shakespearianesque word – a *traitor*. You're still fully in British hands. Just as you're on British – English – soil."

"Why do you want me?"

"Why did *Mantik* want you? Have you never properly asked yourself that? No, you haven't, you see. We don't, do we? We all already know we are special. That's how we survive being *alive*. And thus, of *course* they would single *you* out."

"I'm – I was an errand boy."

"Jargon. My dear Car, do you *really* think that was all they wanted from you?"

"It was just about all I did." (No point in lying, Carver thought. This set-up, whatever it was, had evidently wrung out of him, with the drugs, the darkness, all those Mantik matters they wanted. Though he had not known much. Maybe, thinking him evasive... Had he even been fully tortured? He had no wounds, of course, no pain, and no memories **of** such events. But neither had he recalled the bathing, and cleaning of his teeth – yet it had happened. Whatever they had wanted to happen had happened, But why – why did these people, a surveillance team monitoring Mantik, rescue him – if rescue it had been? Why did *they* want him at all?

"So I'm special," Carver said quietly. "Again, why?"

"Oh, you'll see in due course. Do you remember the woman called Silvia Dusa?"

"She's dead."

"So she is, but a while before that tragic occurrence, she contacted us. She alerted us – to *you*. That was *her* mistake, you see, Car. And yours was in not realising. Silvia had come over to us. She wasn't happy about Mantik's plans. So Mantik set you both up, and then – shall I say *helped* her on her terminal way in that public house. Just as they would have you, Carver, somewhere or other. Also in due course. But that's all over now. You're safe. You're with us."

"Where are we?" said Carver. "England *where*?"

"Kent. That'll do for now."

"*Who* are you?"

"I've told you our nature, but you'd like an actual name? We don't have one. Not even in our official or office slang. We're just – us. Welcome to us, Car. Make yourself at home."

# Thirteen

In the dream, he saw the coloured flowers blotted on the meadows, the wilder walks around the college. White daisies, red and magenta clovers... And then the huge, clipped lawn, with its area for spontaneous rough football, and the river you could swim in. They had taught him to swim, and once or twice he had even played football – those items he had been meant to have had taught to him at the schools. He liked the *aloneness* and the space – and yet keeping the consolidated steady link to the house. It was a big house, and quite old, 17th Century perhaps. Or bits of it. There was an orchard with apples. He had never liked apples before, but these had a sharp sweet acid kick, better than the gin he had once illicitly tried at age ten and a half. He did not ever like booze any way. He did not like or respond to 'teaching' – but here, somehow, he did. He learned other things than swimming and games.

He learned to read properly, that was, to take stuff in, hold and analyse and so find out what it meant. He learned where countries were, and how they worked, or were believed to, and how to calculate mathematically, multiply, qualify, equate. The correlation of numbers, words, codes. To think things through.

He learned that.

Nobody ever forced. Nobody nagged or pursued if you missed some class or talk. But in the end, you did not miss so many. The meals were good, the 'canteen'. He had his own room, and it was of reasonable if hardly giant size. He had a music centre and TV, ultimately use of a computer, only slightly restricted, for recreation or research. The college was not crowded; its students were 'selected' and both male and female. He had sex.

By then, his horizons partnered, both narrowing and expanding. They were becoming *concentrated*. He was altered but altered potentially into *himself*. He seemed to lose nothing he had wanted. But gained extras. He still stole things. He kept them in the desk in his room, which could be opened by his using – not a key – but a sequence of numbers he had chosen and, presumably, (years later he was not so certain of this), known only to himself.

In the dream, he saw the flowers in the meadows. He did not care that they were flowers, or beautiful, or helpful for the environment, but they were part of the new life he had had. They were, (then) the _Now_.

He was by the river next, in the dream. About fifteen, he thought, or sensed. And he glanced up, and on a rise beyond the slow green summer water, he noticed a stone bench. Heavy was sitting there. Heavy, who he had never seen again after that day in the park, after the advent of Sunderland and the college.

Heavy was grown up. Thirty or forty, possibly. Incredibly obese and ungainly, yet somehow he had been poured into a vast and elegant grey suit, the kind powerful guys wore in movies from around 1948. He had rested back his peculiar head, and stretched out his froggish legs, crossing them loosely at the ankles.

Carver was pleased to see Heavy, yet startled, in the dream. He was going to call out to Heavy when Donna moved up close to him across the bed, and put her hands on his spine, and then around him to his stomach, low down, not quite touching his genitals. The dream faltered and started to swirl off.

He woke in the dark. Yes, she was close up against him.

Working on him slowly, softly, with a feline determination. In the beginning, the commencement of their relationship, he had made the advances more often than she. But then it came to be almost always Donna who moved first. Lascivious and eager. It was easy for him to respond, of course. Even once she began to alter, to become more impatient, unreasonable in other areas, even eventually in the area of sex: "You don't like me really, do you, Car? I'm not what you wanted. I saw you look at that bitch in the restaurant. She's more your type. _Isn't_ she?" Or, with deadly 'reasonableness' – "Don't if you don't want to. You're too tired. No. Another night." Although he never did make it 'another night' but always that one, right then, once she had – what? – propositioned him – laid hands on him – her pretty, long-fingered hands, with long painted nails, warm, urgent, fragrant with faintly chemical handcreams, the scent of unreal lilies, of roses, daisy-flowers, clover –

"Donna..." he said, and turned over, the last papery fragments of the dream crumbling from him into thin air.

Her scent was different tonight. It was smoky and deeper – a cello note that had been a staccato piping – her skin – was like – velvet – it – There was a faint light in the room after all. There was no pallor to Donna's skin, or her hair, and under his mouth the texture of her neck was feral but very cool. He lifted away from her. Her eyes were there, abruptly seen, luminous as the eyes of Donna were not. He flung back from her and slammed on the bedside lamp. Both he and she, it seemed, knew to *shut* their eyes then, to protect them from the glare. And then open their eyes and see. They were ice-blue, her eyes. She was not Donna. She was the woman from the breakfast, Angela or Anjeela Merville.

"Good evening," she said, with a softly calm politeness. And then she laughed. "You buzz with electricity. Did you know?"

"What the shit are you doing here?"

"What do you think I am doing here?"

Carver swung himself over, off and out of the bed. He was naked, but the disturbed covers now completely revealed that she was too.

In the low harsh light she looked young, desirable, her full breasts with their black strawberries of nipples, her heavy thighs, the mask of black fur nestled between them. Her hair looked darker too, and longer than he had thought. The smell of her was lush and tasty. Chocolate, honey –

He swallowed, and the smell and taste of her entered him.

"Ms Merville, thanks for your visit. I'd like you to get out now."

She lay looking at him. She said, "No, you wouldn't."

His body had responded to hers. In the lamplight it was absurdly obvious.

"Don't judge a book by its cover," he said.

"Nor you."

Something then – something odd – as if, in this quilted lacuna between the frames of drugged dark and copious alien greeting – anything could *seem* odd any longer – for a second, she looked *familiar*. He *knew* her. But he did not.

"Did Croft send you?"

"No."

"You'll be aware, there will be," he said, "hidden surveillance in this room. Sound, too. They can pump noise, even smells through from the kitchen, for example. So why not the other way with every word intact?"

"If you say so."

"You should *know*," he said. "What is it? Get me to fuck you and take pictures? Why –" he said, "why bother. You – they – have got me, haven't they? Whoever they are. The nameless corporation here, the guards who guard the *guards*. They've got me, though

Christ knows why."

She moved, fluid as a pelt, a silk cord, on to her spine. Her belly was soft and smooth. Her mouth. Her hair –

"Come back to me," she said.

He went back to her.

As he leaned over her she said, so softly he barely heard her, "Remember my name, Car. *Remember* it. *An-jee*-la," she whispered. "*An-jee*la. *Mer*–" But her voice vanished into his mouth. Instead she put up both her hands, taking hold of his body. Now her touch burned him.

He ceased to care about the room and the cameras or the mikes, the Third Persons. He had forgotten Croft. Perhaps he had been drugged also to this intensity of mindless lust and strength. Or it was another dream. It was a vehicle – a car at night, driving straight forward into a wall of fire. You did not stop. You crashed through into the flames. And then it was over. There was nothing more to it, nothing at all.

In the renewal of the darkness she left him. Almost the last of her, her scent, and her voice again, close to his ear,

"A J," she whispered. "AJ, MV." Nonsense, Irrelevant.

But that was nothing either. Everything was nothing. Nothing was anything. He heard the door shut, quietly. How had she got in, the door had been secured... nothing. Anything. Nothing. He did not sleep, yet a sort of trance fell on him. He lay in the timeless quietness of near-dark, thinking of Nothing.

About ten minutes after Croft's pronouncement, the big man had stirred again. As if after a pleasant ordinary interval, a pair of old acquaintances, who had shared a leisure moment in the shade, resumed their everyday procedures. "Let's walk on round the grounds, shall we? We can have a look at the sea from the south side of the house – and there are the sheds. We'll take a look at those first."

The *sheds*.

The sheds, at least from the front, like Russian train carriages.

Like the shed Carver had maintained back at his house in the village. The shed whose windows, by night, glowed turquoise, the exact mixed tone of green (a bluish emerald) and blue (aquamarine) of the lower Second and Third Level Urgency Alerts at Mantik.

Without rush or delay they strolled off through the trees and bushes, going east, away from the sun. The building reappeared, the house, if it was. Aside from its small rear terrace and benches, it was very modern, a box-like construction, and of an odd design (some parts built tall, others of only one or two storeys; some of the roofs angled, most flat). Quite unlike, for instance, the college. There was a gravel drive visible from here that curled off round the house walls. Roses grew in terracotta pots. These flowers were all red, and well-groomed, at variance with the ramble of the rest of the "grounds".

When the rise appeared, and the outlay of the scene matched with the version he had looked at from higher up, in the corridor outside his allotted room, Carver scrutinised the building. He believed he identified the corridor windows instantly. They lacked blinds for one thing. For another they were in the top and second floor of that section. That there were only two floors made sense, as a stair, not a lift, seemed to operate.

After one long establishing glance, Carver turned to survey the rise.

Croft passed no comment. He was already powerfully ambling up the slope between the trees. Carver followed.

The sun caught the sheds, lightly but firmly coupled, like facets of a necklace. Each copied his own shed. He had purchased that shed. *Chosen* it. He did not know why he had chosen a shed of that type, but it came ready-assembled. And why should it not be attractive? There. *Here*. And privacy, he had wanted the shed for that. Outside the house which Donna had had decorated and furnished as she wished, and set with the blaring screens of TVs. Somewhere to store things he stole, too. Naturally. Still a stupid kid. A *theave*, as Heavy would have called him, (only Heavy had never called Carver that), the same way that, for Heavy, a wolf was a *Wolve* and wolves were *Wolfs* – theave, theafs.

Stop. Concentrate.

Say something to the man who named himself Croft.

"What happened," said Carver quietly, "to Robby Johnston?"

As Carver had asked before. Or... had he?

"Who? Ah, yes. The fellow in the diver's suit, the black facemask – or was it a balaclava? Can't remember. I'll have to check."

"He was inside the garden. That night."

"Yes, he was, wasn't he. A bit dottery, apparently. Lucky we could step in."

"I believed," said Carver, "from what's been said, it was Mantik that had the problem with me. Not Johnston."

"Quite. Seems they both did. Not connected, obviously. Had you offended him, this Johnston chap?"

"No."

"Sometimes, Car, we can offend without meaning to. Or noticing we have."

A warning? They had reached the sheds, were less than two metres away. Sunlight soaked them, maple syrup. They glowed. The windows of each one, polished immaculately, gleamed hard as steel. The gleam helped to disguise – eradicate – anything that might be inside. But sunlight no longer affected Carver's eyes. He counted the sheds, from left to right. Seven. Seven carriages, halted at some station beyond Moscow. In reality, or on a movie-set. They were even coupled together, in just that sort of way, or realistically enough. No engine (a steam engine, obviously) to pull them on. Stalled? They could travel no farther.

"You're wondering," said Croft, "why they resemble your own shed from that little suburbanly rural house, yes?"

"Yes."

"Our compliment," said Croft, "to you. They're all for your use. You can come out here and be alone and think. You can store anything here you want to."

"Like what," Carver said without inflexion.

"Things you take. As before."

"Things I stole or steal."

"If you prefer to express your activity in that way."

"It reflects the fact of my activity."

"You've done it since childhood, haven't you, Carver? It started with – what was it, now? Sweets of some sort, I seem to recollect."

"Chocolate."

"Yes, of course. Chocolate in shiny coloured wrappers. And then later, other things. Bits and pieces you never used, or if you did, you took them back, didn't you?"

Carver said nothing.

Croft said, "You're free to do exactly as you want here, Carver. I, we, want you to understand this."

Carver nodded, not speaking, or crediting.

Before he spoke again, some more empty space ebbed by.

Time was moving, the sun was moving, even if neither he nor

Croft nor the railway carriages did.

"What's happened to my partner, Donna?"

"She's fine. She's with her mother. She thinks you're on a special assignment. That's approximately what Mantik have told her. No cause for alarm, and a nice increment in pay."

"She has never known what the office – what Mantik actually involves."

"No. She doesn't now. She thinks it's just some big business deal, with you as a necessary dogsbody. They do know how to play it, Carver. They're *looking* for you, you see. They don't want her in their way. Or, if she knows anything, they'd prefer she panicked and led them to you, not tried to put them off the scent."

"And what will *you* do with her?"

Croft gave a soft gravel-spill of a laugh.

"Nothing whatever. She's of no interest to us."

"When can I see her?" Carver asked sharply.

Croft went on smiling at him. (No, the hair was not a piece... or if it were, it was an incredibly convincing one.)

"Are you saying you really *want* to see her, Car? Are you?"

They had been watching him then some while, and rather intimately. They knew his interest in Donna had cooled to clinker.

"I'd like to be sure she's OK."

"I'll see if I can arrange that, Car. But I have to warn you, you're not going to meet her. That will have to wait."

"Until when?"

"Until our new working relationship has been established."

"Which is?"

"I've told you, dear fellow. We all have to wait a little while for that too. London wasn't built in a day."

(*Something*... Something for sure – the expression was wrong. Croft had said something earlier too that had not quite been in its normal mode – Carver could not think what. Had noted it, until now, only subconsciously. But anyway, Croft might simply be attempting originality.)

Carver said, "So you want me for some use I have, but won't tell me what. And Donna is fine but I can't see her to decide for myself."

"You can't leave this place," said Croft. "Not yet. It wouldn't be safe. Remember, Mantik want you. They believe you are a traitor and that probably you corrupted your colleague, Silvia Dusa, so they had to kill her. No, Carver, I'm sorry, but you must be patient, and settle down. For your own sake. In a few months things will be ironed out, and then you'll be free as air. If rather better paid. Give it time. Relax. Would you like to see the inside of one of the sheds? Choose which. They're all alike."

Carver felt a wave of cold dark dread. He squashed it at once. "All right."

Croft immediately went up the brief steps of the central shed, to the central of the three doors. Precisely the same as the shed at the house in this too, the steps, the way the middle door was triple-opened, inward.

Now Croft came down again, and left the undone door, keys in the last lock, for Carver to go through, alone. No doubt, if wanted, Croft could then slam the door triply locked-shut by remote control, and from any reasonable distance away. Even from inside the up-and-down building. So what? Carver must do as requested.

He went up the steps and walked in through the door.

Nothing had glowed but the woodwork, the flat black roof, the sun on the panes. Within the shed too, nothing was unusual. The doors with door-windows, and four other windows: front; four windows only to the rear. It was empty, both of furniture – and of purloined objects. But Croft, apparently, was quite happy (entirely determined?) that Carver should pocket objects and bring them here. And would a turquoise sheen then begin to rise up from them, as in the *other* shed?

The central door remained open, but when Carver turned back to it and looked out, the tree-flowered rise was otherwise vacant. Omitting farewell, the urbane Mr Croft had taken his large and powerful presence off, noiseless as an iron-grey tiger.

Carver had begun to think about this in the night bed, over and over, the walk, the talk, the neat vanishment; Croft's odd relocation of words, so that in Croft's take it was *London*, not *Rome*, that was not 'built in a day'. Another trick? It was all a sort of trick, surely?

What had they done to him, that he could no longer feel or recapture, or find physical clues to, there in that first space of confining and voiceless and then *vocal* dark? How far off it seemed now, this interlude of void, strapped down, pissing himself, thirst raging. As if it had not happened in relatively recent time – a week, a month – even a *year* before – but many years, two decades. Back *then*, then, when he was thirteen, fifteen, sixteen years of age –

Mind–fuck. Let it go. Some portion <u>of his</u> brain might still unravel it, if left alone to do so. In its shed of skull.

He turned over in the bed. He thought instead of the woman who had entered his room tonight. Anjeela. AJ, MV – The four letters ticked pointlessly in his head. He let them. Was she his sop, a prize, promise of other goodies to come? If he did whatever in Christ they thought they wanted – if even he *could* do it, this obscured and to him unknown thing.

He thought of Donna. The vague image of her flittered by him like a sulky moth. She had gone crazy, or Maggie had. So many crazy people in his life. Sara, his mother. The insane monster that had been his father.

Tick. A.J. Tick. M.V. The moth had disappeared. Tick.

The bedroom was not quite a replica of the spare room at his house. Nothing in it was, quite, either. The bed, for example, was both harder and more flexible, (as intuitively he had found when Anjeela had joined him – a liaising bed for sex. How thoughtful <u>of...</u> someone, or other). It also included, the room, a very small en suite bathroom, rather dissimilar to the bathrooms at his house, but with a shower, lavatory and basin, these a pristine cream, where the other sets had been Arctic white – Donna's decision. (And everything unlike the rabid collection of toilets and sinks and tubs he had shared with Sara, *their* enamel old or chipped, and stained no matter how often she scoured and bleached them.)

He had not noticed the ensuite here, when first he came to. He wondered, now very briefly, if it had even *been* here, or been there but somehow hidden, that initial time. But of course it had been there, and not hidden. He had only been in the last lingering grip of whatever drugs they had used.

Was he still?

The first day of awakening had passed with bacon and coffee, and a steak he had eaten in the room later, brought to him with a salad and a pot of more coffee. And the day had ended, logically in nightfall, and surprisingly in Anjeela's warm-cool smoky edible body. And in her hair, which had seemed to be longer – so he had murmured about it, somewhere in the dark. And had she replied? – he thought she had – "I grew my hair longer for you." Then, "Extensions, Car. It's simple."

And it was all simple, was it not? All this.

The *next* day was very pleasant, nearly restful, with one more beaming girl knocking on the door at 8 a.m., and asking him if she should bring him anything, as they had his 'supper' last night, or would he prefer to go down to the kitchen in this section, (the kitchen through the arch, with the door-occluding fridge-freezer.) Having showered, shaved, dressed, he accordingly went down. There in the kitchen sat the two men, Van Sedden and Ball, and another man they addressed as *Fiddy*, in a sort of boiler suit. *She* was not there. Carver had rather expected that. It fell into place inside the uneasy pattern: Of course Anjeela, having played her intimate game with him (AJMV), would rather absent herself. Then she walked in. Looking, as at the beginning, more heavy than voluptuous, her hair short, her blue eyes uninterested in anything save the coffee mug and her today's choice of white toast and Marmite.

She did not speak to him, he did not speak to her, though he had exchanged brief flaccid greetings with the three men, lacking awkward inquiries this morning on why anyone was here. They were engaged anyway in discussion of a football game, (witnessed on some TV or computer in the building), that seemed to have taken place in the Czech Republic. Naturally they – whoever, whatever 'They' were comprised – would be watching Carver.

He kept it all toneless, not overly relaxed, not visibly tensed. Taking things as they came.

Not much did come of that day at all.

He left the kitchen after eating and took a walk around the 'grounds', (alone, though doubtless on camera), observing, checking over without much expression, body-language under control.

The sea lay beyond the front of the up-and-down building, approximately southward, with a slight bias to the east. On this side some of the upper storeys bulged outward, particularly those some distance from the centre. His would be among those. The bulge would be what had omitted any direct downward view, opening exclusively on the vista of the sea. The gravel drive skirted much of the house; the pots of roses stood on it in formal groups. What seemed the main doorway was central to the sea-facing side. Two large shut wooden doors, behind a shut multi-glazed glass partition. Bullet-proof? For about five and a half metres stretching out from the gravel, there was a width of paved stone, closed along its finish parallel with the house, by a tall, blued iron railing. This was the lookout position, for those who wanted it, the *promenade*, set with the familiar stone, griffin-armed benches. Over the railing the edge of the cliff tumbled off into air, and the sea unrolled bellow. There were gulls, again. Why not, they lived here. One was parading slowly along the railing's flat top. Aristocratically proprietary, it ignored him.

Carver did not investigate to see if there was an easy route by which to descend the cliff, other than climbing on the rail and diving off, (hoping not to encounter any juts or outcrops of cliff-work on the rush down). He doubted the sea, or any beach, would be straightforwardly accessible from here. He looked just long enough to satisfy a perhaps probable unseen watcher. Then moved off, unfast, through the rest of the wooded park.

He spent some hours on this, going back and forth, into, or mostly outward from the building, now and then sitting on some bench. Aside from the railed sea-view he met no barriers, that was, no perceived physical ones. How far did the 'grounds' stretch? Some distance, apparently.

Though occasionally he gazed up, or around, at the trees, he could make out no spy-devices, not even the more subtle ones he had seen demonstrated during his time with Mantik.

He did not bother about lunch. He went in later. It was around 5 p.m. A smiling, friendly, helpful youngish man approached him and explained how he could reach the bar and canteen on the sixth floor of that section – which was the section he had, it seemed, entered.

Carver went, (as expected?), up to the bar. It was very clean and well-ordered, frankly clinical in its own manner, as if alcohol had now become available inside a UK NHS hospital.

Carver asked for, and unhurriedly drank, a single whisky.

He did not want it, but could tell it was a decent one, despite the unknown label and name.

No one approached now, in the clinical bar. The bar staff were attentive and friendly. Anyone who caught Carver's eye either looked at once away, or smiled radiantly at him. (Did he imagine this? Again, the residue of drugs?)

Later he went into the canteen, which resembled, unlike the bar, a plush and rather expensive London restaurant, perhaps belonging to a private political club. He ate a hamburger and salad under the darkly tawny drapes.

He was not tired, only exhausted. He left about eight-thirty. His room had been, as before, and as in the best hotel, immaculately hoovered, brushed and dusted, the bed made up, the bathroom cleaned and aromatic with flowery bleach. New clothes had arrived for him also, still in their packaging, shirts, T-shirts, trousers, underwear. All similar to things he had worn.

Beyond the window a quarter moon lay sideways on the western rim of the sea. Twilight and water. He left the blind up.

Would Anjeela Merville visit him tonight?

Carver thought not.

In this he was correct.

## Fourteen

A series of codes began to move through his head. On the black screen of his mind: letters, numbers. Stupid, simplistic. ABC. 123. U.R.U.I.M.E.

Sara, his – Andy's – mother went entirely mad the day she found out she was pregnant again. Her madness, until then, had been eclectic, and composed of elements that might be explained away, put out of sight. Some things she did were only hysterical – screaming sometimes out of the window of the flat over the off-licence after drunks, once they had gone – or, skittish always, 'making sure' the front door was properly shut three (even six) times after leaving the flat. Small things.

It was just before he took off for the college. Sunderland had come back, and spent about an hour talking to Andy, explaining transport and routine, necessities. After he left, Sara began slowly to seethe and then come to the boil.

"You get everything, don't you? Yeah? It all comes to *you*, if you're a fucking man. You don't even get in the family way." (One of her more prissy expressions.) "Well, I'm not going to have the little fuck. I had enough shit 'cuz of you. That was enough. Or *you* wan' it, yeah? No, din' think so. Just fuck off to your poncy *college*, you little bugger. And I'll get rid of *this* one that's been stuck up me. Once's enough." And she flung her mug and then, snatching it, his, against the wall.

Andy, despite himself, had been shocked. He had not even

known – why, how, should he? – that she had had recent sex with a man, maybe many men. He knew nothing about Sara but the outlines of the past, inside which she had still seemed to move.

He supposed she had cared for, and financially supported him, but she had never had any lasting interest in him ("Why should I?" she might well say, "I never *wanted* you. And what have *you* done?") But she had protected – *tried*, actually uselessly, to protect – him, from his father. She had made him skimpy but regular meals, and washed his clothes and bought him sweets and, when he was little, walked him to vile schools and left him there, skimmed off some of her hard *hard*-earned cash to give him his 'dole'.

Put up with his own indifference and absences. Pretended to like his few (ill–devised?) generosities.

Presumably she did get rid of the second child. Or else she had never been afflicted by it, just a fearful mistake put right by her next menstruation.

Once at the college, he had ceased to see her. He did not need to 'go home'. He did not call her ever. They never wrote. Not even cards.

Then she did write him a letter, when he was sixteen. It was poorly spelled, as by then he could see, and put its words together less ably than Sara did when speaking. She told him she was moving north with someone she knew, she did not specify gender or connection. She called her son, as ever, *Andy*, and she wished Andy luck. She, however, did not sign it 'Mum', as she had with his birthday and Christmas cards in childhood, but with her name, *this* spelled correctly and in full, *Zarissa Maria Cava*.

A.B.C. 1.2.3. 1.4. 1.4. <u>1.4.</u>

Another day arrived, flared blue, green and gold, and sank to darkness in the sea.

Carver spent it, as he had substantially the days before. He had, though, some company in the afternoon.

<u>Following</u> breakfast in the kitchen, Carver lingered. The others, including the non-communicative Anjeela Merville, gradually ebbed away, she in company with the boiler-suited Fiddy. It was a different boiler suit today in deep orange.

Ball was the last to leave. He and Van Sedden seemed scowlingly to have fallen out, did not exchange a word with each <u>other or</u> with anyone else. When Ball rose he glared also at Carver and said,

"Have a _nice_ day, Car, why _don't_ you." Carver nodded and went back to reading the ancient copy of The _Independent_ he had found lying at an empty place on the table. He continued to read a while after Ball had also gone. The paper seemed fairly fresh and crisp, but that must be some treatment – it was dated 2009. (He had noted such or more out-of-date newssheets and magazines in the bar, but that was strangely in keeping with the bar's hygienic hospital ambience.)

The kitchen was vacant then aside from Carver.

He was, he had concluded, expected – _meant_ – to steal something. So he picked up the black mug he had drunk from and walked out with it.

In the cloakroom off the hall below the stairs, Carver annexed an unused bar of hand-soap, dressed in its white wrapper.

Going through the appropriate corridor that he now knew led out to this side of the grounds, one passed a cupboard for office-type stationery, and left unlocked. Carver selected three pens, some batteries and a ring backed notepad.

Carrying everything openly, he went out. There was never any human security on any of the doors, at least, not to be seen.

Outside, it was remorselessly there again, the Wonderful Weather. But this place was some sort of movie-set after all. Conceivably they had finally cracked the scientific formulae for weather control, just as the USA and Russia had been rumoured to have done as far back as the 1960's. Weather control: people control. And here, just sufficient rain, endless warmth and light. Keep the leaves green. Keep summer up and running.

Carver was walking back along the rise towards the line of railway-carriage sheds when the fat cycling enthusiast burst from the trees below, and called out to him.

"Hi! Car!"

They all used the office abbreviation of his name now. It would have been in the inevitable file on him.

Carver turned, stopped, waited for the out-of-breath young man to reach him. This morning Charlie, if that _was_ his name, wore jeans, overstretched from hip to knee, too loose at calves and ankles – he did not, certainly, have a cyclist's legs. Additionally he had on another white tent of T-shirt, this one written over by the optimistic motto _Long Life_. As before, under duress, he was scarlet, and puffing from exertion.

"Some hill," puffed Charlie. He reached out and clapped Carver on the arm, man to man.

Carver waited.

Charlie regained his breath. "How are you doing?"

"Fine." Carver paused. "How's your bicycle?"

"Oh God, she's lovely. Did nearly thirty miles on her yesterday. Getting there. No lie. Getting... Where you headed?"

When Carver did not comment, Charlie decided. "The sheds. I'll trot up there with you."

They trotted very slowly.

"Shame you can't see the sea this side," said Charlie.

The sea lay to the south, the sheds northerly.

"Should you be able to? Is this an island?" Carver asked.

"An isle of adventure, old mate," gasped Charlie.

"I meant, is this place surrounded by sea?"

Charlie stopped, so Carver stopped. Charlie frowned at him and for a moment Carver thought something useful might be said. But then Charlie exclaimed, "You know, old son, you're the spitting image of my dad – I mean, about sixteen years ago,"

"What year was that, then?"

"Oh, when he was younger. You know what I mean."

"So I look like your father. When younger."

"You really do. Although –" Charlie tilted his head, quizzically, "more like my uncle, maybe."

Carver started to go on up the hill.

A jolly dog, Charlie scampered after him, just too out-of-breath to bark.

By now the sheds were clearly in front of them. The sun had not yet topped the higher parts of the building behind. But light still fell on the golden syrup shed-wood in thick separated slices, somehow optically doubling several of them, so seven became eleven.

Croft had left Carver the three-way keys.

Carver undid the centre door of the central (light–doubled) shed.

"I won't come in, OK..." said Charlie, as if anxious not to offend by not doing so. "I'm off to get in some cycling."

"Do you find you have a lot of time for that?"

"Every day, old mate. Regular as a clock."

"What happens the rest of the time?"

Charlie would not, as he had not, give a direct answer. Or would he? Charlie said, "I'm just an errand boy, Car." And for a moment he looked sly. It was, of course, how Carver had described himself.

Then Charlie let out a somehow surprising bray of laughter, spun round and hurtled off down the slope, waving his arms and ungainly as a drunken windmill so that Carver too, for a second, was reminded of someone from the past. Heavy.

Carver went into the shed, and shut and locked the door behind him.

There was a narrow table in there now. A plain, clean, modern table of renewable wood. Waiting to receive anything he might want to set down on it. Displaying, en passant, *they* too had kept keys.

Carver put the pens, batteries, notebook, soap, mug, in a group at the centre. The arrangement seemed very foreign to him. All this was as unlike anything he had ever done as it could be. He too, he felt, was unlike anything he could properly target as himself. Whatever caused this effect, it disturbed him only to a degree. Because perhaps the *different* Carver might find a way out of this mess.

Lunch was a sandwich got from the take-out annexe between the canteen and the bar. He had a small bottle of beer (label unknown) to go with it, mostly for the fluid content. He ate and drank outside, sitting on the bench he had shared with Croft.

Carver sat and thought about Croft, going over all the points he could remember. "London wasn't built in a day." What had been the other off-kilter word or phrase? It would not come. (Charlie too had said something just off the general phraseology. Regular as, not clockwork, but *a clock*. But people got mixed up. Or altered things to be 'clever'.)

None of this was remotely like the takes, adornments, extrapolations, transpositions of someone like Heavy. Theave. Wolfs. Underland for Sunderland. The wind runs backward.

Carver watched the light breeze dapple about in the leaves. He tried to gauge if any tiny giveaway blink or shimmer indicated a spying device. He could not detect anything. Yet he knew they were there. They *had* to be, with such otherwise lax security. And besides he could sense the faint reflected buzz of their electronics on the skin of his bare forearms, his forehead. Sometimes at the tip of his tongue. He had experienced that with women, too, once or twice, when intimately kissing and licking them. Never with Donna. With the black woman he had, Anjeela. He had half expected to. Oddly, suddenly, he recalled Silvia Dusa. The pressure of her hands on his chest, so hot, then the impression of them left behind afterwards, so *cold*. Like the coded numbers, letters, that had splintered over his eyes in semi-sleep, he saw again that terrible image of her mortuary corpse, the inert body eviscerated of life, her riven and evacuated arm–

Carver lurched on the bench. He had been sleeping again now. And now, was awake.

He checked the sky. The sun was deep in the nests of trees. They had not left, or given him, a watch to tell the time, (unlike Ball?), but he could judge reasonably well by the sun. Nearly five again? He planned to go in. He would retreat to his room from the bustle, the beaming smiles and hotelish fake camaraderie – or reticence. As with the college, they all seemed to live in. When darkness arrived he would go into the corridor and look out towards the shed. See if it had begun to glow blue-green. That would not occur, he was fairly sure. But then. Who could say?

As he returned, tramping in along the gravel drive for a last scan of the sea from the promenade-terrace, he heard a furiously whirring mechanical sound. Carver stepped back against the wall of the building as a bicycling Charlie came buffeting past, turgid and erratic, his legs, in their too-tight-but-floppy jeans, labouring like a pair of whipped epic-film slaves hauling rocks. The gravel sprayed up, the split wave of a shallow pool. Some hit the outer glass of the blinded ground floor windows.

Carver did not believe that Charlie saw him. Maybe Charlie could see nothing beyond the weird and possibly ill-advised goal of driving the bicycle on and on at the topmost speed he could conjure, which was about three miles an hour. Charlie's face was dense red again, and angrily fixed. He rained sweat.

His eyes were filmed and blind as the windows.

Midnight. Carver knew, since the small screen he could access behind a panel in the wall, (the helpful food-bringing girl had shown him) gave him the hour, along with a selection of concurrent hours in other time-zones. It was 7 p.m. in New York, around 4 p.m. in San Francisco. No clues there to anything much. He would know without looking. As for it's being 5.20 of the following morning in Cesczeghan, he had never heard of it, though it must lie considerably farther east than Britain.

Carver opened the door of his room and went into the corridor. The blurred amber light that automatically came on there after sunset, reminded him of the sort of stormy gloaming paraphrased in some old paintings. It gave sufficient illumination to find the walls and doors, and just too much to let the unblinded windows keep their views all clear. Carver pressed close to a pane, (a child looking out at the wide world), shading his eyes in against the glass. Now he could see a sable landscape beyond. Black blocked on black, taking a muted glint from the building's lights.

On its hill, the shed was glowing like a torch.

The colour was vivid, not needing any enhancement. (He must have been aware of it *before* shading out the corridor light. And, as before, his *imagination* had mitigated, dismissed the glow. Now nothing but sightlessness could.)

Turquoise. Alert Level low, between Blue and Green.

Even so, a Level of Alert.

There were just seven objects in there, of five categories, unimportant, mundane, adrift in the middle of a wooden table. On a rise in a group of trees, a quarter mile off.

Burning bright.

A loud noise, and Carver stepped back from the window. (It was true, like this, the glow faded, was minimised, might even pass as some security lamp, if your mind was on other matters.)

Into the corridor, from the direction of the stairs, rolled Ball and boiler-suited Fiddy, and then Van Sedden. Then Charlie, even from the stairs pink, if not scarlet, and in a plain black T-shirt over another pair of equally unequal jeans. Anjeela did not appear. Why would she?

"Car, Car," cried Ball, with a drunken happy musicality. "Come join our revel!"

He theatrically bore an uncorked bottle of red wine, one third full. Van Sedden had a bottle of greenish-white, two thirds full. Fiddy carried a bottle of scotch. This was three thirds full, but open. Charlie had a tall glass of what looked like Coke, fizzing. He and Fiddy did not seem pissed, as the other two did, but even so, 'merry', as Sara had been used to say. Car, at bay, stared at them. But there would be surveillance out here too. "Sure," said Car, and let Fiddy hand him the whisky.

# Fifteen

"Pass the port."

"There is no port, you arsehole. 'Swhisky."

"Whisky and wine—"

"Rich and fine—"

"Fucking the fuck shut up and pass the fucking booze, you arrant bloody cunt."

"Pour it out," expanded Fiddy, (this piece of conversation was between him and Ball), "and stick it in."

"Stick it somewhere," grumbled Van Sedden resentfully.

His own white wine was consumed. He had said he did not like whisky. And the _red_ wine – Ball's – had gone down Ball's throat to the last drop, Ball balancing the bottle neck in his mouth, his head tipped right back, a kind of _divertissement,_ (as Sedden had remarked), based on a performing seal.

"Shoulda got more," observed Ball. He could drink, he claimed, "anything". He and Fiddy therefore were by now two thirds down the whisky bottle. Carver – considerately? – had only taken a couple of mouthfuls from it. (The exchange of probable germs did not especially concern Carver. Immunisation was a matter of course at Mantik. And, you assumed, here at this place, too.)

"Fucking bollock they don't keep the bar fucking open after twelve," said Sedden to the terrace pavement.

"True, fucking true, dear swine," (Ball), "though maybe they rightly think guys like you, my prince, need to stop after two bottles of Pinot Grigio and one of Sauvignon Blanc. Eh? D'you suppose?"

Charlie giggled. It transpired his Coke had also contained a double vodka, his fourth double. But he had eked it out.

"Shut the fuck up," suggested Sedden.

And for a while silence dropped.

The five men sat on three of the griffin-armed benches, on the terrace above the cliff-end and the stretching, glinting, now moonless ink of the sea. Stars in the sky were pale as grains of rice, since some dim light still leaked from the building to dilute them. Though none from the shut main doors.

Carver was bored and restless, both these states under firm control. There had been sessions like this at the teenage college. He had swiftly managed to avoid them. Two hours, he estimated, had tonight dragged themselves through and away from the drinking party. In a short while, Carver could take himself also away to his room.

"*You* don't say much," said Ball, waving from the adjacent bench. About a metre separated them.

Carver smiled, noncommittal.

"Why's that?" said Fiddy, "why's he so quiet?"

"What," said Carver mildly, "do you want me to say?"

"Oh, tell us a bit about yourself," said Ball.

"You first," said Carver, amiable.

"Oh, me," said Ball. "Don't get me started."

"No, for fuck's fucking fuck's sake don't get *him* started," muttered Sedden.

Fiddy said, "Go on, Car. We all wanna know about *you*. You're the big star, here."

"Where?" said Carver, gentle. "*Where* am I the star?"

"Up there!" roared Ball abruptly. "Dazzling!" He waved the whisky at the sky over the sea, and Charlie sprang up with curious agility from the third bench and grabbed the bottle from him. "You'll spill it all!"

Then Charlie, standing reasonably steady, tilted the whisky into his own mouth, and gulped two, three, four singles on a breath.

"You're all a pack of cunts," decided Sedden. He too stood up, tottered, held to the back of the stone bench. "I'm go'ff to bed."

"Bye-bye," said Ball. "No loss."

Sedden hauled himself, using the bench as a prop, tottered over and, fetching up in front of Ball, smashed him across the face with his fist.

Ball reeled back. A jet of blood, looking much blacker and wetter than the sea, shot into the air.

"Oops," said Fiddy. He got up in turn and carefully walked some distance along the terrace. There he sat down on the pavement, resting his back on the prongs of the rail, looking at the building's facade, not the sea-view. He seemed soon to fall asleep.

Van Sedden and Ball, however, were now fighting. They staggered about, grunting and moaning, aiming meaty blows that mostly did not connect. Until, lunging to deliver another of these, Sedden fell over. From his knees, and averting his face, he spat out a curtailed string of vomit, then bounded up again and launched himself in encore at Ball. Ball's lower face was a mask of murky blood. His fists struck now, but constantly missing Sedden's head, landing too low on ribcage, shoulders. Sedden swerved at every impact, but did not go down.

From his bench, Carver watched them. If surveillance cameras operated out here, as surely they must, then either the monitors were asleep, or had skived off on some personal errand.

Or else, was that procedure here? Observe always, with no interference. Enough rope for each to hang himself. Or did it make no difference?

It was Ball who fell next. Sedden deliberately dropped down beside him. He sized Ball's head and neck and pulled Ball in that way towards him, as if to kiss his bloodied lips, or lick them. Ball said, slurred and ridiculous, "You've bust my Rolex."

Carver saw Charlie was standing up as well. He appeared steady, if in a rather lopsided way. In total contrast to himself, he was white, and his face shone – not with sweat, you realised. Tears were running out of both his eyes, more urgently than the blood from Ball's nostrils.

"Think I'll have a turn on the old girl," he said, in a choked yet formal voice, the polite little boy in the playground, frightened, but having had it drilled into him he must always do, say, the Right Thing. "Bit of a cycle about. Bloody good."

Carver found he in turn had got up. (Only Fiddy remained on the ground against the railing, snoring sotto voce, as if also trying to be as well-mannered as he could.)

Then Charlie broke the spell – and the whisky bottle, which he dropped with a sharp-dull, smashed-sugar crash on the paving. And without a pause he ran, faster than he had seemed capable of before, along the gravel and toward the far east side of the building.

Van Sedden was dedicatedly banging Ball's head against the pavement.

Carver went over, heaved Sedden up and off and cracked him hard on the jaw. Let go, Sedden sat down on the stone. Lacking the support of bench or railing he then curled slowly over, and lay on his left side, mindlessly gazing at Carver, without interest. Ball was now throwing up. (Carver thought of Iain Cox and E-bone, after Heavy had pushed them. Irrelevant.)

He would go inside, Carver decided. Wake someone and get them out here to clear up.

Before he could take another step, he heard Charlie's bicycle, noisy in the quiet, tinnily whirring and scratching and pumping, furious and laden, back over the gravel. It must have been stationed not so far off, by one of the more recessed frontages, unseen. And look at it now. Coming back along the drive so very fast, faster for sure than it had been ridden earlier, just as Charlie had run so much faster. Whisky or adrenalin.

No holds barred.

In the moments before it happened Carver understood. Carver was not drunk, in no way affected by the double mouthful of whisky. But he stayed immobile and unspeaking and watched with the other two who had kept the vestiges of consciousness; Ball coughing and spitting, squinting, Van Sedden shivering, focus, it seemed, partially restored to his vision.

The bicycle erupted to within a few paces of them, then veered straight out across the short edge of gravel, missing all the rose-pots, and onto the stone paving. Charlie was astride the machine, flying easy as a bird, not breathing either very fast. His legs beat up and down rhythmically. His eyes were huge, and dry. Not afraid. He looked – determined. That was it. A striker about to score the winning penalty, a bomb-happy pilot about to release the bomb-hatch above the darkened, semi-sleeping town.

As Carver already knew they would, man and bike burst on, missing the benches now, and the men, over the pavement, that abbreviated border between earth and water – and air.

They hit the barrier of the rail, Charlie and the bicycle, full on, going in this case at quite a speed.

The bicycle seemed to implode, buckling, condensing.

Charlie though lifted like a gull, up, up, over the top of the railing, up there in the sky of void and stars, the wings of his arms spread wide. Then drifting in an arc, not flapping now as when he floundered down the hill, but caught, appropriately gull-like, as if on some supportive current of the night air. In perceived yet unreal slow-motion once more, but graceful at last and self-possessed, he curved across and downward, to the unseen rocks and shore below. Gone.

## Sixteen

Gelatinously cold, the lights painted the room and its twelve occupants.

It was otherwise hot, the windows shut behind their blinds. (Looking out on all sides at private grounds or open water, why were such blinds necessarily always down, at least on the ground floors?)

Carver sat on the comfortable but business like chairs with the other three men who had survived the night: Van Sedden, Ball, Fiddy.

Even the damaged squashed bicycle had been brought in. It lay on the space of wood-plank floor between the four chairs and the sidelong desk. A fifth witness?

Behind the desk, the other eight; six men, two women. Each wore a dark suit; the women's suits also, visible during their group processional entry from behind the desk, had trousers. One of the women was fat, if not as fat as Charlie had been, though he would be losing weight now, of course.

The other woman was noticeably thin.

As if to make identification – or comparison – between them easy.

The men were all weights, all kinds, and of four clear racial types.

The entire composite ranged from around the age of twenty-five-seven, (the thin woman), to late fifties, early sixties (the tall slim black man in the Oxbridge tie).

It reminded Carver of job interviews he had sometimes, years ago, attended on errands to do with Mantik. Or panels on TV – except for the amount of interviewers in proportion to the – what were they, in fact – *candidates*?

Candidates then for *what*?

Punishment?

There had been excessive alcohol and a punch-up.

A man had ridden his bicycle at, and himself over, the brink of a cliff.

(Night and flight, soaring, arcing down. Seconds of utter release – terror – mesmeric unknowing. After which the hard floor of the world.)

Van Sedden had muttered, as they waited here twenty minutes or so for the interviewing panel to arrive, "Ride come comes before a fall."

And Ball had whispered, "Can it, cunt?"

And Sedden had put his head in his hands and wept. And Ball had got up, sat down, put his arm round Sedden, sat there staring into nowhere as Sedden cried on his shoulder, and Fiddy grunted, and once or twice belched from hangover and bad nerves.

After the panel came in, everyone was pulled together, stiff-upper-lipped, yet quiescent. Soldiers, Carver thought, who would get a beating, (another one), if they did not shine up their gear, stand to attention, wear the masks of discipline, of violence, under total subjugation.

What did *he* look like then, he, Andreas Cava, child of psychopath moron and crazy fool. He who had let the fight go on until its sheer futility had caused him to intervene. And, as the bicycle ran, too late. Poised there, foreseeing what came next, not attempting– Useless. It was not the drugs that had slowed him down. Not the drink, which he had only reluctantly sipped.

He was removed, was Carver. *Always* stood a little aside, a step or two back. Uninvolved. Not wanting involvement. The lizard on the wall. The errand boy. The cool partner. The quiet one. The watcher. A spy-machine.

Even if well-hidden, the surveillance cameras and audio-relay had obviously picked up the scene on the terrace. That nobody had hastened from the building in time to prevent a tragedy was due to – it was suggested – an unforeseen glitch in wiring. (Or perhaps, unrevealed laxity on someone's part?)

They had, nevertheless, been on the spot some two minutes after Charlie descended from view. A ruffled company of men in shirts and jeans, not overtly armed, but unmistakably Security. They had not come from the closed main door.

Everyone present on the terrace, including, till woken, the still-snoring Fiddy, had been 'escorted' inside.

They were shut in a narrow side room, that luckily (or logistically) had access to a lavatory, and here Sedden went to vomit, and then Fiddy, and then around and around again, **one** by one, both politely taking their turns, waiting, gagging in tissues, until the other staggered out from each bout.

Ball had, it seemed, got rid of everything he needed to that way. He sat on the floor – the room had only one chair, and democratically none of them used it.

Whoever was there, aside from seeking and exiting the toilet, kept static and silent. The only noises issued from the lavatory.

(Carver had thought briefly of his father's aggressive, expressive vomitings. Pushed the memory away.)

About an hour after, all of them were ushered to yet another area, a sort of dormitory with ten bunks, and another adjacent wash-room.

Carver lay down, and watched the darkness, which was only a darker light. (None of this was like the period when this 'place' had first taken him.) He drifted asleep once or twice, once woken by one more bout of strenuous puking in the washroom. Donna came to mind now, at the house.

In the first light – dawn presumably – how long had they been here, it seemed more hours than maybe dawn would take to return – five o'clock? Six? – Carver was spoken to quietly by one of the jeaned security men. No names were awarded either way. "Get up, please. I'll take you up." And one more of this labyrinthine warren's steel lifts, and then another succession of corridors, and after these the opening sky in windows, yellowish overcast today, and a view of trees, and surely – the sheds – And then his own allotted room, with its sea view and time-panel.

"Be ready for 10 a.m., please," said the man. "Somebody will be up to take you."

"Where?" said Carver.

The man said nothing. The door was shut behind him. But not locked.

Carver did as he was told, naturally.

By 10 a.m., unbreakfasted, but clean, dressed and 'ready', two men entered who waved him out, and down, and around, (lifts, corridors, annexes, blinded windows), to the hot room with the wooden floor, and the three others and the bicycle and the judging panel. (And *Any Judge's Main Verdict* would be what?)

The thin woman with the slight Italian accent said, "Well, we have listened to you all. From what has been recorded by Security – aside from the interruptive glitching, when sight and sound were lost – your accounts seem to tally with our own."

She was – was she? – a little like Silvia. Silvia Dusa.

Who was dead. Also dead. But no. Too thin. Yet the hair, eyes – that circling gesture of her right hand, expressive and non-English despite the inevitable probability both she, and at least one of her parents, had been born in Britain –

The interrogation/interview/trial had lasted three hours. During the first hour they had been told, over and over, in varying forms, and as if they had not been present, the facts of Charlie (Charles Michael Slade Hemel)'s final bicycle ride. After that a recess was called. The panel walked out of the door behind the desk, three skirt-suited women entered, and Sedden, Ball, Fiddy and Carver were offered by them water, tea, coffee, crisps and sandwiches. Only Carver and Fiddy accepted. Carver ate a little. Fiddy, made more capacious it transpired by barfing, ate three sandwiches and drank a large bottle of Perrier, only then going off decorously to crap and or pee, returning hale and hearty, so Van Sedden cursed him, before being shushed by Ball. (*This* lavatory lay just outside the hot room. You had to knock on the hot room's outer door, explain your mission, and were then let through and subsequently back in. Fiddy had done all without shame. Practiced?)

The next one hour and forty-four minutes, (there was a clock on the wall), entailed each of the four men being told to speak, and speaking, saying what he personally had seen and done, generally prompted, asked to elaborate, or tripped up by the presiding bench of eight-person desk. They all asked questions or broke in with side-long thrusts – "But if you were fighting/ being sick/asleep at that point, how can you be quite certain?"

The man who seemed to be Chinese, and spoke with a soft Mancunian accent, had picked remorselessly on Ball. But Ball seemed, though uneasy and utterly drained, to recognise it all as a gambit. He answered with leaden pragmatism each time. The red-haired Celt, conversely, had it in for Sedden.

Why did they – these people, this 'Place', "Us" – need to act out so much? It decidedly was like a caricature drama of a courtroom, once more on TV. Or a game of charades in a pub.

The fat woman picked on Sedden as well. She drove him mad. In the end he slumped down in his chair and seemed on the verge of fainting. That was when they had the second break, which lasted six minutes.

Carver they neither questioned (interrupted) nor psychologically pawed at.

They let him speak. Listened. Said "thank you" and moved on.

He had, as conceivably they grasped, not been drunk, ill, in a rage or a fight or asleep. But why trust him, why not subject him to the twiddling, needling process the rest had to put up with? They (the 'Place', "Us") knew it all any way. They had the visuals and the sound records. Unless, maybe, there truly had been a major glitch. It seemed unlikely.

When the three hours of hearing and breaks was over, the panel withdrew again. Would they pace back and pass sentence? It seemed not. A woman in a short dress, and a boyish 1940's US crew-cut, danced in and said they could all get over to their 'Work' now. And the outer door was left wide. No Security stood there in its un-Charlie-ish well-tailored jeans.

The bicycle did not get up to follow them out. Nobody had referred to it.

Outside none of them spoke to the others. Not even Sedden to Ball. They wandered off along the corridor beyond the hot room, and the corridor was breathing through a high up open window, showing leaves stitched on a cloudy windless mauve sky.

"Storm," announced Fiddy, portentously.

That was all.

Charles Michael Slade Hemel. C.M.S.H. Something flicked through Carver's thoughts, like a hare through long grass. You knew what it was, but could not see.

He had no idea where the corridor led but followed it round. No need to make plans. Another young woman, blonde in a completely un-Donna way, stood waiting. She too wore a dress but carried a clipboard.

"Oh, Mr Carver. Here you are. Just follow me. Mr Croft is waiting."

Croft sat against the blinded, lighted window, and was in silhouette. An old trick, clichéd – exactly how he had played it the last time. The first time.

"Please sit down, Car," he said. "The nicer chair."

The window behind him, though, today was less luminous, the sun in cloud... His silhouette had faded and drew less significance. Carver had seen its face anyway.

Carver's eyes, now, did not water.

"Nasty business," said Croft pleasantly.

"Yes."

"What did you make of it?"

"I don't know."

"Charlie always had this thing about cycling. Kept a bicycle, but hardly ever got on the machine. They'll have to investigate all the background rubbish, of course. Some emotional problem perhaps."

Carver did not speak. He wondered if they had yet recovered the body from the shoreline below. They must have done. They would be testing it, what was useable, for substances, irregularities, giving *it* the third degree as it was now impossible to give that to Charlie.

Croft shifted. His profile appeared, the large nose and jaw, the heavy-lidded eye that today in the gloom did not glint.

Croft rose. "Why not we go outside, have a stroll. Probably be a downpour later. What do you say?"

As before, Carver went after him to the doorway, the corridor, lift etc.

Not long after they were again sitting on the bench on the rise, where they had sat the first time. The mood of the weather had changed everything. There was no hint of a breeze, nothing moved. The sky had thickly darkened, and the trees had loosely darkened, out of shade into a premature twilight. The world, or this piece of it, seemed to have stopped.

Sara had been frightened of storms. That got worse as the years went on. Carver recalled how once she had run in screaming from the street, seeming to bring the pursuit of lightning and thunder inside with her. She had flown into her bedroom and ripped shut the ineffectual curtains before slamming the door to keep her in. But he had stayed in the outer room, watching at the window.

"We shall just have to get on with things," said Croft, who had not spoken again until now. (What test was this one?) "How have you been, Carver?" as if inquiring after a decent if not well-known acquaintance.

"I've been here," Carver said.

"So you have. Let's see. You asked me one or two questions before, didn't you? I consider, under the circumstances... I might try to reply to some of your concerns. Do you think?"

Croft gave every indication of now pedantically waiting for an answer himself.

"Yes."

"*Yes*. A positive affirmative." Croft's new tactics were odd. But what else? Croft uncrossed and recrossed his ankles. He had not, this time, taken off his jacket. The jacket was a little rumpled. Had he slept in it? It looked that way. Just like the hair of some of the security men, sticking up unwashed and unsmoothed, unready for action –

"You wanted to know why we are so interested in you. Why your Mantik Corp were so interested in you. Apart" (sarcasm?) from your high intelligence rating and other splendid personal abilities, of course. Mantik Corp," added Croft, musingly. He put his hands behind his neck, resting his iron-capped head back on them. "There's a thought. Perhaps you never have thought of this, Carver. Even though that college place where they seeded you wasn't bad, I don't know how much of a classic or etheric education they offered... Mantik–" he paused, "*Corp*. Have you ever heard or read, Car, of the mythic *Manticore* – a fabled beast, dear old chap. In several of the old Bestiaries that gave – you'll know? – lists of magical animals supposedly seen, met with, documented, killed, stuffed and mounted. Indian in origin. Had a lion's body and a manlike face, surrounded by a great mane. Loved eating humans. *What's for Sunday Dinner, Mrs Manticore? Ooh, Manti. It's roast man with a bit of roast man*. They had three rows of teeth, all pointed. And barbs in the tail. Set the table, Mrs Manticore, set the table on a-roar!"

Carver found he stared at Croft. Carver switched off the stare. He glanced round at the trees. Nothing moved. Everything holding its breath.

"No," Carver said, quietly.

"Ever heard of Paracelsus, then," asked Croft, flirtatiously – there was no other word for it.

"I've heard of him."

"Physician-alchemist in 16th Century Europe. Said everyone should fuck or masturbate. Commended the practice as healthful. A man of common sense. He also named an algae that had a certain colour. Nostocaris. Or Nostoc, they have it now. Blue-green. Special properties. Or there's a fish. Its name means Shining Knife. It gives off a blue-green glow in the dark of the deep sea. This scares off would-be predators. But also – and *hear* this, Car, my dear boy – it glows so strong it casts no giveaway shadow – like the Devil, or someone without a soul. And by its own light it can find its prey with enormous ease. They don't get warned by shadow, they're dazzled by glare. And then – *Gotcha!* " Croft smacked his hands – pulled from his head with an almost murderous speed – together.

Carver moved back before he could stop himself. He stood up.

Croft was grinning, laughing up at him, delighted as a three-year-old child with his alarming coup.

"It's energies, Car. That's why your damn sheds light up. And that's why *we* want to eat you alive. You can *conjure* energies. You're like a mast that catches lightning. Only it isn't lightning you catch or that you create. We don't know – I shouldn't tell you this, but I might as well, you're even more ignorant about yourself than we are – we don't know quite what you *do* do, or create. But it's there. It goes off the scale. It has about the potential charge of a little thermo-nuclear device. Only it doesn't go off bang, old boy. It doesn't irradiate or poison or fry. So what *does* it do? Eh, Car? Eh? Any ideas? Any response? Where do we go from here?"

Memory walked with Carver, strangely, through the leafy wooden outland of the 'Place'. It slotted itself, surprising sometimes, between the on-off flutter of codes, numbers, digits that seemed also, if patchily, to need to be there in his head with him, trying either to centre or to faze him. Maybe too wanting to remind him of something, but whether helpfully or simply without logic or relevant meaning, how could he tell? He knew definitely what he was doing. Wandering their 'grounds', as if perplexed and brooding, as if hoping to make sense of Croft's enthused outburst. But Carver had not credited a word of Croft's confidences. They were lies, set to provoke or tangle, all part of the game that went on here, and perhaps – one point of truth – had done so too at Mantik.

The reason for the game was not clear and might not ever (to him) be fathomable. There had been plenty of that before. He had certainly seen Mantik coin such scenarios in which he had had his part, but never knowing more than his particularised role. For now he wanted merely to see if he could find the end of Croft's set-up's 'Place' – the physical geography of this territory set in gardens and bounded only one way by sea. Where was the boundary, wall, barricade? What was its type and what lay beyond? Might it, if not now then in the future, be penetrable from the inside out: Escape. And Carver wore for this search the body-language and general appearance of a man concerned and unnerved, which was reasonably good camouflage. He had not questioned Croft, after Croft's vibrant statement on *energies*. Carver had stared at Croft, as before Carver had not let himself stare. And when Croft rose and, smiling, pleased, (the three-year-old again), sauntered, whistling, away, silently Carver watched him go, standing with his hands loose at his sides, eyes wide open, frowning. The picture of inarticulate insecurity that might well, after all, be sincere.

The storm Fiddy had prophesied did not yet manifest. Yet the darkness of the day, especially between and below the trees, intensified. It was eventually like an afternoon in an English November. Sunset due at about 4 p.m., but a sky so ungiving that by three lights had gone on in the school classroom or the college hall. Even, back then in Sara's flat. And before then too, in the squat where she had lived at first with him, and with his father.

And this was the memory that now walked up beside Carver. Opening some after all accessible door, it soaked gently inside.

And it was a new memory – was it? Something (*something*) not recalled for two thirds of his life – twenty years – or longer. *Never* recalled since childhood...

How old then was Carver, in this memory?

About three, he thought. (An *actual* three-year-old child.)

A dark day, and the one electric bulb in the squat's side room, that dangerous and illegal rewiring had enabled to burn. The flare of it was calmed by a lopsided lampshade of dingy fake pinkish silk. And Sara was sitting on a cushion by the wall, asleep. The air was cold; no heating, but the cold not yet biting or raw. A mild early winter then, back whenever in the earliest '80's of the previous century.

Carver was trying to wake his mother. Who repeatedly, soporifically, shrugged him off. But the man was there then and picked him up. A big man, bearlike, with a dirty unwashed tang to him, which they all, in their individual ways, gave off. How not? There was no water here to wash in, except the cold water from the other premises with the outdoor tap, and this had to be heated on the open fire in the communal room. The child who was Carver had anyway no aversion to the smells. They were normalcy. The man was warm, and held him with a vast protective surging ease.

"C'mon now, darling," said the man, hugging Carver close. "Leave your poor mum to a bit of kip. You sit with yer da. Ah, you're a lovely boy, you are. You'll be a feller, you will, when you grow up. I'll take yer fishin' then. We'll be rich then, your mum and me. And you. We'll all be rich, in a big red house in Hampstead. It'll be warm as toast, and your mummy can have a chandelier in every room to light it all up. Ah, me boy." And the big face, still tan from a summer working on the roads, a big undrunken face full of large green eyes and sheer approval and involvement, laughing down into Carver's child's face, so Carver the child began also to laugh. And the man and he sat by the long cracked window, a French door once, and gazed out at the bare black and grey of a ruinous garden. "Look," said the warm, dirty, gentle bear, "look – a duckie bird!" And there *was*. There really was. A duck with a head green as jade and coriander, and outspread swimmer's wings, flying low over the darkling sky.

Carver, (the man) stopped under the trees of elsewhere and Present Time.

He stared no longer inwards at the memory of Croft. He stared back down and down the staircase of a million adult years, to that moment in November. Was *that* his father, then?

His *father* – before despair and alcohol got their fangs and barbs into him and changed him to what he later became, a violently drunken abuser, a monster from hell. *Him*? *Then*?

A screen shivered inside Carver's brain. Instead of images numbers flowed across. 1. 1. 1. 1. 4. 4. 4. 4.

## Seventeen

Anjeela Merville was standing under a tree, motionless. Her garments matched or coincided with the woodland – dull green, faded black – he might not have seen her, but some freak of punctured daylight had caught her eyes. They shone like bluish mercury. The luminous eyes of a doll, or a cat.

Carver halted. He did and said nothing, for a moment. But this was, in the most bizarre way, like a direct piece of continuity, following somehow instantly on the events that had already passed. Even, indescribably, on the fragment of memory that involved his father. Even on the random and ceaseless snatches of numbers and codes.

"Hello," she said, "Car."

He did not speak. He stood looking at her.

She seemed – different. Her hair again? Yes, it was longer. Just below her shoulders now, thick and curling, liquorice black. More copious extensions, then. But she was slimmer too. Perhaps how she had dressed? Corseting beneath...

She said, "How are you, Car?"

"Did Croft send you?"

"No. Croft is scampering about his section in high good humour. No one sent me."

"You just came after me, then."

"Not exactly."

"Then *what* exactly?"

She said, "Say my name."

He did not. He said, "There are enough games already."

She said, "Aren't there, though. I thought perhaps we could just *play*, without a game at all."

He turned away and began to take long strides through the trees. So far this 'walk', which he reckoned had used up about three more hours, had yielded nothing. From a rise, on a single occasion, he had seen south-westward through the trees, and had a view of the up-and-down building, the sea beyond, and the sun gradually descending, discernible only by a metallic bruise behind the purple cloudbank. And he had found no boundary barrier, no sign he was approaching any. There were no sentries either, of any sort he could detect or concretely suspect. An object fixed high up on a trunk had, for a second, convinced him he at last glimpsed a surveillance device. But it was a piece of metal foil, perhaps pulled up there by a magpie, or other gleam-keen bird-thief.

The sun must be near to going down, he thought. But this twilight did not seem to alter. Only *she* had altered. Anjeela. Presumably gleam-keen on a bit of rustic fuckery in the fern.

Like memory, she was walking beside him now. She had caught up and kept pace with him, matching his long strides without apparent effort. Whatever weight or hair–length, she was fit then. In any sense, he supposed.

"Say my name, Car," she repeated in a while, her breathing serene and unhurried.

"Have you forgotten it?"

"Have you?"

"Yes," he said, ridiculously as a kid of thirteen. "I've forgotten your name."

"Anjeela," she said.

"Merville," he said.

"AJ–" prompting.

"MV," he finished. He stopped again and turned again to look down the few inches into her face. (She was also slightly taller than he had remembered, or wore lifts in her shoes.)

Across his mind, vivid enough as if physically it had flown by between them, the number chain flashed on-off on-off. Code – the code – *J*udges. *M*arket. *A*lways. *A*ble –

She interrupted.

"I want to show you something, Car," she said. Her voice was velvet. Panther voice. He could scent her, cinnamon and honey, ambergris and pure coffee.

He shoved her, with a roughness he never expressed against women, into a convenient tree trunk. "All right. Why not. Undo your pants," he said.

And she gave her panther laugh. Not intimidated, not resisting, not eager or willing or vulnerable, not *useable* at all.

"I want," she said, "to show you *this*."

And she held up her smoke-brown hand, slender and beautifully articulated by its bones and tendons, gemmed with its five mother-of-pearl nails. One of which–

One of which was – was it? – altering. Was – elongating – *growing*, pushing out of the forefinger, slim, straight, displaying its manicured oval tip –

"What –?" he said.

"Just watch, Car," she softly said.

The pearl nail, still smoothly couth, now two-three inches in length – but the – finger too – the finger was effortlessly elongating now, not distorting, merely lengthening, becoming the finger of some non-human being – a finger six inches, one hundred and fifty millimetres – long. The finger ceased to grow. The nail had ceased. They lay there, against his forearm, darker than his shirtsleeve. A perfect finger, not ugly. Only – only – ex-tend-ed. Alien.

"You see it," she said.

"Some drug. I don't know how. In the coffee?" Or in her perfume –?

"No drug, Car. This is really happening."

"It's some trick, then." He brought his own left hand across and clamped the alien finger and its nail between his own. It moved. The faintest quiver. It was warm, flexible; made of flesh and bone and coordinated. "How?" he said. "How are you doing that?"

"Like this," she said.

His eyes skipped back to her face and saw the single strand of shining hair against her cheek, still attached, but its end slipping down, passing like a cord of silk unravelling, unwinding. The end fell on to her throat, slid serpentine down again over her right breast. When it was long enough to reach her waist it twisted and lay still.

Closed against his palm he felt the forefinger flex again. He let go – and watched as, with its own lunatic grace, it withdrew seamlessly back and back into her hand, regaining its proper length, sibling to the rest, the polished oval just a pleasingly coloured and burnished nail. The curl was sliding up as well, up and up, faster, faster, snapping home just under her shoulder with the others, slinking in among them to hide.

He drew away from her. Two metres between them now.

"Very clever," he said. His voice had no substance. It was a mindless and redundant voice. Not even his. Then whose? Who – what – was speaking through him?

She said, "It's what I can do."

He said, "Their cameras will have seen you do it, in that case. Or do they know already?" He thought, *Nothing happened.* It was some form of hypnosis. Or drugs... It will be some drug –

"They don't know. Won't hear. Can't see. Something is messing up the spy-cameras, the clever sound system. Sun spots. *Something.*"

*Something,* he thought. The repeated word from the beginning, from the dark, from – somewhere.

"I'll see you around, Car," she said. She smiled. Her eyes – were not blue. They were – dark. Dark bronze – And then she blinked. Her eyes were blue.

She turned and ran lightly away. *Fleet,* he thought, that old word, fleet as a deer.

*AJ* crossed the mind-screen. *MV.* 1. 1. 4. 4.

Full night had come, by the time he got round to the northern side again, having given up on discovering any finishing line for the 'Place'. He had had nothing with him. Having to go out with Croft had precluded that, nor had he been given any coffee or water, no nourishment, only confusion and its subsequent anger.

Regaining the more inward environs of the 'grounds', Carver found tonight several drinking parties went on. Hardly a wake. An anniversary perhaps. Or seven or so birthdays being celebrated separately but simultaneously. Given Charlie Hemel's death, that was peculiar. But by now, everything was. One seriously sane and reasonable event might, in this climate, be the most suspicious. Carver was enthusiastically offered, and accepted, a drink of apple juice among the loitering festivities he inadvertently passed. Was the juice spiked? It seemed only by very weak vodka. He drank enough to alleviate thirst. The day, and currently the night, stayed weather-wise oppressive, but finally dim thunders were rolling round the sky. Pinkish sheet lightning sometimes opened the black ceiling wide. (A pink lopsided lampshade. C'mon now, darlin', leave your poor mum to a bit of kip. A mast that catches lightning. Look – a duckie bird. Crazy. So many crazies in his life. What memory could he trust, here? How many had been _implanted_? Fingers that grew long like CGI. )

He reached the foot of the rise, (on which the seven railway carriages were stalled), by his own guess around 10.30 p.m.

For some time he leaned on a tree below the hill.

There had been isolated rills of noise rising, sinking, and strings of lights across the woodland, bonfires even. But here, only darkness. So, no doubts.

The shed, just as before, was glowing. The central shed. This was, it went without saying, something else _they_ had done. An organised and chemically-triggered glow. Mantik must have organised something similar. Treating objects he might steal. A slow release, empowered only in one closed area. The shed. No other answer made sense. Why, God knew. He was the errand boy, the _pawn_. Move him here, there. Decoy, bait, shadow, fall guy. _Experiment_?

Tonight, to start with, he did not properly scrutinise the illumination. His imagination had once more stepped in to try to block his intellect. _It's just the same, Carver._ A vivid turquoise. Should be used to it by now, Except, _tonight_, it was in reality – if any of this _were_ real – _not_ just the same. Tonight, the sheen that bloomed like radiation from the shed – was green. Lime-green. Emerald infused by citrine, much sharper than the sting of vodka in juice. A colour that any minute might become solely the yellow of a mid-Urgency, doubtless escalating, Alert.

He sat in the dark, the shed's light burning above him, his back to the trunk of a tree.

The thunder and lightning had rainlessly aborted. There was, in the inert warmth of the air, the taint of burnt wood from the party fires. There had also been some fireworks and Chinese Lanterns for a short while, lifting southward, towards the sea, maybe on the terrace from which the cyclist had taken flight.

Senseless. Even macabre, in an amateurish fashion.

Carver slept a little. And Anjeela had filled her mouth with him, sucking and caressing. But the sharp dream-pleasure woke him, and immediately died, gurning numbly down the darkness, leaving a sour ache; and even that died, losing its way.

The letters and numbers resumed their irritating constellations.

He registered that code, one of the less elusive, which worked the alphabet in two blocks of 1 to 9, and then one last block of 1 to 8 – the letter A counting as 1, B as 2, etc, with I as 9. Then resuming with J as 1 to R (9) and S to Z (1 – 8).

It was the code Mantik had used to warn of the disappearance of a member of the staff. Carver's iPhone had given it as a games clue, *Clue up* being the signal, the *2nd Clue* the code. That morning the second clue had read *Always Justified Marketable Value*. You took the first letter of each word, in this instance AJMV – and that gave you, conversely, on the 1 to 9, 1 to 9, 1 to 8 principle, the numbers/letters A – 1, J – 1 and M – 4, V – 4.

The code's numbers and letters presented showed all the *other* alphabetical instances – while leaving out all remaining letters that themselves would be numbered 1 or 4. They were then S and D. The subject therefore had such initials. In other words, Silvia Dusa.

A very straightforward code, transparent enough, and one of hundreds Carver had had, over the years, to learn. Strange therefore, really, he had not, until now, picked up on its recent reissue – *here*, both on his mind-screen, and spoken aloud to him by the blue-eyed black woman who had had sex with him in the bed, and later, out in the woods, grown her fingernail, and finger, and one coil of hair, like an effect in a movie.

But ignore the effect – doubtless stage-managed and sensibly unbelievable. The main question now was another one. Anjeela

Merville had stressed, many times and by differing means, the two first and second syllable letters of her name. And they made up the very same code clue as the others from Mantik. A and J and M and V left SD. So what – *what* – was this woman's connection with Dusa, who had betrayed Mantik, and shopped Carver, and died as her reward?

# Eighteen

Yellow.

Straight through and done with turquoise and lime. Yellow now: 4th Level Alert.

Carver had dropped asleep, drugged this time by silence and the surrounding wrap of the dark. He thought he had dreamed of Anjeela again, standing under a magenta maple tree that had burned through the greenness of the woods. "Drop your pants," Anjeela said. As *he* had said it. But that was all.

The morning light was coming back now too. And above, the yellow glow in the shed was dissolving. Did he only imagine it had become fully yellow? Or did he imagine it was <u>*not*</u> yellow, or lime, that it was the same greenish blue as it had been before or did he–?

"<u>*Energies*</u>." Croft's voice, distinct as if physically heard. "<u>Nostocaris. That fish. Shining Knife. Casts no giveaway shadow. Someone without a soul</u>."

Carver got up. His body felt stiff and unwieldy for a moment. But he was physically well enough trained this went off at once.

He was hungry and dry and his bladder angry. He pissed against the tree, thinking of late revellers going home from the pub through the village woods around and behind his house there, that house he had owned and lived in with Donna, and how the drunks peed on the trees, as if this counted for anything.

He considered Johnston also for the turn of one thought. What Johnston had been doing, and why, and what had happened (forget fake reassurances) to Johnston when Croft's army, the nameless Us, arrived to grab Carver. And what had happened to Donna, Maggie. And who had really assisted, or themselves only facilitated Silvia Dusa's blood-letting death.

By then he was walking directly south towards the up-and-down building. The unwieldy shape was soon clearly visible, some of its night lights still on, and the day returning in pale waves. There seemed a lot of smoke going up in a solid column on the far side. The smell of old burning was stronger now. A hundred large wooden things – logs, chairs, tables – thoroughly consumed, a thousand bacon sandwiches crisped to ashes in their flaming hearts.

Drawing nearer to the building, Carver found he went by and through small herds of people sleeping, or beginning fretfully to wake, on the ground. There was a scatter of campers' tents, some of which, inadequately erected, had collapsed. The remnants of the fires lay on seared black mats of scorched turf. One or two had kept partly alight. He saw at least five that had at some point got out of hand and spread – marks of fire-extinguisher wet, damage to tree trunks and foliage, a blackened creeper.

To the south side, even so, at least from here, the smoke pillar actually seemed less; its stench hung low. All this was like the aftermath of a poorly run music festival. Along the edges of the gravel drive a couple of the rose urns had been broken. Flowers spilled, showing their thorns.

Now and then, as he passed, he had encountered a burst of random abuse, the sort you might get from an unknown drunk dissatisfied in the street. Up close to the building, Security was roaming about. The men looked as they had after Charlie Hemel's death. They were untidy, as if dressed and assembled in unexpected haste, asked to act, and employ methods they were entirely unused to and had not ever practiced.

One man came shouldering over to Carver. The man's hair had been slicked back impatiently and flared up in misaligned quills.

"Where have you been?" he rapped.

"For a walk."

"Where are you going?"

"Inside," said Carver.

"Get in and stay in," said the security man.

"Why? What's happened?"

"Don't fucking argue. Get in, go to your room, and stay put."

"Sure," said Carver.

He went past the man who, he was aware, turned to stare after him, making certain the returnee did as ordered.

Other people were milling around a side entrance when Carver reached it. They were quarrelling fiercely, dedicatedly. One of the men was in tears of frustration. "You think too much, you don't *listen*–" Carver went by them. They seemed not to see him. But as he moved into the as yet still night-lit hall space beyond the door, one of the women ran after him. "Wait! Wait!" she cried. She flung her arms around him. He tried gently to ease her off but she would not let go. "Why have I had to wait so long for you?" she asked. There was less recrimination in her voice than sadness. He did not know her, could not recall even noticing her before. She was fairly ordinary, pretty, slender, average age and type. "Don't leave me," she said, piteously.

Drugs again, this time used on her, or by her on herself? Alcohol? She did not seem particularly drunk or high. Only – upset.

"What's the matter?" He could hear the caution in his tone.

So did she. "How can you be so cruel to me? After all this while – You and me. *Everyone* recognises that – why can't you?"

She was insane. Something, or someone, had driven her mad. Just as the bicycle had driven Charlie Hemel to the cliff's edge and over.

"OK," Carver said. He patted her shoulder. "We need to talk, then."

"Yes!" she exclaimed. "*Yes*."

"I just have to see Croft," said Carver – would she remember who Croft was, his apparent significance? It looked as if she did, thank Christ. "I'll be about half an hour. Then I'll meet you here."

"Can't I come with–"

"You know what he's like."

She appeared puzzled then, already losing the thread because it made sense and so, to her now, was meaningless.

"See you soon," said Carver. He moved from her grip and she let her arms fall.

As he got into the first lift he could find, he did not glance back. She was crying now, like the guy outside. Like Van Sedden. (Donna, Sara.) Too many tears.

The lift went up three floors only. Carver got out on the third, tramped down an empty corridor that had coloured photographs on the walls of ships and castles, and no windows. Turning into another corridor, lights on and lined by closed doors, Carver picked up a low buzzing sound, some machine, and farther on several voices shouting, words lost. No other evidence of life. But there was a second lift. It would descend, judging by its placement, to a different area of the building than the hallway where the mad girl waited. Carver got in the lift.

When the doors opened on the next floor down, another of the security men stood there, and beckoned Carver brusquely out.

"Daddy wants you," he said jeeringly.

Croft? Presumably. Or someone else who claimed to be in charge.

This was a madhouse, Carver thought. Whatever organisation had nabbed him that night in the village, was more than merely a collection of watchers or rivals or, possibly, enemy agents at war with Mantik. Whatever these unnamed operatives were, or had in mind, entailed something (*something*) indecipherable.

Even should all this latest oddness prove to be some massive and choreographed set-piece of mind-fuck, meant solely to break and remodel Carver, they themselves would have to be genuinely crazy to waste so much theatre on him. There was definitely no purpose to it. Carver was not a "*Star*". He knew nothing and had access to nothing of any true value. So – did they then mistake him for some other one who *did* or *had*? *Scar*, he thought. *Three Scars. And I am what?* Say maybe the Second Scar. *But they think I am the First – or the Third* – The one that really *counts*.

## Nineteen

The beaming girl in the front office of Croft's section was not beaming. She wore a cream kimono-ish dressing-gown and her bare feet were up on a desk while she sat drinking tea.

"What?" she asked, as the buttons by the metal door let Carver and the man in. "We're not open yet, you know."

"You're open. Mr C wants this one."

"No he doesn't."

The security man pointed out a chair for Carver to sit in. "Park yourself there and wait."

Carver again obeyed. The guard shot a look at the girl. "Stupid bitch," he said, in a tepidly analytical manner.

The girl ignored him. He went out.

The door shut.

The girl began to colour her toenails vivid phosphorescent

crimson. From the polish the long room filled with an acid and chemical odour. It seemed to Carver nail varnish, as with hair lacquers, conditioners and similar things, had carried a less raucous smell in his childhood. This stuff was like paint-stripper.

"Do you fancy some sex?" the girl asked, squinting up, if remaining beamless.

Carver did not reply.

"Well?" she demanded.

"No thanks."

"No. It's too early isn't it? Maybe later," she added vaguely. "I'll see how I feel then."

From outside, and six, seven storeys down, there came a sudden rush of noise, a seawave smashing on the blinded windows.

Carver got to his feet, walked to the nearest window and slammed the blind upwards.

Beyond the pane, below, the generalised vista of grass slopes, trees, and – currently – the debris of the previous night's celebrations. A large, burned patch showed baldly off to the left. Between that spot and the building, a strip of the gravel margin and another urn in pieces, petals lying like torn out, freshly coloured toenails.

Small figures, dwarfed by distance, were fighting. Empty wine bottles were being used to bash heads in. Even as Carver scrutinised the scene, a man fell face down on the gravel. Another two men, laughingly, kicked him. A woman, unseen, was screaming. ("*Cunt! Cunt!*")

"Is Croft up here?" Carver asked.

"Oh yes," said the girl. "Why don't you just go in? You can find your own bloody way. I'm sick of traipsing about after you all."

A broken glass sound splashed from below. An object flew up also, very fast, flung towards the window, running on air but falling short; a woman's high-heeled shoe.

Carver, having left the window, put his hand on the panel by Croft's door.

The door undid itself and there was the inner room, the orderly chairs, and the desk, the large window behind it with its blind firmly down. Croft was standing by the window. In silhouette, but already moving away, coming out towards Carver.

"Thank God you're here," said Croft. "I thought they might have trouble locating you."

His voice was calm, but heavy. His face, now daylight described it, the same. It was a fact, he did not look particularly English, but that meant nothing. Legally born and bred in Britain he could be citizen and patriot, until proven otherwise.

His *hair* was real. It had become dishevelled enough that had it been a piece, gaps would be discernible and were not.

"Did you have much trouble?" Croft asked.

"In what way?"

"Coming through the building, or – were you outside?"

"Yes."

"Something has happened," said Croft. "I don't know what and getting any info through has become a nightmare. Communications – out or in – are no longer feasible. Most of the IT has gone down. The computers will only – what was it they said? – yes. They'll only let you play games on them. Fantasy games. Kill the Giant, Rob the Wizard, virtually buy a virtual farm. That kind of enterprise. Nobody's phone works. Mine certainly don't. None of them."

Carver waited, but Croft now paced across the room to the left, back to the centre, back to the left. He stood there, then, by a steel-fronted cabinet. He stared into the steel, clicking his teeth.

"Do you know," Carver said, "what–"

"What's caused it? No. Nobody does. Or, the ones that are still compost mentis don't–" (Did he say that? Compost not com*pos*?) "And the rest of them," said Croft. "Well. You've seen. Something introduced," Croft elaborated, "through the water system perhaps, although that is, of course, supposed to be inviolable. All Security is supposed to be. Or it's something in the air, a gas, maybe... Nobody spotted so much as a hot-air balloon... But it has caused anyway trouble. You've seen. We're in trouble. And getting worse. We have," said Croft, "you and I, to get out of here, Car. Quick as we can."

"All right."

"Just us," said Croft. "The rest – anyone who's still in working order – will have to fend for selves. You and I. We're important."

Fantasy computer games, Carver thought. Escape from the Danger Zone. And how, precisely? He had noted there were no cars, no sort of real transport, anywhere visible – perhaps some big underground parking facility existed. He had not, of course, been shown.

"But it won't be done without trouble," said Croft.

*Trouble*. He had said the word three, four times now. "Just play it cool, Carver. We play it cool."

"Sure."

"Cool. You and I."

The door opened and the un-beaming girl stamped in with a tray. There was a coffee-pot and a jug of water. The pot rattled emptily, and the slopping water did not have its courteous ice-and-slice. She set the tray on the desk.

"Thank you," said Croft stonily, not as he had on that other occasion.

The girl now said nothing. She went out again, failing to shut the door.

Croft shut it. "We'll take the lift down to the side terrace," said Croft. "That part of the grounds has as a rule less traffic – with luck, not enough of them will be out there to cause immediate concerns. This is going to be tight shit, Carver. Can you handle that?"

Carver nodded once. He thought of Anjeela a moment, wondering where *she* was. But his brain was by now mainly exploring the abrupt new idea: that Croft could enable them – Carver – to leave the confines of the 'Place'. For there *was* a boundary, a way out – there had to be – and Croft would know where it was and how to use it. Chaos had come. And as any of the gods in any proper fantasy game (even in the Bible) knew, from chaos might be created – anything.

## TWENTY

Croft and Carver travelled down in the lift that was corridor-attached to Croft's room. Six – seven? – levels below, they emerged onto the terrace with steps and handrail. They descended the steps to the grass. No one was there. The whole area, including the lush wilderness ahead, seemed held in a unique pocket of unmotion and blurred quiet – though raucous shouts and other disturbances were audible, they sounded removed and irrelevant; noises off. On the slopes, and among the trees, no burning was to be seen, and nothing stirred in the windless, smoke-dried airlessness. Already the day was too warm. The sky had a glaring pallor. Nothing moved there, either. The gulls were gone.

Then four security men ran out of the trees up ahead. Their advent was so unannounced Carver suspected they had been hidden from sight, waiting for anyone – or two specific persons – to come down the steps.

Carver stopped dead. Croft also. They watched as the four men – coordinated, expressionless – bounded towards them.

None of the four carried a weapon, but all were no doubt armed, and with a selection of devices. This was like the schools. Carver, almost mindlessly now, seeing in pictures not words – one or two boys on their own, hoping it was OK, and abruptly confronted out of nowhere by the bullies. But here the bullies had been *cloned* – they all looked alike. The man with the spiked hair was not included.

About five metres from them, the gang came to a halt.

Croft spoke. "Yes?" His voice was steady and pitched, and kept a balanced authority. He was in charge. That was all there was to it.

Or not.

The face of the slightly taller security man sagged to let out a ribald laugh.

"Hello, Crofty. Look, it's Crofty. Who'd have guessed?"

Two of the others laughed, softly, not minding.

The fourth man stared hard through round unliking glassy eyes. "Well," the fourth man said, "he can frenchy kiss up his own shitty arse."

That made all four men laugh. Even the glassy-eyed man who had said it.

The taller one said, "So. What'll we do with him, boys?"

Croft did not speak now. To speak was very likely useless.

Carver readied himself for what must come next – a fight with professional strong-arm balletics, the utilisation, probably, of instruments intended to subdue, if not – essentially – to kill. He did not look at Croft. To look at Croft would not be useful either.

Short and incongruous, a firework cracked, somewhere around the building.

It was not a firework.

As one, the four-man gang altered, everything about them changing.

Their faces had resumed likeness, blankly serious and fixed. Only "Shooting–" the glassy-eyed man murmured, as if explaining to himself, giving his body an extra split second to respond. And they all broke into motion, running, sprinting at and then past the two men who had seemed to be their quarry. Off they raced, away along the wall of the building, the shortest of them leaping a low bush that had encroached.

A litter of several more disembodied shots fractured through far-off air. Then quietness reassembled, and the sense of total distancing.

"This place smells like badly-smoked haddock," remarked Croft, "don't you think so?"

Carver did not answer.

Croft began to stride up the incline, more or less in the direction he had led Carver before. Carver followed. Nobody else, nothing, sprang from the trees. At least, not yet.

"Hiding," said Croft, "in plain sight."

They had met no one at all, though they had not paused at the griffin bench on the slope, but progressed around, by the rises and dips of the higher ground, towards the northern side. To the sheds. Carver's sheds.

Although Carver had been left with keys, unsurprisingly Croft had another set.

He unlocked the central door of the central shed.

Inside it was cooler than the woods. (*Cool*. Play it...)

Carver looked around him. He had been about here last night till dawn, had sat below, looking up, or sleeping, under the yellow eye of the 4th Level Alert that the glow in the shed had become. Unless he had imagined this, as he had imagined, or been made to imagine, that Anjeela Merville could grow her hair and fingers to unusual lengths.

The shed had, it was true, also changed somewhat. In addition to the table, on which he had put the small random group of 'stolen' objects, three chairs were instantly notable. They had been arranged against the walls. Plus there was a miniature white fridge, working on batteries, whose door Croft at once flung wide. "Good, good," said Croft, with sombre gratification. And drew out a large bottle of vodka with a white and brown label, its pedigree written in Russian characters. A filled ice-tray came next, and a dish of anchovies. Everything began at once to smoke as its frigidity met the surrounding warmth. Croft set the bottle and fish on the table and pulled up two of the chairs.

Carver now noted another much lower table had been positioned under the main table, with a dozen glasses standing on it. "My apologies, they didn't bring the coffee, as I asked. I know you're not enamoured of alcohol, Car. That was your father, was it? There is bottled water in the fridge, nicely chilled – yes?"

"All right," Carver said.

Croft went back and drew out a two-litre bottle that had lain on its side due to the cramped space. Its label also was unknown. It seemed to be in French and bore the reproduced pen-and-ink illustration of a fairy-tale well.

"Come," said Croft, as he seated himself. "Sit." Carver remained where he stood, just inside the door. "Shut the door, please, old fellow," added Croft. "Perhaps you should lock it – I have the keys here."

"In case someone comes by, you mean," said Carver.

"Hiding in plain sight," Croft repeated. He had poured a short thin glass full of vodka, and knocked it back, picked up two anchovies in his fingers and set them in his mouth, savorously rolling them about his tongue before biting down.

Carver shut and triple-locked the door. He retained the keys. "I thought," Carver said quietly, "we had to get out of here. Away."

"We do," said Croft, through the fish. He chewed further, then swallowed, poured another drink, and swallowed that, again in one mouthful. He poured a third glass, and now added the miniature ice-cubes. Put it down, only running the edge of his large and manicured hand lightly, kindly, against its frosty sides. Petting it before drinking it.

"Then why," said Carver, "are we in here?"

"Common sense. They have gone mad. They will look for me. For us. Initially in the sections. Then outside. They will expect that we attempt a straight route for the outer world. They will be massing at every exit."

"What *are* the exits? *Where* are they?"

"I'll show you the best ones. In a little while. You must be patient, Car, dear boy. Have some water – or *can* I tempt you to this tasty water-coloured beverage?"

"Where does it come from?" Carver asked.

"Somewhere in Russia, I assume. Legally imported. Perfectly valid, patriotic and safe. No treason in sampling foreign drinks or food. These are good, these anchovies. Yes? No? Your loss, dear boy. Caviar would be delightful, of course." He ate more of the fish, then raised and tipped the glass between his lips. This time he emptied only half, crunched on an ice-cube. Turning in the chair he pierced Carver with a grimace of sudden and intense malevolence. "Sit down, boy. What do you think you are doing? *Sit*. Drink your water."

Carver glanced over his shoulder through windows, out of the shed. The slopes were sullen and shadowed yet still seemed vacant of people. But the trees had not shown the security gang until the four men chose to emerge. And if Carver left now, he had no notion of any safe way to get across the wild extensive grounds, at speed and in the right direction.

He walked to the table, positioned the second chair and sat; reached for the water and the second glass. (The keys were in his pocket and Croft might have forgotten them.)

"We must just be patient," said Croft thoughtfully. "*We* can do that. It's the fashion now, everything must rush so fast. It was better in the past. The past went slowly. Perhaps even you remember how slow it went when you were young. Minutes that were hours, hours that were years." He finished the glass, sucked in another of the ice-cubes. Deciding to speak again, he spat the cube out on the floor. He had devoured all the anchovies, and now wiped his oily fingers on the sleeve of his severe and costly suit, whose jacket, even in the heat, he did not slough. "Let's pretend, shall we?" said Croft, resuming a smile, almost drowsy with a goodwill as sudden as the flash of malevolence. "Let's pretend we're in a Russian novel – Tolstoy, say. Or a Chekhov play, that might be better. *Platonov*... *The Cherry Orchard*.... *The Seagull*. Ah, that would be the life. All that elite glamour and passion and fuckingly glorious angst, and then a conclusive and mindlessly magnificently fearless death. Anna and Platonov with their trains, and so-and-so with his pistol – Drink up, Car. Nothing like good vodka." His mind had mislaid, it seemed, that Carver's drink was water. Carver drank amenably. His heart thudded heavy as lead, like leaden bullets loaded in his chest, playing now Russian Roulette, slipping round, with the empty click of escape, but in the end the explosion would come, more silent than any silence of the living earth.

Croft refilled his own glass.

The bottle was half empty, one more chamber of the gun. When all the single-glass-deep chambers of the bottle were empty, the explosion would yet come.

Whatever was happening in this Place was plainly happening to Croft as well. Did he know? Did any of them? – the girl with her blood-dipped toenails, Ball and Van Sedden fighting and weeping. Charlie Hemel. Anjeela–

And he, Carver, he must have it too, this madness. That, his madness, was why he had seen her hand alter, and her hair. Did he now only *imagine* – *pretend* – Croft partly lay there in the wooden chair, his jacket smelling of vinegar and salt-fish, and his real hair falling over his vast, mournful and bitter eyes.

Croft drank. "Car," said Croft. "You know, dear boy, it's been hard on me. My son – it was – years ago. They killed him. It was during conflict, the great battle, hearts, minds. It was then. He was so young. About your age once, Car. When you were young, like that. I wished so much he hadn't died. If it could have been me. If someone – if someone had said to me, we must kill one of you, Peter. You, or him. I'd have – I – would have said, me. Let it be me. But no – nobody asked. He was my son. I never saw – Not enough left of him to bury. *What's that?*" Croft had lurched about, almost falling, spinning up from the chair which itself did fall, on its back. He rushed to the nearest window and gaped out, panting as if he had run for miles across a minefield. He put both his hands up on the glass, as a child might, staring out. And then he threw himself on the floor, below the window level, not to be seen.

Carver rose cautiously, and approached the other closer window, keeping to one side of it. He could make out nothing in the view that had not already been there. No intruders, other than trees, in between. But, as he had already decided, that might not prove a thing. He eased away from the window. Really, the shed being constructed as it was, with so many windows on both sides, to hide in here was fairly nonviable. Croft, going crazy, glossed over this. Or else it made for him a facet of some necessary pattern, inescapable after all. Just like the building and its grounds.

Far away though now it was, the up-and-down building in fact ended the vista from the shed. About a quarter mile off below this hill. The windows of the corridor outside his room would be identifiable, if he searched for them – he did not.

Croft was getting up from the floor. He stood without unease and crossed unguardedly in front of the windows as he returned to right his chair and sit on it. He looked a moment at the vodka bottle but did not refill his glass.

Croft's face was strangely both very old and very young. The features, sockets and lids of the eyes, might have been carved. He seemed tired but restless, feverish.

"What were we talking about? Ah," he said. "Chekhov. Have you read the plays?"

"No."

"That's a pity. Nobody reads now. Nothing like that, like Chekhov. But you'll have seen the plays acted–" Carver did not reply, or need to. "You'll know what I mean. There comes a junction, a crossroads. You have to choose. Jump under the train, blow your brains out. Ibsen has it too. *Hedda Gabler.* You can't go on. The jackals are gathering, the starving black wolves that want to rip your guts and gnaw your bones. Or you can avoid them. A crash, a flame, nuclear detonation of the brain and skull. All over. Oblivion. Peace."

Croft lifted the vodka and poured himself another glass. He sipped it, laid it down with tender care.

"I think it was quick for him. My boy. They said it was. So young. So quick."

Croft sat and did not say anything. Carver did as Croft did. If Croft finished the bottle, he might lose consciousness, or at any rate become less *intransigent*, could be dealt with.

If there was time.

Odd the rest of them had not come here. Something more intriguing for them to do, obviously. Searching the building. Massing at the exits–

Would Carver have to kill Croft?

And others, would he have to kill others, too?

He was untrained in that. Self-defence to a point, of course. Not murder.

But he reckoned he could, if he had to, and got the chance. Most human things were capable of that.

Was Croft starting to go to sleep? His long lids were almost shut. He slumped in the chair.

Outside, at the windows, a blink of transparent lightning. Downhill, through the intercessionary trees, a low flat *boom* resounded. Underfoot, faint yet not to be missed, vibration trembled the floor of the shed, and the adjacent sheds rattled at their couplings, softly, as if – for a second – the train would be travelling on.

Something had been blown up. Going on the impact, probably not the entire building.

Carver went back to the window. The building was not visible. Instead another pillar of darkness was copiously gushing upward, tinged a muddy orange at its base. The smoke was already, blown not by any non-existent wind but by the charge of the blast, swirling uphill towards them.

As the smoke thickened round the sheds, the tremble below ground ended.

Croft had revived. He sat upright. He drained his glass, poured another drink and tipped it down his throat.

"**No** time to lose now," he announced very clearly. "Got to get out, you and I. OK, Car, OK, old man?" And from inside the jacket, from under his arm, he drew out a slender handgun, and set it down by the nearly empty bottle and the empty plate.

Carver, not meaning to, half rose.

"Sit, my friend," said Croft, his voice musical as any fine actor's. "Even like this, I'd be too quick for you. You have to trust me on this."

Something – *something* – yes, Carver trusted him on this. Croft would be too quick.

One hope. His aim might not, under these circumstances, be so very splendid. Not now. So hold quiet, and judge the moment. The moment to dodge, to dive – or to die.

"The thing of it is, Car," said Croft, turned in the chair, and watching him, black eyes wide open, burning and abnormally clear, "I do *mean* to escape. But how about you? Do you want to come with me – over the mountain and far away? Oh Christ, Carver," he said, and the bright clear eyes filled up with tears brighter than the vodka, or the eyes. "I see it now. I see it. My son. It's you, Carver, you, my dear son. Poor boy, poor boy– Say, then, dearest boy, do you want to escape with me?"

It was gibberish, but not all. Carver had seen at last what Croft's escape plan must be. Either there *was* no other path left out of this Place, or else Croft could no longer access the path. And so the only route was through the gun.

"No," Carver said. "I don't want to escape that way."

He spoke calmly. Reasonably.

It might not, could not work. It did.

"Good luck then, my dear son. Take care. Get out now, please.

And close the door."

Carver got up and walked to the door and opened it and at every step he felt the blazing bullet shear home through him into head or heart. But no bullet came. Only the smudged greenness outside, the leaves, the patched clearness and the smoke like fog, old fogs someone had once told him of as a child.

And peculiarly, through the patches in the fog, an irrelevant fact came to Carver now, that only this central shed had two steps up to it. The others, either side, stood on slightly higher ground, and were stepless. This was the first time he had noticed.

Carver did not look in at Croft as he closed the door.

Carver was down the two steps, just on to the turf and tree roots, the smoke catching in his throat, when the gun thundered behind him. Carver stalled, but the bullet had not been for him. Its noise was unconvincing even so, the one bad special effect which, after all, had spoilt the play's final act,

## Twenty-One

But another act was due to begin. After an interval.

In the interval, Carver walked off from the sheds, across and over the rise, and down its further side. The acrid smoke became less here. The woods were thicker, the scent of leaves and grass persisted. No sun showed, but from the position of the glare that now and then seared through the overcast, he thought it must be noon.

He sat under a tree, as he had before. He waited, not for another theatrical surge, (explosion, shot), but perhaps for his brain to catch up. It did not seem to. It maundered around the edges of the plot, the storyline, veering off as if bored, to other, tinier events – an ant on a blade of glass, indifferent to the larger world and intent on its own life-drama; an increasing awareness of his own tiredness and physical hunger – when had he last eaten? God knew – which the cold water had not alleviated.

However, the fact of the unfinished water bottle was what, in the end, made him get to his feet. He needed more fluid, he thought, and besides there might be something palatable in the fridge, aside from anchovies.

So, back up the slope Carver went, and straight up the steps to the shed door.

Only as he opened it did he properly understand, aside from a mere concept, that a man lay dead now in the wooden room, or dying even, if Croft had got his last move wrong.

Croft had not. He had been infallibly perfect. The chair had fallen again as the power of the gun propelled him from it. Croft lay a brief space from the chair, and the gun too had separated from both the chair and the man, done with them, and its role temporarily concluded.

One could not mistake that Croft was dead, either. He had known what he did, had maybe practiced it earlier, (dress rehearsals). A smear of blood had ebbed from his mouth, a fragment of a tooth. His face otherwise was only closed, as his eyes were; more a shutter than a face: No one home. The back of his skull, and some of its formerly internal cargo, had flown free to strike the wall.

The smell that hung there was bizarre yet over-intimate, human discharges of different inevitable sorts. The visual effect, despite its utter conviction, contained an intense element of unreality. Carver found he was *not* convinced. Although he *knew*, with intrinsic built-in knowledge, as of life and death themselves, that the procedure had been achieved and was complete.

Nor could he move. He did not have full liberty. For example, now, he could not – or would not – go to the fridge. Somehow, but speaking aloud, he ordered himself to the table, and grabbed the bottle of water.

Then he found it hard to leave the table.

Where was he going? To the door, and out again.

Leave this – this room – area – stage-set – leave it to the remains on the floor.

"*Come on*," Carver said aloud. His voice was iron, emotionless.

*My son*, Croft had said. But not to Carver, however it had seemed. It was to the past Croft had referred, the past that went by so slowly.

My son. Years ago. They killed him. Not enough... to bury.

Carver turned, gained the door, went out. He shut the door carefully and locked it with the triple keys.

The smoke was getting less. How much time had gone by now? The sun, or its implication, had shifted. Below, through the trees, he could just make out movement around the building. Nothing nearer. And nothing there was distinct enough anyway to ascertain what damage had been caused.

He must get on.

Try to reach some aperture of escape, even if he had not ever located anything on his forays. He should have taken the gun. He knew sufficient to fire one. Go back in then, into the shed, approach the body, take the gun.

He was not afraid or anxious about the body. It was not that. And yet somehow it would not be possible to go back into the shed again.

Carver walked down from the rise once more the other way, away from the building, the sheds, northward. He got now about two hundred metres. There was a bench, not stone with griffins, only plain wood, backless, no arm rests. Carver sat on the bench.

Drink the water. Pull himself together. (They had been fond of that expression at the schools.) Why did no one else come in this direction? But they would. In a while. He should have taken the gun. Or perhaps it had held merely a solitary bullet. No, at least two – Croft had offered to kill Carver. There must therefore have been at least one more – or did he know Carver would not consent, or did –

A bird called from the tops of the trees, shrill and angry.

Carver drank the water.

The interval was concluded. Carver found he had lain down full length on the bench and slept. Had the water been drugged? No. Stop that. Exhaustion, that was all. And carelessness – due to what? Shock? Fear? Insanity – yes, no doubt that. The chemical or viral madness that struck this Place – introduced–

All the trees had changed to a smoky copper. Red Alert, 6th Level – only sunset. Pull yourself –

He sat up, and the empty plastic bottle fled from him, dissociating itself, as the gun had from Croft.

Somebody was standing on the rise, where the sheds were, above Carver, and looked over at him. The figure was painted, on its right side, a sunset, nail varnish red. A woman. Then she dropped down, the way a cat or dog might have that had been standing on its hind legs to perform a trick – He could not see her now.

Carver did not shift from the sitting position. Not aware of it, still he knew the woman was springing down the hill towards him. As she broke through the mix of shadows and shapes on to the apron of the weedy turf, he nodded. "Hello, Ms Merville. Out for a run?"

She had halted.

She stood knee-high in fern, wild geranium, the taller grasses. Despite her contemporary jeans and T-shirt she had, with her long dark hair and curiously rhythmic stasis, a look of something classical. She was slimly curved against the light. Her hair reached her waist. Her eyes were not blue – they were – some freakish overlay of the dying light.

"Car," she said, "come with me, back to the sheds."

"No," he said pleasantly. "I don't want to, thanks."

"I know what happened," she said. "I saw him through the window. But there are six other sheds. One of those."

"We've all gone fucking mental, Angie," he said. "Better get used to it."

"You're wrong," she said. Her voice, as his had previously been, was expressionless. "You haven't. I haven't."

She was beside him. She had advanced so smoothly somehow he had not properly seen her do it. Her hand rested on his neck, was gone. Where her hand had touched, a coolness spangled. She smelled wonderful. Her eyes were not blue. Her hair hung to her waist. She was like a beautiful snake.

"Get up, Carver," she said, and now her voice was metallic and cruel, and he had got to his feet.

The sunset stayed as they walked up the rise, a rich Burgundy red, diluting and sinking only on the right, while they climbed.

The sun was going down on the wrong side of the sky.

Or – the sun was going down – twice–

At the top of the rise, there were the sheds again, repetitions, facile. Carver saw the pieces of sky and the sun was already just down, and in the proper quarter, westward, over there to the right. All else was twilight, and greying. But here. The rose-red varnish went on.

The central shed. To the left of them. Or course. The shed had raised its profile through blue and green and yellow and orange. It was scarlet-crimson now. As he had predicted before: 6th Level Urgency Alert.

"Yes," she said. "Car, the keys work the same on every shed. Open this one." This was the last shed to their right, nearest to the greying west, the seventh.

He found the keys, undid the central door of the seventh shed. When they were in he locked the door shut. It was dark inside, nothing in it, empty of tables and fridges and Croft. Just over there, the stain of red soaking in, strengthening as all the dusk went out.

Velvet black of night, with a ruby fastened to the collar.

Anjeela had brought food, ham and cheese rolls, Greek salad, and a thermos of black coffee – these self-evidently obtained from the (probably now defunct) take-out annexe.

He ate sluggishly, a sullen kid not wanting to give in. The coffee had kept most of its heat. That was better. When he offered her a share she shook her head. She stuck to the lukewarm litre bottle of water she had brought. They all knew him, his preferences. His weaknesses. They *had* known. Now she did. Just her. And himself. If he anyway knew anything – either about himself or anything at all.

When they had finished their meal, about half of which was uneaten, she set the leftovers neatly to one side, covered protectively by their wrappers. (He had seen Sara do this, never Donna. And not so many other women. But they had never had to "Watch the pennies" as Sara had sometimes said.) (Had Anjeela had to watch them? How did you, anyhow, watch a penny? You would lose interest.)

In the dark of the seventh shed, with only that red neon blotch to remind him, he watched this woman as carefully as any penny. Her own light-complexioned darkness had an alluring visual effect. A figment of night made into a woman–

For a long time, aside from his thanking her for the food and offering to share the coffee, he had not spoken. She had not spoken at all since they came in here. She sat on the floor as he did, and across from him, again faintly side-lit by the glow, that also aureoled her hair. Which definitely was much longer. Not extensions, he thought. A wig perhaps – but the hairline had no look of a wig. The hair had grown silky. It moved loosely when she did. She had very beautiful hands. The paleness of the nails against the dark skin... But neither her nails nor fingers extended themselves.

Without preface, a savage and raucous wailing and bellowing

broke out in the distance, the sound of exultant rage and agonised protest so generally and often heard – and seen – on such TV stations as Al-Jazeera or the British BBC.

"They're still some way off," she said at once, as the inhumanly human notes quavered and abruptly fell apart to nothing. Was she reassuring him? *Seeking* reassurance –?

"Yes," he said, "How long for, do you wonder? Before they come up here."

She shrugged. "When they do, they do."

"You're happy with that."

"I accept it will happen, sometime."

"Pragmatic, then. You're pragmatic. Christ, we shouldn't be sat here, *waiting* for them–"

"I am not," she said, "waiting for them. I am *waiting* to tell you something, Mr Carver. Something you will need, and ultimately must understand. Though very likely not at first. That will be difficult for you."

"Oh, difficult. Sure."

He got up and went to one of the windows. Any lights might possibly not be spotted through the red smoulder from the central shed. Where the ground descended, surely only the blackness of the moonless, starless overcast night paid out its folds. The up-and-down building, what might be left of it, seemed now to offer no locating illumination. Even the smudges of fire had died. It was, like this, invisible.

"Well then, Anjeela. What is it you have to tell me? You're pregnant perhaps–" He was astounded by what he had just said – redundant, crazy – oh, crazy, of course – "rather soon to know, isn't it?"

"No, I am not pregnant, Mr Carver. Nor, incidentally, is your partner, Donna. She never was. As you suspected, I believe."

"Why," he said woodenly, "are you calling me *Mr Carver*."

"What would you prefer?" she asked. Almost as Sunderland had said it that time, so long ago, a hundred years, in the flat with Sara shut in the kitchen, and the world changing so fast – so fast – "*Car*? Andrew? Andy? *Andreas*?"

"I don't care what you call me. I wondered why you'd *altered* what you called me."

"I thought you might prefer more formality at this moment Mr Carver. Given what I have to and am going to say."

"So now this is a hospital, and you're the specialist, right? You're going to tell me I have three months to live. Or two. Is *that* it?" Between fury and unexpected terror – he felt such emotions sweeping in on him, and horror, that too, that extra primal sense of the darkness and the *redness* – the 6th Level Alert, only one below Armageddon – one quarter minute to midnight on the nuclear clock –

She kept silent. She let him *fall* silent. She let the silence open wide its awful wings and threaten to devour them both.

And then, out of the silence, she said, "You might prefer I told you that, Mr Carver. But it isn't that. Your last medical check showed you healthy and very fit. Everything in perfect working order. Much, much better even than for many much younger men. But this other matter. That's different. Sit down, Mr Carver, please. It will be easier then, on us both." And he left the window and sat down.

As she spoke to him, she ceased to be beautiful, or anyone he (even slightly) knew. She became only her voice, and then the voice smoked off into the dark and the red. Her voice became only what it said to him, and told him, the pictures this summoned. Sometimes he thought he interrupted to ask her questions, or to contest what she said. Did she reply? Or not–? Conceivably *he* did not speak. Afterwards, though he could recollect his asking, denying, challenging, he could not remember hearing his *own* voice. Therefore, maybe he had only listened, dumb.

"*Scar*. You've read the file and the other notes on *Scar*. No need for subterfuge. Please credit me when I tell you this, no one can presently either see or eavesdrop, let alone record, our talk or actions. All Surveillance, and affiliated systems here, have failed, or are in the full process of it. Security and visio-audial went the first. As with any type of Third Person. Of course, this is enemy sabotage, and connected to the other effect which has taken hold, the generalised irrational behaviour of almost everyone on site, the – *madness* I may as well call it. It amounts to madness, sometimes in its most pronounced forms. And in this case, perhaps, to judge a book by its cover is only common sense. What else but mad was poor Charlie Hemel? Or any of the several others who have done similar or worse things in the past forty-eight hours? But you've witnessed a lot of madness, haven't you, Mr Carver? Enough to recognise it without too much prevarication. Accept, then, the mechanisms are also out of their minds. And I can say freely what I must say. And you should listen in turn as freely and openly. There will be no record. Not that a record of this particular lesson is required. It must simply occur. *Scar*, then, the curious clue to some unprecedented espionage or conspiracy, some terrorist or conjunctive plan. Scar. A name for a mark on the skin, a landscape feature. A family name. And the *Third Scar*, the enigma – the final item – at which the deadly curse, as in a story of Mr Sherlock Holmes by Mr Arthur Conan Doyle, will fall. I won't now unravel the leads in this piece of nonsense. It was and is a very open code, and meant to be suspected, if perhaps not entirely solved. It was leaked, of course. In the same way that Silvia Dusa – do you remember Silvia? – was intended to desert Mantik and go over to the opposition, or rather to the branch of the opposition in whose faltering stronghold you and I now find ourselves. Silvia Dusa had her own mission, which she fulfilled rather well. She sold you to the enemies of Mantik, the outfit here. And when Mantik had tangled you up sufficiently – the faked and incriminating recording of you and Silvia, her death, the implication of your exclusion – and left you unprotectedly alone, the opposition, under the aegis of Mr Peter Croft moved in, and took you and brought you here, to this cliffy retreat. And no, though in a way you are in Britain, we are not in Kent, Mr Carver. Hopefully in a while, sooner or later, you'll get a proper overview of where we are. But that's for future reference. Meanwhile, fully to clarify *Scar* for you, the *Third* Scar. There are indeed three subjects. Not marks of old wounds, nor outcrops of cliffs, nor, in themselves, influences, curses. They are three people. As for the family name given them, I'm afraid this is someone's little joke in very bad taste. Maybe it even halfway suggested itself to you, and you dismissed it, not unintelligently, as meaning nothing. Except, it does, you see. Or, you will see in a moment. Take your mother's name, now. Zarissa, originally. But she anglicised it, a common self-protective measure among foreign immigrants to any unknown country; either the parents do it, or the children at last. Molinsky becomes Mollins, perhaps, or Goldman – Oldman. Petre or Pe'ta – Peter. Cava becomes Carver with the last A replaced and thrown off, and Andreas – Andrew. And Zarissa – Sara. Sara Carver. S. Carver. SCARVER. Loose the last three letters. _SCAR_."

"It passes down through the mothers, it seems, the relevant gene. Though the women themselves are not, at least as is so far known, imbued with its powers. Rather like the disease haemophilia, which passes through the mother and, again, as is so far known, affects mostly her sons. Though an occasional daughter has, it was eventually determined, also been afflicted by the ailment. So it crosses from family to unrelated family, through sexual union in or out of marriage. The woman herself ungifted, or unpoisoned, dormant, only the conducting agent. In this case now, the three people referred to in Mantik's scheme do include two men and one woman. All of them fairly young, in their early or mid-thirties, as are you. Of course, as are you. Since you, Mr Carver, are the third of their number. Let me make clear at once that the skittish use of your mother's name to identify both you and the rest of the English trio, does not mean Sara, your mother, gave birth to all three. Indeed not. Her only child, at least this far, has been yourself. The other male's mother was an English woman, who died during his infancy in Europe. And the female member of the Scar Trio – well, her mother is still alive, though perhaps not for too much longer. A frail woman, this mother, and extensively vicious to compensate her for her frailty. How do I know to offer such a personal insight? Why, because the bitch is my mother, naturally. Since I am the Second Scar, Mr Carver. Drink some more of the coffee now, Mr Carver. It will help you. Yes, good. Rest your back against the wall. Good. I will wait a moment or two. I think we have time."

"There are estimates of between four hundred and six hundred other people of this, our, type, so far identified, or largely analysed as probable, across the accessible and investigable world. Some of these are still children, of those many are less than ten years of age. Rather randomly then, twenty adult candidates are scattered about the northern United States. Approximately the same number in South America. Thirty-six or thirty-eight have been verified, or are rumoured to have been, through Russia and her satellite countries. In the Middle East one hundred and ten, (the bulk in Iran). In the Scandinavian countries ten to seventeen. In China, the Koreas, and Japan, jointly, seventy-five. Australia, at the last count, eighty-one. There are, or seem to be, un_count_able others in India, where indigenous religious beliefs and mysticism may both camouflage, and conversely, falsely promote, their activities. Most of Africa is in a complementary state. By and large no data, however carefully collated, can provide an exact, numerically accurate list. Even so, from information now available, and fully validated, the fact that such persons exist is proven. What do they matter though, this strange random and polyglot tribe, of which you and I, Mr Carver, are part? They matter, and we, I and you matter, because of the genetically bestowed powers I have mentioned. _Powers_, Mr Carver, Natural abilities of various sorts, all of them quite extraordinary, and of differentiated and – shall I use the word? – there is no other – _miraculous_ scope. There have always been, so legend and history both inform us, such people. Miracle workers in the literal meaning of the words. They can read minds, or move objects without physically touching them, take on animal forms, levitate upward into the air, heal – or harm. Cure. Or kill. You've seen, Mr Carver, something of what _I_ can do. _Shape–shifter_, that would have been the name for me, back in ignorant years. I will show, in a little while, when there is more time to spare, something of the full gamut of my abilities. It started when I was eleven years old. I saw a movie – who was it? Some pretty girl – I wanted to be blonde like her. My hair was black as coal. When my mother saw me, she beat me. Extra spitefully. She thought I had used bleach from the kitchen. She thought I had wastefully and time-wastingly endangered myself, and wasted the bleach, and that blondes were scum from the Devil's fundament. In the morning, of course, I had healed my cuts and bruises – not from any non-existent bleach but from her hands and the implement she had wielded, a fish-slice. But my mother forgot what she had done. If she'd recalled I think she would have accused _me_ of 'harming myself'. (This had happened, this false accusation after one of her attacks, before.) But by the morning also I was brunette again. When _they_ began to investigate me, I did not know – I was twelve. An agent of Mantik's – Mr Preece he was called – visited me when I was just fourteen. I had been discovered later than the first of the two men, I was the second discovery. The third and last of whom is you. And so we arrive at you, Mr Carver. _You_."

Carver thought, afterwards, he said to her then, "You healed your bruises and turned back into a brunette. And your eyes are dark now. They used to be blue. Not shape-changing. It's called personal delusion. And wearing contact lenses."

But presumably he did _not_ say it. He had already stopped seeing her; she was only a voice, and words, and images that formed from them.

Besides, by then also he knew, or something in him knew, that to fight any longer was useless. And outside the night was black and red and made no sound, as it crept towards them up the hill.

"Preece, like certain others who would finally contact such people as myself, and you, tend themselves to minor but fascinatingly odd talents. Preece could undo locked doors without keys. Sunderland was like this too. Do you recall Sunderland? I don't know what he was good at. Something. But what you'll want to know, or you will feel that you must _have_ the knowledge of, a decision that is valid, is what _is your_ personal – power – _skill_, shall I say? _Your_ special and major talent. Mr Croft mentioned something?"

"Energies," Carver (afterward) thought he had scathingly, wearily, said. But he had not said anything.

"Croft – his name, too, was altered in childhood – he derived from an area off the Mediterranean, unaffiliated with either the Arab nations or the Jews, let alone the Russian political landmass. Mr Croft was born in Britain. But that was in the past. Now, in the recent days here, when he began firstly to feel the effects of the induced _madness_, as we must term it, he became somewhat fulsome, unwise... enough to alert you, maybe, or not. I suspect you are so accustomed by now to the extreme behaviours of others. Their unreliable and occasionally dangerous sillinesses. Hysterical women. Eccentric men. Even the terrible and brutal rages of your father. But Mr Croft no doubt told you, you could summon and release energies, the nature and direction of which none of them, here in this stronghold of Croft's organisation, had quite been able to solve, let alone take _precautions against_. A pity for them, that. Mantik, on the other hand, solved the puzzle some while back. Then, you may think unkindly, wickedly, they allowed certain aspects to proceed, exposing to your particular _skill_ persons of assembled types, to see precisely the _results_. Do you recall the man nicknamed _Bugger Back-Scratcher_ at the place on Trench Street? The man who always, too intimately, felt the male workers up, when performing their security checks? He was one of the people Mantik left open to your skill. No, no, of course you had no notion. Believe me, take it in and don't let go of it, you were, during all these events, innocent. *Mr Back-Scratcher* finally sexually assaulted a man on the tube, in front of witnesses. Mantik hushed up the business. They rescued *Mr Back–Scratcher* from the force of the Law, recompensed the assaultee. *Mr Back–Scratcher* is elsewhere now. Treatable, apparently. His exposure was limited and intermittent. And, obviously, some persons, as with any – shall I say, *diseases*? – will be much more susceptible than others. It has been noted, nevertheless, even once a formula for general protection was developed for use by Mantik, passed off as one more essential ordinary medical shot – against 'flu, MRSA – there were always slight discrepancies. You may, for example, have noticed that some people, when they are with you, even if not acting in any overtly peculiar way, are still prone to *silly* little affectations and mistakes. Repeating some word over and over – that's a favourite. Jack Stuart found it very amusing, that. He found, luckily for Mr Stuart, that once he left your vicinity, this blip quickly corrected itself for him. Mr Carver, I have to say, even *I*, who am virtually totally naturally immune to your skill – your unconscious, and innocent and *deadly* skill – seem to be repeating certain words, phrases, as I've sat here with you. Full, for example even, if in different syntactical forms. *Forms*, even. *Even*, even. But you know, don't you, you've *known* in some way all your life, that people close to you, *exposed* to you, and inevitably those that work with you, live with you, sleep with you, fuck with you, seem to lose their reason."

Carver (afterward) thought he did not speak. Not now.

"You produce, Mr Carver, an energy, decidedly, and of a sort largely unquantifiable. Although by now heightened by Mantik's chemical treatment of certain articles and objects – things you might, given your tendency, appropriate – steal. The chemical, by the way, is in itself harmless. The rest of Mantik's crew, or anyone, remain impervious, having no reaction to or with it. Which, evidently, is not so for *you*. Evidently also, the chemical formula was allowed to pass into the hands of Croft's people, so that once they got hold of you, they could apply it and immediately witness the unmissable result. The augmentation reacts *with* and *on* you, Mr Carver. Your astonishing power is galvanised. And, incidentally if most effectively, this is what produces the extravagant side effect, the coloured glow that filled your private garden shed, and now lights up to the left of us, here. Your own unease and dread, Mr

Carver, have changed its nature, (you see, *nature* repeated by me yet once more), turned it through the colours of the Alert, blue-green right through to scarlet: 6th Level High. And the volume of your deadly, (deadly, again), power is now also raised to a phenomenal level. It goes perhaps without saying, Croft's outfit did not in any form understand precisely what it indicated – or what that power entails. They were hoping to learn. Obviously, once they had you here, certain people were set specially to watch you. I was one. Mr Van Sedden and Mr Ball were the main operatives. And as we see, they were affected very rapidly. But I must add, even when you were first held here, drugged and investigated, *helpless*, your power worked on all and everything around you. Unconscious, Mr Carver, you were and are as lethal as when fully aware. Even your prime interrogator, I've heard, lost purchase after only a day and night. They thought it was a breakdown. It *was*. Your work. As I say, Croft and his people hoped to learn what you were, and what you could accomplish. They have. I though am, as I said, immune. Ninety-nine percent immune. As, very probably, the other member of our trio is, or perhaps *any* of our kind. But nobody, Mr Carver, *nobody* else. And that is why no one has yet come up the hill, to us here. A purely animal response. They sense *you* are here. But also, Mr Carver, that is why they will, eventually, irresistibly, arrive. Your skill, your genius, Mr Carver, is to bring insanity. And by now you can affect machines too. Am I correct – your cars frequently needed repairs, your phones – other items? Even – it has been mooted at Mantik – you can upset the *weather*. But your main talent lies with people. Your main talent lies in driving your fellow humans mad. To start with, your father and your mother, the most and worst exposed, and as your power erratically and blindly grew, caught in its blast. Later, if more patchily, fellow students at your schools, even certain adolescents and teachers at the special college, though by then you had become even more solitary, and Mantik, too, was already experimenting with antidotes, several of which had some helpful effects. Nevertheless, you have seen what you can do with the entirely unprotected. Donna, even Maggie, Donna's mother. Even Mr Johnston, your neighbour in the village. He was one very susceptible victim, who did not have much contact with you at all, though of course, generally meeting you at the garden's end, by the *shed*, where – naturally – your ability was itself augmented. Mr Johnston went mad and acted out the fantasy of a dangerous intruder. Even manipulating his injured leg to move with an unusual fluidity it should not have been capable of – and for which he has paid physically, since. He might even have murdered you that night, if Mr Croft's battalion hadn't stepped in first. Madness. The infliction of madness is your power. You can drive insane. You can even drive to suicide. You have always been a gun, Mr Carver, but now the bullets are in, you are loaded and primed. You are a missile, Mr Carver, and now the clock has struck midnight, the hand of authority has turned the key and pressed the button. Mantik. They perfected your talent and let their enemies – their Life-Long Enemies – seek and find and take you. And so you destroyed these enemies of Mantik, as you were intended to. Not even knowing, Mr Carver, what you did. Forgive me," she said, the *voice* said, gentle now, sorrowful and sorry. "Forgive me, Car. For telling you the whole truth at last."

*White*.
White flashed, cracked, burned, blanked.
Out of the redness, blind whiteness. The ruby glare had flared to Diamond. Top Level Alert. Annihilation. Terminus.
A second later, pale and amorphous, offering no competition, real lightning clawed across the hill. And instant thunder detonated less from the sky than underfoot.
As with the explosion, the earth shook. And the central shed's blind white glare went out.
Carver, in the darkness, could *see* her now, again. Anjeela. Her voice had stopped, and so *she* returned. And – she was no longer Anjeela. In the dark, after the bursting of the glow had died and the lightning melted, he could make out this woman had herself grown luminously pale. Her skin had become ethnically European, her features the same, nose, mouth. Her shadow eyes. He knew her, even so. Knew the one that now she was *fully* changing herself into.
Beyond the windows and doors things like strands of shiny foil-covered wire were rushing rustling down. The rain had come. And in the rain, over the slope of the hill, hundreds of fireflies danced: solar or battery torches, the colour of a cheap bad Sauterne, (the sort his father had drunk), sliding upward through the deluge.

## Twenty-Two

Rain rushed, noise of thin silver and rusted tin; the thunder dragged its heavy train carriages around and around the sky. They sat, facing each other, the man, the woman, on the shed's floor. Neither spoke now. Beyond the square of darkness they inhabited, the other dark made sound enough. And soon, through the windows, light bloomed, shattered by drops of water on the glass. And the shapes appeared through the broken pebbledash of light and night and water. They were like ghosts. So many, a great gathering, not speaking, either, making no sound he could distinguish. But closer. Close and closer, close as the windows. Up against the glass in the windows and the doors. (Just as Croft had stood before, that was it.) Pressed up to the glass, the *faces* pressed to it, and each pressing to it one or both hands, their palms flat... On both sides of the shed. Nothing visible outside now but men and women, the tops of their bodies and their faces and rained-through hair, and hands, and behind them other bodies, faces, wet hair, hands – standing just like Croft. But all these Crofts facing *in*, at the man and the woman seated on the floor. Unmoving. Unspeaking. And otherwise only the rain and the thunder, and the million bits of pebbled torchlight.

"The door," he said. But it was futile. He did not continue.

"The door's locked, Car," she said however. Her voice was calm and miles off. "You locked the door."

I know, he said, but he did not say it.

They could break in, the mad ones outside. The shed was only wood and glass. They could break in, would break in, the mad ones, the ones he had driven mad. If he had, if that was what he could do, if he could – something (*something*) something had. Him?

He had never known himself. Now he saw himself, as if he also were outside himself, looking in through a rain-speckled and unclear pane of glass.

He saw himself and did not know who he was.

And she, he saw her too, and she was not her but someone else.

The shed trembled. Thunder. Or the pressure of flesh and bone. Only slight. But it would not take much.

"Car," she said. The woman in the shed with him.

What? he said. He had not said it. "What?" he asked her aloud.

"In a moment," she said, "you must get up, go to the window, and look out at them."

Why? "Why?" he said.

"I think it may make them draw back," she said.

He did not get up.

Then he got up.

He walked to a window.

All the faces, the eyes. He stood, not close to the glass as Croft had, or as they did, but a couple of steps back. It was completely straightforward to look at them, even into the eyes of them. They did not appear real. Like Croft, too, Croft as now he was, there seemed, behind each face, each pair of eyes, nothing. No one was home.

But, as she had suggested they might, they began to shuffle and slip aside, away. The rain-tide of them was slithering off. And the ones behind were also withdrawing. Not so far, maybe the space of a metre, another half metre, left at this one window, between the shed wall and the crowd of mad people.

Carver recognised one or two of them now, men and girls seen inside the building or the grounds previously. The unsociable ones and the smiley ones. *There* – the girl with the clipboard who had last taken him to Croft – a man who had greeted Carver in the plush restaurant-canteen – "Hello, Car – enjoying that? That's a good steak, that, Car–" And there, the fatter woman from the judging panel that followed Hamel's death.

If he moved from the window, would the tide of them merely flow in again right up to the glass?

Carver left the window, crossed to another. Here too, instantly, the crowd began to shift and sidle away – and when he glanced, the first window had stayed unoccupied. He went from glass to glass. As each emptied, he went to the next, and none refilled.

They were indeed all moving off even a little farther, about five metres now, on the first side, and there, see, a distance down the south-facing hill, twenty metres, twenty-five –

The woman, not rising, had craned her neck to watch him.

When he left the windows altogether he did not return to the area of floor where she sat. He sat against a wall, under one of the cleared windows. Then recalled he had in fact moved back to sit here previously, when she told him to rest against a wall...

How did you know? But he did not ask her.

*It's stage-managed, that's how she knows. Do this, she'll say, and it will work*. *He* had not driven anyone mad. It was *their* game, their theatre production, during which *they* would drive Carver insane.

But he thought of Sara, shrieking, and his father – he thought of the girl at the college he had first had sex with, who had reached her climax clinging to him, and told him how wonderful he was, and then, later, would not leave him alone, and then later again one day took off all her clothes, and danced naked on the unsafe fire-escape, cursing everyone till a medic came with a hypodermic, and Carver had not known why. And a thousand instances, all of which could be explained away.

The rain fell.

Lights flickered outside, more distantly.

What time was it?

What time is it?

"What time," he said, "is it?"

"About midnight," she said, "I think, by now. Try to get some sleep," she said.

He leaned his head back on the wooden wall. He was trapped in the body of an unknown man.

*I don't know you*.

He did not know–

*I don't know*–

What did his name mean? A butcher, someone who carved inscriptions in stone, a sculptor, a psycho with a knife–

He was walking through a corridor full of mirrors, and in every one he passed there was a faceless shadow with black gleaming eyes, his height, his build, keeping pace with him.

He could crawl or he could run, but the shadow would keep up with him. It would be Carver himself, of course, who could not keep up with the shadow.

Nothing seemed changed when he woke... except the rain had stopped. And there was a lightening to the sense of the dark, if not actual light.

When he looked around him, he noted the woman had altered her position to sleep. She lay curled up on the floor, on her left side, both her arms folded in to cushion and support her neck and skull, her knees drawn up against her stomach. As if unconsciously to protect herself, or she was cold.

She did not react when he got up. But that might not mean

anything. She might well be wide awake, her eyes closed but all of her alert and listening, to see what he would do next.

The rain-spotted windows were empty of faces.

Carver went to each pane. The crowd had stayed back, twenty, thirty metres down the hill, to the south and the north, on both sides. They had revised their position, but were intransigently there. Like the woman on the floor.

Carver regarded the crowd, the mad people, as he patrolled quietly round the shed, and round once more. They were, all of them so far as he could tell, quiescent, and not making any noise. Some of them sat on the drenched earth, others stood.

Most of the torches had been kept on, highlighting portions of their group mass, or here and there gone out – maybe only the batteries had failed – and in these patches casting irregular shadows, blots of night, visually ominous but unmeaningful.

Every face that he could focus on, however, had stayed fixed toward the shed. Those to the north looked upward to the south, those to the south looked upward to the north.

It was like – what in God's name? – yes, some emphatic Biblical movie. The Tribes of Israel turning as one to stare at the mountain as Moses descended to them with the Tablets of the Laws of God. Or the Sermon on the Mount, for Christ's sake, the multitude gazing up at Jesus.

The imagery, its symbol – of need, savage belief, utter attachment and expectancy, and – if only momentary – total dependence – was repellent and frightening.

How long had they stayed like *that*?

As long, it might be, as he had slept.

Carver's guts griped harshly. Not only in distaste and alarm. The everyday processes of elimination were asserting themselves, demanding to be attended to.

It would be wiser and more prudent to crap and piss inside the shed. But the woman – less through embarrassment and social reluctance, more some curious protective impulse – made him bolt and bar bowels and bladder against compliance.

Instead, he went to the central door, unlocked it, stepped out and locked it shut again.

He had gone to the windows and met their faces and their eyes, and they had withdrawn. What now would they do? Rush up and tear him in pieces, perhaps. Or only sit and watch their too human saviour as he squatted by some tree? *He* was the theatre finally, they the audience.

Carver moved out and down the slope of the hill. Southward first. What did it matter? They could kill him, or only sit there, or someone else would come – some crazy leftover security man, or crazy woman who thought he had got her pregnant or had knocked her daughter about – No. Irrelevant.

Irrelevantly then, the crowd on the hillside began to climb to their feet, some clutching out at others, some calling out in thin lost voices – and they started to scatter away from him, Carver, the single advancing figure, to run now, some screaming, some falling and pulling others over, but most scrambling up again and plunging on, down the slope between the trees and their stumbling roots, through the knots of soaking grass. Running away. It was not Carver, after all, apparently, who was afraid. *They* were afraid. They fled him, or what they thought he was, or what he really was. He did not have to proceed very far. When, after no vast distance, he stopped, still they poured on, shouting and crying, away. He watched them drain down the hill, like more spilled water.

When even the nearer tumbling figures had grown very small, he walked back up the rise, past the shed, next repeating the manoeuvre on the northern side. It was not very different. Seeing him approach, panic and headlong flight. More fell though that side. A few very certainly did not get up. They were trampled, he believed, by others. But by now he felt nothing, they were not anything to him he could empathise with. No one, nothing, surely – was. Ever had... been.

He relieved himself in privacy among the bushes, cleaning up afterwards in the prescribed pastoral manner the rule books suggested. The collected rain was very helpfully cleansing. Lavishly it went on dripping and streaming down from foliage and branches, up out of the grass, enough to clean off the shit of a whole squadron of desperate men.

The sky was paling also. Perfect on its cue: sunrise. A lovely new late summer, early autumn, late fall, God-knew-what- season day. And in the intensifying flare of predawn, little things were glittering, catching the gleams: a slender silver broken bracelet, a broken shoe, part of a sleeve, a thick chunk of hair torn out by a low bough in the panic-flight; pale indeterminate hair, dawn colour, with one High Level Red Alert of blood along its strands.

Carver reached the shed. He stood with his face against the windowless western end of it. He felt nothing at all, but he wept. Or it was only the rain that had somehow filled him too and now, like the excrement, and the humanity, must leave him.

## TWENTY-THREE

She had woken and was sitting on the floor. She looked clean and fresh, even her lustrous hair – not like the piece caught outside on the tree – brushed. But she dealt either in true physical transformation, or delusion. She could, demonstrably, cope with all things, put anything personally physical right. Probably she would not even need a toilet. It seemed not. She appeared at ease, and did not mention any necessary excursion from the shed.

He had locked her in – to protect her? Maybe. He did not analyse the fact. Coming back in and finding her, he left the door unlocked.

"They've gone," she said, "yes?"

"They ran away. When I went out to them."

"Yes. That could happen. Drawn near to you, or scared off. An animal with a campfire."

Carver did not ask her why or deny what she said. That was over. He crossed to the remainder of the food, took a roll with ham and began to eat it. At this she too reached out and selected the last of the salad. She ate it with her fingers. There was nothing left to drink.

He was not thirsty, the air was lush with moisture. She perhaps did not need to drink. Or eat, come to that. She did such stuff only as camouflage. Passing for human...

The flamboyantly ridiculous idea hopped about his brain, glad not to be either challenged or confirmed.

He stood, leaning back on the shed wall. He finished the dry bread and ham.

"Well," he said. "What next, Silvia?"

She looked sidelong up at him. *So you have noticed*, her look seemed to say.

"Or," Carver said, unemphatic and banal, "I suppose you could explain why you now look like her. Sound like her. Silvia Dusa, I mean. She's dead. You're aware of that, you told me you were. So is this some sort of memorial tribute? The way ordinary people might send a card, or leave a flower or a teddy bear? Like that?"

"Or," she said, "while you slept Anjeela Merville slunk out of this shed, and Silvia Dusa took her place?"

"That's a chance, certainly," he said. "You looked this way when I first saw you earlier this morning. So you two swapped over. But she's still dead. So I take it, Ms Dusa, you are a fucking corpse." His tone was only conversationally interested, as if to be civil.

Equally everyday she replied, "But how do you know Silvia Dusa is dead, Car?"

"I saw her." As he said it, surprising him – he had thought himself past such an inevitable hurdle – a coldness sank through his brain and spine.

"I believe, Car, you saw a *picture* of her. On a computer screen."

"I saw the picture of her *dead*. She'd cut through the vein of her left arm."

"No. She *appeared* to have done so."

"It wasn't some make-up job – some cosmetic mock-up for a film effect, CGI – it–" Carver broke off.

As the young woman rose and moved towards him, he retreated a step. But his back was already to the wall.

Silvia Dusa rolled up her left sleeve and held out her left forearm.

"*Don't*" he said. His voice vibrated with fury and threat.

But she shook her head, a delicate party-girl quivering. And on the creamy honey her skin now was, the vein in her arm seared up blue and *unzipped* itself with the swift ease of a party dress –

The blood ran. It was red. Red. It was red.

Then the blood stopped. The vein puckered, gaped, (emptied), a riverbed in drought, blistered and ruined.

"I can cry at will. Bleed at will. I can do this, Car. And while I do bleed, I can also apply an internal tourniquet to safeguard my life – invisibly. Plus, if you wish, I can turn my face and body, every inch, to the look-alike of a dead woman on a mortuary slab. I can reduce my breathing and heart-rate to match. And I can hold that persona, that pose, for anything up to thirteen minutes, while the authentication is accurately collected."

Carver made a sound. He sprang forward. He took her by the throat, with a killer's clutch. Glaring into her face, her eyes – But here, with and in her, someone _was_ at home. Oh yes. Behind the face and eyes of dead Silvia Dusa, a very living creature watched him. Her eyes were black, gold, bronze. His hands turned to putty and dropped from her. His legs gave way. It was she who caught him, eased him down. They kneeled together now on the floor. She put both her arms – each of them alike, whole and unmarked – around him.

"Car," she said. "Again, I am so sorry. But you have to know. There's only one way now, for any of us. Lies don't help. Lies are over, at least between _us_."

## Twenty-Four

One, two of them, buzzing across the open sky, giant insects with firm grey bodies and long tails and a windmill each of spinning wings above their backs. The first chopper was bigger, heavier.

Carver stood out on the hillside, watching them circle, far above the trees.

Below, once only, he saw what he guessed must be people running, the way startled antelope or zebra might out on the African plains. No one else was near, except for the woman. She had stayed farther up the hill, beside the sheds. In full daylight, a softly lambent late summer's morning, nothing looked particularly unusual here. Just the helicopters. And a quarter mile off, through the vegetation, the black jagged stain over the up-and-down building.

She had said, the woman, they should remain on the rise, and wait. The new arrivals would deal with the rest of it. His work, her work, had been accomplished.

(He thought he had asked her questions, as they kneeled together in the shed and she held him in her arms. But, as before, very possibly he had not. She must only have told him other – things, elucidating what she had already said. There were bits of information seemingly pushed randomly into compartments of his mind... Mantik and Croft's outfit were rivals, Croft's people _not_ the guards that guarded the guards, but an undermining force set to spy on, corrupt and ruin Mantik's function of guardianship. Life-Long Enemies for sure. Yet Croft's force had not been active for the assistance of enemy foreign governments, instead they operated on behalf of the more obscure *interior* interests – commercial, political, religious – inherent in the Free Democracy of the sprawled British Composite – these words, Carver seemed to recall, the woman who was now Silvia Dusa had stressed were not her own; she was quoting them from the manuals of Mantik.)

The chugging helicopter rasp grew louder. The bigger one was descending, shaking the air in chunks off its windmill blades. The smaller aircraft stayed high, sedately going on in its repetitive circle.

(She had said also, he thought, that she had *had* to appear to die. Her death would confirm Mantik's enemies' belief that she had sold Mantik out. Meanwhile the other personality, Anjeela, had already been partly established with Croft's people. Sloughing her – by then 'dead' – Silvia-persona, Anjeela was next absorbed into the stronghold by the sea. She was in reality to be Carver's back-up and liaison. (Or overseer.) And since she was a *shape-shifter*, of course, of course, her disguise was absolute, no giveaway anywhere.)

Yes, the bigger chopper was going to land – Carver altered his position – that solid flat roof, probably, there, and more towards the eastern blocks of the building.

(And she had digressed briefly on what she could do, her *changing* – surely she had spoken again of this? Comparing her ability to what happened anyway, to anything that was born and went on living. The child expanding from baby to adult, which adult might grow its hair or gain a tan, fatten or become thin – eventually aging, backbone diminishing, flesh sagging, hair – long or short – losing colour. And what *she* did, Silvia-Anjeela, that was just the same. Merely accomplished faster. And they had, she said, none of their kind, (his, hers) at least those of them who had been found out in their talents, no choice. There was nothing to gain in struggling against such masters as Mantik. But they, she, *he*, were more than valuable, they were priceless, and precious. They would be – providing they complied, obeyed – protected. But they must grasp and accept both their powers and, with equal clarity, the *use* to which all this would be put. That was their only hope. The three of them. She, the other unknown man, and Carver.)

The chopper had landed, a locust-wasp of grey metal. Its rotor blades were slowing, coming visible. Men were gliding out of its womb. Or insectoid lava, they might from this distance be simply larvae –

The mission had gone to plan. All it needed now was a bucket and mop to clean up the mess – They were pouring down the side of the building now, touching earth, racing forward, outward, and in. About a hundred, one hundred and twenty, men, Carver estimated.

How many of Croft's people were still alive, or even physically able? No need for an army to cope with what was left.

It would be very easy, perhaps, finally to mop them up. To stamp on them.

(He could not care. But he had never got close to anyone. Not Sara. None of the women. No men. Nor to himself. How prudent. His instinctive and only protection.)

(She had held him in her arms there on the shed floor. Close as her lover. But they were not lovers. Nothing. All this was nothing.)

About twenty more minutes passed during which vague veils of shouting rose from below and, once only, the note of guns – improved by the amphitheatre acoustics of the terrain. Then the other helicopter began faultlessly to descend, sunlight smoothly passing over its carapace. Everything was so simple.

Not long after, one of the military units reached the top of the rise. They were polite. In plain uncamouflaged 'camouflage', twelve dog soldiers panned out around the sheds, coordinated as dancers, just as when they had swarmed up the hill. Their leader saluted Silvia Dusa. (Carver was not surprised. Surprise was over.)

"You're well, ma'am?"

"We're well," she said. "However, there is a dead man in the central shed."

"Very good, ma'am." The tall young officer turned and barked, and five of the others sprang in against the shed. After staring through the windows, two men immediately kicked in the middle door. No, it had not taken very much to break it down. Splinters rained outward, scattering the light. Into the shed the two soldiers glided, catlike and fast, the light now glinting on their weapons.

A few invisibly abrasive yet mostly inexplicit sounds resulted. One man came out.

"Dead as a turd," he said, "sir."

"That's Peter Croft," said Silvia Dusa.

"Yes, we reckoned so," said the captain. He turned to Silvia, "Mr Stuart thought that would be Croft's way. He's not the only one."

Both soldiers had come out of the shed. One was talking via his ear-piece, asking for a "bob" for a grade A corpse. The second man added, to nobody particularly, "At least Crofty got it right."

"Yes," said the captain to Silvia. "Some of the others of 'em mucked it up good and fucking proper, ma'am."

Presently he and three of his men escorted Silvia and Carver down the rise and through the woods, back towards the lower grounds and the building.

There was a large room, perhaps used for conferences, or widescreen shows of planned future events – a vast black screen was positioned at one end. The area had been tidied up, made pristine. Nor was there any smell of the burnt smoke permeating, it seemed, the rest of the building. This room stank of perfumed disinfectants. The sun beamed in at tall and currently blindless windows. Outside, the green lawns were empty of anyone except the occasional unit of dog troops patrolling or standing in alert ease along the gravel drive. (A single urn had survived. Just the flowers were torn out, and even those had now been cleared away.)

Latham sat far up the room at the screen end, at a long table surrounded by chairs. He was his normal self, or seemed to be, in a light suit and silk tie, drinking coffee from a freshly brewed pot. A couple of chairs away sat another man, ample, unyoung, casual, slightly flushed. He was contentedly drinking from a magnum bottle of red French wine which, as they entered, he decanted for himself into a plastic coffee mug. For a moment Carver could not identify him. Then he did. It was Alex Avondale, the sentimental old glutton with the estate, in Scotland. He and Carver had had that dinner at Rattles in London. The night Carver went home so late and Donna went so entirely mad. (Or seemed to; she had already been mad, of course, for years. Carver had done that to her. As to so many others.)

Avondale smiled warmly at Carver and Silvia Dusa as they walked up the pristine, disinfected room. Latham did not smile. But he had on his benign and _porcine_ face. At some point it would, as ever, alter to his _other_ face, the lizard-like mask. Ah, now it did, as his eyes focussed on Carver. And then the lizard recoiled again inside Latham. And in his most plummy tone, he called, "Welcome, Carver, Silvia. Come and sit down. You've had a heavy night." And he half rose.

They sat. Silvia close to Latham, obliquely facing Avondale. Carver did not sit.

"What will you have, Silvia?" Latham inquired.

"Coffee, thank you."

Latham selected another white plastic beaker, filled it with coffee, carefully pushed it over to her with a sachet of brown sugar. She accepted both. He knew her taste in coffee, then. Or thought he did, and she obliged.

"And Carver – coffee, yes?"

"No," Carver said.

He leaned across, took a beaker from the remaining stack, and picking up Avondale's wine bottle, poured the beaker full, about two glasses worth. Carver, still standing, drank all the wine straight down. (It had an odd flavour, from the plastic probably, the mellow flintiness sweetened wrongly.) When the beaker was void, he refilled it about halfway, and went with it along the table to the farther end. There he sat. They had turned their heads to watch him, and now resumed facing forward at each other.

As if nothing uncharacteristic had happened, Latham said, "You've both done superlatively well. Jack Stuart said I should be sure to tell you how impressed and appreciative he is. And how satisfied Mantik is. You'll be in line for some very splendid perks, when we all get back to base. Incidentally, we should be able to leave here inside a few more hours. I regret any delay. Can't hurry things."

"Why not?" Carver heard himself say.

And Latham showed him once again his reptile face, which only slowly dissolved into goodwill.

It was Avondale who laughed, friendly and sympathetic.

"The impatience of youth. Don't worry, Carver, we'll make it. You'll see the lights of London long before the dark moves in."

(Avondale, who had shaken his hand outside the restaurant, and called him 'son'. As Croft would do, before Croft blew his own brains out of his skull.)

Carver swallowed more mouthfuls of the wine. Not many. Then put down the beaker.

"What makes you think," said Carver, "I'm going with you?"

Avondale smiled on and averted his gaze, as if to save Carver humiliation.

Latham did not remove his attention. He said, "Because,

Carver, you have nowhere else to go."

Carver said, "That didn't stop Croft."

Latham said, "It was you, Carver, who stopped Croft. As intended. Yes. Obviously we have used you, ruthlessly. It was essential. Their nest here was a danger to us, and to the security of the whole country. But no longer. Your debut has been a total triumph. You'll get used to your success. Everybody does. Or... the ones that want to survive do so. What you have to get into your head, Carver, is that you are completely safe with us—"

"That is what Croft said to me."

"Naturally. But in the case of Mantik, it is *true*. You *are*, with us, entirely safe. And that is because we, at last, are entirely safe with *you*. We've made ourselves so. You can't hurt us. And we, Mr Avondale here and I, for example, Ms Dusa, and all our other members, are now in that same fortunate position. Oh yes, you could, just conceivably, harm any one of us with some amateurish physical violence or other. But I don't advise you to try. Because without us, Car, you're really on your *own*. Do you see yet? Do you? Anyone else you will now almost certainly destroy utterly, from the brain outward. The same way you destroyed every person working here, even those who had no direct contact with you. But *we* are *immune*." The tone, at last, not jammy anymore, lizard voice of silver scales. The firm father with the hard hand, though not blind drunk or crazy. Blind sane. "We are your only family now, Car. Just as, in another way, we are, say, a family for Silvia. But in your case, Car, additionally we're the only solid refuge you can go to. We didn't cause your ability, Car, we didn't *make* you. But we *developed* you. And there isn't, now, any other cunt of a person or fuck of a place you can run to that won't end up just one more *here*, and one more Peter Croft."

Carver found he himself had looked away.

He stared into the deep red pool of the wine in his beaker.

No, he did not want to drink any more of it. Or get up and go anywhere else.

He sat, letting his eyes fill with redness.

And heard Avondale say, quietly and affectionately, to a nice mother with a rather difficult child, "Maybe, keep your eye on our friend, eh, Silvia... Can we leave that with you? No hurry. There's time. Take your time."

"Is it Avondale then?" Carver asked, ten minutes or thirty minutes later. By then the other men had left the room.

"Avondale ...?"

Her voice had remained Silvia Dusa's.

"You're the Second Scar. I'm the Third. Is Avondale the First?"

She chuckled, quiet, no edge to it. "No. But he's pretty high up in Mantik. Higher than they usually let on. He checked you out that night you two had dinner in London. Checked the *effect* you had. Yes, he was protected, but he's one like Preece, or Sunderland – he has certain – developed sensitivities. He could tell better than a machine. His report on you was the final deciding vote. Then Mantik got you properly lined up, and everything went into action."

"Including you,"

"Including me."

"Dead on a slab."

She did not reply. He did not look at her.

(The wine seemed miles deep now, how far did it descend into that other dimension it seemed to occupy? A bottomless henna lake.)

"Who's the First Scar, then?" Carver asked. He had no knowledge why he did. He did not care.

"I don't know him. I mean I've never met him. I was told a little about him." She paused. When Carver said nothing, she continued slowly, thoughtfully. Maybe she was improvising, making it up as she went along. "He was born in Europe, somewhere between the Middle East and Russia. Three quarters English, one quarter something I can't remember, some eastern European nationality, from his father's side. The father was half and half, with a fully English mother. Apparently, there was something wrong with the boy – defective genes, learning difficulties. Physically he was, well, odd. But she loved him, the woman, and the father came to love him. He was a very loveable infant for them, it seems. Phenomenally so. And his mother called him this unreasonable name – I was told it was something extremely religious, something like – was it *Paradise*? No, it wasn't. But *that* extravagant and unsuitable. A curse of a name for a kid. For anybody. And then there was bad trouble out there, where the father was posted – he worked for the British government – and both parents were killed. But the boy survived. And it became obvious he had something special, exclusively astonishing. So Mantik took him on. He grew up in Britain, somewhere. He's far younger, by the way, than Avondale. Of the three of us, apparently, I'm the oldest, if not by much. He's about your age. Car. Thirty-one-two-three – whatever. I can't recall his name."

"Paradise."

"I'm sorry. It wasn't that. *Kingdom of God*–? Was it that? No. You see, I can grow my hair at will or turn it blonde—"

"Or be a corpse."

"–Or be a corpse, yes. But I can't remember the name of the first member of our trio. Perhaps you should ask Latham."

"Ask Latham." Carver smiled. His facial muscles simply did this. He did not know why, or why he spoke to her at all, this reasonable and couth young woman.

"There's no restriction on him telling you, Car. Not now. Or *I'll* ask, if you like."

Like...

The pool of henna reached down and down. You could effortlessly drown in it. That was why they drank it, after all. To drown. It in you, you in it. Either/or.

A movement. Her chair shifting back.

"Let's go outside, shall we?" she asked.

Why? Why not? Go outside.

Carver rose. He picked up the beaker and poured the last of the wine out on the cleansed floor. Only a trickle now, about deep enough to drown a fly.

The room opened on another lift. They descended two floors. The lift door drew wide on a sunny courtyard, shut in by the building on one side, and by walls nine or ten feet high on the other three sides. Tree tops visible, sky. Hint of sea-scent and faint putrid linger of smoke, with – here – the mildest tinge of human death in it.

The yard was paved, plain concrete squares. Tubs around, the plants undamaged, some with flowers. Two sets of garden tables, four chairs apiece. No one there.

Another door, metal, with a button to push, confronted them in the third wall. Presumably it led out to the grounds.

But Silvia had sat down on one of the two tables. She shook back her malleable hair and raised her face to the sky, eyes part-closed.

No noises anywhere. But neither did the birds call. Still no gulls flying over.

On either side, blank windowless angles of the building restricted further view.

In a corner, beside one of the tubs, a smashed bottle (overlooked?) sparkled happily.

The woman spoke.

"Try to relax, Car. We'll be leaving fairly soon. Around two in the afternoon at the latest."

Avondale: *You'll see the lights of London long before the the dark moves in*.

London. What was London?

Carver pulled out a chair from the second table and sat on it. He would not, he supposed, be able to get rid of the girl. She was his (un)official minder. And she was strong enough probably to manage him, was she? He would not want to try, would not want to harm her. Even if, in the shed –

Too late, Croft. I should have said *Yes*. Yours was the only way out.

Beyond the wall with the door there was a sound. Nothing to it, in fact. An *ordinary* sound. A couple of voices were talking without urgency or raised volume. And then, instead, a girl's crying, but not that loud either. And then a male voice, but so very low, no meaning could be made of it except a sort of – kindness. The crying faltered and stopped. "Thanks, mate," said another male voice, audibly.

Following which the silence returned. They, whoever they had been, had gone away.

And yet –

Something had *not* gone away.

Something stayed there outside the shut metal door. *Something*.

Not meaning to, not knowing what it meant, Carver had got up again. Silvia also had swung herself about on the table, her back to Carver, staring it seemed towards the shut door. Which sighed. And slid open.

## TWENTY-FIVE

Mainly sunshine filled the space, a starburst of white-gold. But against and out of the sun –

A silhouette evolved. Forming up and filling in, until substantial. Though advancing, it was at once reminiscent of a man seated against a blank lit window. An old trick. Filmic. Effective. A big shape, a big man, tall and excessively broad-bodied, thickly built of flesh. *Croft*? It was Peter Croft, animate and alive, and without the rear of his skull blown off.

He came rambling forward unhurriedly out of the light. Not only big, then, *this* Croft had ballooned into fat. And the suit was a tent, yet tailored and not graceless. The fashion in which he moved, too, had an almost absurd – *elegance*. The body did not seem either to mind or to be hampered by its potential obesity. Its lack of coordination was *coordinated*. Another species, and automated in its own unique way. Valid in its own unique right.

Shaggy hair, not grey, well-cut yet tufted, framed the profound countenance of a huge toad. The enormous eyes, river-brown rather than dark, were definitely not Croft's, but bulbous. They glowed, having consumed some ray of the sun.

"Loandy," the toad-being said. "You've all grown up." And stopped, positioned on the paving. Where instantly it was a fixture, cast from iron and set there to last forever.

As Carver's vision adjusted, he saw over one of the bulbous shoulders. Two paramedics were leading a woman away along a line of trees. She appeared tranquil, going along brightly, without regret. She was not crying anymore.

Silvia spoke.

"I remember," she murmured, "the name."

"Yes," said Carver. He too had realised what it must be, the name that implied Paradise, and had been altered by morons to fit apparent earthly circumstance. "Heaven. That's his name."

On the wide-screen of Carver's mind the truth unrolled, some extravaganza of fiction that was fact. Suddenly he had it all. There could be and were no doubts. As, however reluctantly, one recognised oneself in a mirror.

Born in that other country far east of the Med, the trouble in the city or the town, the bomb-blast that negated the diplomatic building, Croft's living quarters with it. Croft must have been elsewhere. He had not seen. His wife, the English woman, detonated into fragments like broken glass, and the child – the unwieldy impaired child Croft had begun by loathing and fearing, until those states altered into amazed love – shattered so small, as only a child's body could be, not anything could be found. _Not enough left of him to bury_. Except they had _lied_. The British employers of Peter, or Petre Croft, _Mantik Corp_. The child had survived the blast. No one could figure out how. They had been together in that room, the mother and her son she had called Heaven out of the passionate belief she had in him. But where she and the room and all else had perished, the child, two, three years of age, he was untouched. Just as, those other years later, he would be untouched by the racing traffic on that suburban road, and with him the black puppy he had snatched, and known by then how to shield by his ungainly miraculous curled-up body.

And Carver could see – the three-year-old child wandering through the bombed rubble, and how he floundered to the hurt and howling, the screaming, the dying, and floppily touched them with his small ugly ungainly disgusting beautiful hands. And they grew serene and lay waiting, for death or rescue. And maybe some of them slept, or even laughed. Not minding, unafraid.

So Mantik, when they entered the scene, took the child with the obscenely perfect name. They carried him off as evil wizards do in some TV series for the fantasy-minded under-twelves. And they told Petre Croft that both his wife, _and_ his son, had been killed. But Croft, though he believed it, on some other level, in some obscure way, sensed – _smelled_ – the stench of treachery. And that was why he had, eventually, turned to other work, anything that might bring Mantik crashing down.

Carver knew, almost in words, always in pictures, how Heaven, by then known as Heavy, was allowed to grow up, supervised and guarded – yet left experimentally to the non-mercies of the mundane world. And while he was, Mantik, like all the cruellest and most cold-blooded guardian gods, noted every nuance of his development, and his – _skills_. His _powers_.

Subsidiary to which, they had seen him connect himself, unwanted, then welcomed, to another boy, this one the dark and sullen and uneducated little thief, Andreas Cava. And by that straightforward means, they learned bit by bit, that Carver too was worth taking up and manipulating, for future and relentless use. Heavy, Silvia, Carver. One, Two, Three. Scar, Scar, _Scar_.

_He's informed me of this, shown me, Heavy. That's how I can see it, and_ *know for certain.*

Carver stared into Heavy's eyes. Does *he* know? Does he know *what* Mantik are – *does he understand?* – The men were standing rather as they had, when boys, in the park, the very last occasion of their meeting. Not far off, nor close. May all the good be happy. And all the bad be good. Oh Christ, Christ.

"Your father's dead. He's wrapped up in a grade A body bag," Carver jaggedly said to Heavy. "Did they bother to tell you?"

"Yes," Heavy answered. "'S all right. He's fined now. And I'll be able to be talking with him, like I do with moth–ah."

Carver could feel the unexcitable warmth from Heavy. It was like the sunlight. And he could feel Silvia's presence, now at his back, hot and cold like heating or freezing, fire and Arctic waters.

"She can change shape," he said to Heavy. "And you can change – anything. But I – ruin and drive insane. And we are all Mantik's slaves. Their *whores*."

Heavy put out one of his awful, fat and misshapen hands, and touched Carver on the shoulder. Only an instant. There was no feeling at all from this, less than a leaf falling –

"Leafs do fall," Heavy said, in a low unheard murmur.

– And after the fall – something...

*Something.*

What?

"I must go now," said Heavy. "Lots man need helpful up there. It will be fined, Andy. Will be fined. Belief it. We are not too many. See you next soon."

Above, so high, so far, a shape, and a shadow falling like a leaf, and then another, and another. And then the wild amused screeching of a gull.

Heavy raised his heavy head. He grinned into the sky with joy. "Gully birds," approved Heavy. "They pull the sun."

Up from the flat roof the second lesser helicopter lifted. The fair-skinned sky was open wide, and any gulls, sensibly, had veered to the west. The shrill-singing racket of the aircraft filled Carver's ears like glue. Under and about him the rear seat vibrated and jarred. He was on the left, Silvia to the middle. Avondale occupied the right-hand place. He seemed, mollified by his drink and the general success, to be nodding off. No conversation started. There were no questions. Heavy was gone. In front, by the pilot, Latham sat. He was close enough you could pull his hair. It was the school bus.

Swiftly sky-borne, astoundingly high. The colossal blueness and the transparent gleam. And below, the building, some original wieldy house bought up and soullessly extended, erratically decorated, recently very blackened, here, there, by arson.

Carver could see now, the multiple extension of carefully planted and nurtured 'grounds', woods, rises, valleys. And then, a reduced yet shaking swing of the chopper revealed hillsides northerly, and behind, huge barren chunky crags collapsing statically downward to moorlands, grey-green and purple, miles beneath.

Where *was* this place? Scotland – some outpost of Avondale's folly – No. Unless he had passed it over to the LLE – the true Life Long Enemies, to Croft's organisation, some deliberate ploy – but it made no sense. What did?

As if it knew it had suggested too much, the chopper manoeuvred again, and the forward and side-view were solely of the south margin of the cliff. One last glimpse of the building and the lawns, the south terrace (so tiny now, toyland.) Then all the earth dropped away into an incredible abyss. At the bottom of which was not red wine, or eternal darkness, but the sea. Emerald near the narrow shoreline, curving over into outer ocean. And there the waves were a single thing, a glistening sheet of turquoise.

But it was not turquoise, of course. Not much is what it seems. Some things are not even – what they are.

# EXHIBIT NINE
# GREEN WALLPAPER

# GREEN WALLPAPER

O God! I could be bounded in a nut-shell, and count myself a king of infinite space, were it not that I have bad dreams.

— William Shakespeare, *Hamlet*

The spirit, finally, will always conquer the sword.

— Napoleon Bonaparte

Below the equator and above the Tropic of Capricorn, a speck in the widest nowhere of the Atlantic Ocean, built from the tall black debris of an ancient volcano: the island. Too far from Africa, too far to matter – and from Europe as far it seems as hell is from the earth, once one has been cast down into it. Winds that are fevers blow in this place. The humid grey heat shatters only on icy, greasy rain, which smokes as the heat resumes. Yet a colonial town goes on about its business here, and private houses scatter the heights. Hundreds, it is true, have supposedly died of the climate, of the very remoteness. And no one with a choice ever stays long. Yet the island is the possession of a great worldly power, and so tons of soil were long ago deposited and spread, and gardens and woods planted. They grow quite richly now, pasted all over the rough, badly finished plaster of the black rock. Like green wallpaper.

He has been thinking... or dreaming, he isn't sure, of that second woman who was his wife. Curious, really. His first wife was several years older than he, the second a lot younger. Some sort of balance in that, maybe. The first wife he had loved, and she was barren, and had betrayed him over and over with other men – but in the end she clung to him, was jealous, *wanted* him – died without him. While the second *never* wanted him, pretended, was entirely faithful while they were together – as far as he knew, and he *would* have known if she were not – quickly providing him with a son. But then, when his star fell, and everything crashed about him, she ran away, taking his son with her, robbing him of his child – his future – and now she lies in bed with some nobody of an Austrian officer. *She*, his empress, who had shared his throne. Just as the first wife had been his empress before.

Yes, a balance, probably.

As in a mathematical problem.

It's all like that.

He sighs – he sighs often – and hauls himself up from the wooden chair, pushing back from the wooden table. How heavy he feels. Legs, arms. Lack of enough exercise. Lack of – everything.

He walks round the room, once, twice, picking up a few objects, two books, a quill. A small coin someone's found. Heaven knows, they need any funds they can get.

He is indulging in one of his five-day stints of seclusion. Later, very likely, he'll call one of them in, dictate a little more of his memoirs. But he finds increasingly, if he is honest, that now the desire to put the record straight is offset by the need – to do nothing.

## Nothing!

He, hero, general, king, emperor, once almost master of all Europe. Oh, he could have had the world. It was running toward him as eagerly as he ran with his armies to seize it.

But then…

He feels he has lived a long time. His life seems to stretch back forever, in tumults of battle and pageantry, and in cosy domestic scenes, power and glory and content and grief. But not forward, of course. Never that.

His belly hurts, but it always does. Always did. Confound his body. Men have obeyed him, but the machine of his body would seldom fully obey. He had had to break it to his will and now, as sometimes even in the past, it outwits and overcomes him. At last, like all the rest, seeing him fallen, it too creeps forward like a cowardly hyena, to paw and rend.

Some noise outside? What's that? Marchand, his manservant,

calls softly through the door that leads into his private rooms. Apparently the English governor, Lowe, had called again, wanting to speak to him. That ginger-haired, crawling thing. Has he gone? Yes.

He says, absently but with a flicker of old firmness, "See that anything is wiped over, if he's been near it."

The house is very high up on the bleak tableland among the diseased and arthritic gum trees. Here the winds really blow, like trumpets. Another new tree lost its branches in the garden only three nights back. Up here, it's more difficult to cover over the grey and black with green.

Besides this house – this *place* – it comprises a cowshed, washhouse, and stable, inadequately cobbled together and ineffectually disguised as being fit for human habitation. The floors break, leaking moisture, stinking of old manure. Rats dance in cupboards, chewing the mahogany that slowly rots anyway, along with all the books, due to the damp. Every day the silver lamp in his bedroom is cleaned, briefly removing a perpetual dull film. The rest of the silver's gone, of course. He had had to part with it. But it was sold cheaply to the evil Lowe, who would allow no one else in the town to buy it. The town is always full of notices warning the townspeople that none must fraternise with the French enemy on the height. He is legally restricted to a few miles' radius that stretches about the 'house'. Sometimes he absconds – but no, he hasn't bothered with that for a long while. He used to ride or walk all day. When his belly prevented him from riding on the Russian campaign, among those mud- and snow-smothered steppes, he strode league after league with his men instead.

He thinks of Moscow, burning. That beautiful, domed city put to the torch only to spite him and stop him. They would have seared all Russia off the face of the earth if that had been the only way. He recalls the tsar whom he had charmed and enticed into treaty, like a silly girl into bed.

Outside the grey brightness is fading to gluey greyish-blue. The sun must have set. There's only the evening now to cope with. One more victory, then. One more day tossed onto the rubbish heap of history.

Of course, when first delivered up here, he had thought frequently of some means to escape. The notion of escaping still haunts him, even now, just as it haunts the obnoxious Lowe, who himself sneaks about the area continually. Yet escape is out of the question.

He believes he is resigned to this.

Therefore, only his mind can escape into books and memories, his thoughts, his dreams.

Something moves softly.

Is it a rat, shifting along the bookshelves, or under the camp bed in the adjacent room?

Generally, the rats are more bold, noisier.

The two chambers are otherwise empty. The man who lives here has moved out into the dining room, where his fellow exiles have tonight made the effort, all of them, to join him for supper.

It is full night now.

The soft rustling, fluttering, comes again. Perhaps a large moth, a bird even...

Something ripples, there – there – *under* the brownish nankeen that swathes the walls of the bedroom. Or is it only a trick of the half dark? The muslin curtains are undrawn and some kind of outer glow – a lamp, the clouded stars – gives partial light but not enough.

No, after all, the nankeen covering is quite static.

Yet something *is* here.

And it does move, if only faintly discernibly, and that moving being noticed more by the sense of *touch*, like a quiet breath over the rooms, a sigh, that goes *through* things – furniture, carpet, a wall.

It looks into the dining room.

Yellow candlelight, and the crowded table surrounded by people with once fine clothes and creased faces, one beautiful woman and one less so: a young boy, a noisy baby now being carried out – men in medals that commemorate triumphs.

The supper looks frugal. Earlier today, at dinner, the meat was rancid again. The governor sees to that.

What looks in – looks without eyes. Invisible, and yet not *completely* so. Somehow a sort of shadow is present that's cast by nothing in the room, so the beautiful woman suddenly starts and says a creature is there, is it a lizard? Send it out, kill it...

But then the shadow *isn't* there, isn't anywhere, and only one man puts his hand to his cheek, feeling a mild moist breath smooth over it, perfectly clean, except for a little mustiness, perhaps...

Rustum, the servant who has just crossed an outer room, feels something slide over him – now like a weightless, silky shawl. His eyes glitter as they follow intuitively what they can't see. Tonight, should he sleep against his master's door, as he has so often in the past? No. It will be no use. The elder people from whom Rustum descends, they have names for such things and know neither a door, nor a man, not even a sword, can keep the demons out. No precaution or act will work.

"Fah! This wine is putrid!" exclaims one of the younger men angrily. He adds. "Sire, we should slaughter that villainous little fiend, Lowe."

"The English would love that, their representative, my gaoler, murdered," says the one addressed as sire. "What do you think they'd do? They're faithless." He's no longer an emperor, but still he must be called 'sire', although such a title, he has said, means nothing, and never did.

The two women are stiffly arguing in an undertone. Someone shushes them.

The ex-emperor wants his coffee. Then he will want to play chess or cards. Then read them a Greek play or a French play by Racine, talk to them about bygone days. Always it is like this. He keeps them up half or all the night, wears them out, drains them, exhausts them, casts them aside. Even when he dictates the accounts of his life and battles, he can go on and on, pacing the rooms, paying out his acute and finely-tuned phrases, for the classical education of his youth has informed his syntax, just as much as once it did his genius in war, despite the accent, which he's never lost. *He* then can continue in this recital ten hours or more, but his secretaries collapse, fall asleep, faint even. Then he calls in another. Wears *them* out, drains *them*. The ex-emperor is a sort of vampire. He's never known, and would be enraged and would disbelieve, if told. He has seldom – ever? – been able to empathise. For he is the centre of the world. From the beginning, until the end. They – all other things – bit players, useful, magnetising, inadequate.

An invisible shadow now hangs up on the ceiling like a cobweb. It still looks down, attentively watching. Some ebb of its formless form unravels, trails negligently along the floor. And a single rat, sidling from the mahogany sideboard into a space under the planking, slinks aside to avoid all contact.

He's dreaming... or thinking... the fires of burning Russian villages or the campfires burning in Paris across the Seine, that night at the beginning or the last act of downfall – the city full by then of his foes, and his young empress already fled...

Fires. Genius, the fire from heaven – not every brain is equipped to receive it.

He smells a delicious perfume. He knows it – less the unguents with which she would lave herself, and which she would rub into the curly reddish darkness of her hair – than her own *personal* sweet odour. Oh, yes. He had written to her once – *I am hurrying toward you – do not wash.* She was one of those rare women who never had an impure smell, not even her breath when first she spoke in the morning – sweet, always sweet, the loveliness only heightened when she refrained from the bath.

Marie-Josephe. Joséphine.

He opens his eyes and through the dim dark of the small bedchamber, *sees* her standing there by the fireplace. She's dressed in a white gown. It isn't one of the scandalous gowns that she and some of her cronies used to wear at Malmaison when he was well away, the kind that, when sprayed with water, became transparent; this was the garment of an empress. And on her head, the royal golden wreath he himself had crowned her with. She had worn her diadem for him that night after the coronation, he and she alone.

Joséphine.

"Here I am," she says. She is the age she was when first they met, her early thirties. Pearls glimmer in her ears. Her skin is juicy, ravishing. Beautiful woman. The only woman he had ever truly loved – almost that.

"You haven't missed me at all," she says.

"Always."

"Never, once I grew old."

"Ah, Joséphine. But now... you're young again."

"All this while I've waited for you. I saw you at Malmaison once, you sat there alone, mourning for me. Don't you want to be with me now?"

"More than I can say." He sighs. "To lie in your arms. To rest against you."

"Then why won't you come to me?"

Some element penetrates, hard as a bullet. The old wound in his

Achilles tendon – such a blatant emblem – stings. He raises himself on his elbow and feels too the throb of the anguish in his gut and knows he's wide awake after all.

## "WHAT ARE YOU?"

"I am Joséphine! Remember the house, and the red geraniums pouring over from their pots, the flowers I brought all the way from Martinique. And the Temple of Love, in the gardens..."

He tries, properly, to push up from the bed, and finds it difficult. His head spins, a common ailment in this fever-drenched pest hole the English have sent him to, to make sure he dies.

When finally he gets his feet onto the worn carpet, he turns again and she's gone.

Yes, it's fever. That's all it is. A brief delirium. But it was so like her, wanting him to kill himself and hurry to meet her – he must assume that was what the hallucinatory Joséphine had required. She always wanted him away at first, so she could have her fun with all the others. And then, when he fell in love with his Polish girl, *then* Joséphine had wanted to be there with him. And now, in some place beyond the world that could not exist, impatient, she asked: *Why aren't you here?*

He shakes his head. Outside stars are blazing in a brief opening of the cloud. He remembers remarking once, "Say what you will of the absence of a creator, but who made all *those?*"

When the candle's alight, he gets up and goes to inspect the area where the apparition stood. On the floor there seems to be the faintest dusting of white powder – the sort she had used on her face and shoulders – but no, it isn't anything... loose plaster, no doubt.

Panting, his unhealthy fatness that has little to do with diet making him sweat, he climbs back onto the bed. A stab of infernal agony drives through his belly like a claw. So bad now. He supposes it can only get worse. Tomorrow, to soothe it, he will spend several hours in a scalding bath.

But even now he can fall asleep at will, like an animal. He falls asleep and dreams of Joséphine among her self-imported geraniums. His little son, that the other one gave him, the traitorous Austrian woman, runs by her side.

Something floats over him, a cloud that in sleep he does not see. Then the nankeen ripples behind the bed. In the morning, Rustum and Marchand both, coming in, will notice this brownish wall cover has become a little green in tone. Naturally, in this climate, there's mildew outdoors and in, lichen even, everywhere.

All of his companions here argue continuously among themselves, and some of them come to him raving or whining with complaints. At certain times they have only communicated with each other by means of written notes.

What is all this inanity? His canvas had been the world – now he's trapped in a nutshell, with these persons who seem unable to understand that his eternal suffering does not need to be augmented by their pettiness. *Oh, let them all go, for God's sake.* If there were a God.

He thinks of the other two islands, the rugged, forested country of his early childhood, and the island of his first exile, this one mantled with stone pines, fig trees, shapely crags, walking among whose vineyards he had lamented: *This place is very small.*

Something must have been listening. If not a god, then some other imbecile tyrant. If Elba was small, what is *this* tiny dot?

And his mother had been permitted to come to him on Elba, and brought him all her carefully saved money, enabling him to finance a voyage back toward the coast of France.

He thinks of the loyal guard they had let him keep on Elba, shouting for him, and the army he had raised there besides. He thinks of the march back to Paris, and all the troops sent out to impede him, thousands upon thousands of men, and how he had gone out alone before his little force, stood there with cloak thrown back, weaponless, and bellowed: "If you would kill your emperor – here he is!"

Which brought those thousands rushing to his side like liberated happy dogs: "Life to the emperor! Life and glory!"

He reads a play by Sophocles.

He recalls the coronation, setting the laurel wreath on his own head – he who has been crowned by gold and iron.

The day goes. Eleven o'clock. He can resort to bed.

When he wakes about three in the morning, Joséphine is there, lying beside him.

He looks into her chestnut eyes.

"Go away," he says quietly. "I'll be a ghost soon enough. But I don't want you yet. And this bed isn't wide enough for us both."

As she fades, he remembers how her little hound, Fortunate – fortunate indeed it *had* been, the brute, that he'd never killed it – would constantly get between them, biting him, jealous.

There is no sugar for the breakfast coffee again. He stands looking at the portrait of his Austrian wife and their son, and at his silver alarm clock that had belonged to a mighty Prussian king.

He can hear the two Corsican servants arguing now, in an outer room.

The ship should arrive tomorrow with more books.

At the afternoon dinner he eats in the English soldiers' barracks. They always welcome him with respect and great politeness, even though he has little English. Soldiers are all the same, once their mettle is proven. And they know the miracles he's wrought and value him for them. He was a worthy foe. Worthy. The English prince should never have treated him in this way. He'd thrown himself on English mercy – and received none.

He thinks, sitting there in the drab dripping heat, of the ship *Bellerophon* (harsh name – Bearer of Darts) and how he had won her officers over, and they had seemed to promise him a safe retirement in England.

It's never occurred to him, and doesn't now, that after he had sworn to wipe England's status and future off the face of the world, it was unlikely England *would* harbour him.

He hears the old revolutionary anthem in his head, the *Marseillaise*, despite the fact he himself had banned the singing of it. It spoke too much, he had said, of violence and the wrong issues.

Something moves the curtains. A slight breeze. For a moment he sees his own cannon, under his orders, mowing down French citizens in the streets – the rabble – but that, so long ago. Before he became their father, their protector.

His eyes focus on the curtains to blot out memory.

How inventive. The curtains seem to have taken on the shape of his young Austrian empress. She had been quite succulent – one could forget the slight pockmarks on her face. She's nicely dressed. Satin shoes. Little buckles.

His eyes are tired and playing tricks, for the figure in the curtain looks solid, pink and ivory, smiling in her playful, spiteful, catlike way.

This damned malaise. Perhaps he can ride off the fever. Even inside the narrow twelve-mile limit of the cordon that legally restricts him.

Yet when they bring out his horse, he sends it back It looks as feverish and tired, as forlorn and crestfallen, as he. And he notes it's been bitten by a rat.

The exiled party at the makeshift house on the tableland is now much smaller. They are always leaving him, these loyal adjuncts of his – their health gives way, they're urgently needed elsewhere. And they, of course, can choose. The one sane, reliable physician, O'Meara, has left too, some while ago. The other, inevitably, is useless.

It isn't so much that he has become used to the dreams that seem to arrive even when he is awake, it's that he doesn't dislike them. For that reason too, probably, he who talks and writes about every aspect of his all-consuming life and self doesn't record them. Exactly as he always refuses to hear, or to tell, a bawdy tale. They must be secret too, then, as relations with a chosen woman. And possibly tinged with something he himself is partially ashamed of. Maybe only his own weakness. He's old, in his fifties, fat and in pain, sluggish. Bored. He is entitled to a few private dreams.

All of them have come to him now, his women – Joséphine and Austrian Thérèse and Maria, his exquisite, dovelike Polish mistress – generous and thoughtful as always, since she even brought with her the illusion of a ballroom sparkled with champagne and candlefire. There have been a handful of others... girls from here and there, blondes, brunettes.

He has turned them all off. It goes without saying. Joséphine with the frankness of familiar habit. Thérèse perhaps unkindly – but then even in the dreams she refused to bring his son to see him. Maria with a tenderness fitted to her patient, undemanding simplicity. The rest only needed a snap of his fingers – sizzle! Gone... They always return anyway.

Only this afternoon, walking into his study, the floor carpeted by new books recently read cover to cover and then cast away, Maria is standing in the bedroom doorway.

"What shall I do about you?" he asks her. "You have a good

husband now. Why steal away to see an old fat fellow who has lost everything and is exiled to a rock?"

"But I miss you," she says gently. "Can't I come to visit you?"

A thought strikes him uncomfortably. "Are you sick, Marie? Tell me you're not dead, like the Empress Joséphine."

She blushes as if he had made a sudden – wanted amorous – advance. "No, no, my dearest lord. I'm well."

"And your boy?" With her too there had been a son, but too late. All too late.

"He's well, dear wise one."

She loves him. It's clear in her lambent eyes. Poor child.

"I think I hear our son calling you, Marie," he playfully says, and she turns her lovely head and indeed seems to hear someone call, and then she turns entirely and entirely vanishes.

And then he's sorry. Before, strictly, he pulls himself up.

He slumps at the wooden table. He is being courted by ghosts both living and dead. A harmless pastime? Or just a persistent fever?

Take medicine, then.

Get better.

For there's still a chance his world may change, his chains struck off, his eagle wings able to open once more to flight…

*No, old fool. Be still. That's over and done.* Even should the poison-tongued English relent, and witless France come to her senses, what could he do now, shut in this sack of blubber and worn bones? *Here's my true prison – my own flesh.*

*He walks to the mirror and surveys himself.* Once I resembled, closely, the Roman Emperor Augustus. Who now is this scarecrow?

In the mirror too, over his shoulder, he sees Maria lying naked but for an enticing, modest shawl, on his narrow bed.

He shuts his eyes, undoes them. She's gone. His old enemy Talleyrand sits there instead, swinging his courtly white-stockinged leg, clicking his gold braid, leering and laughing at him.

A flash like cannon shot passes through his blood. He almost runs at Talleyrand, clever, traitorous Talleyrand, to wring his chicken neck.

But he doesn't. For *this* Talleyrand isn't real.

Later there is a storm. And in the flame of the lightning, he sees one by one his family members about the two rooms, his mother, Laetizia, in a chair; his brothers that he made kings, and the one brother, Lucien, he made nothing, posed on silent duty like wet birds; his feckless sisters in their gowns worth thousands of francs, his stepdaughter in her diamonds... His worst enemy, Bernadotte, parades by the bookshelves, and Fouché poses, shouting didactically until the lightning punches a hole right through him, and he shatters like a glass.

O'Meara, the physician who left, might have been spoken to about all this. But there's no one now.

Again he thinks of escape – will these futile thoughts never leave him? How could he do it, unless he were invisible? He smiles drearily. Death will provide the escape route, then.

To Marchand, who arrives in the aftermath of the tempest to say another of the newly planted trees has lost a limb, and then peers anxiously at him, he says, "Yes, the pain's bad tonight. But there we have it. Only *Napoleon* can overthrow Napoleon."

"Sire..."

"Ssh. Light the candles. The wind blew them out. The dark's a strange place to inhabit. When I shut my eyes, every mistake I have made marches before me. Whole battalions pass."

"Your noble life, sire, was..."

"A ballad, Marchand. A saga. The hero always dies."

Something...

...there it goes...

Rippling like a sea wave behind the wallpaper. If anyone troubled, if they noticed, they would take one of his candles from its eagle sconce and go and stare very hard at the badly damp-stained nankeen on the bedroom walls.

It had a Chinese pattern once, now faded to marks like those large insects might construct.

It is very green, nearly the colour of the ex-emperor's old coat. Half close one's eyes and the impression is of a jungle growing over the material of the nankeen and the plaster. When it moves – seems to move – the idea is very strong of a forest shivering at the passage of a muscular wind, or of some large, predatory creature.

He lies tossing about under the wall. He's dreaming of circumnavigating the Alps in a torrent of an army, of the iron crown of Lombardy, of a sullen fortress in a desert that would not yield, sitting alone on his horse in the waste of sand while his legions marched away – only he having the courage to gaze at what he was unable to defeat.

The current doctor believes this once omni-powerful man is a liar, who pretends, for politically manipulative reasons, to pains in his belly and teeth. The doctor treats all symptoms with bitter and useless things dissolved in water. But unlike damp, clean water too is scarce here. The governor – always he – has made sure of that.

But this sick, tossing man can always sleep, deeply.

Something...

...flows out of the green on the wall.

Now it's beside the bed, positioned there, still rippling faintly, an image like that of a breeze over a lake. One couldn't say it *stood* on the floor. It simply *is*.

Formless and translucent and much less green than the stain it's brought out on the wall. There's a light herbal smell, rather like scythed grass, or wet trampled ferns.

Presumably the preliminary contacts, although inconclusive and so unfulfilled, have strengthened it, for it was invisible before, and limited in revelation to that sense of a thick cool breath or a piece of silk or an obscure shadow. Even where he has seen it directly, they haven't yet touched.

It's also fed, lightly, on all the others in the house. This had made them extra fractious, draining them, affecting their well-being. Just as he has done, if it comes to that. But remember, hundreds have died here of those fevers and ailments that haunt the island. The apparition is itself a sort of fever that preys on human things, or on animal ones when nothing else is available. Its existence began as the plants grew upon the barren rock. It was brought close to the present victim when he had his garden made, just out there against the house, and when he tended and watered it so assiduously. Ever since, *this* has looked in at his windows, slid in at his walls. Had it needed to be invited? Then he *has* invited it. His need, his *hunger* calls out to its own. Hundreds have died through both of them, because of the ex-emperor on his inadequate camp bed, and because of the demon that quivers beside him.

Like attracts like. Vampire lures vampire. It isn't always essential to draw them in with voluble welcome across a threshold. Recognition is one of the most potent introductions.

A lizard runs abruptly down the farthest wall. It squeezes

through a crack in the planking beneath the carpet and has escaped. But the shimmering greenness has taken of the lizard no notice whatsoever. It bends lower toward the fallen emperor, *drinking* his dreams, feeding superficially and deliberately, for the best dish is now, without doubt, already being prepared.

The life of a happy man, this man had said, is a silver sky, spoiled only by a few black stars. An unhappy man's life is like the ordinary sky all men see by night – black, with only the spreads of silver stars to mark his separated moments of joy.

The strangest thing... opening his eyes he sees the sky of dawn beyond the window. It's shining clear and brilliantly silver just before the rising of the sun – and a handful of little black clouds litter it, scarcely visible, like dim black stars.

Then a figure moves between him and the window.

"Good morning, sire," says the young man who sits on the end of his bed. The young man's mouth quirks with an ironic smile, amused, but it's not a face for humour especially, more priestly and stern, although very handsome, the thick, dark hair not yellowishly powdered today, but hanging silkenly to his collar, his blue-black eyes intent and steady as those of a trained gunner – not surprising, for he had been such a gunner.

For a few seconds the ex-emperor does not know him. Or rather mistakes him first for several others in turn – friends of his youth, his brothers – even an enemy he can't name. Recognition, then, doesn't always provide the instant introduction.

Yet they are eye to eye.

## I TO I.

The young man is his younger self.

He speaks quite tenderly. "You didn't want any of the others I showed you, did you? You want only *you*. And so, he is here."

Every one of the few left here know now the man who was their emperor is sick – to death. Even Governor Lowe is sure, and rushes to the house, and desires very imperiously and repeatedly to see the captive, for how else can the staunch and suspicious governor be certain the prisoner hasn't escaped? The governor becomes quite certain, in fact, and takes to his heels when the prisoner bellows at him, unseen, from behind his locked door.

"So," he says to the apparition on the end of the bed. But it isn't an apparition. More convincing than any perfume, he can smell its youthful and healthy body, and the freshness of the clean linen he had always insisted on, once he could. "So, you can haunt me at daybreak too, then."

"I'll always haunt you. I am you."

"No. No, you are *not*. You called me *sire*."

"Courtesy. Until you grew used to what you saw."

He's silent. The other, the younger him, turns and points out of the window. The sun is coming up, the silver sky giving way to gold.

"From the east," says the other. "The sun, beloved of the bee and the eagle, and the Lion of Leo, our birth sign. Think of the East. Do you remember?"

He sighs. He sighs so much. "Yes."

"Egypt, the gateway. That campaign which, if wholly successful, would have split England from her Eastern empire. Then on to the lands of fable – Arabia, Persia, India. Your goal, our goal. The same road that was taken by the mighty Alexander of the Greeks. He almost conquered and ruled all the known world. As we did, almost, our much larger world. Is this not true?"

"Perhaps," he says. "But there was too much to do. The farther I went, the more I had achieved, the more complex and petty the ramifications. Surrounded by fools and foes... No, I'm my own worst foe. And if you are myself, you phantom, then maybe you *are* that worst foe, externalised."

But the man sitting on the end of the bed shakes his head so the shiny feathers of his young hair fly.

"Think of it this way," says the younger man. "As you grew in knowledge, expertise, and power, as your genius was burnished and jewelled by experience, time trampled you and you aged. Me you left behind – a genius also – but untaught by that experience, *unleavened.*"

"If you were left behind, it wasn't ever my choice. All men age. I before my hour, I believe. I've lived life more than most certainly, lived enough life perhaps for two men. What am I? Fifty-one years. Then in truth I must be one hundred and two. Small wonder I should look and feel it."

His stomach gripes, agonisingly, as always now.

His other self watches with a curious apparent mixture of concern and impatience. "It was all that fasting and famishing in our youth," he murmurs, as the face of the older man gradually clears. "That will upset all the mechanisms of a body. The fat on you comes from that, too. We were poor and starved for years. Then we ate. Such things never work out."

"Yes, yes, I'm fat enough. Soon I'll be bone thin."

"So you resign yourself – ourself – to death."

"I can do no other. I always scorned to take my own life unless all hope was gone. I travelled through Russia with a black bag of poison around my neck, ready. Now life and hope depart together."

Outside the door a soft scratch, and Marchand clears his throat.

Where the younger self is, a smoky flicker appears in the air. He has vanished, yet even as the door opens, the ex-emperor hears his own young voice whisper at his ear, "Tonight, put out the chessboard. I'll play a game with you."

Marchand, troubled, for he thinks he's heard his master not only talking to himself, but muttering answers, advances into the room with a little hot water and the accessories kept for shaving.

And his master looks very ill this morning, Marchand thinks. The yellowish tone of his skin seems heightened by the horrible glowing mossy shade of the wallpaper, and the heartless brilliance of the morning sky.

That evening after supper, he doesn't want to dictate or debate any reminiscences. Nor to read aloud the play by Racine he had placed nearby. He smooths the play regretfully. Its soul-searching drama calls to him even as he moves away.

In the bedroom he stands in his red slippers. Night covers the imprisoning island, flecked, in only a very few areas, by silver stars.

Instead of getting into bed, he goes back into the outer room where he has arranged the chessboard with its array of fierce figures.

How childish to put this out, expecting a phantom to join him. Then, oddly, with the same little ironic quirk of a smile his own other self earlier displayed, he sets a glass of the thin wine on either side the table and lugs the other chair into position.

Something laughs, up in the ceiling.

He knows the laugh. His own.

Turning, he's just in time to see the green mist that blooms against the dirty brown wallpaper, and how it lightly opens, like a curtain, and out of it, and down, as if descending a brief stair, unerringly runs the short and slender form that long ago was his.

Dreadfully – it startles and shames him – the ex-emperor's eyes expand with tears.

He blinks them back.

But the eyes of his other self are wet also.

The other self holds out its hand.

Frowning now, he clasps it. The hand is warm – strong, calloused as he – anyone – would expect, from swords and guns and reins – and as real.

They sit down. Both raise their glass at the same instant, and both drink. Both view the board carefully.

"Tonight," says his other self, almost flirting, "I shall be Russia."

"Then what am I?"

"Napoleon," says the other self. "What else *need* you be? Life to you, Emperor! *Play to win.*"

Yes, it *is* a flirt, this thing. *I am you*, it says, then courts him. Despite its words of being left behind without his learning, perhaps his experience is already being drunk down by it out of the air.

They play.

The pieces slide and click across the squares. Hours melt like candlewax from the clock.

Neither can win. How could they? They employ the same strategies. Ah yes, it *has* learned.

"You see after all," admits the young man, nearly shy but not unwilling. "Now I've gained your mature cunning."

"And I've lost all my edge."

"Here it is, your edge. It is *me.*"

How young or old precisely is the other? The ex-emperor considers him judicially. He doesn't need the other to say to him, as soon he does, "Do you remember Toulon?" – it merely confirms the idea his younger self is approximately twenty-three or twenty-four.

"After Toulon, the beginning of your ascent to power," says the ex-emperor rather drily.

"While yours collapses and ends."

"All things end."

"Not all. Of course, not all."

He considers this. Then, looking at the board, suddenly he sees the younger man has left him an opening – perhaps left it purposely – or not. He makes his move and wins the hours-long game.

"So, you've taken Russia," gravely announces the young man. "Soon you can claim the East as well. Not only a united Europe, but a united earth. An end then to *all* war. The wings of the eagle will cover everything and keep it safe."

"Hush, it's lost, that great game. Soon I'll be dead."

The other says disdainfully, "You're not dying. You will live on. True, in vicious pain, in cruel frustration and unhappiness, losing gradually not only yourself, but every faculty you still command – no longer able to ride, then no longer able to walk, no longer able to *think* – a fat old grasshopper all withered up in this prison cell atop the tiniest islet in the world. Do you believe by now you shouldn't already be dead? The English gaoler has tried enough, and always, to starve and wound and break and so kill you. In spite of your weakness and despair, and the rat that gnaws in your guts, you have the constitution of a lion. Yes, you'll live. Another five, ten, fifteen years. On and on into increasing debility and old age – without teeth or sight or sense – until, as you say, finally you die and crumble to dust. But it's far away. A long and arduous road to reach your grave."

He smiles, bitterly. "If I'm to live, I have no choice. I'd trusted this misery was almost over."

"It can be," says the other, flippant. And abruptly standing up – he's gone.

"Come back, you rogue you devil…!" he catches himself calling it to return. And sighs again.

There is the smell in the room of newly cut greenery, and he recalls the oily scent of broken geraniums by the Temple of Love at Malmaison.

But Joséphine won't visit him again. It was true; he hadn't wanted her, or any of his women. Nor his enemies. His son he had wanted. He'd thought possibly this haunt or demon, whatever it was, might have presented his son to him. If only once. But also now it's too late for that. It knows it has fascinated him entirely in this one shape.

Even though he thinks this, he doesn't believe in the demon, which is perhaps why he isn't afraid of it. Naturally, he has played the chess game against himself, and drunk both thimbles of vinegary wine.

He lies down on the bed. Sleeps. Dreamless, now.

"Do you remember Toulon? Mondovi, Mantua, Alexandria, Austerlitz?"

Yes, he remembers.

The demon returns, returns. They relive the campaigns, the chess pieces becoming whole armies. Once more he dashes forward into battle, skilled, braver than lions, risking all and taking all. Careless, too, sometimes, determined, as if, stripped of weapons, still he would bite his way through the enemy ranks...

The demon isn't real.

It is a fever dream.

They talk of Corsica, his birthplace. He sees it appear before him – a mirage – the tree-covered heights, the polished shores...

"You didn't want your women, not even your mother – not even your son – oh, be honest. It's this you want. Your past. And me. You want me that is yourself and your youth, when you grew upward into the light of victory."

The demon is correct.

He watches it – himself – narrowly. And so makes more mistakes at the chess – *loses* at Toulon, *loses* at *Austerlitz*... "Once you allowed me to win," he tells the demon. "Our first game."

But the demon checkmates him without answering, leans across the wooden table and, casting its own convincing shadow, clasps his hand, warmly, strongly, once more.

## "I CAN TELL YOU HOW TO WIN."

He sits back then, and the creature lets him go. It speaks softly in his own inventive, fluent French, accented always with Italian.

"You must tell them you're dying."

"I do so. I am."

"That's good. But I've watched you. You must say it with more conviction. Make out your will."

"A wise thought. I shall, God help me."

The spasm in his belly rears and racks him, and he doubles over in a cold thick sweat, retching once or twice. The demon waits politely for some while, until the agony withdraws.

"Yes. It will be easy," the sick man grates.

The demon replies, "Easier than you know. You have only to give me yourself, and then I shall be yours."

He straightens. Wipes his face. Through the door he glimpses the unnerving wallpaper.

"You want my soul," he suggests.

"*Souls!* You don't believe in them. This is a bargain of the flesh. I have all your youth, and now all of your wisdom. What you would want therefore is to be me. And I..." The whisper falls like drops of water in his ears. "What *I* want is the renewal of my self, through the vitality of your remarkable blood."

The older man lets out a long, hoarse laugh.

"My blood's rotten. I have the canker in my guts, like my father before me."

"Nothing of the sort. Your blood is of the best. Why else should I want it? I've supped all these years off the vital fluid of worthless men, or off the gore of rats and reptiles. But you – *you* tempted me. The blood of a hero and a genius."

The old man watches his adversary now. The old man's eyes, though bloodshot, and the whites a little discoloured, are still dark. They seem to see at last very well what the thing is that appears to be himself, and that has learned to speak in his voice. How peculiar, the mouth – his own – avid now as his had never been, no, even in the throes of great rage or passion, and the young eyes themselves glittering like those of a rabid fox.

"You'll drink my blood, then."

"I don't drink." Disdainful. "I *absorb.*" The human phrase somehow disturbingly apt, even on that fox tongue. "Some are simple to drain. Not you. Without you allow it, I can do little."

Avid. He sees it is avid, and it permits him to see, through every non-corporeal atom, the avidity made concrete by its seeming physicality. As a man lets a woman see his lust, knowing it will move her, when she is attracted.

## *YET,* WITHOUT YOU ALLOW IT...

After all a threshold, over which this fiend must be specifically invited.

"I say again," says the old man, grey from the bout of pain, but ever steady-eyed, "if you have my blood, I'll die."

"No. You will become what you see before you. Your former self. The world will lie at your feet again. When you're strong enough to seize it."

He lowers his eyes. The vampire can probably see him thinking. It would seem, however, not *what* he thinks. For he knows it lies, of course. The exchange will result in strength for it, and an end for himself.

In the window, a hint of morning.

"How long," asks the old man, "will the process take?"

"Not long."

He rises, clumsily. The pain has left an afterglow of scalded horror. He's tired. It takes too much, this long road.

"I shall make my will," he says again to the thing across the table. "Come back when it's done. Then you can have what you want. Understand me, I don't believe in your bargain. But I've done enough. They took my means of a swift death from me, along with all my power and possessions. You then shall replace the little black knot of poison I carried for such a while. You shall be my suicide. As before, only torture and death stand waiting for me. No Roman could do more, or less, than I. Come back when I've seen to my will."

He watches it gleam suddenly through all the solid and human flesh and life it's put on to woo him. Will that disguise adhere, if wanted? But it fades anyway, smiling its fox smile. In its excitement, it has forgotten a moment *only* to resemble him.

Fighting exhaustion and pain he makes the will, filling the testament with lies, recriminations, accusations, and tricks. This takes days. He dispenses fortunes that maybe will never be honourably extended to the beneficiaries. These riches include hidden stashes of francs, gold, quicksilver, his hair, and his silver lamp, which he leaves to his mother in Rome. Unshaven, he lies spent on the bed. One of the remaining companions comes sometimes and reads newspapers to him. He gives his gold snuffbox to the untrusted doctor, with a demand for a prompt post-mortem autopsy. It seems the ex-emperor actively wishes his body cut open, disembowelled – as if to be sure it can never reengage itself.

At close, regular intervals, the stomach spasms convulse him. Between them, he dreams and tells those in the room Joséphine was with him but wouldn't embrace him. She had instead assured him that soon they would no longer be parted.

Not long, then. Not long before death sucks him down. Behind the bed, a backdrop, that wallpaper must always have been so green, and with the strange marks on it, which must be a pattern, surely?

"What a vast time... you've made me wait," the sick man says.

"And you, what a time I have waited for you." There it is, bending over him, himself, the other, twenty-three, twenty-four. The other murmurs, "Are you prepared?"

"One last – tell me, how is it I must *allow you* this? Couldn't you have taken my blood otherwise?"

"I've said. With others. Weaklings. Not you – a worthy adversary. I've tasted your ichor in superficial sips, from your dreams, memories…"

"From my thoughts?"

"Not those. Your kind of strength shuts doors. Only your longings – and even there I misjudged, didn't I, until I knew you better. But now I shall feast on you. Are you afraid?"

"No. I always had a curious nature. Mathematics, the sciences intrigue me. This too has a sort of mathematic, so I believe."

The thing that wears his shape bends closer and closer. The sick man, scenting skin, linen starch, hair, sensing its warmth, again notes how well it has made itself to please him. In further proof, his own young hair brushes the sick man's face. And at this instant he feels the essence of his blood begin to drift away from his veins and heart and brain, unhurtful and terrible, into the substance of the demon. He sees the creature too, lit with a kind of bloom, like a plant well-watered, and how its eyes – his *own* eyes – bulge and fixate. It gives a strangled moan. Delight? Satisfaction? Then he hears it shriek, far off as a gull above the tableland. Yet the words are clear. "It burns! Your blood – it burns!"

The sick man, not quite so sick as he's pretended, puts up his arms as if to clasp a beloved son, and seizes the vampire by the waist. He finds he is still strong enough to surprise himself – to surprise both his selves. He hauls it down on top of him. It thrashes, but already something's amiss with it and with its timeless procedure.

He gives it no space either to draw back or to recover. He sinks his own sore teeth into its throat, mauling and biting, snapping through until he can taste the blood of *it* – green as sap, boiling and slippery, not unpleasant, like herbs or medicine, or geranium leaves in a salad…

The vampire is thrashing and screaming on the bed. Something has occurred. As the emperor, swallowing one ultimate mouthful of green wine, rolls aside, letting the creature go, he beholds how the vampire has been altered.

It's bloated – and changed both shape and colour. It is no longer that film which floated from behind the wall, nor is it any longer in the form of the young and handsome man who had operated the guns at Toulon. Now, flopping over onto its back, it is a swollen man-fish dragged, engorged with fever and internal venoms, from some awful sea, sallow and fat-bellied and broken, the sunken face old before its time, the dark eyes bloodshot and the whites liverishly yellow.

Yes. Still the vampire is himself, but now his aged recent *ruined* self. Nevertheless, still fleshy, and if not warm to the touch, more clammy, yet able to *be* touched, and handled.

His blood. His *ichor*.

He had seen men in the desert as they marched, days without water, forcing gallons between their lips at some oasis and then foaming at the mouth, vomiting, dying. The vampire had waited so long for his blood, only *sipping*. Then taking it fast and in such quantity, greedy, *thirsty* – *too* much. *It burns!*

It kills.

The creature, poisoned by the power of light that lingers still in every hero, even those who make mistakes and grow old. Only Napoleon can conquer Napoleon.

The emperor stands by the bed, shaking back the lush silken hair that hangs to his collar.

In every muscle, artery, and bone, he feels the shining sap of the vampire bounding and coursing in a wonderful mad ride, metamorphosing him back through time, making him young again, perhaps forever. What from him has poisoned the fiend has, from the fiend, done the hero only perfect good.

Centre of the universe – how could he ever properly have credited he could die? He was immortal.

But the palpitating lump of apparently human wreckage on the bed rasps from its rattled throat, "You knew... You knew..." petulant as a child.

He replies. There is space for it, now. "Not certainly. But it was worth the risk. I built my life on such risks. And on charming my adversaries. Then. But now...?" He pauses, wonderingly. *"I am a private citizen of the world. No island can contain me, only the earth herself..."* The young man stands there, his head lifted. Everything beckons to him. Will his life be like his former life? Or quite different? God knew. "My God," he says, turning to the window, "look at the stars!" And *vanishes* into thin air.

The bargain, although it has not transpired as intended, is fulfilled, it seems.

Moments later, one of the ex-emperor's attendants rushes into the room, having heard weird distant cries he had, at first, taken for those of a night bird.

As he runs forward, the dying remnant on the bed leaps upright and grips him so tightly, astonishingly, that the attendant can't even shout for assistance. But the doctor, hearing wild thuds, presently intrudes and pries the man from the invalid's uncannily strong grasp.

The ex-emperor collapses back on the bed. Behind him, the wallpaper stays an intransigently faded green.

He survives only another day, while rain smashes against the cowshed house and greenish mist streams through every one of the wet, noisome rooms. Sometimes, he seems to crave drink, but can swallow nothing. That evening another tree is uprooted by the wind.

Late the following day, as the sun sets wearily into the Atlantic, they find the heart of the ex-emperor has also gone down into the dark.

Bribed by the gold snuffbox, and surrounded by witnesses, the doctor cuts deeply into the body cavity of the corpse, exposing and removing certain organs. If anything has lived in this body, undeniably it can no longer do so.

The verdict as to the cause of death is variable and inconclusive. It will remain a topic of debate for at least two centuries.

Long after, the body, buried on the fever-blighted island of St.

Helena, is disinterred and rehoused, with some ceremony, inside a tomb of sable and crystal, in the heart of France.

Napoleon, they say with sad irony, is once more in Paris.

Is he?

# About the Author

Tanith Lee (1947-2015) was born in London. Because her parents were professional dancers (ballroom, Latin American) and had to live where the work was, she attended a number of truly terrible schools, and didn't learn to read – she was also dyslectic – until almost age 8. And then only because her father taught her. This opened the world of books to her, and by 9 she was writing. After much better education at a grammar school, she went on to work in a library. This was followed by various other jobs – shop assistant, waitress, clerk – plus a year at art college when she was 25-26. In 1974, her career as a writer was launched, when DAW Books of America, under the leadership of Donald A. Wollheim, bought and published *The Birthgrave*, and thereafter 26 of her novels and collections.

Tanith was presented with a Lifetime Achievement Award in 2013, at World Fantasycon in Brighton. During her lifetime, she also received the World Horror Convention Grand Master Award, as well as the August Derleth Award and the World Fantasy Award for short fiction (twice).

In 1992, she married the writer-artist-photographer John Kaiine, her partner since 1987. They lived on the Sussex Weald, near the sea, in a house full of books and plants, and never without feline companions. She died at home in May 2015, after a long illness, continuing to work until a couple of weeks before her death.

Throughout her life, Tanith wrote around 100 books, and over 300 short stories. 4 of her radio plays were broadcast by the BBC; she also wrote 2 episodes (*Sarcophagus* and *Sand*) for the TV series *Blake's 7*. Her stories were read regularly on Radio 4 Extra. She was an inspiration to a generation of writers and her work was enormously influential within genre fiction – as it continues to be. She wrote in many styles, within and across many genres, including Horror, SF and Fantasy, Historical, Detective, Contemporary-Psychological, Children and Young Adult. Her preoccupation, though, was always people.

# Books by Tanith Lee

## Series
The Birthgrave Trilogy (The Birthgrave; Vazkor, son of Vazkor [published as Shadowfire in the UK], Quest for the White Witch)
The Blood Opera Sequence (Dark Dance; Personal Darkness; Darkness, I)
The Flat Earth Opus (Night's Master; Death's Master; Delusion's Master; Delirium's Mistress; Night's Sorceries)
The Lionwolf Trilogy (Cast a Bright Shadow; Here in Cold Hell; No Flame But Mine)
The Paradys Quartet (The Book of the Damned; The Book of the Beast; The Book of the Dead; The Book of the Mad)
The Venus Quartet (Faces Under Water; Saint Fire; A Bed of Earth; Venus Preserved)
The Vis Trilogy (The Storm Lord; Anackire; The White Serpent)
The FOUR-Bee Series (Don't Bite the Sun; Drinking Sapphire Wine)
The S.I.L.V.E.R. Series (Silver Metal Lover; Metallic Love)

## Novels and Novellas
34
The Blood of Roses
Companions on the Road
Days of Grass
Death of the Day
Electric Forest
Elephantasm
Eva Fairdeath
The Gods Are Thirsty
Kill the Dead
Heart-Beast
A Heroine of the World
Louisa the Poisoner
Lycanthia
Madame Two Swords
Mortal Suns
Reigning Cats and Dogs
Sabella
Sung in Shadow
Vivia
Volkhavaar
When the Lights Go Out
White as Snow
The Winter Players

## Young Adult and Children's Fiction

Animal Castle (picture book)
The Castle of Dark
The Claidi Journals (Law of the Wolf Tower; Wolf Star Rise, Queen of the Wolves, Wolf Wing)
The Dragon Hoard
East of Midnight
The Piratica Novels (Piratica 1; Piratica 2; Piratica 3)
Prince on a White Horse
Princess Hynchatti and Other Surprises
Shon the Taken
The Unicorn Trilogy (Black Unicorn; Gold Unicorn; Red Unicorn)
The Voyage of the Bassett: Islands in the Sky

## Story Collections

Blood 20
Cold Grey Stones
Colder Greyer Stones
Cyrion
Dancing in the Fire
Disturbed by Her Song
Dreams of Dark and Light
Fatal Women
Forests of the Night
The Gorgon
Hunting the Shadows
Nightshades
Phantasya
Red as Blood – Tales from the Sisters Grimmer
Redder Than Blood
Sounds and Furies
Tamastara, or the Indian Nights
Space is Just a Starry Night
Tempting the Gods
Unsilent Night
Women as Demons

# Tanith Lee Titles Published by Immanion Press

*The Colouring Book Series*
Cruel Pink
Greyglass
To Indigo
Ivoria
Killing Violets
L'Amber
Turquoiselle

*The Blood Opera Sequence*
Dark Dance
Personal Darkness
Darkness, I

**Novels and Novellas**
34
Ghosteria Volume 2: The Novel: Zircons May Be Mistaken
Madame Two Swords
Vivia
The Heart of the Moon

**Collections**
Animate Objects
A Different City
Ghosteria Volume 1: The Stories
Legenda Maris
The Weird Tales of Tanith Lee
Venus Burning: Realms: Collected Short Stories from 'Realms of Fantasy'
Strindberg's Ghost Sonata and Other Uncollected Tales
Love in a Time of Dragons and Other Rare Tales
A Wolf at the Door and Other Rare Tales

**Of Interest to Tanith Lee Enthusiasts...**
Night's Nieces

*This anthology is a tribute to Tanith Lee, comprising short stories written shortly after her death by some of her writer friends to whom Tanith was a profound influence and inspiration: Storm Constantine, Cecilia Dart-Thornton, Vera Nazarian, Sarah Singleton, Kari Sperring, Sam Stone, Freda Warrington and Liz Williams. With an introduction by Tanith's husband, the artist John Kaiine. Illustrated throughout by the contributors and with photographs from Tanith Lee's personal collection.*

# Immanion Press
Purveyors of Speculative Fiction

### A Wolf at the Door by Tanith Lee

Includes 13 tales, most of which appeared only in magazines or rare anthologies. 'A wolf at the door' implies hidden threat – until the door is open, we don't really know what's out there. And now the beast is upon you, scratching at the wood, its hot breath steaming on the step. Will you survive the encounter? Perhaps, once the door is opened, what you might have thought to be a threat turns out to be something else entirely. But of course, it can also be a werewolf…
ISBN 978-1-912815-04-3, £11.99, $15.99 pbk

### Coming Forth by Day by Storm Constantine

This book explores the myths of Ancient Egyptian gods and goddesses – showing how their stories relate to aspects of our lives, hopes and aspirations, and how we can learn from these ancient narratives. Through 28 deep and evocative pathworkings and rituals, the author provides a rich and vivid system of magic that the practitioner – whether experienced or a novice – can utilize in the search for self-knowledge, and to help themselves, others and the world around them. ISBN: 978-1-912241-11-8 Price: £12.99, $16.99

### Breathe, My Shadow by Storm Constantine

A standalone Wraeththu Mythos novel. Seladris believes he carries a curse making him a danger to any who know him. Now a new job brings him to Ferelithia, the town known as the Pearl of Almagabra. But Ferelithia conceals a dark past, which is leaking into the present. In the strange old house, Inglefey, Seladris tries to deal with hauntings of his own and his new environment, until fate leads him to the cottage on the shore where the shaman Meladriel works his magic. Has Seladris been drawn to Ferelithia to help Meladriel repel a malevolent present or is he simply part of the evil that now threatens the town?
ISBN: 978-1-912815-06-7 £13.99, $17.99 pbk

www.immanion-press.com
info@immanion-press.com

## The Blood of Roses Volume 1: Mechail, Anillia by Tanith Lee

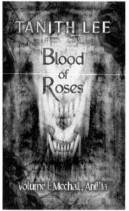

In a rich, complex epic set in a grim fantasy world, Tanith Lee explores in her distinctive style the excesses of religion as well as the dark pagan roots of earlier times. While the Christerium might believe it wields the greater power and keeps the people under control through brutality and oppression, the older cunning ways lie hidden in every forest glade and in the hearts of those who worship the Great Tree, nourished by the blood of willing sacrifice. But then the Tree is destroyed, in the midst of a sacred rite, unleashing a potent and vengeful magic. This vivid, macabre epic was only ever published in the UK in a hardback edition – to most readers it will be a completely new title, which Immanion Press is proud to present in two paperback volumes, with illustrations by Danielle Lainton and cover art by John Kaiine. ISBN: 9978-1-912815-07-4, Price: £12.99, $16.99, €15.99

## The Blood of Roses Volume 2: Jun, Eujasia, Mechailus

Against the backdrop of a savage world, in which the bloody religion of the Christerium holds power, strange creatures have formed and stalk the fearsome and magnificent chambers of the great cathedrals. Three characters take up the tale that began in *The Blood of Roses: Volume 1*. With Jun, the original sacrifice to the Great World Tree, the story begins to unfurl – how the dark priest Anjelen came to be and acquired such great power, how he managed to subjugate and tame a towering and oppressive regime to do his bidding. Eujasia takes the reader deep into the secret world of these fluid and mysterious characters – where nothing is as it seems, and personalities appear interchangeable. Eujasia seeks Anjelen, but for what ends? Mechailus is the sum of all stories – and in this enigmatic, kaleidoscopic being the reader learns the truth. This book brings to a conclusion the sweeping, macabre epic of belief and desire, once available only as a hardback edition in the UK. This Immanion Press editions gives all readers access to one of Tanith Lee's most complex and chilling works. ISBN: 978-1-912815-08-1, £12.99, $16.99, €15.99

**www.immanion-press.com**
**info@immanion-press.com**

Milton Keynes UK
Ingram Content Group UK Ltd.
UKHW031522050224
437298UK00003B/637